T0387888

the norm. A beautifully written story, with plenty of mystery and just enough red herrings to keep the reader guessing. And, in my case, utterly captivated. I very much hope this isn't the last we hear of Piper Sail. I can't wait to read more of her story!"

HANNAH CURRIE, author of the Daughters of Peverell and Crown of Promise series

"A delightful whodunit mystery that will have you flying through the pages and wishing the indomitable Piper Sail could be your best friend. I loved everything about *The Secret Investigator of Astor Street*, from the 1920s setting to the sweet romance and the suspenseful anticipation Stephanie Morrell expertly builds with every chapter. A highly recommended read for all ages!"

LORIE LANGDON, author of the Disney Happily Never After series

"*The Secret Investigator of Astor Street* is a sparkling blend of wit, danger, and vintage charm, sweeping readers into the glittering and gritty streets of 1920s Chicago. Stephanie Morrill delivers a heroine you'll cheer for in Piper Sail—clever, bold, and unwilling to accept silence when truth is on the line. Smart, stylish, and full of heart, this book is a must-read for fans of mystery, jazz-age stories, and strong heroines."

JILL WILLIAMSON, Christy Award-winning author of the Blood of Kings series

"In *The Secret Investigator of Astor Street*, Stephanie Morrill distills atmospheric prose, the nuances of grief, complex family drama, undiluted emotion, and the shadowed back-alleys of 1920s Chicago into an intoxicating YA mystery riddled with more twists than a speakeasy escape tunnel. If you're in need of a private eye with moxie and heart, the secret investigator of Astor Street is on the case!"

ANGELA BELL, author of *A Lady's Guide to Marvels and Misadventure*

"Piper Sail is back with a new case to solve in this supremely satisfying sequel! Morrill delivers another captivating and compelling mystery with a smart and gutsy heroine you'll love rooting for, set against the glitzy backdrop of Chicago's Roaring Twenties. Mafia, secrets, and societal expectations for young women clash, and one twist after another had me compulsively flipping pages long into the night!"

GILLIAN BRONTE ADAMS, author of
The Fireborn Epic series

"Welcome back, Piper Sail! With the gumption of Enola Holmes and the savvy street smarts of Veronica Mars, Piper's misadventures in mystery and romance are well set in a lively 1920s Chicago thanks to the winsome, humorous, and wholly captivating pen of Stephanie Morrill. I hadn't realized how much I missed Piper, Mariano, and Sidekick until I stepped back into their world. With a delicate blend of light and darkness, vulnerability and wit, *The Secret Investigator of Astor Street* is rich in history and romance and destined to lure back Piper fans while delighting the uninitiated."

RACHEL MCMILLAN, bestselling
author of *The Mozart Code*

"The fact that it took me so long to come up with the words to express how much I adore Piper Sail should say everything you need to know about this story. Mystery, intrigue, romance—what more could you want? *The Secret Investigator of Astor Street* is one you won't want to miss."

ALISON GERVAIS, award-winning author

"Delightful! Captivating! Since the day I closed *The Lost Girl of Astor Street*, I have anxiously awaited its sequel, and Stephanie Morrill does not disappoint! *The Secret Investigator of Astor Street* gives us more of spunky Piper Sail, who, through almost no fault of her own, finds herself once again scrutinizing mobsters and other unsavory characters populating 1920s Chicago as she seeks to uncover the truth behind a mysterious death. Morrill's wit and style mark every page, and there are plenty of twists to keep readers guessing. I can't wait to see what Piper Sail will get up to next."

SHANNON DITTEMORE, award-winning
author of *Winter, White and Wicked*

A PIPER SAIL MYSTERY

THE SECRET INVESTIGATOR OF ASTOR STREET

STEPHANIE MORRILL

BLINK

BLINK

The Secret Investigator of Astor Street
Copyright © 2025 by Stephanie Morrill

Published by Blink, 3950 Sparks Drive SE, Suite 101, Grand Rapids, MI, USA. Blink is a registered trademark of HarperCollins Focus LLC, a wholly owned subsidiary of HarperCollins Publishers.

ISBN 978-0-310-17581-0 (hardcover)
ISBN 978-0-310-17587-2 (audio)
ISBN 978-0-310-17583-4 (ebook)

Library of Congress Cataloging-in-Publication Data

Names: Morrill, Stephanie, author.
Title: The secret investigator of Astor Street / Stephanie Morrill.
Description: Grand Rapids, Michigan : Blink, 2025. | Series: A Piper Sail mystery ; 2 | Audience term: Teenagers | Audience: Ages 13 and up. | Summary: Eighteen-year-old Piper investigates a possible murder case that takes her into the criminal underworld of 1920s Chicago.
Identifiers: LCCN 2025005664 (print) | LCCN 2025005665 (ebook) | ISBN 9780310175810 (hardcover) | ISBN 9780310175834 (ebook) | ISBN 9780310175872 (audio)
Subjects: CYAC: Mystery and detective stories. | Murder—Fiction. | Mafia—Fiction. | Chicago (Ill.)—History—20th century—Fiction. | LCGFT: Detective and mystery fiction. | Historical fiction. | Novels.
Classification: LCC PZ7.M827215 Se 2025 (print) | LCC PZ7.M827215 (ebook) | DDC [Fic]—dc23
LC record available at https://lccn.loc.gov/2025005664
LC ebook record available at https://lccn.loc.gov/2025005665

HarperCollins Publishers, Macken House, 39/40 Mayor Street Upper, Dublin 1, D01 C9W8, Ireland (https://www.harpercollins.com)

Cover Design: Jennifer Showalter Greenwalt
Cover Illustration: Dawn Cooper
Interior Design: Denise Froehlich

Printed in the United States of America

25 26 27 28 29 LBC 5 4 3 2 1

To Ben. Thank you for being my safe place to fall and for always getting me back on my feet. I love you.

CHAPTER

ONE

DECEMBER 1, 1924

CHICAGO, ILLINOIS

I gaze up at the Applegates' imposing brick house and take a bracing breath. Mrs. Applegate has never liked me—the feeling is mutual—but Rebecca Jensen's disappearance is far more important than our petty disputes over the years. I glance at my watch. Only five minutes until I should start walking to Presley's for the awards ceremony. I could delay this conversation until after . . . but doing so might impact how fast we find Rebecca. I'll just have to be late for the ceremony. When someone is missing, every minute matters.

I unlatch the wrought iron gate and tug on Sidekick's leash. He plants his rear on the sidewalk despite the snow, and gives me a look that clearly reads *no*. Gone are the days of Sidekick giving me timid glances or shivering in the cold because he was malnourished. His once lanky body is now thick with muscle and covered in a fluffy coat of fur the color of sun-bleached sand.

My exhale is visible in the early December chill. "Believe me, I understand. She likes you better than me, though."

With another pull and some scratching of his floppy ears, I convince Sidekick that walking through the gate is something he can do. I adjust my cloche and survey my attire to make sure there's nothing about my appearance that Mrs. Applegate will find offensive. I'm unusually tidy, thanks to my morning plans. My coat covers most of my drop-waist dress, but even so, it's clean and a tasteful shade of burgundy. I already know she hates my bobbed hair, but I can't do anything about that. I *am* wearing stockings rather than bare legs, which will hopefully count for something.

I inhale, exhale, and rap on Mrs. Applegate's door.

Sidekick edges toward a potted evergreen, eyeing the festive red velvet bow. I wrap his leash around my hand an extra time. "No."

He looks up at me with woeful eyes.

"I'm sorry, but you'll ruin the whole interview if you eat her Christmas decorations."

From the other side of the door, footsteps approach, and I force a polite smile onto my face. There's probably no amount of politeness that can make up for an entire rambunctious childhood of living next door to Mrs. Applegate, but it doesn't hurt to try.

Mrs. Applegate opens the door. She's a large woman, tall and solidly built. Her steel-streaked hair is wound into a large knot on the crown of her head, and her brown eyes are magnified behind thick eyeglasses. She takes one look at me and frowns.

"Hello, Mrs. Applegate." I use the sweet and courteous tone I always heard Lydia use with our neighbors, which is why everybody adored Lydia. "How are you this morning?"

"I'm fine, Piper." Her critical gaze runs over the length of me. "Is something wrong?"

"Yes, actually. Do you mind answering a few questions for me?"

Mrs. Applegate's sharp gaze flicks from me to Sidekick and back to me. "Is this about Rosamund's granddaughter?"

In recent months, I've spent some time practicing an *I'm not surprised* look in the mirror, because it seems like that could be useful during investigations. I try it now but have a feeling I fall short. "So, you've heard that she went missing yesterday? When did you last see her?"

Mrs. Applegate looks at me in a way she never has before—with a hint of a smile and a sheen in her eyes that, if I had to label it, I would say is compassion. "They found Rebecca safe and sound last night. She fell asleep on the train and missed her stop. That's all, Piper."

I inhale deeply. It's the first easy breath I've taken since last night, when I heard that Mrs. Jensen's fourteen-year-old granddaughter boarded the train for Detroit but hadn't yet arrived, despite it being hours past when she should've. "You're sure?"

"I'm quite sure. I spoke with Rosamund this morning, who spoke to her daughter-in-law. Rebecca is home."

"I'm so relieved to hear that." My eyes brim with tears. "I'd feared the worst."

Mrs. Applegate nods, and her gaze drifts to my scarred cheek, which I did my best to conceal with liquid makeup this morning. "Of course you did."

I take another deep breath. Rebecca is home. I can go to Emma's award ceremony without having to worry about what happened to Mrs. Jensen's granddaughter or where she might be.

I check my wristwatch and step back from the door. "Thank you, Mrs. Applegate. Sorry to rush off so quickly, but I'm headed to Presley's. Emma Crane has won the Service to School and Others award, and the ceremony is this morning."

Mrs. Applegate's eyes light. "How wonderful for our Emma! You've been so fortunate as to have the loveliest of friends."

An unvoiced question lingers in her compliment of Lydia and Emma. *Why are these lovely girls friends with you, Piper Sail?*

But I just smile and say, "Yes, I'm very lucky," before I turn and dash down the final steps. "Good day, Mrs. Applegate!"

Though if I were truly lucky, Lydia would still be here with us. She wouldn't have been kidnapped, right here in the Astor Street District, and killed a short time later. This morning, Astor Street appears magical, with its manicured trees balancing ribbons of snow on their branches, the sky a bright blue overhead. I've lived here for most of my life, so I often overlook how picturesque my neighborhood is. These days, it's hard for me to notice the beauty without also noticing the shadow it casts.

Last night, I'd laid awake for hours making lists of everyone in the neighborhood I'd seen Rebecca speak to during the week of Thanksgiving. This morning, I telephoned the train station, asking about options for traveling to Detroit, and then I'd gone so far as to place a long-distance call to the Detroit station to ask about arrivals from Chicago. I knew the call would take a chunk out of my weekly allowance, but if I could help find Rebecca before anything horrible happened to her, the expense was well worth it.

And as it turns out, none of that was necessary, because the girl had, thankfully, just fallen asleep on the train. I'm grateful, of course. But I'm something else too. Something I can't quite label.

Something I don't have time to dwell on, because I need to get Sidekick back inside and grab my handbag. Hopefully, I can still make it to Presley's somewhat on time.

I run up my front steps and burst through the door. As I loosen Sidekick's leash, I look up to find my father's wife, Jane, in the living room. She sits at the small desk and works on something that involves both a monthly calendar and a notepad. In the not quite six months they've been married, Jane has heartily embraced the life available to Astor Street wives. She's likely planning some sort of tea or fund-raiser or another similar gathering that primarily serves to keep a woman's mind needlessly and harmlessly occupied.

Jane looks up with a smile fixed on her face. Her appearance is lovely and ladylike, as always. Her raven hair is freshly trimmed at her chin, and the forest-green shade of her dress makes her hazel eyes appear lighter.

"Piper." She says my name with surprise. "Where have you been?"

"They found Rebecca."

Jane blinks at me several times, and it's clear she's trying to interpret my meaning without having to ask.

"Rebecca Jensen," I add. "Mrs. Jensen's granddaughter? They found her."

"Oh yes." Jane chuckles. "Yes, I know. She fell asleep on the train, silly thing. Rosamund came around late last night to let us know. You'd already gone to bed."

Jane goes back to her note-taking and I stare at the top of her head. "You should've told me that. I've been really worried."

Jane looks up, eyes wide. "I'm sorry, I didn't realize." Her gaze is assessing. "Though I should have, shouldn't I?"

I snatch my small, beaded bag from the hook. "I need to leave. Sidekick has already been walked and fed."

"Piper, I really am sorry."

I intended to slam the door behind me, but Jane's tone—sincere, regretful—makes me pause. I scrub the last of the anger from my voice and say, "All that matters is that Rebecca is home safe."

I pull the door closed as Jane is saying something else— likely an inquiry about when I'll be home. She likes to pretend to have a maternal role in my life even though to be my mother, she would've had to give birth to me when she was nine.

As I trot down my front steps, I flip up the collar of my red plaid coat to keep the wind's chill off my neck. I glance again at my watch, as though it's going to tell me something besides *you're already running late.*

I'll walk fast. It'll help keep me warm.

I've just closed our front gate when a male voice calls out, "Piper!" from the Buick parked along the sidewalk.

I know the voice instantly but have to draw closer before I can see Jeremiah Crane's face in the driver's seat. He wears his trilby the same as always: skewed slightly and paired with a smirk that implies he's God's gift to the ladies of Chicago. Jeremiah's handsome enough to get away with such a look, but I would absolutely never tell him that.

I bend so I can speak to him through the open passenger window. "How are you?"

"Emma said you need a ride to the ceremony."

I frown. When I mentioned to Jeremiah's sister that I'd be relying on public transportation this morning, I hadn't intended for her to pass that information along to her older brother. "That isn't entirely accurate—"

"Do you have a ride to the school or no?"

I instinctively hold my cloche to my head as a breeze kicks up, a reflex for all Chicagoans. "Well, no, but—"

"Okay, then." Jeremiah starts the car and calls over the thrum of the engine, "Hop in."

The direct order to get inside Jeremiah's Buick makes me bristle. For a moment, I imagine myself turning and walking away, my shoulders square and my chin high. "Stubborn to a fault" is how my mother used to describe me, and she wasn't wrong. It's one of my many flaws.

With a sigh that's kept private thanks to the engine's continued growl, I open the passenger door and climb inside. "Thank you," I force myself to say.

Jeremiah exhales a scoffing laugh. "You do *not* mean that."

I forget sometimes how well Jeremiah knows me. How similar we are. "You're right." I bite my lip to keep from grinning. "But I probably *am* appreciative. Deep inside."

His laugh is a warm rumble, and the look he casts my direction is so admiring, I turn away, cheeks burning. "Mariano wanted to come this morning, but he's working. Otherwise he would have driven me."

This isn't much subtler than flat-out saying, *Do not look at me like that. I'm dating someone else.* Something had to be said, though.

Jeremiah's smile cools and he nods once. "I'm sure he would've."

He fixes his gaze on the road as he waits to turn onto Lake Shore Drive, and an uncomfortable silence buckles itself into the seat between us.

Once upon a time, whenever Jeremiah paid attention to me, I flirted back. Or I at least attempted to flirt back. Our conversations involved too much bickering to be considered "flirtatious" in the classic sense of the word. When it comes to flattering boys, I've always felt like I'm an elephant stomping around, inadvertently crushing egos. But Jeremiah also has a rather antagonizing style of conversing—of doing everything, really—and we might've been good together, if we'd had the chance to try.

"It's kind of you to come support Emma this morning," Jeremiah says as he navigates the busy street.

I fuss with the hem of my coat, trying to cover as much of my legs as possible. "Emma was nice enough to extend an invitation. How could I say no?"

"In my experience, it's very easy. *No* is a single syllable, same as the word *yes*."

I smile. For Jeremiah, saying no really is as simple as that, and I suspect that his unemotional, confident decision-making serves him very well at *The Daily Chicagoan*, the newspaper his father started two decades ago. Jeremiah works there now as a reporter, and he'll someday run the whole thing.

"It isn't as though I wanted to say no. Or like I have a busy schedule these days." I press my teeth into my lower lip. What an awkward thing to say. When will I learn to think before words shoot out from my mouth? "Did you hear Rebecca Jensen arrived home safely?"

"No." He drags out the word. "Should I know who that is?"

This response isn't too surprising, considering Jeremiah no longer lives in the neighborhood.

"Mrs. Jensen's granddaughter. Her family was here from Detroit for Thanksgiving, and then Rebecca stayed on a few more days. She was supposed to return home yesterday, only she never got off the train." I look out the window at the wide, choppy waters of Lake Michigan. "Everyone was panicked, understandably, but it appears she fell asleep and missed her stop. She's home safe now."

"I'm glad to hear everything turned out okay."

"Me too."

My throat constricts as I think of Rebecca, and then of Lydia, who was also missing but then stolen from us forever. While I'm relieved about Rebecca, relieved for her family and kind Mrs. Jensen, I can't deny there's another feeling wrapped around that relief. I couldn't name it initially, but I can now: disappointment.

I'm not at all disappointed that Rebecca's safe, of course, but for the few hours while I was searching for her, I felt useful in a way I haven't since solving the mystery of Lydia's death. If only *that* were a career option for women—being a detective.

I glance at Jeremiah and find he's once again looking at me with unwarranted affection. Instead of pointedly reminding him of Mariano once more, I reach for the unromantic subject of the Chicago crime scene.

"I read your article on the brewing war between the North and South Side gangs. I can't believe you called out specific mobsters by name."

Jeremiah winks. "Pretty brave of me, don't you think?"

"I was thinking it was pretty stupid of you, actually. And Emma agrees with me, by the way."

"Traitorous sister," Jeremiah says with a laugh. "Well, it's either stupid or brave. Time will tell."

My diversion works. For the next few minutes, Jeremiah shares details of another piece he's working on, this one about the consequences Prohibition has had in Chicago, and he's still talking about that as the high limestone walls of Presley's School for Girls come into view.

My chest tightens. I spent my four years as a student longing to be done with the place, and yet now there's something inside me that yearns to be a Presley's girl once more. Why is that?

"Finally," Jeremiah says as he spots a space wide enough to park the car. "Sorry, I should've dropped you off at the door. We'll have to walk a bit."

"I'm fine. I originally planned to walk to and from the L station, remember? I'm not going to complain about a trek across campus."

I collect my beaded handbag from beside me, and it feels pointlessly small in my grasp. I've grown accustomed to carrying a leather shopping bag that was once my mother's instead of these tiny, stylish bags that hold nothing more than pin money and a lipstick. Well, and a pocketknife. I refuse to go anywhere without that.

I exit the car before Jeremiah can do anything needlessly chivalrous, like open my door for me, and then I again take in the familiar building. Maybe my longing to be a student once more is normal nostalgia rather than a sign of immaturity or cowardice? Maybe I would feel this way even if I had left to attend Bryn Mawr or one of the other universities I'd been accepted to but never confirmed.

Throughout childhood, as I navigated the narrow, ordained path of one grade leading to the next, I'd assumed the moment I graduated would feel like blissful freedom. That the whole world would feel wide open to me. I didn't know that instead it would feel terrifying and lonely, as though I've taken an incorrect step and ended up living the wrong life.

"Ready?"

I startle. Jeremiah looks at me, hands in his pockets, eyebrows raised. I swallow the truth: *No. Not at all.*

"Yes." I put on a smile and take a step forward, wobbling slightly as my heel presses into the slick ground. "I'm ready."

CHAPTER
TWO

The ceremony is held in the Grand Salle, which I was told is French for "large, important room." Why this one room at Presley's was given a French name when none of the others were has always been a mystery to me, though I suppose the name fits. The Grand Salle is a big box of space with a stage on one end that's used for theater productions, the annual fashion show, the fall and spring award ceremonies, and other similar school events.

Jeremiah and I arrive as the students file in. Many of the girls look at him and then look away, blushing or smiling. A few appear to be trying to catch his eye. I glance at Jeremiah to see how he's enjoying being the center of attention—prepared to inform him that this happens with all male visitors at Presley's so he shouldn't feel too flattered—but he's oblivious. Or he at least *appears* oblivious. He's probably just ignoring them.

His gaze scans the room and then stops. "I see my parents. Looks as though they've saved us seats."

He presses a hand into my back, urging me to the left, but from the right I hear a girl say, "Piper!"

I turn to find Hannah LeVine, Lydia's younger sister, seated in the back with the rest of the freshman class. I rush to her. "How are you?"

"Fine. Bored. These things always feel like a waste of time." Hannah flutters a hand, indicating the room in general. "Why are you here?"

"Emma Crane is receiving one of the awards. How are you doing? How do you like Presley's?"

Her shrug is sharp, and a strand of hair comes loose from her faux bob. Only a faux bob because Dr. and Mrs. LeVine think a girl cutting her hair short is, at best, a foolish fad and, at worst, a sin. Lydia was always compliant enough to not publicly rebel against them, but Hannah is the type who might come home one day with not just a bob but also trousers.

I take in her fierce expression, the emotion simmering in her eyes, and the way her arms are crossed like she's holding herself together. "Hannah, are you okay?"

But from the stage, Headmistress Robinson taps the microphone. "If everyone could please take their seats, we're going to get started shortly."

"Piper," Jeremiah says, his male voice cutting through the din of chattering girls.

"I'll be right there."

But when I turn back to Hannah, she says, "I'm fine," with a smile on her face. A smile that I don't believe for a second is genuine. "I really am."

"You don't seem like it. You seem . . ." *Furious* is the word that comes to mind, even though she's smiling at me. "Upset."

"No, it's just . . ." Hannah's gaze drops to the floor. "I heard some upsetting news about Mrs. Jensen's granddaughter. She boarded a train yesterday to go home, but—"

"They found her."

Hannah looks up. "Really?"

"Yes. I spoke to Mrs. Applegate just before coming here, and apparently Rebecca fell asleep on the train and missed her stop, that's all."

Hannah exhales, and her shoulders loosen from their rigid stance. "That's good to hear. I barely slept last night. It reminded me of . . ."

Her jaw trembles and I fold her into a hug. "I know."

Hannah squeezes me tight, her fingers clutching at the fabric of my coat as though if she loosens her grip, she'll fall.

"If everyone can take their seats," Headmistress Robinson repeats, "so we can start on time, that would be very appreciated."

Still, I hesitate to walk away. "We can talk more later?"

"I'm fine." Hannah smiles in a way that looks distinctly forced. "Good to see you."

She turns away from me and retakes her seat. Even so, I linger a moment longer before turning back toward Jeremiah. I expect him to look exasperated or impatient, but instead he appears concerned.

"Something wrong?"

I shake my head. "She was worried about Mrs. Jensen's granddaughter. She hadn't heard yet that she's safe."

"I'm glad you were able to tell her." Jeremiah's gaze skims toward Hannah. "I imagine every situation like that hits harder when you've been through what she has. What you *both* have."

The look Jeremiah gives me is tender, and I feel it then—the monstrous weight of my grief over losing Lydia. I feel how easily I could break into sobs right now, into screams, and I push it all away. Back down where it belongs in the dark recesses of my soul, with the lid screwed on nice and tight.

The grief used to be harder to control. There had been moments where it felt like the lid popped off, and the grief spilled out—dark and hot and unwanted, like coffee sloshing on a white rug. I would feel the agony of losing her as I flailed, desperate to stuff the memories away again. Thinking about Lydia is still excruciating, but when the memories do unexpectedly rise to the surface, at least it feels easier to keep everything inside and give the lid a nice tight twist.

I turn on a smile for Jeremiah that probably looks every ounce as genuine as the one Hannah showed me. "Let's go find our seats."

Emma rushes across the Grand Salle to hug me. "You're such a dear for coming."

"I wouldn't have missed it. And"—I murmur directly into her ear—"I cannot believe you sent Jeremiah to pick me up."

Emma's grin is mischievous. "Yes, you can."

Her wide-set eyes and freckled nose make her look naïve as well as young, but that's deceiving. Emma is certainly sweet as sugar, but she's shrewd too. That's the award I would've recommended for her if the school had asked me—Sweet but Shrewd. The services award, however, is the highest of all Presley's honors and will look better to colleges.

"Oh!" Emma's fingers clutch my arm. "Have you heard anything more about Rebecca Jensen?"

"Yes! Right before I came. She's home safely. She fell asleep on the train and missed her stop."

"Isn't that a relief?" Emma rubs a strand of light brown hair between two fingers. "How are you? I rang to check on you last night, but the line was busy."

"Probably my father. Thank you for thinking of me." My fingers curl around the silver locket that holds Lydia's senior portrait. "The whole situation gave me a feeling of déjà vu, as they say."

"How could it not?"

Over Emma's shoulder, I see Headmistress Robinson socializing with several mothers. She wears what I think of as her uniform—a long, straight skirt, a white blouse buttoned up to her neck, and the dark stockings women wore a decade ago. She probably wears this exact same outfit to bed, high-button boots and all.

"What are you smirking about?"

I return my focus to Emma and step slightly to my left, blocking myself from Headmistress Robinson's line of vision. "Nothing important. What's the rest of your day like?"

Emma snorts. "They're going to make me go back to class soon, and I do not want to talk about boring stuff like my school day. How are things with Mariano?"

"Good," I say, more out of reflex than anything else.

Headmistress Robinson comes into view again, and this time she's greeting a closer group of parents. I take another step to the left, keeping Emma between us.

"Good?" Emma echoes. "That's all you have to say?"

"Yes, things are good. And that's all the information you get, because after that stunt this morning, I don't trust your motives."

Emma rolls her eyes. "Sending Jeremiah to pick you up was not a stunt, thank you very much. And, frankly, it just seems like Mariano is busy a lot, that's all. And after the whole ordeal in October . . ."

I inhale sharply.

Emma either doesn't hear this or ignores me. "I want good things for you."

"Mariano *is* a good thing for me, even if he is busy." *And even with what happened in October.* But Emma and I have argued about that situation enough. "It's an especially hectic time for him with the O'Banion murder and all."

Emma gives me a blank look.

"Dean O'Banion," I repeat. "The florist gangster? This was on the front page of your father's paper, for crying out loud."

"Yes, yes," Emma says. "I just needed more context. I don't typically—"

"Good morning, Miss Sail."

Blast. I'd hoped that even if Headmistress Robinson *did* notice me, she would wish to avoid me as much as I wish to avoid her. I put on a polite smile. "Good morning, ma'am. How are you?"

"I'm well, thank you. I'm very proud of all our award winners. Especially you, Miss Crane." Headmistress Robinson's gaze sharpens on Emma. "Shouldn't you be headed back to class?"

Emma bobs a slight curtsy. "Yes, ma'am."

With one more quick hug for me, Emma turns on the heel of her black saddle shoe and retreats. My chest tightens as I watch her leave, so sure of herself and of where she's going.

Headmistress Robinson clasps her hands and fixes her attention on me. "What a pleasant surprise to see you, Miss Sail."

If the headmistress ever expressed pleasure in seeing me before, I don't recall the occasion. "Thank you. It's nice to be back."

Headmistress Robinson stares at me for a moment, her silver eyebrows arched. "Tell me, what are you doing these days with that active brain of yours?"

There's a tugging sensation in my stomach, like I've been caught on a hook and a fisherman is about to reel me in.

"I keep very busy."

Her mouth hints at a smile. "With?"

Fortunately, I have practice with making nothing sound like something. "All kinds of things. I help my father in his office, and I nanny for a family around the corner from us." I swallow and say again, "All kinds of things."

I can't stand to look the headmistress in the eyes and tell her that with my Presley's education, I have done nothing. Outside of spending an afternoon organizing my father's files, and accepting a two-hour job of watching the Barrow boys back in September, I have a daily routine that makes my life feel like not-nothing: several walks for Sidekick, long mealtimes with the newspaper or a book, a radio program in the afternoon, but in essence, it amounts to wasting time.

"I see. And what are your plans for this next season of your life?"

I cast my gaze about the room, hoping Jeremiah will observe my panic and come to my rescue, but his back is turned to me. "I'm still exploring options."

Because I cannot very well say to her, *I'm trying to figure out how to be a detective.*

There's a moment's pause. "You mean you don't know yet."

My jaw reflexively clenches. "I mean I'm still exploring options."

"What do you think of coming to work here?"

A laugh climbs up my throat and I try to keep it contained, but some slips out as I say, "Here at Presley's?"

She nods. "Mrs. Osbourne learned last week she's in a delicate condition. We need a secretary, and we need one right away. What do you think?"

Mrs. Osbourne was so thin, she could've effectively hidden behind a broom in a game of hide-and-seek. I struggle to imagine her round with an expected child. "I don't know anything about being a secretary."

"Being a good secretary is about knowing how to be with people. How to speak to them and how to hear them. I think you're capable of those things."

"I'm sure it's more complicated than that."

"There's some typing involved, but you received an A in that course, so I'm not worried."

"You checked my grade?"

Headmistress Robinson nods. "I was going to ring you up this afternoon. You were the first candidate that came to mind, if you can believe that."

I blink at her. I cannot believe that.

"While you do sound very busy, if you're curious, the hours are eight to four, Monday through Friday. Salary of five dollars a week."

Five dollars a week. That's double my weekly allowance from Father, and taking money from him has felt different ever since I learned he makes his living not by defending the innocent from unjust punishment, as I'd always assumed, but from protecting members of the mafia from deserved consequences. The idea of earning enough to move out on my own, to no longer have to live under the same roof as Jane, is certainly appealing. Though I'm not sure how feasible that is on just five dollars a week.

"Our housekeeper makes nine a week," I say.

Headmistress Robinson fixes me with narrowed eyes. "Your housekeeper probably knows what she's doing."

"She's the best." I rock back on my heels and then land

flat-footed again. "And the poor woman had to raise me. Even so, you need someone soon, and it seems to me that eight dollars a week is more fitting."

Her stare hardens. "Six dollars."

"Seven."

Headmistress Robinson's mouth purses. "Six dollars and fifty cents."

I consider the increase and nod.

"Good. I'll see you tomorrow morning at eight. Keep in mind, Miss Sail, that you will be representing Presley's School for Girls. None of your tomfoolery of the past will be tolerated."

"You don't need to worry," I say. "I've outgrown all that."

Her only response is, "Hmm," before she moves on to speak with someone else.

When I share my employment news at supper, there's silence in the dining room. The corner clock ticks away each awkward moment.

"But," Father says, "don't you want to continue your education, Pippy?"

Jane looks from Father to me and then returns her focus to buttering a slice of bread.

"Maybe. I'm not sure what I want to do."

This is a lie.

I know exactly what I want to do. I want to find those who have gone missing or bring about justice for those whose lives were taken from them, like I did for Lydia. But there's no option for a woman—especially a young one—to become a detective. The closest I can get is *marrying* a detective. This isn't a completely unappealing idea, of course. But becoming Mrs. Piper Cassano doesn't seem like a good aim for my career.

"It's perfectly acceptable to enter a university and not know what you want to do," Jane says as she pokes a cube of zucchini with her fork. "A college campus is the ideal atmosphere for a young woman to explore possibilities. And to meet young men her own age."

Father makes a gruff sound that's maybe a laugh and maybe a protest. "I'd prefer that Piper stop meeting young men her own age, actually. There are too many fluttering about as it is. Jane said you arrived and left with Jeremiah Crane today."

I push the undesirables out of my medley of vegetables, leaving the green beans and roasted potatoes in the pile I intend to eat. "He did that as a favor to Emma."

Father smiles as though I just told a moderately funny joke. "I doubt that."

His implication dangles there, gangly and awkward, until Jane says in a bright voice, "The fund-raiser is coming together nicely. I met with the caterer this afternoon."

Father asks about the menu, so I suppose we're done talking about my new job at Presley's. Including the two of them, I am now three for three in receiving disappointed responses from those I've told.

Jeremiah had also frowned when I shared the news as we walked to his car. "Isn't that a little beneath you?"

"What do you mean?" I asked with a laugh. "I have nothing but a high school diploma."

"I guess." Jeremiah shrugged. "Even still. You solved a murder this summer. Taking a job as a secretary seems like an unsatisfying next step for you."

"I can't just go around the city solving murders, Jeremiah."

"I don't know why not. Chicago has plenty to choose from."

"And how, exactly, would that work? Am I knocking on people's doors asking if they have any murders they need solved?"

He chuckled and shrugged again, but then admitted, "No, I guess not. And I didn't mean you should be solving murders anyway. Obviously."

Obviously. Because I'm a girl.

What will Mariano say when I tell him about the job? He typically calls in the evening after he's home from work, so I'll find out soon.

I finish my dinner and carry my plate into the kitchen. Not so long ago, Joyce would have been in here, cleaning up or eating her own dinner with her son, Walter. There were a number of years when Father and my brothers were busy, and I ate dinner with Joyce and Walter more nights than I did my own family.

But Walter resides in California year-round now, playing for a minor league baseball team, and Joyce has her own place. With my brothers and me all grown and Jane moving in, there's no need for live-in help like there was five years ago when my mother died. Joyce still comes several days a week to do housework and the bulk of meal preparations. To me, it looks like Joyce does the hard work, leaving Jane to throw together the prepared ingredients and soak up all the credit.

When I said as much to Joyce, she just shook her head. "I'm doing my job well if I help Mrs. Sail to look her best. Don't you worry about me, Piper."

After I wash my dishes, I take Sidekick for his evening walk. When I return, I learn that Mariano still hasn't called. I travel down the hall to Father's dark and empty office, and without stepping inside I reach around the corner and fumble for the light switch. A second later, the room illuminates with a soft glow. Sidekick stands beside me and paws at the wooden floor planks. He won't step into the room, and I don't blame him.

Father had his office rearranged and redecorated following the events of early summer, but even still it's hard to go inside. If the telephone is ringing or Father is in here, I can walk in without hesitation. But there's something about *deciding* to enter the office that makes me feel like I have ants marching up my spine.

I take a deep breath and walk briskly to the desk. I turn on the new desk lamp and reach for the candlestick phone. While I wait for someone to answer at Mariano's apartment, Sidekick remains at the door, watching me with wide, alert eyes. Keeping me safe.

"Hello?" Jack's voice, not Mariano's.

"Hi, Jack, it's Piper."

"*Buonasera*, Piper. How fortunate that you would call right now."

"How so?"

"Mariano isn't here. That means I get you all to myself."

Mariano's roommate's flirtations are easy to ignore because Jack is incessant and generous with them. If you're female, he will flirt with you.

"He isn't there?" My eyes flick to the clock on Father's desk. Eight thirty. Mariano should've been home hours ago. "Is he still at work?"

"No. With his family for supper, he said."

I frown. Sidekick paws at the ground another time or two, as if urging me to leave the room before I get hurt again. "Is something wrong?"

"He didn't say. Should I have him call you when he gets home?"

"If he's home in the next hour, yes. Otherwise, I guess I'll just speak to him tomorrow."

Jack and I exchange good-byes and then I hang the earpiece back on its hook and stare at the telephone. As normal as a family supper might sound, that isn't something Mariano does. Mariano loves his father and siblings, but they're mafia and he's a detective, promoted at an absurdly early age *because* of his mafia roots and knowledge. Cassano family gatherings aren't casual or regular affairs for him.

And that's been even more true since the events this autumn, the family wedding followed four weeks later by the arrival of a baby. Both things I also learned from Jack *after* they happened. There's an ache behind my sternum that's hard to ignore.

Sidekick whimpers at the door, a plea for me to leave.

"You're right." I stand and flick off the lamp. "No need to be in here now."

His tail wags as I approach the door, like he's delighted to see I've escaped the room. I crouch on the floor to scratch his ears, and he nestles against me, licking my hands and wriggling as close as he can.

"You don't need to worry about me," I murmur into his ear. "All of that's behind us now."

THREE

When I return to Astor Street after my first exhausting day as Presley's secretary, I find Mariano seated on my front steps, Sidekick beside him. He hasn't seen me yet, and I take a moment to soak up Mariano's narrow, unassuming build. He's hunched forward slightly, like the world weighs heavy, and his jawline is sharply defined. He must be clenching his teeth. Out of worry or anger? The effect of the harsh silhouette is softened by how his dark hair curls a bit on the back of his neck. Past due for a haircut, as usual.

Sidekick spots me first, and his tail thwaps as I draw closer. Mariano looks up and the sharp lines soften into a smile. "Did you take the L today or get a ride from someone?"

I smirk. "Hello to you too, Detective. I took the L."

He frowns and fusses with the knot of his tie. "Jane told me about your job, and I really think you should be taking the Ford."

"Nick took the Ford when he moved out."

Mariano's frown deepens. "Maybe Jeremiah could give you rides. Does he still bring Emma home?"

I sink onto the step beside him and loop my arm through his. "This is our first face-to-face conversation in days. Is this how you want it to go?"

Mariano holds my gaze. The moment his eyes slide ever-so-briefly to my scarred cheek is barely perceivable.

"There's been an increase in muggings on the L. I don't like the idea of you riding alone."

"I'm fine. I carry a knife." I pat my dress pocket, where I keep the knife that used to be Nick's but has been mine for months now.

Mariano rests his forehead against mine and huffs quietly. "Frankly, I worry *because* you're the type of girl who thinks to carry a knife."

"You don't need to worry about me."

He tucks a loose strand of hair behind my ear. "I don't know how to not worry about you."

We sit like this for a minute, maybe two. I don't want to break the magic of the moment, but I can sense the heaviness he feels. The weight that's bowing his shoulders.

"Are you upset I didn't tell you about the job?" I ask. "I tried to tell you. That's what I called about last night."

His forehead rubs against mine as he shakes his head. "No, of course not."

"What's wrong, then?"

"Nothing."

My lips twitch upward. Does he really think I'll believe that? "Lie."

Mariano replies with a ghost of a smile and pulls back from me. "Nothing that isn't always wrong, I should say." He fits an arm around my waist, keeping me close. "The city is crazy. There used to be a civilized way of doing business, even among criminals, and now . . ." He shakes his head. Sighs. "Even my own family, God have mercy."

I lace my fingers through his and stare at my fair skin contrasted with his olive. "Jack said you had supper with your family last night. Is something going on?"

Mariano barks a laugh. "Always. Nothing for you to worry about, though."

He squeezes my hand and smiles at me, but it doesn't cast away the shadows in his eyes.

Chaos is the best word to describe my new role at Presley's. Girls are constantly in and out of the office, needing to turn in forms, to use the telephone, to threaten and complain, or to sometimes threaten that their parents will complain.

"Aren't you a student here?" a few of them ask, looking me up and down like I might be pulling some kind of trick.

"No, I graduated in May," I say the first few times, and then eventually I start replying, "Yes. This is my punishment for bad behavior."

Halfway through my second day on the job, I'm beginning to wonder if Headmistress Robinson thought of me for the position because she knows being a school secretary is basically thankless torture with a bit of typing thrown in for good measure.

When Hannah LeVine comes into the office, a mouse of a freshman girl trailing behind her, she greets me with, "Piper, we need to talk to you."

I sigh. Even Hannah LeVine is going to come in here and yell at me.

I swallow the bite of peanut butter sandwich I've been chewing and reach for my notepad. "Okay, what about?"

"This is my friend, Louisa Dell." Hannah gestures to the girl, who meets my eyes only briefly before looking away. It's possible Louisa isn't mousy but only appears that way because

Hannah is so intense. "She has a problem, and I told her that you can help."

"I'll try." I press my pencil to the paper and write *Louisa Dell* so that I know for whom I'm changing a second semester class or a lunch period or whatever request it is that Hannah has brought me. "How can I help, Louisa?"

Louisa has round eyes set into a round face, accentuated by a bob of dark hair that curls under her chin, the two halves almost touching and creating a circle of hair. She glances at Hannah, who nods, encouraging.

"It's my older brother," Louisa says to the ground. "They say he took his own life."

My pencil lead snaps with her last words. "I'm . . . so sorry. That's terrible."

Louisa's eyes rest on mine for a few seconds. They're a striking green color, like a soda bottle. "I don't think he did." Her voice is quiet but strong. "I think the police have it wrong."

For a moment, all I can do is stare at the girl. Does she mean she thinks her brother was murdered? And Hannah brought her to me because . . . why? Does she think I can help? I look to Hannah, who nods at me, expectation clear on her face. An expectation to do *what*?

"I'm so sorry to hear that." The words come out breathless, as if I just ran a lap around the office. We are the only three people in here, but even still, I lower my voice. "Why do you think the police are wrong?"

"Because Clarence was happy. I just can't imagine he would've done something like take his own life." Louisa clutches the edge of my desk. "He was always joking around and smiling. He never would've harmed himself like that."

Hannah's gaze flicks to my notepad and back to me. "Shouldn't you be writing this down?"

I look at her expectant face. "Hannah, what exactly do you think I can do about this?"

"Figure out what happened to Louisa's brother," Hannah says in a tone that implies she feels this is obvious.

"What? I can't do that."

"Of course you can. You solved Lydia's murder, didn't you?"

"I did, but—"

"And you were trying to figure out what happened to Mrs. Jensen's granddaughter too. Mrs. Applegate told my mother that you knocked on her door and everything."

"That's different."

"I don't see how." Hannah presses into my desk. "Louisa will tell you everything you need to know about Clarence. That's how it works with the police when someone is missing and they think the person has been murdered. They ask questions, and they figure it out from there."

"But I'm not the police." How strange that I feel the need to speak that sentence. "I have no training for this. Why don't you try talking to the police again? See if they'll reopen the case."

Louisa's shaking her head before the words are fully out of my mouth. "I've tried a couple of times."

"Maybe I could try asking?" I roll the pencil between my fingers for a moment. "I know a policeman. He's not in Homicide, but maybe he would know who to talk to."

"Do you think we'd be talking to you if the police were an option?" Hannah snaps. "They've said this is a suicide and they won't do anything else."

Louisa bites into her lower lip, and the skin between her eyebrows puckers.

Hannah looks from her friend to me, and her expression is so intense, I lean away. "Why not look into it yourself?"

"I could, I guess, but I don't have the kind of experience that the police have—"

"Stop being so scared." Hannah's eyes blaze. "Piper, if you don't help her, who will?"

The stubborn set of Hannah's jaw is a jarring reminder of Lydia.

In the justice system, like all elaborate systems, there are cracks. Bad guys lurk in the cracks, like crooked cops or the mafia or defense attorneys who get rich protecting the guilty and powerful. But good people like Louisa fall into the cracks too. People who need help or want to challenge a decision, but they're too small for the system to acknowledge.

Hannah's right. Nobody else is going to crawl into that crack with Louisa. What does it hurt to let her talk a bit? It doesn't mean I have to *do* anything.

"Okay." I drag out the word as I reach for a pencil with unbroken lead. "Tell me about Clarence."

I sit on the L and look over the notes I took during the two minutes I had with Louisa before the phone rang and I had to redirect my attention to my job. To my *real* job.

Clarence Dell. 22. Found dead in apartment October 30 by roommate. Left a note. Dinner with Louisa: Michigan Automat, Tonight 6:00.

I stare at the words and shrivel into my seat. What am I doing, agreeing to have a chat with Louisa about Clarence's death? As if I have any right to do that. As if stumbling upon the truth about what happened to Lydia means I can figure out what happened to a guy I never met. As if I know better than the trained police, who ruled his death a suicide.

When I meet Louisa at the restaurant tonight, I really need to make it clear: *I don't know what Hannah told you, but I'm not sure if I can really help you.* I refold the paper into fourths and stick it into my leather shopping bag.

When I get off the L, instead of walking down Astor Street, I head for the Cranes' house on the street behind mine. Jeremiah's car is parked out front, so hopefully Emma is inside and doesn't mind the idea of taking a walk, despite the cold. The sun is out, at least.

Not only is she inside, she answers the door with a smile. It's funny; before I really knew Emma, I thought of her as being an ordinary-looking girl. Now I can't figure out why I ever thought that, because Emma is absolutely lovely.

"Hi! Come on in."

I hitch the shopping bag higher on my shoulder. "Do you mind if we walk instead? I've been sitting behind a desk a lot of the day."

"Of course. Just let me get my coat and tell Mother. Would you like to come inside while you wait?"

I shake my head. "I'm fine here, thank you."

Emma's eyes roam my face for a moment. "Okay. I'll be right back."

I walk back down to the sidewalk and tighten the belt of my coat. Fortunately, I don't have to wait long before Emma opens the door and bounds down the steps, a blue plaid coat over her

Presley's uniform and a fur-trimmed cloche pulled over her sandy waves.

"What has you all bothered?" she greets me as she threads the last of her coat buttons.

I came to Emma to talk, but now I'm unsure of how to begin. "Do you know Louisa Dell? She's a freshman."

Emma frowns. "No. Why?"

"Her older brother died at the end of October. The police said suicide, but Louisa doesn't think that's true. She's friends with Hannah LeVine, who brought her to me because . . ."

The idea sounds silly and yet makes me feel so strangely vulnerable, I can't even bring myself to verbalize it.

"They want you to investigate." Emma isn't asking.

"Why did you assume that?"

"It's not so bananas, you know. I once asked you to investigate someone for me. Remember?"

I definitely do. At the time, Emma was seeing a fellow she really liked, but she knew he was hiding something. Turns out he was hiding his profession: undercover Prohibition agent. With his cover blown in Chicago, Robbie was transferred away at the end of July. Emma was upset, but Jeremiah told me that the rest of the family was relieved since Emma still has another year of high school. I was relieved too. I had never fully trusted Robbie, especially not with something as precious as my friend's heart.

"I just don't know that I can do it," I say. "I don't know Clarence. I don't know Louisa. I don't even know where to begin."

"Maybe with getting to know them?" Emma suggests. "And don't you think Mariano could help you out a bit?"

"I can't ask him—he's a professional. He'd probably think it was ridiculous anyway."

Emma tucks her hands into her coat pockets. "Would he?"

I open my mouth and then snap it shut when I realize she's right. Back when Emma asked me to look into Robbie, I laughed about it, but Mariano didn't. *Who else is she going to ask?* he'd said to me. Not too far away from what Hannah said this afternoon. *If you don't help her, who will?*

"I'm surprised you're not happier about this." Emma frowns at me. "Not too long ago, you and I were talking about how you didn't know what to do next. How, even if you wanted to do this kind of work, you can't just go to police school, like you could if you were a man. And now you're being asked to investigate something. Why are you hesitating?"

"I don't know." We reach the street corner, and the wind plasters our hair across our faces. I wait until we've crossed the street and are shielded by another row of houses before continuing. "It isn't as though I can charge her for my work, though. Can I?"

"Why wouldn't you?"

"Who am I to charge people? What if I can't figure anything out? She shouldn't have to pay me if I can't solve what happened to her brother."

Emma retucks her hair behind her ears. "I'm not sure that's true. Don't the police have frozen files, or whatever they call them?"

"Cold cases."

"See? There are enough times that the police can't figure out what happened that they've come up with a phrase for it, and I imagine the same is true with private investigators. Nobody is perfect at their job."

"I'm supposed to have dinner with her tonight at the Michigan Automat. Maybe if I just explain to her that I don't really know if I can help—"

"Why would you do that, though?" Emma gives me a look that's a cross between amused and exasperated. "What's the harm in listening and trying to help her, same as you did me?"

"I just think Louisa needs to be clear on the fact that I'm not anybody official." I press my hat firmer onto my head. "Yes, I figured out what happened to Lydia, but it isn't as though anybody has granted me permission to investigate crimes."

Emma blinks at me. "Whose permission are you waiting for, Piper?"

My mouth opens on instinct, but no sound comes out. I can't think of a reply. A minute ticks away, and I finally admit, "I don't know."

Emma links her arm through mine. "Maybe the only permission you really need is from yourself."

FOUR

Louisa stands just inside the Michigan Automat, wearing a green wool coat and a fur-lined turban over her dark brown hair.

"I wasn't sure if I should get a table or wait for you here, but it wasn't too crowded when I arrived." Louisa glances about the room. "It's starting to fill up, though. Should we get some food?"

We walk along the wall of entrée options, all tucked behind individual plate glass doors. Louisa chatters about the different offerings, and I wave away her offer to buy my dinner as I slide a nickel into the slot beside a plate of chicken pot pie and mashed potatoes. Louisa selects macaroni and cheese, then we gather mugs of apple cider and pick an empty table for two that offers some privacy.

I unbutton my coat and hang it over the back of my chair.

"I like your dress," Louisa says.

"Thank you."

I smooth the pleats of my black drop-waist dress and hope she can't tell how deeply I appreciate the compliment. I had surveyed my options for an embarrassing amount of time, searching for a dress that makes me look like I can be trusted with something as serious as an older brother's death, but also doesn't look as though I take myself *too* seriously. Like I think I'm a *real* detective or something.

"I can't hardly wear black anymore without thinking of

funerals." Louisa scoots her chair closer to the table. "My mother still wears black anytime she goes out."

As I lift my fork, Louisa bows her head slightly. A moment later, she crosses herself, then spreads her napkin across her lap and lifts her own fork.

"The thing you need to know about Clarence is that he wasn't suicidal." Louisa spears a pasta elbow. "He was happy all the time."

I anticipated us exchanging some polite conversation before we broached the subject of Clarence—especially with how chatty Louisa has been since I arrived—but apparently not.

I reach into my bag and fumble for my notebook. "Surely not *all* the time. Nobody is happy all the time."

"Maybe not, but Clarence came close. He laughed a lot, and he was fun to be around. There's just no way he would've taken his own life."

"But there was a note?"

"Yes."

I hold her gaze, but she simply stares back at me. "How do you think the note got there?"

She shrugs. "Whoever killed him must've written it."

"Was it written in Clarence's handwriting?"

"Yes. Or at least, what looked like his handwriting." She gathers a bite of limp green beans onto her fork. "But he or she could've faked his handwriting. That wouldn't be too hard."

I take a bite of pot pie and chew thoroughly to delay asking the unpleasant but necessary question. "And . . . how did he die?"

"Poison." Louisa grimaces. "Arsenic is what the autopsy came back with."

"Did the autopsy show anything else in his system?"

"Alcohol and chocolate pie."

I make a note of this. "Not a very common combination."

"No. The police said he probably mixed the arsenic in with the alcohol to make it more palatable."

"What about the chocolate pie?"

Louisa fiddles with the ends of her dark hair. "He ate dinner with us Wednesday night to celebrate Mother's birthday. I sent a slice home with him. It was his favorite."

I add a few notes about the pie before looking up at her. "What do you think happened to your brother?"

She inhales deeply. "I think someone must've put poison in his drink and then wrote a letter to make it look like self-harm. Even if Clarence was going to kill himself—which he never would have—he wouldn't have chosen arsenic."

"Why do you say that?"

"Arsenic poisoning involves a lot of throwing up, apparently. Clarence hated throwing up. I know that nobody *likes* it, but Clarence really hated it. He'd do a lot to keep himself from vomiting."

"Can you actually do that? I never think of it as a choice."

Louisa shrugs. "Clarence always swore that he could stop it, and that he did. He never would've picked poison."

I write this down and consider the words for a moment. "What did the letter say?"

Louisa averts her gaze to her dinner and pokes at the noodles. "That he 'just couldn't anymore.'"

"Just couldn't . . . what?"

"I don't know. It doesn't even sound like him. Clarence is detailed. He never would've left behind a note like that."

"Okay." I lean back in my chair. "Let's say you're right. Who were Clarence's enemies? Who would've wanted him dead?"

"Nobody. Everybody loved Clarence."

I hope she can see the issue without me pointing it out, but Louisa just blinks her green eyes at me.

I lean forward. "Well, Louisa, if you're correct and he didn't take his own life, then *somebody* must have disliked him enough to want him dead."

Her brow puckers. "I know, but I don't know why anyone would want him dead."

I take another bite of my pot pie and chew as I think. Even if I do manage to figure out what happened to Clarence, neither option—suicide nor murder—is going to be pleasant for Louisa.

"Tell me more about him." I shoo several crumbs off my notebook. "Everything you can about his life. Where he lived, where he worked, who his friends were. That sort of thing."

Louisa nods and clasps her hands on the table, looking like a teacher's pet who finally understands the assignment. "Clarence lived up north a bit with his best friend, Daniel. They've been friends since high school, so when they started at Loyola, they got a place together."

"Where did they go to high school?"

"Harvard School for Boys. In Kenwood?"

I nod. Rich boy school. "Yes, I know it."

"They graduated in . . ." She considers a moment. "Twenty-one, I guess. And then both went to Loyola to study finance. Or something like that." Louisa pokes at her macaroni and cheese but doesn't seem keen on eating it. "Clarence always had a head for numbers, just like my father. He works for the federal reserve."

"Clarence did?"

"No, my father. Federal Reserve District Bank. He talked about Clarence working there too someday."

I touch my pencil to the *1921* written beside the name of Clarence's high school. "He would've graduated from college this coming spring, then?"

"Well." The color in Louisa's cheeks rises and she pops a bite of macaroni into her mouth. "Originally, yes. But he wasn't enrolled this semester, so . . . no."

The back of my neck prickles. We're talking about the real Clarence now. Not the version you polish to a shine and then tell others about. "Why wasn't he enrolled?"

"I don't know." Her voice is tight. "Mother and Daddy weren't happy about him taking a break, but when I asked Clarence about it, he said to not worry. He said a lot of students took a break in college."

"What did you think about that?"

"It didn't seem like him," Louisa admits.

I make note of this and then push my fork through the pot pie's flaky crust. "Did Clarence ever say he wasn't happy at Loyola?"

"No. Not to me, anyway."

I frown. Why else might he have taken a break? "Did he have bad grades?"

"Absolutely not," Louisa says, as though I couldn't have asked a dumber question. "Clarence had top marks all the time."

"What about friends? Did he have friends other than Daniel? A girlfriend?"

"There was a girl he saw briefly in the fall, but she was a bad egg, so they broke up. Mostly, he talked about Daniel, though recently he'd made some friends at work too. Liam is the only one I ever met."

I write *Liam* on a fresh line. "What do you know about him?"

"About Liam? Not a lot. He gave us his spare tire one day when Clarence and I were headed to a Cubs game. They saw each other mostly at work, I think."

"Where did Clarence work?"

"A smoking store that wasn't too far from his apartment, Foxglove Smoke Shop. Clarence didn't talk about it much, but all his clothes smelled like cigars." Louisa wrinkles her nose.

"Had he worked there long?"

"Since early summer."

I take a large bite of my dinner to give myself time to think. My eyes wander over the notes I've taken. Does any of this even matter? When it was Lydia, it felt different. I knew her secrets and where to start poking around. I can think of plenty of questions to ask Louisa, but how do I know what will be useful?

Louisa blinks at me expectantly. I have to ask *something*.

"Is Clarence your only sibling?"

She shakes her head. "No, I have a sister who graduated from Presley's two years ago. Joanna?"

She says the name as a question, but I don't know anyone by the name of Joanna Dell. Lydia always socialized widely and was well-liked, but I was primarily known as "Lydia's friend." Well, until early in our junior year when I took a rather infamous ride down the school banister wearing my bathing costume.

"What's Joanna doing now?" I ask, like I know who she is.

"Being perfect." Louisa stabs a stubborn noodle. "She's at Vassar, dating a man from Yale."

"What did Joanna say when she heard the news about Clarence?"

Louisa glances up at me, and then back to her dinner. "She was surprised."

"And your parents?"

"Also surprised."

"Have any of them expressed doubt that Clarence took his own life?"

Louisa purses her lips and looks away. "We were all surprised when the call came."

"But that isn't the same thing. Does anybody else in your family think Clarence didn't really do it?"

Louisa reaches for her mug of cider, but instead of lifting it, she rotates it slightly over and over. "The others in my family . . ."

When Louisa trails off, I have to bite my lip to keep from prompting her to finish her sentence. I take a bite of mashed potatoes so I won't be tempted.

She stops turning the mug and lifts her gaze to meet mine. "You know how in school, teachers don't like it if you ask too many questions? As a student, your job is to listen. To take notes. You're not to question if what you're being told is right or wrong. The teacher said it, and so it's a fact."

I nod. "Sure."

"Well, that's what my parents and Joanna are like. With the newspaper, the radio, and certainly the police. If they say, 'Clarence died by suicide,' my parents and sister might ask questions, but they're not going to question what they're told. Do you understand what I'm saying?"

I nod slowly. "That your family doesn't question authority."

"*They* don't. Clarence and I always did. Maybe it's why we got on so well." Louisa pushes her half-eaten meal to the side and folds her hands on the Formica table. She fixes me with a hard look that makes it clear she's not the mousy girl I first assumed her to be. "I know my brother. I know he didn't do what the police said he did. I *know* it. And I'm the only one left who will ask questions, because he's gone."

Her voice breaks on the word *gone*.

Looking into her round face, I see something familiar. Something I saw in my own reflection shortly after Lydia went missing—a mixture of grim determination and responsibility. I knew I probably wouldn't like what I found, but answers had to be found anyway, and I needed to be the one looking for them because nobody else cared like I did.

"Okay." I intend to sound confident, but instead my voice comes out hushed and raspy. "I'll see what I can find out about Clarence."

CHAPTER
FIVE

Mariano is late.

I stand just inside the B/G Sandwich Shop, where I'm out of the cold but will be instantly visible to Mariano when he arrives. *If he arrives.*

I brush away the voice of doubt. He *will* arrive. The one time he canceled last minute, he eventually called the restaurant to get a message to me, so it's not as though he actually stood me up.

The customer at the register orders the roast chicken sandwich with potato salad—my usual order—and my stomach growls like an irritable cat. I peek at my watch again and learn that Mariano is now twenty minutes late, not just nineteen minutes late like the last time I checked. Should I go ahead and order so at least I'm not quite as grumpy while I wait for him?

His delayed arrival feels extra irksome because as I was leaving to meet Mariano, Louisa brought a banker's box full of items related to Clarence. To be on time for our Saturday lunch date, I left the box unopened in my bedroom. I could've had twenty minutes to peruse what Louisa brought me, but instead I've been standing in the B/G entrance waiting on Mariano.

He gets another two minutes, and then if he hasn't arrived, I'll order myself a sandwich and take it home.

This B/G is about halfway between Astor Street and Mariano's apartment on the edge of Little Italy. Sometime during the fall, we started referring to it as "our place." Probably around the time that the cashier, Norma, took to greeting us by name whenever we arrived. It's a typical B/G on the inside—a long counter where you place your order and small Formica tables for the few who don't take their sandwiches to go. Norma never seems to mind the rare occasions that Mariano and I occupy a table for multiple hours. Sometimes, she even refills our drinks or brings out slices of pie and coffee, no charge.

I look at my watch again. Twenty-two minutes late. Looks like I'm taking my sandwich home.

I march up to the counter and make an effort to not scowl at Norma, because it isn't her fault Mariano hasn't arrived. Norma is in her early twenties and is saving up money for secretary school. She keeps her finger waves of short brown hair pinned back from her face and wears more makeup than anyone I know. It doesn't look bad, exactly, but it does give me the feeling that I don't *really* know what she looks like.

As I approach, she purses her cherry-red lips. "No Mariano today?"

I feel the thinness of my smile. "I guess not."

"Something must have come up at work, because I can't imagine any other reason Mariano would miss— Oh, speak of the devil."

I whirl and see Mariano rushing toward the glass B/G door, one hand pressing his homburg tight to his head as the winter wind pushes against him. He whips open the door and steps inside with a wild-eyed look.

"Traffic was terrible," he says between pants for breath. Did he run here from wherever he parked? "Sorry to keep you waiting."

Most of my irritation crumbles away, but some stays stubbornly in place. "I'm glad you made it."

"Me too." His hand rests on my back. "I hate that it cuts into our time together."

"Some time is better than no time," I say, parroting our refrain that was born of his excruciatingly busy fall.

"The usual for both of you?" Norma asks.

Mariano pays for our sandwiches, and we take our second-favorite table because our usual corner table is occupied. I squelch the petty urge to say that it was still open twenty minutes ago. Bad traffic isn't his fault.

"How are you?" His cadence is rushed, as though trying to cram as much into our time together as possible. "Aside from being irritated with me, of course. How was your morning?"

"Fine." My own voice is still stiff. I've always been exceptional at clinging to my anger. *Let it go, Piper.* "Sidekick ate a bag of peppermints Jane left out, so that should be interesting."

Mariano winces. "I imagine he's eaten worse before, so he'll probably be fine."

Sidekick lived on the street for an unknown amount of time before I adopted him—or before he adopted me, really—so he probably really *has* eaten worse. "Probably so. Jane was furious."

Mariano's smile chips away the last of my irritation. "I'm sure you were sorry to see her upset."

"Of course I was." I shed my coat. "I don't find it funny at all when she gets angry and her voice turns high-pitched."

Mariano grins.

Instead of calling out our number, Norma delivers our sandwiches to the table with a smile and an "Enjoy."

On each of our plates is a chocolate chip cookie that neither of us ordered.

"Good ol' Norma," Mariano says fondly as he lifts his sandwich.

"Indeed." I gather potato salad onto my spoon. "I have a question for you. Have you ever come across a death that looked like suicide but was actually a murder?"

Mariano's roast beef on rye is halfway to his mouth, and it hangs there as he stares at me, unblinking. He exhales a sound of amusement as he places the sandwich back onto his plate. "I wonder at what point in our relationship I'll stop being surprised by questions you ask me."

"I'm just wondering how common it is."

"It won't be today, apparently." He takes a drink of water. "I'm still surprised by you today."

I shift in the hard wooden seat and feel a touch of embarrassment that Zola, Mariano's ex, probably didn't ask questions like that. She probably asked nice, normal questions like how his day had been or what he ate for breakfast. Not that I think Mariano would rather be sitting here with her, but I'm not sure this is his favorite trait of mine.

"It isn't a random question," I say. "I have a reason for asking."

"I assumed. And what is that reason?"

My heart flutters. Will he laugh when I tell him? Grow angry? "There's a girl at Presley's whose brother took his own life in October according to the police report, but she thinks he didn't. That he was killed."

"Oh, jeez." Mariano leans back in his seat. "That's awful. Did you know him?"

"No. And I don't really know her either, but she's friends with Lydia's younger sister, and . . ." I shrug.

"She thinks since you solved Lydia's murder, you can do the same for this girl."

"Something like that."

Mariano's smile is soft. "And because you're you, you want to help."

I nod and take a bite of my sandwich. There's nothing special about the roast chicken sandwich at B/G, except that I'm almost always with Mariano when I'm eating it, so in an odd way it's become one of my favorite foods.

Mariano still hasn't said anything more.

I swallow. "Do you think that's silly?"

"Not a bit of that is silly. Not the sister struggling to accept what the police are telling her, nor you wanting to help." Mariano offers me one of his french fries. "Why does she think her brother didn't do it?"

I accept the fry and pop it into my mouth. "She says he seemed like his happy, normal self right up until the end."

"Mmm." Mariano considers this. "We hear that a lot."

"I wondered. Poor Louisa. She's sure that Clarence wouldn't have taken his own life, but also sure that nobody would've wanted him dead."

Mariano grimaces. "We hear that a lot too. Typically, it doesn't take much digging to find the victim isn't quite as saint-like as the family insisted. Was he still in school? Working?"

"A little of both. He'd been in college but was taking a break. Apparently, that was very upsetting to his parents, which doesn't surprise me because he's a Harvard School boy. Not the university, the one in Kenwood."

"Living back at home, then?" Mariano asks, then takes a massive bite.

"No. He shares—shared—an apartment with a friend, and he worked on the North Side at a place called Foxglove Smoke Shop."

Mariano pauses midchew and swallows, even though there's no way he was ready. "The Fox? You're sure about that?"

I frown. "She said Foxglove Smoke Shop. Why? What's wrong with that?"

Mariano pushes his chair onto its back two legs. "Foxglove Smoke Shop—or The Fox as it's commonly known—isn't a smoke shop. It's a North Side casino."

North Side . . . meaning mobsters. Was Louisa's brother involved in the mafia? Surely not. "Are you certain?"

He loosens his tie as he brings his chair back down on all four legs. "Positive. It was owned by O'Banion, but I don't know who runs the place now. North Side has been a bit chaotic these last few weeks." Mariano tightens the tie he just loosened. "You're like a magnet for organized crime, Piper Sail."

I hold up my hands, as if surrendering. "This is the first I've heard of any of this. I figured it was an actual smoke shop. It isn't as though I'm going out looking for mobsters."

"I'm not saying it's your fault. Organized crime is the heart of our city right now, honestly. None of us can completely escape." He sweeps his hand through his hair, which is the darkest of browns. "Even if you're *not* choosing to date the son of a mobster."

Irritation flares inside me. "That is *not* who you are, Mariano."

Mariano's eyebrows raise. "Piper, that's exactly who I am."

"Okay, maybe, yes. But that's not *all* that you are. I wish you'd stop saying things like that." I reach for my glass of water. "It isn't as though my family is squeaky-clean, you know."

Mariano shrugs and drags several french fries through ketchup. "What your father does isn't illegal. The sixth amendment states—"

I hold up a hand to stop him. "Do not quote the sixth to me. That was Nick's defense when I spoke to him about Father."

Mariano smiles, but it doesn't reach his eyes. "Okay." He glances at his watch and winces at what he sees. "So, are you going to take the case?"

He asks me with the same tone he would use to ask if I'm taking the L home or what I might have for dinner. It makes investigating Clarence's death seem like an okay choice to make.

I nod as I swallow my bite. "I am. Not sure I know what I'm doing, of course, but she really doesn't have anybody else she can ask."

"She's lucky to have you." Mariano's words warm me all the way down to my toes. "And to answer your original question, suicide is hard to fake. There are just . . ." He gestures with a hand, as if trying to pull words from the air. "Details that are unique and hard to replicate. Patterns. Angles. It isn't impossible, but I wouldn't say that it's a common way of trying to get away with murder. How did he die?"

"Poisoning."

Mariano ticks his head from side to side, considering. "Do you know what kind?"

"I think she said arsenic. I'll have to look at my notes."

"Hmm. Well, if you're going to fake suicide, that isn't a bad way to go. For one thing, a lot of people choose arsenic for suicide, so that isn't a red flag for a suspicious death."

"Louisa said Clarence hated vomiting and he wouldn't have chosen poison."

Mariano frowns. "Don't we all hate vomiting?"

"That's what I said. She said he hated it more than most, though."

His frown persists a moment longer and then he shrugs. "Regardless, arsenic is the most common poison you'll see in a suicide because it's easy to get hold of. But if you wanted to murder somebody with it, there are some advantages. It doesn't have much of a taste, so it's easy to mix into a drink or something similar. And its effects usually take place some time later, which gives the murderer plenty of time to put space between himself and the victim."

"How much time later?"

"Depends on how much you take. Was there a note?"

I nod. "Though his sister said it didn't sound like him."

Mariano frowns. "That's pretty common for suicide too. People don't feel like themselves when they're writing them." He looks at his watch again and sighs. "I'm really sorry, but I need to go. Can we talk about this more—"

"Mariano?"

We both look up at the sound of his name and find a woman in her late fifties approaching our table, a paper-wrapped sandwich in hand.

"*Buon pomeriggio*, Signora Randa," Mariano says as he stands. "How are you?"

"Good! Very good. I was visiting Bruno. He has an apartment not far from here."

Signora Randa glances my way, which Mariano takes as his cue to introduce me. "This is Piper."

I offer my hand. "How do you do?"

"Nice to meet you." Her gaze travels down me, but not in a way that feels unkind, just observant. She grins at Mariano. "Lots of excitement in your family right now, *si*? I saw Zola out with the baby just a few days ago. She's grown so much already!"

The baby.

I can't see Mariano's face in full, but even at this angle I can see how his smile freezes, how his shoulders stiffen.

"Babies do that, I hear," he says.

"What a fun Christmas your family will have this year! Babies make everything feel more festive."

I nibble at my sandwich and try to arrange my face in a normal expression. One that doesn't make it obvious my heart is racing, and that I want to cover my ears and sing *la, la, la* so I don't have to hear anything else about Zola or the baby.

"Well, I need to get back to work—"

"Of course." Signora Randa squeezes Mariano in another hug. "I'm sure I'll be seeing you soon." She nods to me. "Lovely meeting you."

Smile normal. Talk normal.

"You too."

She walks away and Mariano turns to me. He doesn't quite meet my gaze as he says, "Sorry, but I really do have to go."

Keep smiling normally. Keep talking normally. Both of which would be easier to do if Mariano smiled and spoke normally whenever his brother, Zola, or their new arrival came up in conversation. The topic doesn't arise often—we both avoid it—but every time it does, I sense a widening crack in our relationship.

And out of the crack oozes questions that I can typically keep buried: If he no longer has feelings for Zola, why didn't he tell me about the wedding or the baby until after both events had occurred? Why does his smile stiffen and his voice tighten whenever they come up? And on the heels of those questions, there are always others: Was he late for dates with Zola or is he that way just with me? Did he tell her he loved her, and if so, why doesn't he say it to me? Is it because he doesn't?

The questions make me feel like I'm holding a mouthful of sour wine. I swallow and put on a smile. "I understand."

He holds my eyes a moment before bending and kissing my forehead. "I'll call you."

"Okay."

Mariano stands there a moment longer, then turns and strides out of B/G, leaving me to sit alone in my tangle of emotions.

CHAPTER
SIX

The box of Clarence's things sits in the middle of my bed, heavy enough that my mattress sags. After my lunch with Mariano, I'd been eager to get back to my room so I could look inside, but now that I'm here, I can only lean against my headboard and stare at the box. Sidekick hops up onto the bed and rests his furry head in my lap. I thread my fingers into his cream-colored fur and scratch between his ears. His eyes slide closed, content.

"I put everything in there that I thought might be helpful," Louisa told me this morning as she transferred the heavy box to my arms. "Yearbooks, photographs, his financial logs. I didn't know what would be helpful."

So long as the box lid remains on, Clarence Dell is just a story I've been told. Once I take the lid off, he will become a person to me.

I squeeze my eyes tight for a moment and then open the box.

On top is an envelope labeled *photographs*, and I start there. The first that I pull out is of Clarence in his graduating year. He has a sweet, pleasant face. Round like Louisa's, with ears that stick out a bit, light hair and eyes, and a round nose that will probably turn bulbous in his old age.

No, that *would* have turned bulbous. An ache unfurls in my rib cage.

A family photograph shows Mr. and Mrs. Dell sitting in fine clothes with their three children gathered around them. Judging by how Louisa appears in the photograph, I'm guessing the picture is only a year or two old. Maybe taken around the time that her older sister, Joanna, graduated. Joanna looks very similar to Louisa and Clarence, and I imagine if Mr. and Mrs. Dell had ten more kids, they would've looked just like these three.

I set aside the photographs and pull out a bulging composition book labeled *1923*. Some sort of diary? That would be useful. But instead, the inside is full of receipts. They're taped in chronological order to nearly every page with notes like "Lunch with Daniel" or "Gift for Mother" on the sides in tidy, all-caps handwriting.

"You are very detailed, Mr. Dell," I say as I flip the pages.

Or maybe this is normal? Maybe when you have a bank account and money to track, this is how you're supposed to do it? My only experience with money is budgeting my weekly allowance, and I have no bills or financial responsibilities.

I flip to a fresh page in my notebook and write, "How do men keep track of their money?"

Then I rummage through the box in search of 1924's composition book. When I find it, I open to the last recorded entry.

October 29, the day before Clarence was found dead, he bought socks and toothpaste at Woolworth's. I stare at the itemized receipt, written in the loopy writing of an anonymous cashier. Socks and toothpaste? If you're thinking of ending your life, would you also be thinking about clean teeth and fresh socks? And if you've lost the will to live, would you take the time to document the expense?

Even though I've never considered suicide, I've known times of deep sadness where it felt as though life would never again be normal. After Lydia's body was found, I was so consumed with grief, I had to lie to myself in order to get out of bed in the morning. I certainly didn't think thoughts like, *I could use some new socks.*

But Clarence Dell isn't me. Maybe purchases like this and the habit of documenting them were so ingrained in him, they happened regardless of his mood.

I flip back a few pages. There are no pay stubs the way there had been in the 1923 book, when Clarence worked at Carson's department store. Instead, Clarence recorded "+$20 from work" every week, I assume from Foxglove Smoke Shop. If the business is what Mariano says it is—a North Side–run casino—then they probably pay in cash and there would be nothing official like a pay stub.

Twenty dollars a week is an excellent amount of money, far more than he made at Carson's. But it doesn't look as though Clarence lived an extravagant lifestyle. The most money he spent was in August and September, when there's a lot of *Lunch with ELZ* or *Movie with ELZ* or *Gift for ELZ* written in his blocky handwriting. E.L.Z. could be the girlfriend Louisa said he dated. *Who is E.L.Z.?* I write on my list.

I keep digging through the box, impatient to see it all. I find four yearbooks from Harvard School, several sweet birthday cards he gave to Louisa, a ring with two keys—one small and one larger with a label of *3F*—and then an envelope labeled *Note*.

Note?

I lift the flap of the envelope and look at the unassuming rectangle of white paper inside. Oh. *That* note.

I just can't anymore. I'm sorry. —Clarence

I don't even know Clarence, and the words make me feel like the time Nick kicked me between the ribs. I flip the paper over to see if there's more on the back, but that's it. Clarence Dell, who had so much to say about where his money went, had surprisingly little to say about why he chose to leave life behind.

If, indeed, he *did* choose.

I reopen one of the cards he wrote to Louisa and compare the handwriting. They sure appear to be written by the same person. If it's a fake, it's a good one.

There's a sharp rap on my door, startling me so much that I yelp and Sidekick gives a reactive *woof.*

"Piper?"

I sigh. Just Jane. An irritated Jane. "Come in."

My door opens, and Jane pokes her head inside. "Dinner's ready. I've been calling you."

"Okay, I'm sorry." I look at my wristwatch, surprised by the late hour. The stiffness in my legs and lower back confirm that I've been going through the box longer than I realized.

Jane is already trotting down the last of the stairs when I exit my room. By the time I reach the dining room table, she's in her seat across from Father. There's still steam rising from the plates, so they haven't been sitting here all that long.

As soon as I've slid into my seat, Father says a standard blessing over our food.

"I'm sorry, I was working." I spread my napkin across my lap. "I didn't hear you calling for me."

"It's not a problem," Father says, though Jane—who climbed the two flights of stairs to retrieve me—clearly disagrees. "I often get so focused on what I'm doing that I don't hear people calling for me either."

"Did Presley's send work home with you?" Jane asks.

I hesitate, but yes, that's easier. "A little."

"It's good that you enjoy work, I suppose, because it's likely you'll need to continue if you carry on with this path." Jane primly slices a green bean in half. "I don't think detectives make much money."

I freeze. How does she know that I'm investigating a case? Did Louisa say something to her? Did—

"Honey." Father's term of endearment has a note of exasperation. "Piper and Mariano have barely begun dating. It's far too soon for Piper to be thinking about marriage."

Oh, *that's* what she meant. Relief sweeps through me.

Father looks at me, expectation in his eyes. "Right?"

"Yes." I nod. "Absolutely."

Obviously, Mariano isn't thinking about marriage. He's never even said that he loves me.

But Jane laughs. "Timothy, surely you know better than that. Young ladies are always thinking about marriage. I never went out with a man unless I thought there was some chance I might marry him, and I'm sure Piper is the same way. It's the only respectable way for a young lady to date."

Father's gaze shifts my direction, as if waiting for me to confirm this.

I shrug and poke at my potatoes.

Jane, thankfully, shifts the conversation to an article she read in the paper about an old South Side neighborhood that I'm unfamiliar with. How they're building a factory right there in the neighborhood, and what a tragedy it is.

My mind wanders back upstairs, to the box of Clarence Dell's belongings. Can I really do this? With Lydia, I had just poked about, stumbling along. Eventually, I poked around enough that I bumbled my way into the truth about what happened. But can I do that with someone I don't know—just "poke around"? And even if I can, is that really the way to go about an investigation?

"I charge fifteen cents an hour," I had told Louisa at our dinner Thursday evening. I invented this on the fly when she asked how much to pay me. "You can pay for several hours in advance, and then when the funds run out, I'll apprise you of my progress. At that point, you can decide if you want me to continue the investigation."

This had all seemed sensible while sitting across from her in the automat, but now it seems crazy that she immediately handed me money for six hours, like I know what I'm doing.

But I'm smart. I can figure this out.

Speaking to whoever E.L.Z. is seems like a sensible beginning, considering how much time they spent together recently. Clarence's address book was in the box, but there were no entries under Z. Louisa might know if E.L.Z. refers to the ex-girlfriend, and if Louisa doesn't, the best friend/roommate, Daniel, probably does.

Yes, Daniel. Daniel is where I should start. Daniel, who found the body and who was Clarence's best friend.

"Piper," Father says, and I have the impression it isn't the first time. He chuckles as I blink at him. "What are you thinking about so deeply over there?"

"Work." I busy myself by scooping potatoes onto my fork. "Just thinking about work."

CHAPTER
SEVEN

Louisa keeps up a string of words as we depart Presley's after school the next day and walk to the L Station. With minimal breaks for breathing, she carries on about her classes, the book she's reading, and a show she saw last Friday. She's clearly feeling more comfortable with me than she did at our first meeting.

While we stand on the platform awaiting the train's arrival, she leans so far over the tracks to peer down the line, my hand instinctively reaches to take hold of her.

"Not sure when I rode the L last. Mother and Daddy aren't fans of me being on public transportation by myself. Though I'm not by myself, I suppose. I'm with you. The last time I rode the train, I was with Joanna, and— Oh, is that it?"

Her mouth actually closes for a moment, and I hear the approaching noise too. "It's *a* train, at least. Not sure it's *our* train."

"I hope we don't have to wait too long. I don't want to keep Daniel waiting. He's really nice. You'll like him. He can be brusque, so don't take that personally. I haven't seen him in a while. I'm a bit nervous." Louisa clutches her handbag and glances at me. "When I'm nervous, I tend to talk a lot."

I smile. "Really?"

She nods earnestly, not seeming to notice my sarcasm. "I do. My father will say to me, 'Time to button your lips, Louisa,' and I'll bite my lip, like this." She presses her top teeth into her lower lip. "I suppose that's what I should do now. I'm not even sure *why* I'm nervous. It's just Daniel."

"Right." I tug at her arm so she'll take a few steps back from the edge, especially now that I can see the approaching train is ours. "You're really just there to introduce me."

Which is what *I'm* nervous about. Last night, I spent way too long trying to decide on my outfit for today. I finally selected a pearl-gray dress and a charcoal cloche that I hope say Take Me Seriously. If only I could do something about my age or gender.

"The last time I was in the apartment was September," Louisa says as we take our seats on the train. She tucks strands of hair behind her ears over and over, and I want to take both her hands and settle them in her lap. "Clarence was still alive."

Maybe it isn't Daniel she's anxious about, but rather being submerged in memories of Clarence. Maybe she's afraid of her own grief. If so, I can certainly understand.

"If you don't want to go up to the apartment—"

Louisa shakes her head. "I can handle it."

"Of course you can. But if you don't *want* to—"

Louisa turns to me, her bottle-green eyes bright. "It's for Clarence."

I nod, and that's that. Because I recognize that expression, that emotion. When of course you don't want to do something, but the love you have for that person is more powerful than all the fear and grief churning in your gut.

I turn and look out the window, corralling my thoughts away from Louisa and directing them toward Daniel. Inside my shopping bag is my notebook with a list of questions, but I don't want to look at it while I'm talking to him. I run them through my head—*Where were you on the thirtieth? When was the last time you saw Clarence alive? What was he like? Had you noticed any changes in his behavior?*—and audition follow-up questions depending on how he might answer those. That is, if Daniel lets me ask him anything at all. He might take one look at me, laugh, and refuse to answer anything. And what then?

"I haven't seen Daniel since the funeral," Louisa says as we walk along Sheridan Road. She's no longer speaking in rapid sentences, but she's twisting her gloved hands together as we navigate the sidewalks.

I skim the address of the closest building. We're still several numbers away from where Clarence lived. "Is that unusual?"

"He was at our house all the time when they were in high school, but that changed in college. They were busy." Louisa shrugged. "It's to be expected, I suppose."

Her hurt feelings simmer below her words. Though I've never adored either of my brothers the way Louisa does Clarence, I can remember the first summer that Tim didn't come back home but instead got an apartment in Champaign with several others planning to go to law school. While it's natural for families to evolve, to break apart and eventually form new families, I've always thought that evolution must have felt different to Tim, the first of us to break away, than it did to me as the youngest still living at home. Natural or not, to me it felt as if Tim had abandoned us.

"Here we are." Louisa points to a four-story brick building that looks identical to the other brick buildings. This area is densely packed, though some effort has been made to plant trees and install a few benches. There's a Thompson's Cafeteria, a laundromat, and a Woolworth's within sight. *Socks and tooth-paste*, I think when I see it.

Inside the apartment vestibule, Louisa pulls the small lever labeled *3F.*

"It'll buzz inside the apartment," she says, as if I'm unfamiliar with how these things work. "Then Daniel will come down and let us in."

"Okay, great." I instinctively tighten the belt on my red plaid coat and then stuff my hands into my pockets to hide how they tremble.

A few seconds later, the locked door opens and a young man appears on the other side. He smiles at Louisa without showing his teeth. "Hi, Lou-Lou. Come on in." His gaze shifts to me. "You must be Louisa's friend. I'm Daniel Becker."

"Piper Sail." I hold out my hand to shake and pray my palm isn't sweaty. "Nice to meet you."

He nods and offers a polite smile. "Likewise."

Daniel is only a few inches taller than me, probably five foot nine or so, with a thicker, stockier build. His hair is brown and—despite his youth—thin. His eyes assess me as we shake hands.

Louisa glances between the two of us. "Piper is helping me investigate Clarence's death."

Surprise flickers on Daniel's face, and he drops my hand. He frowns at Louisa. "Are you serious?"

Louisa tugs at the fingertips of each of her gloves. "Last summer, Piper's best friend was murdered and she's the one that figured out who killed her."

My mouth falls open at this. Nobody ever speaks so bluntly about Lydia, and an irrational anger wells up inside me.

Daniel looks at me. "I'm sorry to hear that."

I swallow the rage Louisa's words dredged up. Daniel also

lost a best friend, and us being here is going to surface some horrible memories for him too.

"Thank you," I say. "I'm sorry for your loss as well."

"Thank you." He hesitates a moment and then looks at Louisa. "Why don't we go upstairs, where we can speak privately?"

Daniel leads us up two sets of utilitarian stairs and then holds open the door for apartment 3F. His gaze sweeps over me as I pass through. What did Louisa tell him about me when she set up this meeting?

The apartment is even smaller than I expected and smells strongly of coffee. Upon entering, I'm in a square of a room that serves as a kitchen, dining area, and living room. The kitchen isn't much more than a cupboard, a sink, and a small oven and cooktop. There's a round table shoved close to the icebox, but the majority of the room is taken up by a rocking chair and a couch that seats two.

"Sorry for intruding on your afternoon," I say as Daniel closes the door. "We won't stay long."

I glance at my watch: 4:10, but it's ticking slowly. I'm abysmal at remembering to wind it.

"Not at all." He gestures to the round table barely big enough for two, where there's half a cup of coffee and an open textbook. "I'm just studying for my final exams, so I don't mind taking a break."

The clock hanging above the kitchen sink says 4:15. Daniel follows my gaze. "Don't trust that one." He glances at his wristwatch. "Four twenty-three."

"Thank you." I adjust and wind my watch, and then nod to his textbooks. "How many final exams do you have?"

He grimaces. "Four."

Louisa removes her hat and clutches it in her hands as she looks around the apartment. "Everything is just as I remember. It's hard to believe so much has happened since September."

Daniel's expression is guarded when he looks at Louisa, making me think of how I feel when my one-year-old nephew, Howie, comes for a visit. I never feel sure of how to interact with him.

Daniel takes a deep breath and shifts his focus to me. "Miss Sail, I'm not sure what Louisa has told you, but Clarence's death . . ."

For a moment, the only sounds in the apartment are the ticking of the poorly working clock and a neighbor's radio program. Daniel seems to be struggling to find the words he wants to use, and I let him.

"She knows about how he died," Louisa says. "She also knows that I believe he didn't kill himself."

Daniel exhales a shaky breath. "Lou . . ."

Her jaw sets stubbornly. "I *don't*."

Daniel's Adam's apple slides down and back up. He looks at me as if I'm part of the problem. If Louisa wasn't standing here, I might spin him a story to put him at ease—claim I'm not *really* investigating Clarence's death, but rather I'm indulging her. *Poor kid just can't believe her brother would've done this*, I might say, before I started to pry for information. But there's no way to silently communicate that strategy to Louisa.

I put on a smile that I hope makes me appear sweet. "If I can just ask you a few questions, Mr. Becker, we'll leave you in peace."

Daniel tweaks the cuffs of his shirt. "That's a nice thought, but I haven't experienced peace since I came home that day."

That day. It's how I think of Lydia's death as well. For an instant, my throat cinches so tight, I can't speak. I swallow and ask a strangled, "Where were you on the thirtieth?"

"Class all morning and work until five." He shakes his head absently. "If only I'd been here . . ."

"When did you see Clarence last?"

"Alive?" Daniel scratches behind his left ear, then his right. "That morning before I left for class. Of course, I had no idea it was the last time we'd ever speak."

His eyes become glassy.

I feel my emotions rise as I think of my own last moments with Lydia, her standing at her door, waving farewell. I grit my teeth and shove the thought away. *Not now*, I think, though it honestly never feels like a good time to take the lid off, to let the grief out.

"Had he been acting any differently?" I ask, teeth still gritted.

Daniel looks confused, probably because of my strange tone.

I unlock my jaw. "Was he cleaning up after himself around the apartment? Was he eating, sleeping, bathing regularly? Did he talk about future plans?"

His mouth purses slightly as he thinks.

Louisa clears her throat. "I've already told her that Clarence seemed like himself right up until he died. That he didn't seem depressed at all."

I try to send Louisa a look that says *Please stop answering questions meant for Daniel*, but her eyes are locked on her brother's friend.

"I mean, that's what's so strange about the whole thing, right?" Louisa twists her gloves in her hands. "He was perfectly fine. He was *Clarence*. And then he was dead."

Daniel regards her for another few seconds before opening

his mouth. "I'm sorry, Louisa." The words are slow. Regretful. "But that isn't really true."

Louisa's round eyes, which perpetually look surprised, widen even further. "How can you say that? I saw him the night before, and he was completely normal."

"Yes, but I lived with him." The gentleness in Daniel's voice isn't going to help this go down easy. "I saw sides of him that no one else saw. I know this is hard to hear, but Clarence hadn't been himself since what happened at school."

"What happened at school?" Louisa and I ask simultaneously.

I shoot her a look that she doesn't see. If she goes anywhere else with me, we're going to have a talk about who should be asking the questions (not her) and who should be answering them (also not her).

Daniel's brow furrows. "You know he wasn't at Loyola anymore, right?"

"Of course. Mother and Daddy are so sore about it." Louisa shakes her head. "*Were* so sore about it, I mean."

"He'd been different ever since then." Daniel scratches the back of his neck. "Which is understandable. I just wish I'd realized he was taking it so hard."

I open my mouth to ask, but unsurprisingly Louisa beats me. "Taking *what* so hard?"

Daniel blinks at her. "Getting made."

"Getting *made*? What do you mean?"

"You don't know, do you?" His gaze flicks to me, as if remembering I'm still here, then goes back to Louisa. "Loyola suspended Clarence for cheating."

Here we go. Just as Mariano said, the real person is never as saintly as the family portrays them.

"For *what*?" Louisa's voice turns shrill. "Clarence would *never* cheat. He would never need to! He was so smart."

"I know it's tough to understand, Louisa, but college isn't like high school. The classes are harder. The stakes are higher. A lot of people do things to get by that they never would've imagined they'd do." Daniel swallows hard. "Don't think too poorly of Clarence."

"No." Louisa's hands press onto her narrow hips. "There is no way my brother cheated. He never would have done that."

Daniel opens his mouth. Shuts it. He looks to me, as if he thinks I might come to his aid.

I adjust my bag on my shoulder, wishing I could whip out my notebook and start firing questions at him. "When did the suspension happen?"

"Right before spring exams." Daniel ducks his head, revealing a shiny bald spot on his crown. "He had mimeographed answer keys for several classes and—"

Louisa stomps her foot. "No. He *never* would have cheated, and you know it."

Daniel's cheeks darken as he looks at her. "I know it's hard to accept what happened. It's hard for me too. But this"—he gestures to me—"isn't gonna bring Clarence back. No offense intended, Miss Sail."

Louisa huffs. "I know nothing will bring him back, but I want to know what really happened—"

"We know what really happened." Daniel's voice turns sharp. "And we don't need some fake schoolgirl detective poking around and getting everyone worked up again."

My face stings as if Daniel slapped both my cheeks. *Fake schoolgirl detective.*

Louisa opens her mouth, but I rest my hand on her arm. She actually understands and closes her mouth.

I inhale slowly, as if I can breathe my way through to the other side of the shame. "I know this is painful, Mr. Becker, and that Clarence's death is probably the last thing in the world you want to revisit. I understand that. But if you can please show me where you found Clarence, we'll leave straight away."

Daniel looks at me and appears to be considering my request.

"Okay." He jerks his head toward a stumpy hallway. "This way."

I turn to Louisa, who shakes her head at me. She doesn't want to reenter her brother's room.

I nod. "I'll be right back."

The hallway only takes a few paces to cross and contains three doors, one of which is closed. Daniel puts his hand on the doorknob and turns. The door opens soundlessly.

The room is cold and empty. Sunlight weakened by winter and obscured by the city skyline filters through the window, illuminating dust particles as they float through the space. Nothing of Clarence's remains.

"This is where you found him?" Even though I pitch my voice low, it still echoes slightly in the empty room.

Daniel gestures to the floor. The bed was moved recently enough that there are still indentations in the carpet. "He was lying here." Then he nods to the right. "His nightstand was there, and that's where the note, the glass, and the rat poison were."

"Rat poison? Louisa said they found arsenic in his system."

"That's what rat poison is mostly. We kept a box under the kitchen sink."

"Oh." I frown at the room, trying to visualize how it looked with the furniture. "He wouldn't have just taken a spoonful of rat poison though, would he?"

Daniel shakes his head. "He mixed it into a glass of scotch."

"Where was the pie?" I ask. "Louisa mentioned there was pie in his system."

Daniel shrugs. "There was no pie when I came in here, just the empty scotch glass, the rat poison, and the note."

I look around the room, but there's really nothing else to see. "Louisa said there was a lot of vomit."

He grimaces. "The bathroom was a mess. Poor guy."

"Did you find that odd?"

"No, I think it's a normal reaction when you've poisoned yourself."

I shake my head. "I meant, did you find it odd that Clarence chose poison? Louisa said he hated vomiting and avoided it at all costs. That even if he was going to take his own life, that's not the method he would've chosen."

Daniel's gaze skims my face, as if assessing. "Look, I don't know you, and I'm not trying to be rude, but I'm worried about this whole situation with Louisa."

His voice is barely louder than a whisper, and his mouth is close to my ear. Uncomfortably close, considering I don't really know him and the bedroom door is mostly shut. "Maybe it's because she didn't know about Clarence's cheating, but it's concerning that Louisa still refuses to believe the truth about him. Things like this—like you, taking her seriously and acting like Clarence might not have taken his own life—just make everything worse."

Fake schoolgirl detective. I feel my face flush. "I'm not trying to make it worse. I'm trying to help her find some answers and some peace. That's all."

Daniel looks away from me. "I just don't know that there's peace to be found here, Miss Sail. Not for any of us who loved Clarence."

Losing Lydia like I did was hard enough. But if I'd been the one to *find* her? And if it's true that Clarence was in a bad enough place to take his own life, as the person who saw him daily, Daniel must feel so much guilt.

"If there's nothing else"—Daniel keeps his gaze on the ground—"can we please be done in here?"

"Yes," I say and retreat to the door. "The only other thing I wondered about was if you know someone with the initials E.L.Z."

"E.L.Z.," Daniel echoes. "Not without context, no."

"August to early October, Clarence spent a lot of time with someone who he referred to as E.L.Z. A girlfriend, maybe?"

"August to early October," Daniel repeats. Recognition lights his eyes. "Oh. I think you mean Elz, not E.L.Z. Her name is Elz."

"Elz?" What kind of a name is that? "Is it a nickname of some sort?"

"I don't know. She's Polish, I think. Or Hungarian. I can't remember now. I never met her." Daniel shrugs. His expression turns pensive. "Clarence seemed happy when they were dating, and I thought things were going to be better, but then the relationship was over. Very suddenly. He never told me why, really."

"Did Clarence seem upset?"

Daniel considers this and nods. "He didn't say much about it, but yes. I think he was really upset. And that was just a few weeks before . . . everything."

So, Clarence had been booted from college because he was caught cheating, and just weeks before he died, his relationship suddenly ended. Louisa hadn't exactly painted a full picture of her brother.

"Interesting," I say. "Can you think of anybody who would've wanted to hurt Clarence? Anybody who he'd fought with or who wished him harm?"

"No." Daniel's chuckle is dry and humorless. "Everybody loved Clarence."

For a moment, I forget myself. I forget I'm just a fake schoolgirl detective and I say, "I'm going to leave my phone number with you. If you think of anything else that might be helpful, give me a call."

Daniel blinks at me, and a smile plays at the corners of his mouth. "Okay, Miss Sail."

He's amused, and I'm glad that I can turn my back to him and walk away before he sees how my presumption stains my cheeks red.

CHAPTER
EIGHT

"Daniel's wrong. That's all there is to it." Louisa crosses her arms over her chest, and her elbow jabs me. "Clarence wasn't that upset about splitting with Elz. Honest."

"Or he didn't tell you he was upset. I don't think it's out of the question that he might've shared different things with his best friend than he did his little sister."

Louisa turns toward the train window, her nose in the air. "Elz was a bad egg. We all knew that. Nobody expected them to last, even Clarence. He never bothered introducing her to his friends or most of the family."

"If 'everyone knew' Elz was a bad egg, why was Clarence seeing her for two months?"

Louisa gives me a look. Not a cold look, exactly, but sharp.

"Ah." I smile. "I'm guessing she isn't ugly?"

Louisa snorts a laugh. "Not a bit. And in addition to that, Elz was fun and flirty. She's the sort of girl that a fellow might take out a time or two, but not one they would be serious about. Surely you know the type."

I do, though according to Clarence's financial diaries—or whatever they should be called—he took Elz out far more than two times. "How did they meet?"

"She worked at the smoke shop."

The casino. If Louisa can't accept the idea of her brother getting suspended from school for cheating, what's she going to do when I break the news to her that the smoke shop isn't really a smoke shop? I'll save that information for another time.

"Does she still? I'd like to get in touch with her."

"That's a waste of time. He wasn't serious about her."

"That doesn't mean she wasn't serious about *him*."

The hard façade Louisa has been wearing on our train ride softens at this. "Yeah." She says this slowly, like she's trying out the idea. "I guess that could be true. Or she might know people at work who had something against Clarence."

"Exactly. Because if you're right that Clarence didn't take his own life, that means I'm looking for someone else who did."

To me, this is obvious, but Louisa seems to need regular reminding.

"Her address might be in Clarence's book that I gave you." Louisa's face scrunches with concentration. "I don't remember her last name, though. Something strange."

"I'll see what I can find."

The train grinds to a stop, but this isn't our station. Several from our car exit and several others enter—a tired-looking woman with hair from the last decade, a Black man in a fine-cut suit and a trilby like Jeremiah's, and an older man with a horseshoe of gray hair. I file them all away, like Mariano taught me.

"I can tell Daniel thinks this whole thing is silly," Louisa says softly. "Like *I'm* silly."

She isn't wrong, exactly, but I think the situation is more complex than that. "Daniel's concerned for you."

"He doesn't need to be." Louisa pulls at a loose thread on her coat's cuff. "I'm not naïve; I just know my brother."

I consider not pressing her—she's a paying customer, after

all—but I can't leave the point alone. "Everybody has secrets. Clarence didn't tell you he'd been kicked out of Loyola."

Louisa purses her mouth. "I'm sure that was a mistake, because Clarence wouldn't have cheated. He never would've needed to. He's always been a whiz at school."

The train lurches as we pull out of the station.

"Louisa, do you think it's possible that you didn't know Clarence as well as you thought you did?"

I try to ask the question gently, but Louisa still gives me a dagger of a look. "I thought you believed me."

"I believe that *you* believe everything you say about your brother." She turns away from me, but I press on. "You hired me to find the truth, Louisa. Not to blindly trust everything you say. I *have* to ask questions. I *have* to dig."

In the reflection of the glass, I see Louisa's jaw tighten.

A minute ticks by. I stop waiting for Louisa to reply and instead recite to myself the things Daniel said that I want to write down as soon as I have some privacy.

Louisa finally turns to me, the darkening cityscape framing her stern face. "Okay, fine. Dig. Ask. But you know what you're going to find when you do? You're going to find out that Clarence is everything I've said he is, because I. Know. My. Brother."

Once again, I look through my notes from yesterday afternoon's conversation with Daniel. And once again, I feel a swirling, almost sickening sensation as I try to figure out what to do with any of it. Maybe if you receive formal training to be a detective, they teach you how to keep track of all the details that get thrown at you. Do the instructors teach how to sift out what's important? How to connect information? How to reconcile conflicting details?

The telephone rings, and I jump as if the phone doesn't ring all day, every day here at Presley's. I push away my notebook and pull the mouthpiece close.

"Presley's School for Girls, how may I assist you?"

As I take down notes about a student who needs to leave early today for a doctor's appointment, Headmistress Robinson marches through the office.

When I end the phone call with the mother, the headmistress says, "Miss Sail, I need to speak with you."

My stomach wriggles. "Yes, ma'am?"

She pierces me with her ice-blue eyes. "It has come to my attention that you've been calling Ms. Underhill by her Christian name."

"Oh." The corners of my mouth twitch. There's a laugh in my throat that fights to get out. "Um. Should I not do that?"

I swallow and pray fervently that I won't giggle. Whenever I enter the teacher's lounge, Ms. Underhill looks so annoyed by my presence that I can't seem to help myself from saying, "Hello, Mary. Fancy seeing you in here," as I make a show of cleaning the percolator or tidying the box of teas.

I lose my battle with the giggle and try to make it sound more like a cough.

Headmistress Robinson sighs. "Please address all staff formally, Miss Sail."

"Yes, ma'am."

The headmistress taps her stack of mail on the edge of my desk, squaring up the edges. "Outside of that, you've stepped into this role nicely. I think this job suits you well."

Her voice is gruff, as though she doesn't really want to give me a compliment.

I reply with only a dip of my head, because I don't want her to see how much her words mean to me. When I look up again, the headmistress is exiting the office as Miss Bianchi, the new history teacher, enters.

Miss Bianchi takes a look at my face, then at Headmistress Robinson's retreating figure before saying quietly, "Are you okay?"

I nod and finish filling out the early dismissal pass before I forget. "I've been a little lippy with Ms. Underhill is all. I've been using her given name."

Miss Bianchi laughs and then covers her mouth. "Sorry, but that woman invites it, if you want my opinion. Surely the headmistress knows that."

"I'm pretty sure the headmistress knows everything."

She grins. "Well, you have permission to call me Isabella."

I wish Miss Bianchi had been my history teacher instead of Ms. Dull, who lived up to her name. Miss Bianchi—Isabella, I guess—is young and lively, with an easy smile and quick wit.

She smiles now. "You were a student here, yes?"

I nod.

"My first teaching job out of college was my alma mater." Isabella leans against my desk. "There were many things I liked about teaching there, but it was hard for some of the staff to accept me as a colleague. I knew if I stayed, I wouldn't be seen as an adult until all my former teachers were gone."

"That's probably true for me at Presley's too. This is just a temporary job for me while . . ."

While *what*? While I get my own private investigator business going? While I wait to get married?

Isabella doesn't seem to mind my incomplete sentence. "I hope you stay, but sometimes you have to start walking down the road before you can see where you want it to take you. As Marcus Aurelius says— Oh, there she is."

I turn to see who prevented Isabella from sharing Aurelius's wisdom and find a short woman striding through the main doors. She's wearing a turban that looks more suitable for evening wear, and the large buttons of her coat sparkle. The only thing not glamorous about her is the brown bag she's carrying from Thompson's.

She smiles broadly at Isabella as she enters. "You're already in here! I thought I'd have to come find you."

"No, because you're late. Five minutes of my lunch break have already ticked away, thank you very much."

The woman rolls her eyes. "Can you believe her, Betty?" She looks at me for the first time and startles. "I'm so sorry. I just assumed you were Betty."

"Betty is in a family way and had to leave her position." Isabella gestures to me. "This is Piper. Piper, this is my sister, Chiara."

"How do you do?" I say.

Chiara blinks rapidly. "Goodness, aren't you a doll? You look like you could be a *student* here."

"Chiara," Isabella says with a sigh. She looks to me. "Sorry. Chiara prefers to talk first and think afterward. Or to just *not* think."

Chiara laughs at this, seeming unoffended. "Apologies, Piper. How do you feel about oatmeal cookies? I brought an extra one for Betty, because she never liked having to go find Isabella for me, so I always felt like I had to bribe her."

"I will happily eat the cookie you were going to bribe Betty with. Thank you."

Chiara grins at me and digs in the bag, while Isabella surveys the clock hanging in the office. "I'm now down to twenty-three minutes to eat my lunch."

"Oh, stop being such a flat tire." Chiara presses the paper-wrapped cookie into my hand. "Nice to meet you."

I watch them leave the office with a pang of regret that I don't have a sister of my own. Not only that, the one person who was like a sister isn't here any longer.

Grief for Lydia descends like a shove, pushing hard on my chest. My eyes burn and I press my palms into them, blocking the tears from coming out. *Not now. Not here.* I inhale a rattling breath through my nose, as if I can suck the grief back down into my lungs, deep into my body. *Just not now. Later. You can feel it later.*

The telephone trills, and I reach for it with such gusto, I nearly knock it over. "Presley's School for Girls, how can I assist you?"

By the time I'm off the phone with the parent who wants to set up a meeting with Headmistress Robinson, I'm back to breathing normally. The only remains of the grief are a slight ache in my chest, similar to how my calves might ache after a day full of walking.

The experience leaves me longing for the sound of Mariano's voice. Mariano, the one good thing to have come from losing Lydia.

I ring the station only to be told that he isn't in right now.

"Would you like to leave a message?" asks the gravel-voiced secretary.

I hesitate. The last time Mariano and I spoke was at our rushed lunch on Saturday. Today is *Tuesday*. Why hasn't he called me, especially when our lunch ended on such an uncomfortable note?

"No." I lower the earpiece back to the hook as I speak. "No message."

Is this how breakups begin? A missed date or two. A few days between phone calls. Oh, and a major family event that he just plain never told me about. That I had to find out about from *Jack*, of all people.

My eyes sheet with tears and I blink them away. I'm making too much of this. We aren't splitting up; these are just normal problems that arise when you're seeing someone. Nothing to worry about.

Yet several hours later, when I answer the Presley's telephone and it's Mariano sounding apologetic, something within me relaxes.

"Sorry I haven't called since Saturday." His voice drags with fatigue. "I've been getting home after ten every night."

I perform an unnecessary tidying of the writing utensils in my pencil cup. "Has it been since Saturday? I hadn't noticed."

"Really."

His tone is amused because he knows. Of course he does. He knows I'm mad, and he knows I'm pretending to not be mad.

His reading me so easily only makes me madder. "I'm busy too, you know. It isn't as though I spend my days sitting by the telephone."

"That's funny. I thought that's what Presley's paid you to do."

"Well, yes, in a sense that *is* what I do every day, but I'm not sitting here wondering if you're going to call or thinking about how it's been since lunch on Saturday that we spoke."

He chuckles. As I get frostier, he seems to get warmer.

"A lunch you were late for, by the way," I add.

"It's been a terrible week, and we can both agree that I'm a terrible boyfriend." Mariano's voice is now serious, though maybe only to placate me. "Even so, can I come over tonight? I think I can get out of here by seven."

I suppress a smile, because even though he can't see me, I'm sure he'll be able to hear it in my voice. "I suppose that'd be fine."

"Thank you. I should be at your house around seven thirty."

Just a few hours away. Before I can stop it, hope flutters in my chest. Even though I know it's more likely to be eight or eight thirty and that it's possible something will come up and Mariano won't be able to come at all.

Even as I think this, the hope continues to flutter. Hope is stubborn that way.

I'm stubborn that way.

CHAPTER
NINE

My breath fogs the glass as I stare onto lamplit Astor Street. Snowflakes the size of quarters have just started to fall, dissolving as soon as they land. It's 7:25 p.m., and there's no sign of Mariano.

"I'm going to take Sidekick out for a walk," I announce.

Sidekick's head lifts at the sound of his name combined with one of his favorite words.

Jane looks up from the issue of *Vogue* she's been flipping through. Her gaze flicks toward the dark windows. "Now?"

"Yes." I pull my red coat off the hook and slip my arms through the sleeves.

"I don't know that . . ." Her gaze drifts down the hall. "Maybe ask your father?"

"Sidekick needs to go out again, and the snow isn't sticking yet. We'll just go quick around the block."

Sidekick stretches as he stands and then trots over to me, tail wagging. I clip the leash to his collar just as I hear the gate unlatch. I pull the front door open enough to confirm that it's Mariano.

"Mariano is here, don't worry!" I call back to Jane, closing the door before I'm even done with my sentence.

I open my mouth to greet Mariano, but the words die on my tongue. He frequently looks tired—he has a tiring job—but I've never seen him wear the fatigue so obviously. His beautiful brown eyes are puffy and bloodshot. His shoulders are rounded, as though somebody placed upon him the weight of Chicago's many sins.

When he smiles at me, the corners of his mouth barely lift. "Hi."

The remains of my anger dissipate, and I wrap him into a hug and squeeze. A moment later, his arms come around me. We stand there in the lamplight, anchored by each other as the city and snow swirl. Sidekick gives up on his walk and plops beside us.

"Some days"—Mariano's voice is slow and deep in my ear—"you are the only person in the world that I like."

I smile into the black wool of his coat. "You're nicer than me. *Most* days, you're the only person in the world that I like."

I feel his laugh rumble against me. "You didn't sound as though you liked me when we were on the phone earlier."

"That's just bluster." I tip my head back so I can see him. "Bluster and pride."

He doesn't return my smile. "I'm very sorry that we haven't spoken since Saturday. Especially with Signora Randa and all her talk about the baby."

I shake my head. "We don't have to talk about it."

"I know it's uncomfortable. I know *I* made it uncomfortable."

Our time together is so limited, I don't want to spend it talking about this, especially with how defeated he already looks. "Mariano, everything is fine."

His eyes scan my face, and when they catch on my scarred cheek, I duck my head. I don't want to see disappointment dim his eyes. Not disappointment about my appearance, but that he didn't keep me safe from the one who caused the scarring.

"Can we go for a walk?" he asks. "Or is it too cold?"

I tug Mariano toward the gate and Sidekick leaps to his feet, tail wagging once again. "Sitting in my living room with Jane would be far chillier. Tell me about work."

Mariano groans. "No. I'll talk to you about anything *except* work."

"Okay. Tell me your deepest, darkest fears then."

He grins, and it's wonderful to see him looking like himself. "That's much better, though a lot of my deep, dark fears are related to my work." Mariano takes my hand, which feels a little silly since we're both wearing gloves, but it's nice too. "Why don't you tell me about *your* work?"

"Which job?"

"Either."

We pause while Sidekick investigates the base of a streetlamp.

"Headmistress Robinson gave me a compliment today, which was strange. Of course, it came on the heels of chastising me for how I was speaking to Ms. Underhill, so I suppose it evens out."

"And how were you speaking to Ms. Underhill?"

I shrug. "Like a colleague."

Mariano makes a grunting noise that suggests he doesn't believe me.

"Like a *sassy* colleague, sure, but like a colleague. She takes offense to being called by her given name, apparently."

"That's my girl. Winning hearts wherever she goes." He squeezes my hand. "How's your other job going?"

"Fine?" The syllable curls into an unintentional question.

He arches his eyebrows.

"Yesterday, I met Clarence's best friend and roommate. The Clarence that Daniel described is a little different than the one Louisa told me about."

"That tends to happen. What did Daniel say?"

"He says Clarence hadn't really been himself once he got kicked out of Loyola in the spring for cheating. And that Clarence didn't take it well when he and his girlfriend split in early October, just weeks before his death."

"That *is* different."

"The way Daniel explained everything made me see why his death was classified as a suicide. Clarence's circumstances—his cheating coming to light and losing his girlfriend—probably did leave him feeling hopeless." My thoughts flit through the time at Daniel's apartment, landing at his descriptions of how he'd found Clarence. The rat poison, the scotch glass, the note. "But also, there are details that don't seem quite right that Daniel clearly isn't interested in exploring. He doesn't want to think more about what happened to Clarence, which I understand."

Mariano nods, his mouth set in a grim line. "I'm sure it's unpleasant. I hate to ask this, but can he be trusted?"

I consider the question. "I think so. More than I can trust Louisa, most likely. She adored her brother, and I think it blinded her to who he really was. She didn't know about the cheating, and even when Daniel told us about it, her instinct was to say that he never would've cheated. That he was too smart for that. And Daniel says that Clarence was really upset about the breakup, while Louisa says he wasn't. That he never expected that relationship to last. She gets defensive anytime I suggest Clarence might not have been an angel."

"A lot of people say they want the truth, but they really don't." Mariano brushes snowflakes off my shoulders. "What they really want is for you to confirm what they already believe."

I wrap Sidekick's lagging leash around my hand a couple

times. His enthusiasm for the walk has waned, which is okay because we're almost back on Astor Street. "I just wish I knew who was telling me the truth. I think they're both telling me what they believe is true, but I don't know how to reconcile both their truths. And I feel like I'm taking all these notes and I have no idea what's important."

"That's normal. When you're mining for gold, you get a lot of silt in the process."

"How do you know what's gold and what's silt?"

He shrugs and tightens his grip on my hand as we turn into the wind. "Keep shaking the pan and see what ends up at the bottom."

I think about that for a few seconds. "No, I need *real* advice. Not a metaphor. How do I know what's important and what's not?"

"You won't always, and that's especially true in the beginning when you're gathering everybody's statements. But as you start laying them side by side, you'll see inconsistencies, or bits that don't seem quite right. Like how the sister insists her brother was this saintly guy, and yet he's working at The Fox. I promise you, there are no saints working at The Fox."

"Probably not."

We're back on Astor Street and nearly at my house before I share what's bothering me most of all. "I worry that I'll do all this work and Louisa won't like what I find."

Mariano nods. "That's very possible."

"Being at Clarence's apartment felt really sad, and I hated asking Daniel to relive the whole thing. I mean, I've been the best friend who—" I swallow hard. Mariano squeezes my hand.

When I'm sure the wave of emotion has passed, I add, "And I didn't know what to tell Daniel about who I am."

Mariano frowns. "Who you are?"

Daniel's words reverberate in my head. *Fake schoolgirl detective.*

"I mean, I can't call myself a private investigator. I haven't earned that yet."

I expect Mariano to agree with me, but instead, his frown deepens. "When will you have earned it?"

We stand outside the gate, neither of us moving to unlatch it. The snow is getting heavier, so it can't be put off much longer.

"I don't know. But even if I *do* earn it someday, I'm never going to be able to swagger into a room the way you do."

He smiles fully. "I do not swagger."

The first time I saw Mariano, he was at Presley's on official business. Maybe he didn't swagger in the classic sense of the word, but he moved like someone with authority.

"But you have the badge. I have nothing."

Mariano's arms circle around my waist. "That's not true at all. You have something far more powerful than a badge or a title."

"And what's that?"

"Almost everyone you meet will underestimate you." He rests his forehead against mine. "And that is exceedingly valuable, Detective Sail."

When Sidekick and I come back inside, Jane is exactly where I left her, only she's deeper into her magazine. I towel dry Sidekick's fur, though as soon as I release him he still shakes himself out and then rubs his body along the rug. Typically, that behavior causes Jane to sigh heavily or outright say, "I wish he wasn't allowed in here," but tonight she's absorbed by her reading.

As I hang my coat, Jane says in a tone as crisp as a green apple, "You didn't mention that Mariano was coming over."

I pause untying my boot to look at her, but her focus is on her magazine. "Was I supposed to?"

"It would've been nice."

I keep looking at her, this woman who invaded my childhood home. Am I supposed to say sorry? Mariano coming over tonight impacted her in no way that I can see.

Jane's gaze flicks up. "Were you trying to keep his visit a secret?"

A disbelieving laugh slips out. "No. That's why I said to you, 'Mariano is here.' I didn't think it mattered because he wasn't planning to come inside—"

"And why wasn't he planning to come inside?" Jane gives up her pretense of reading and lowers the *Vogue*. "That's what a proper young man should do when he's seeing a young woman."

Propriety. Of course that's what this is about. What others might think.

I take a deep breath and say as calmly as I can, "Nothing improper happened—"

"Nothing improper? You were kissing him on the sidewalk! Anybody could've seen that."

"So what if they did? Anybody who knows me knows that he and I are seeing each other."

"It doesn't matter." Jane's cheeks have turned bright red. "Your father may let you run loose, but—"

"You're not even ten years older than me. Do *not* act like my mother."

Jane leans back as if I shouted, though I didn't. Her mouth is open, but she doesn't speak, just stares at me.

Father's footsteps come down the hall, and both Jane and I turn to look at him as he arrives in the living room doorway. His glasses are low on his nose, and he's dressed in a sweater and old trousers.

His eyes flick between the two of us. "Is something wrong?"

Jane looks away from him, and I do too. When your father is a lawyer, you learn quickly that keeping your mouth shut is often the best way to go.

"I thought I heard raised voices," Father continues.

Sidekick, oblivious to the tension, continues to roll around on the floor.

Father frowns at my dog. "Why's he wet?"

"Mariano and I took him for a walk, and it's snowing."

"I see." Father smiles at me, but it seems strained. "Pippy, will you come into my office?"

I try for a light tone. "Sure."

I silently follow him down the hall. On his desk is an array of items: an adding machine, a manila folder full of small bits of paper, an open notebook, and an empty whiskey glass. Father was clearly in the middle of something when he decided to intervene.

"What are you working on?" I ask as he takes a seat behind his desk.

"Something I'm sure you would find boring." He closes both the folder and the notebook, which upon closer inspection I realize is an accounts ledger.

"Oh, are you doing something with money?"

Father's eyes widen slightly at my obvious interest. "Yes, I'm reconciling my accounts."

"How often do you do that? Every day? Every week?"

Father's head tilts slightly, as though trying to figure me out. "I'm not *that* disciplined about it. Typically, I get around to it every couple of weeks."

"And do you keep all your receipts? How do you store them?"

"I only keep receipts if I think I might need them later." Father's gaze is steady on me for a moment. Searching. "Why are you asking these questions?"

The lie comes so swiftly, it's almost scary. "I'll receive my first paycheck on Friday, and I need to open a bank account. I need to know how to do these kinds of things."

Father rocks in his chair several times. "I hadn't thought about that. We'll have to go together. I don't know if they allow girls to have their own accounts."

"So, I have the right to vote but not the right to have my own bank account? How does that make any sense?"

"I think some banks allow it, but I'm not sure about any of the *good* banks. Even so, you won't need to bother with all *this*." He waves a hand at his desk. "Money isn't something you need to concern yourself about right now."

"That's a little old-fashioned, don't you think?"

"Maybe." His smile is thin, and when he opens his mouth, I sense that he's about to usher the conversation in a different direction.

"A friend of mine keeps every receipt taped into a notebook. Would you say that's normal or strange?"

Father considers this. "I'm not in the habit of asking my friends how they track their expenses, but I don't think it's normal. Or necessary. Why does your friend do that?"

"He's from a banking family, so maybe that's why? Maybe it's normal if you're in that line of work."

The creases of Father's forehead deepen. "What boy are we talking about?"

"Just an acquaintance of mine. The brother of an acquaintance of mine, actually."

Father's frown persists. "And he's telling you details about how he tracks his personal finances? That sounds like a boy who's trying to impress you, Pippy."

"No, it's nothing like that. He's just . . ." I grapple for how to explain Clarence to my father. "He's enthusiastic about money is all."

Father leans back in his chair. "Piper."

Oh, that doesn't sound good. He doesn't use my real name too often. "Mm-hmm?"

"I'd like to talk to you about Mariano."

"Okay."

Father looks at me for a moment, and then leans forward and rests his elbows on his desk. "How are things going?"

I don't know where this line of questioning is headed, but I don't like it. "Good," I say brightly. "Very good."

"Very good?"

My mind flits to October. To Jack's expression as he realized I had no idea. *Wait, he didn't tell you about the wedding? What about the baby?* "Yes. Very good."

"Good. That's good." Father leans back again and smooths a nonexistent wrinkle on his sweater. Then again. "Very good."

I take a step back from his desk. "Well, it's getting late, so . . ."

"Piper, I understand Mariano was there for you during a very traumatic season. I know he means a lot to you. He's a good man." Father hesitates. "Considering."

Considering? A protective feeling rises inside me, as though my relationship with Mariano is inside a box and I'm sliding the lid into place to secure what's within.

"But I just wonder," Father continues, "if in the long term you wouldn't be happier with someone . . . different. Not that I don't like Mariano, of course. He cares for you, and he really does seem to be very principled."

"He does," I say evenly, "because he is."

"He'll never make much money, obviously, being a cop with principles." Father smiles grimly. "But maybe that's okay."

This is so classically my father; eloquent when speaking to a group about the law or politics, reluctant when talking one-on-one about matters of the heart.

He looks at me, as if hoping I'll share more.

"I'm glad you feel it's okay." I take a step backward. "I have work tomorrow, so I'm heading upstairs to bed."

"Yes, smart idea." Father props his elbows on his desk and steeples his fingers. "It's just that I've been thinking more about what Jane said—about young ladies and only dating those whom you'd seriously consider marrying. There are qualities about a person that might seem important or unimportant to us when we're young that later feel much more important. Like money, for example. Right now, it might not feel important to you that Mariano doesn't make much, because you live in a nice house, you have lots of beautiful clothes, you don't have to prepare your own meals, and so on. You have to consider what that will feel like five, ten, or fifteen years into the future, though. Imagine the two of you have five kids—"

I reflexively grimace, which makes Father smile. "It's just an illustration."

"Can we illustrate with fewer kids? Or maybe no kids?"

Father sighs. "All I'm saying is to consider how you might feel in the future, not just how you feel now."

"Okay." I take another step toward the door. "Good night, Father."

Father hesitates and then says, "Good night, honey."

After I escape, I stop in the kitchen to get a glass of water, then walk through the living room to the stairs. Jane still sits on the couch, reading her magazine beneath a small pool of light in the dark living room. She says nothing as I pass through, Sidekick clicking along behind me.

She looks lonely, and I'm surprised by the sympathy that tugs at my heart. I hesitate at the bottom of the stairs. "Good night, Jane."

Without looking up, she says a frosty, "Good night."

Well, I tried.

After washing my face and brushing my teeth, I retreat to my room and pull the box of Clarence's things onto my bed. With my housecoat wrapped around me, I take out Clarence's address book and begin flipping pages in search of Elz. I've nearly given up on finding her when I flip to the Ws. *Elzbieta Wójcik* is written in Clarence's blocky, all-caps style.

"There you are, Elz," I murmur into the quiet of my bedroom.

Her address is in Chicago, but I don't recognize the street name, and there's no telephone number. If I want to speak to her, I'll have to find her on a map and then drop by.

I pack away the address book and slide the box back into its hiding place beneath my bed. As I stand upright, I catch sight of myself in my full-length mirror.

Round, youthful face.

Unbrushed hair.

A flannel housecoat, worn thin at the elbows, and lumpy woolen socks.

The reflection looking back at me isn't one that inspires respect and deference, but perhaps Mariano is right. Perhaps being underestimated by others isn't something to be continually irritated by, but rather an advantage to capitalize upon.

CHAPTER
TEN

As the L rattles westward, I look at my dim reflection in the window. *Hi. I'm here to speak to Elzbieta Wójcik. I'm a private investigator.*

I raise my chin and try for a stern don't-mess-with-me kind of look, but all I manage to do is put my scars directly in the rays of sunlight slanting through the window. I flinch away from the sight. Mercifully, I have no memories of being dragged into the waiting car and receiving the actual wounds, or of the doctors later picking out the gravel with tweezers, but there were months of bandages and salve and more bandages and salve. And still there are scars.

Maybe I should skip the private investigator act and try for a softer approach? *Hi, my name is Piper. Is Elzbieta here? I'd like to speak to her about Clarence Dell.*

Of course, whoever answers the door will say something along the lines of, "Who are you?" and I'll have to say *something.*

I think the words repeatedly as the train pulls into the station closest to Elzbieta's. *I'm a private investigator. I'm a private investigator. I am a private investigator.* This feels as convincing as thinking over and over, *I'm a strawberry.*

The houses in Elzbieta's neighborhood are all classic brick bungalows, squashed together like the houses downtown. It looks to be a neighborhood of working-class families, but one that takes pride in owning a home, in keeping it nice. A few homes are showing some age with their chipped paint or broken fence posts, but most are well-kept with curtains in the windows, Christmas wreaths on the doors, or rocking chairs on the front porch.

Elzbieta's house has the debris of childhood strewn about the front yard—a discarded jump rope, a tricycle—and I frown and double-check the address. Perhaps Elzbieta has younger siblings, because I'm sure Daniel or Louisa would've mentioned to me if Elzbieta had children of her own.

I mount the front steps and knock on the door. A moment later, footsteps approach. When the door opens, a woman not much older than me stands on the other side. Her dress is faded—the kind of dress you wear around the house when you don't think you'll be seeing anyone that day—and her hair is unstyled. Even still, she's striking. Big hazel eyes with thick, dark lashes. Thin eyebrows that arch just right. Cheekbones that give her a sleek, unique appearance.

"Hi." I clear my throat. "I'm looking for Elzbieta Wójcik."

She blinks at me. "I'm Elzbieta."

Her voice is lower than I expected, like if caramel had a sound.

"Okay, great. My name is Piper, and I am . . ." I swallow. "I . . . work for a private investigator."

I *work for* a private investigator? That's the angle I'm going with?

Elzbieta's expression turns guarded. "Is something wrong?"

I can't think of a way to take back the lie, so I will have to stick with the path my tongue chose. I straighten my shoulders. "No. I mean, nothing *new* is wrong."

Elzbieta pulls back slightly and narrows the door opening.

Why hadn't I thought through anything past how I was

going to introduce myself? "This is about Clarence Dell. I've been hired—or rather, my *boss* has been hired—to look into his death."

At Clarence's name, Elzbieta's face drains of color. "Clarence? But didn't he . . .? I mean, I was told that he . . ."

"Took his own life?" I supply. "That's what the police said, yes. But I've—we've—been hired to take a second look at what happened to Clarence."

Elzbieta's teeth press into her lower lip as she regards me. She swallows hard and then speaks in a voice even lower than her usual timbre. "Clarence was very important to me. How can I help?"

"If you have some time right now, I'd like to ask you a few questions."

"Come on in." Elzbieta opens the door fully. "I would offer to take your coat, but I imagine you'll want to keep it. It's chilly in here."

The house is noticeably cold, and the floorboards creak as I step inside. The first thing I see is a steep staircase that is littered with knit hats and stockings and doll shoes. Or perhaps the shoes of an actual baby. When Elzbieta closes the front door, I peek into the living room and see the fire crackling in the fireplace. Two young girls have a deck of cards between them, but they ignore it and blink at me.

I attempt a friendly smile. "Hello."

"Who are you?" one asks.

Elzbieta had been pressing a blanket along the front door's threshold and now stands upright. "This is my friend . . ."

"Piper," I fill in.

"Yes, Piper." Elzbieta fixes the two girls with a firm look.

"We're going to be in the kitchen. Do not disturb us, and do not get loud. I just got Zofia to sleep."

Elzbieta doesn't look older than twenty, and she has *three* kids? How could she possibly have time to date?

Elzbieta gestures for me to follow her through the living room and into a narrow kitchen. At the far end sits a rectangular table, laden with dirty dishes and silverware from a previous meal.

"Sorry, this will have to do." Elzbieta pulls out a chair for me and wipes several crumbs to the floor. "This is my sister and brother-in-law's house. Privacy is impossible, but it's what I have."

The girls are her nieces. That makes much more sense.

"I understand," I say. "I grew up with six people living in the house."

No need to mention that one of those people was our live-in housekeeper or that I have an Astor Street address. But Elzbieta's eyes skim over me, and I feel as though I might as well be wearing a sign that says "I have money." While I didn't put on my fanciest dress and shoes for this interview, I only own nice clothes, and their designs and constructions have certain tells that are picked up by those who pay attention. Elzbieta appears to be the type to pay attention.

"I'm moving out January first, and I'm counting down the days." Using her fingertips, she sweeps breadcrumbs away. "Clarence. Did his parents hire you?"

Elzbieta punctuates the question with a searing look. I open my mouth because for a moment, I forget that I don't have to answer her. That I'm here to *ask* questions. I close my lips and pull my notebook from my shopping bag.

"It would be very helpful to understand the nature of your relationship with Clarence at the time of his death." I try for a stiff, formal tone like Headmistress Robinson uses, and I feel my shoulders straighten.

Small lines form on either side of Elzbieta's mouth as she frowns. "Well. I assume you're here because you know that Clarence and I dated for a little while."

I nod. "When did your relationship end?"

"Early October. I'm sorry, but—" A tremble works its way into Elzbieta's voice, and I look up from my paper. "But if you're investigating Clarence's death, is that because you think maybe he *didn't* take his own life?"

"We're looking into several possibilities."

Elzbieta stares at me with her intense hazel eyes, noisily inhaling and exhaling several times. "But that would mean you think someone . . . did *that* to Clarence?"

When I nod, she swallows hard and then looks away, blinking rapidly. I catalog her reaction. She seems sincere, but that doesn't mean she is.

"I know it's hard to hear, Miss Wójcik. And it's certainly possible that Clarence really did—" I cut myself off when Elzbieta's eyes flick toward her nieces in the living room. "But there have been some questions raised, and this is the kind of thing you want to be certain about."

Her jaw clenches. In the living room, the fire gives a loud *pop* and one of the girls giggles.

"And I'm the ex-girlfriend," Elzbieta mutters, "so of course you need to talk to me."

I smooth the blank page in my notebook. "We're talking to everyone who was close to Clarence. Anything you can tell me about him, about your relationship, about who he was close to, who disliked him—any of that would be helpful."

She nods, her eyes fixed on the floor.

When the silence stretches, I say, "Let's start with you. When did you last see Clarence?"

Elzbieta is silent for so long that I'm about to repeat the question when she says, "October twenty-seventh. We were both at work."

"Is that how you met? Work?"

Elzbieta nods.

"And how long were you in a relationship?"

"Our first date was August fourteenth, and we broke up on October fourth."

"That's very specific."

Elzbieta finally looks me in the eyes. "Isn't that what you want?"

"It is. I was just surprised, I guess." I smile, hoping to put her at ease. "I'm not sure I could give you the specific date that I started seeing my boyfriend."

She goes back to surveying the dirty dishes on the table. "Clarence was special."

The pain in her voice surprises me. "Who ended the relationship?"

"He did."

"Really?"

Her gaze snaps to mine. "Why do you say it with surprise?"

"His roommate said that Clarence had been depressed since your breakup. From that, I assumed you broke up with him."

Her lips press thin. She seems to consider this for a moment, then shakes her head. "No."

Hmm. I'll come back to that. "Where do you work?"

"The Fox. Foxglove Smoke Shop. It's a casino."

"And what's your role there?"

"I'm a cigarette girl. Clarence did the books."

"The books?"

"He managed the money. When he started, he was only doing the accounts for The Fox, but Dean saw real fast what an egghead Clarence was. He had Clarence doing all kinds of money stuff for him before long."

"You mean Dean O'Banion?"

"Yeah."

"Clarence worked directly for him?" It's one thing to work within an establishment that's controlled by a mobster, but working for the boss himself . . .

"He wasn't a bad fellow, really." Elzbieta picks at a cuticle. "He really thought Clarence was the cat's pajamas. That caused some problems, actually. Mostly with Tubs."

"And who is Tubs?"

"He runs The Fox. He was Clarence's boss." Elzbieta's expression shifts, and she sits up straighter. "You should definitely look into Tubs. He really didn't like Clarence."

A dozen questions wrestle their way through my mind, all wanting to be the first out of my mouth. "Why didn't he like Clarence?" is the winner.

She presses her lips together in thought. "Probably because Dean liked him so much. Tubs felt threatened, I imagine, but he couldn't very well fire Clarence after what had happened."

A dozen *more* questions bloom in my mind. "What happened?"

"You don't know about this yet?" Elzbieta uncrosses and recrosses her legs. "It's mostly North Siders working at The Fox, although there are people like me and Clarence too. Not really part of it all, you know, just trying to make a buck. Anyway, Clarence found out there were some South Side fellows hanging around. They weren't obviously Italian, so they slipped by. Clarence overheard them plotting against Dean, and he told him. Dean was real appreciative, as you might imagine."

"This was in September?" I ask.

Elzbieta nods.

Only to have Clarence die the following month. Is that a coincidence? "Do you know if Clarence was rewarded in any way?"

Elzbieta shrugs and toys with a loose thread on her cuff. "Maybe. I don't know. Probably. Dean liked throwing money around."

I make a note to myself to check Clarence's ledger.

"Do you think Clarence might've been killed by one of the South Side guys who . . .?" I trail off because Elzbieta is shaking her head. "Why not?"

Elzbieta shifts in her seat. "Because Dean took care of them."

Something icy slides down my spine. "Oh. Yes, I guess that's to be expected." That's how it works in this world, isn't it? And Mariano had been complaining just the other day that it's only getting worse, the killings less discriminate than they once were. "Do you think someone else on the South Side might've retaliated for *that* by taking out Clarence?"

Elzbieta considers and then shakes her head. "Not against Clarence, I don't think. What happened wasn't widely known. Even Tubs probably didn't fully understand what Clarence had done to win over Dean. Oh!" Elzbieta's eyes light, but she brings her voice back down to a hush. "I just remembered another reason you should talk to Tubs: Clarence was pretty sure he was skimming from The Fox. I don't know what happened with that, because Clarence and I split, but for a while Clarence was trying to figure out what to do."

Tubs skimming, C knew, I write. "So Tubs already hated Clarence, and that was *before* Clarence found out he was stealing from The Fox?"

"Clarence suspected he was, anyway. I don't know if he had proof. I was so upset when he broke up with me, I'd completely forgotten about that until just now." Elzbieta shakes her head, as if scolding herself.

"So, you don't know if Clarence ever confronted Tubs, or . . . ?"

"No. Liam would probably know."

I put a star next to Tubs's name to remind myself to ask more about him, then ask, "Who's Liam?" I remember Louisa mentioning him, though she hadn't known much.

"A good friend of Clarence's." Elzbieta's expression darkens, and she shakes her head almost imperceptibly.

That's interesting. I set aside my planned questions about Tubs. "Tell me more about Liam."

"He's . . ." Elzbieta's jaw hardens once more. "He's always been a good friend to Clarence."

When she doesn't elaborate, I ask, "He works at The Fox too?"

She nods. "As a bouncer. Keiran too. The three of them were good friends. It was always a little funny, these two broad-shouldered North Siders and then Clarence, with his big brain and private school upbringing." A sheen forms over her eyes. "He was so smart."

Her face has lost the stormy expression she wore when speaking of Liam. I tap my pencil on my paper and consider where to steer the conversation.

Elzbieta shifts her weight in her chair. "The thing about Liam is, he's . . . interested in me. Has been for a while now." Elzbieta tucks her dark hair behind her ears and wipes her palms on the skirt of her dress. "And sometimes he would joke . . . Well, I mean, it sounds strange to say it now, but it really *was* a joke. He would say, 'If I could just get rid of Clarence, I'd have a shot with you.'"

She glances at me, then her gaze flits around the room. "Obviously he doesn't say that now, and he was as distraught as I was when Clarence died, so I really don't think . . ." She swallows hard. "But he *is* a Finnegan."

A Finnegan.

My thoughts wrap around the surname and squeeze. "That's Liam's last name? Finnegan?"

Elzbieta nods. "It's why I always turned him down, even before Clarence came along. I don't want to get mixed up with all that."

Neither do I, and yet the Finnegans are like a nightmare I can't seem to escape. The whole time I was looking into Lydia's disappearance, the Finnegan name kept rising to the surface. Patrick and Colin Finnegan are brothers and the most dangerous brand of gangster—small-timers posturing as big-timers.

And now here they are again. Mariano's right; I really am like a magnet for organized crime.

"I'll need to speak to Liam." I tap my pencil against my notebook. "And Tubs too. That isn't his real name, is it?"

She exhales an amused laugh. "No, but that's what everybody calls him. I can't even remember his real name. Something like George or John or Michael. Something really common. He lives at the corner of this street, actually."

I smile. "In the brick house?"

She catches the joke—they're all brick houses—and says

dryly, "That's the one. Brick house, green door and shutters. Lives there with his wife and daughter. At least I think his wife and daughter still live there."

"What about Liam?" I ask. "Where does he live?"

"I don't know. Farther north, I'd guess."

"Do you know when Liam works next? Maybe I could speak to him at The Fox."

Elzbieta considers me for a moment and then says, "The only girls hanging around at The Fox are performers and cigarette girls. There's no one like you." Her eyes do another appraising flick down and back up my outfit. "Maybe your boss could talk to Liam and Tubs instead?"

I keep my eyes on my notebook. "He's busy with other cases right now, so I'll have to be the one to talk to them." I imagine knocking on the front doors of Liam's or Tubs's home, or showing up at their work as someone who works for a private investigator. I can't imagine they'll be as willing to answer my questions as Elzbieta has been. "Although, it might be best if I can talk to them without either knowing they're being investigated."

Elzbieta nods and considers this. "Can you sing? I could speak to Tubs about booking you."

I laugh. "Not at all. I would clear the place." I remember Isabella's sister arriving at Presley's with lunch a few days ago. "What about if I visited you at work?"

Elzbieta's eyes widen.

"If you were willing to help, I mean. You could introduce me to others as your . . . cousin?"

"Like I said, we don't have female patrons. The fellas are there to gamble and drink. If you really wanted to see inside The Fox, well . . ." Elzbieta leans back and takes me in. "You don't look much taller than me. I could maybe squeeze you into one of my uniforms."

A noise of surprise sticks in my throat.

"I could tell people I'm training you. My boss will be away next Monday night, so that might work. If Liam is in that night, of course. Tubs is almost always there, but Liam only works a couple days a week."

My brain whirs with the idea. I've never been inside a casino. The closest I've ever been was a speakeasy, The Green Door Tavern. Even with Walter there, I'd managed to get into more trouble than I would've liked, and this time, there will be no Walter.

And what do these uniforms look like exactly?

"I don't know, Elzbieta." The thought of going turns my stomach into a beehive. "It's a nice offer, but I don't want to get you in trouble with your boss."

"I can take care of myself," Elzbieta says, and I don't doubt her for a second. "And this is for Clarence. If you're right and somebody really did hurt him, then I want to do everything I can to help you figure out who did it. I can get you inside The Fox, and I can help you get close to Tubs and Liam."

I study her for a moment, this girl who glows with loveliness even in a faded dress and unstyled hair. Louisa had described her as fun and flirty, as a bad egg, but that isn't how she strikes me at all. She seems genuinely heartbroken over Clarence's death.

"Okay," I say slowly. "Thank you."

Her serious face flickers into a smile. "Do you know where The Fox is?"

"Only vaguely."

"On Diversey Street. Ground floor of The Foxglove Hotel. My shift starts at nine, so why don't you come around eight forty-five?"

"That's eight forty-five p.m.?"

She smirks. "You didn't think gambling happened during the respectable hours of the day, did you?"

I smile in response, but my thoughts are churning through how I'm going to get out of the house—and back *into* the house—without letting Father or Jane know what I'm up to. I'll have to figure that out later, because this is too good of an opportunity to pass up.

I take a swift, bracing breath and nod once. "Okay. I'll be there."

CHAPTER
ELEVEN

After handing Elzbieta my telephone number, I knot my scarf and walk along the sidewalk with my head ducked. While I'm in the neighborhood, it seems a shame to not take a closer look at where Tubs lives. Obviously, he won't invite me inside for a cozy chat the way Elzbieta did, but maybe I could learn *something* from knocking on his door.

As I approach the corner, I take in Tubs's house. The two-story brick bungalow looks much like its neighbors, with evergreen shutters and a wooden chair on the front porch. Not the type of chair where you would sit and enjoy fine weather and a glass of lemonade, but one for practical purposes like smoking or haircuts. There's nothing particularly inviting about the place—not even the warm glow of a lamp, despite it being four thirty and sunset quickly approaching. Mail nearly overflows from the box that hangs alongside the front door. Not only does it look as though no one is home now, it looks as though no one has been home for days. Or at least if they are, they haven't bothered with gathering their mail.

I hesitate a moment, and then venture up the walkway and onto the porch. No sound comes from within. I knock, just in case anyone is watching, and then eye the mailbox.

Opening any of the mail would be a federal crime, but what about looking through somebody's mail? There's an envelope in the front that I can't help but see. It's from Cook County Hospital and is addressed to Michael Murphy. I touch the corner of the envelope, bending it forward slightly so I can see what's behind. The next envelope is also addressed to Michael Murphy but from State Street Salary Loans. Even more interesting. After two catalogs and a utility bill, there's a third official-looking envelope, this time from North Side Salary Lenders, another one of those quick-loan places. The type where you walk out with cash, but also with sky-high interest. And where you turn to when you're in a financial jam.

Somebody is coming to the door.

I yank my hand back from the mailbox, but I can tell I'm not fast enough. The man who opens the door—tall and thin and dour-faced—looks from me to his mailbox and back to me again.

"Who are you? What are you doing?" He is one of the tallest people I've ever seen, easily over six feet tall, maybe even halfway to seven feet.

"Uh." I put on a bright smile and nod to the stuffed box. "Some of your mail was delivered to us, Mr. Murphy."

"Next time, just leave it." Without stepping outside, he reaches into the box and grabs the thick bundle.

"Yes, of course. Sorry."

I duck my head and spot a postcard that's fallen. On the front is a photograph of a large brick building with striped awnings. *Superior Bathhouse, Hot Springs, Arkansas* is printed down below. I bend and pick it up, flipping it over as I do and taking in a few words scribbled on the back before stretching it out to Michael Murphy. *The waters have been so restorative for Polly. Can you please send money to—*

He snatches the card from my hand and closes the door in my face.

I turn and retreat from the front porch, the cold biting my cheeks. The walk to the station is several blocks, and as soon as I arrive, I copy the details in my notebook with my ice-stiff fingers. Was the postcard from Tubs's wife? Who is Polly? What kind of restoration was she finding in Hot Springs, Arkansas?

I make notes of the other pieces of mail I saw. Michael Murphy—or Tubs, I guess—really might have been skimming from The Foxglove Smoke Shop, because all the evidence says he's in debt. And if Clarence had found out and threatened to turn him in to a fellow like Dean O'Banion? Well, that seems like a pretty good motive for wanting Clarence dead.

I'm attempting to type a letter of thanks for a donation, but my brain keeps wandering away from Presley's to the Clarence Dell case. To how genuinely sad Elzbieta appeared two days ago when I sat beside her at the kitchen table. To the name Finnegan dropping into the conversation. To the postcard from Hot Springs, Arkansas, that I handed to Tubs. To the idea of donning Elzbieta's cigarette girl costume—whatever that looks like—and walking around in a smoke-filled North Side casino.

Venturing into dangerous or unknown places in the city isn't new to me, but I've always had Mariano or Walter along as protection. This time, I'm not even sure I'll have a pocket to put my knife in.

But how else will I get close to Liam? To Tubs? This *has* to be done.

I nod at my typewriter, confirming the decision, and resume typing.

Not that I know what I'm going to say to either of them to get them to talk about Clarence. I can't exactly sashay through The Fox, offer Liam Finnegan a pack of cigarettes from my tray, and say, "That'll be five cents, and how about you tell me everything you know about Clarence Dell?" Hopefully, Liam is at least chattier than Tubs. He looked like he'd rather spit on me than talk to me, which is unfortunate because he's the best suspect I have.

Maybe at work he'll be different. Maybe I can—

My fingers freeze atop the typewriter keys. Do I hear . . . screaming?

I listen a moment longer. Yes, that's definitely screaming. I push back from my desk, rush to the office door, and fling it open. The screams bounce off the hallway's walls, a full-bodied, unrestrained sound. Whoever the girl is, she's screaming actual words, but I can't understand any of them.

I hurry along the hallway, resisting the urge to cover my ears as the sound grows louder. When I turn the corner, I find Isabella with a firm hold on the arms of a girl who is doing more stumbling and flailing than she is walking.

"I hate her!" the girl shrieks. "I'm never going back there! I hate her!"

Isabella pulls the girl along, and I catch a glimpse of the student's face. It's Hannah LeVine. For a moment, I'm too stunned to move. Hannah is throwing a tantrum like she's still the four-year-old girl I once knew. Her blonde hair flies in wild strings as she thrashes, and her face—which has so often reminded me of a porcelain doll's—is as red as an overripe tomato.

Isabella catches sight of me and throws me a look of desperation. I break into a run toward her.

"Can you get the headmistress?" she calls.

I shake my head. "Let me take Hannah."

"The headmistress!" Isabella yells, trying to be louder than Hannah. She probably couldn't even hear what I said, not with Hannah screaming right into her ear. "Get the headmistress!"

"I hate her! I hate her! I hate her!" Hannah wrenches away from Isabella's right hand. "You can't make me go back! I won't go back!"

"Hannah." I slide to a stop directly in front of her and reach out.

She swats my hands away like they're wasps. "You can't make me go back!"

"Hannah!" I yell right into her face and grasp her shoulders. "I'm not trying to make you go anywhere. Let's calm down, okay?"

Hannah blinks at me. Her red face crumples, and she grabs me into something akin to a hug, only more desperate. Like she's drowning and I'm the buoy. She clutches me—tighter, tighter, tighter—and then releases a guttural scream that I feel in my teeth.

"It's going to be okay, Hannah." Tears sheet my eyes. "It's all going to be okay."

Her face mashes into my shoulder. The screaming ends, and a moment later Hannah is sobbing.

Isabella says something—likely that she's getting the headmistress—and then hurries down the hall toward the office. Every teacher along this hallway has come to peek at what's going on. Some stand in their doorways with their arms crossed, looking annoyed at the interruption. Others poke their heads out of their classrooms, their expressions alarmed.

I rub my hand in circles against Hannah's back, like my mother used to when I was upset. "You're going to be okay."

"No, I won't." Hannah's voice is wet and rough. "She's gone forever, Piper. Lydia's gone forever, and that will *never* be okay."

My eyes slide shut. *Lydia.* The tears that had been building spill over as my own grief oozes out of the cracks of the container where I keep the memories. Lydia, giggly and shy because her family's new chauffeur is really cute. Lydia on Oak Street Beach, squealing as I drag her into the icy waters. Lydia, stubborn as she sits in my living room and tells me she's going to tell the chauffeur how she feels before her parents send her away to the Mayo Clinic.

I clutch Hannah close to me and struggle to not devolve into a sobbing tantrum of my own.

Presley's telephone is strangely silent, as if nobody wants to call and disturb me right now. Isabella paces back and forth, her shoe heels making a soft sound against the wood floors.

"How did you know what to do for her?" Isabella laces her fingers together and then unlaces them. "Everything I said made it worse."

"I've known Hannah a long time." My voice sounds like I scrubbed it with a Brillo pad. "I was best friends with her older sister."

Isabella looks at me then, perhaps hearing the *was.*

"She died." The syllables are an unintentional whisper.

Isabella's eyes soften. She opens her mouth, but the door from outside flings open before a sound can emerge. Mrs. LeVine strides into the office wearing a pleated black dress, no coat, and blazing eyes. In an instant, I'm ten years old and fumbling through an explanation about how Lydia fell out of the tree that I talked her into climbing.

"Where is she?" Mrs. LeVine demands in a low voice.

When I stand, my knees tremble. "She's with the headmistress. They're waiting for you."

"What happened, Piper?"

"I don't know, really—"

Isabella steps forward with an outstretched hand. "Mrs. LeVine, I'm Isabella Bianchi. I'm the new history teacher here, and though I don't have your daughter in class, my classroom is next door to Home Economics, where Hannah was at the time. I'm not sure what happened, but there were a lot of raised voices, so I went to see if Ms. Underhill needed help. When I entered her classroom, Hannah was . . . Well, there was quite a bit of yelling, and she was also throwing things."

Mrs. LeVine closes her eyes. Exhales.

Isabella glances at me and then continues. "I was afraid she was going to hurt herself or someone else with the way she was carrying on, so I tried to get her out of the classroom. Thankfully, Piper heard the commotion. She was the one who finally calmed Hannah."

"Somewhat," I add. "She was still crying too much to get an explanation out of her. I don't know what sparked her anger, but whatever it was, it had to do with Lydia."

"What *doesn't* spark her anger these days?" Mrs. LeVine says. "Thank you both. I apologize on behalf of Hannah for the interruption to your afternoon. How she behaved was inexcusable."

My throat aches, and I'm afraid if I open my mouth to respond, I'll cry.

"No need to apologize, ma'am." Isabella gestures to the door. "May I take you to the headmistress's office?"

"Please."

Mrs. LeVine nods a farewell to me, and then follows Isabella out of the office. I sit and stare at the half-finished letter in my typewriter. I have no memory of what I intended to say next, so I just sit and listen to the white-and-black wall clock as it ticks away the day, unperturbed by the events of the last half hour.

Lydia is why I will risk going to The Fox.

Clarence is to Louisa what Lydia is to me, to Hannah. And what risk would I not have taken to find the truth about Lydia?

Much as I wish I could, I can't do anything else for Lydia. She's gone and her case is closed. But I can still find answers for Louisa and figure out what happened to Clarence, and in doing so, I can honor Lydia and what she meant to me.

TWELVE

When Mrs. LeVine comes back through the office with Hannah, I'm on the phone and unable to speak with either of them. Mrs. LeVine keeps her arm tight around Hannah's shoulders, as if shielding her from a harsh wind. Hannah's head is ducked against her mother. I try to catch their eyes as they move toward the door, but Hannah doesn't look at me and Mrs. LeVine only glances in my direction.

The final hours of the school day drag, but at last the bell rings. Even though I still have another half hour before I can leave, that bell is one of my favorite sounds of the day, especially on a Friday.

Minutes later, the hallway door pushes open and Louisa comes into the office, her green coat making her bottle-green eyes even more vibrant. "Is now an okay time?"

"Of course."

We're alone in the office, but even still Louisa waits until she's at the edge of my desk before saying, "Did you hear about Hannah?"

"I didn't just hear *about* Hannah, I *heard* Hannah. I think we all did."

"You're probably right." Louisa shakes her head. "Poor thing."

"Do you know what set her off?"

She nods, sending her dark hair swinging forward. "We were in Home Economics and Hannah was rude to Ms. Underhill. I didn't hear what she said, but it must've been pretty bad because

Ms. Underhill said, 'A dead sister doesn't give you an excuse to be disrespectful.'"

I gasp. "She didn't."

Fury ignites in my chest. I am absolutely calling her Mary the next time I see her; I don't care if the headmistress *does* fire me.

"And then it was like Hannah turned into a wild animal. She started screaming and throwing spools of thread and dumping out her sewing basket. We all froze, even Ms. Underhill. It was terrifying, to be honest. I've never seen anyone like that."

I think of Hannah raging in the hallway, of the way she screamed, and my jaw aches. "Me neither."

Hannah's fury over what happened to Lydia has been simmering—festering—ever since Lydia went missing. I suppose Ms. Underhill's comment was the proverbial last straw and Hannah finally lost control of the anger she's kept trapped inside. Or *mostly* trapped inside, really.

"Perhaps this isn't a good time." Louisa casts her eyes downward, as though embarrassed. "But I wondered if you have any news for me about Clarence."

"Yes, actually." I glance through the glass partitions of both doors to be sure no one is about to interrupt us. "I met Elzbieta on Wednesday, and it was a very useful meeting. She mentioned two people from work at The Fox who—"

"The where?"

"That's what they call The Foxglove Smoke Shop." I hesitate. "It's not really a smoking store, but a casino."

Louisa blinks rapidly. "Is it really? I always assumed it was a store that sold cigars and pipes and such."

"That's what I assumed too, but no." I tap a pencil against my desk. "It's also owned by the North Side Gang."

Louisa recoils as though I threw a punch. "What?"

I can't tell if her question is rhetorical or not. "I've now confirmed this through a couple of sources."

She frowns and gives a slow shake of her head. "I bet Clarence didn't even know."

Oh, Louisa. The sweetest, most loyal sister I've ever met.

"What he knew and didn't know is unclear, but Elzbieta gave me some good information about a few coworkers. I'm going to follow those leads."

Louisa gives one succinct nod of her head. "And what about Elzbieta?"

"She was really helpful." I lean back in my chair and stretch my neck from side to side. "She's going to help me get into The Fox so I can get closer to those who might have wanted to hurt your brother."

Louisa continues to gaze steadily at me. "Sure, but what about Elzbieta? What's her alibi on the day Clarence died?"

I stop stretching. I don't know the answer because I didn't think to ask. Elzbieta hadn't acted guilty—she'd seemed sad about Clarence and was a fount of information—and because of that, I'd forgotten to ask some of the most basic questions possible. Like, "Where were you on October thirtieth?"

My stomach churns like I swallowed something acidic. "I'm not sure."

Louisa's sigh sounds impatient. "Well, find out. She's not a good egg. We need to know where she was the day he died."

Being told how to do my job—especially when I missed something this obvious—has me feeling like a feral cat protecting territory.

"Something interesting I learned," I say as though I need to prove my capabilities, "is that Clarence had some issues with his boss."

"What kind of issues? Clarence always got along well with teachers."

If Louisa can't accept that Clarence knowingly worked at a casino, I'm not sure what she'll do with the information I've gathered about Clarence and Tubs and Dean O'Banion. Better to save that until I've had more time to investigate Tubs.

"I'm figuring that out still. I also learned that Clarence broke up with Elzbieta."

Louisa doesn't react.

I add, "Daniel said that Elzbieta broke Clarence's heart, and he'd been depressed over the end of their relationship. Because of that, I'd assumed Elzbieta broke things off."

Louisa tilts her head, considering this. "I just think Daniel's wrong. Clarence wasn't upset, so I'm not sure it matters who called it off."

"It might matter." I absently tap my pencil against my desk. "If Clarence broke up with Elzbieta before she was ready for the relationship to end, that suggests a stronger motive than if she'd ended things."

"Yeah," she says with more enthusiasm. "Yeah, maybe she was really steamed about Clarence ending things. Maybe if you're a girl like Elzbieta, you're used to being the one who calls off relationships." Now Louisa looks absolutely excited. "Maybe it made her angry. *Really* angry."

A girl like Elzbieta. I turn Louisa's phrase over in my mind. Yes, Elzbieta is beautiful, but she isn't exactly living a charmed life. I think of her as she was on Wednesday, wearing her faded dress, sitting in a cold, crowded house that needs a good scrubbing, and appearing very tired. Elzbieta looked as though she'd seen plenty of hardship, not like a girl who would snap because a boy lost interest in her.

I lean back in my chair again. "I'll be sure to find out where she was the day Clarence died, and I'll give you any additional information I learn after I go to The Fox."

"Do I owe you more money yet?"

I hesitate. If I were billing honestly, absolutely. She would've owed me starting about halfway through my conversation with Elzbieta. But should I charge for the hours that I spend going through the box of Clarence's things over and over? For time that I spend just ruminating on the case, pacing my floors, trying to connect dots that maybe don't have a connection?

"No," I say. "Not yet."

Louisa gives me a skeptical look. "Are you sure?"

The office door pushes open, and the groundskeeper, Lawrence, lumbers inside with a box of something in one hand.

"Afternoon, ladies," he says in his thick Texas drawl.

I smile. I've always liked Lawrence. "Hello, how are you?"

"Glad it's Friday."

"Same here."

Louisa hitches her bag higher onto her shoulder. "I'll see you later," she says to me before rushing out the door.

Lawrence watches her go, then glances at me. "Did I chase her off?"

"Not at all." I stand and take to closing the manila folders still open on my desk. "We'd said everything we needed to. Do you have plans this weekend?"

"Nothin' too excitin'. I think the missus volunteered to watch our grandbaby, so that'll be most of Saturday."

As Lawrence speaks, he uses a gloved hand to pull a crust of bread out of the box he's carrying. He places it in the corner of the office.

"Are you making sure the mice have plenty to eat over the weekend?" I ask.

"Yes, ma'am." He smiles his gap-toothed grin at me. "I hope they eat every last bite. Rolled these crusts around in some rat poison."

Rat poison. My thoughts fly to Clarence, and I force myself to smile. "Does this mean I'll have some fun surprises waiting for me when I come to work on Monday morning?"

"Of course not, Miss Sail. They typically make it back to their hidey-holes before they die."

"How considerate of them." I thread my arm through one sleeve of my coat, then repeat for the other. "How long after eating the poison does it take effect?"

Lawrence shrugs. "Doesn't say on the box. Can't be *too* fast actin' or they'd die right on the spot. The idea is that they make it back home before it kills them." He waves at the crust. "Don't worry—you won't find these Monday morning either. I'll come back 'round Sunday evening and pick up whatever they didn't take."

"Thank you, Lawrence."

"You have a nice weekend, Miss," he says over his shoulder as he heads deeper into the school.

"You too," I call after him.

I button up my coat and secure my scarf before heading outside. Old snow crunches beneath my shoes as I make my way to the L station. When I arrive, I realize I have no memory of my walk there. My thoughts had been too absorbed with what Lawrence said about the rodents having time to make it back home before they died.

What if the empty glass on Clarence's bedside table was just an ordinary glass of scotch? What if the rat poison sitting there was more a prop than anything else, set out by the murderer to make the room look like everything about his death was contained to that time and space—as I and almost everyone else have assumed?

I still don't know how Clarence spent his last day, but what if the murder was put into place hours before he entered his room? Only much like the mice, he didn't know yet that at some point in his afternoon, he'd consumed a murder weapon?

On a whim, I board the northbound train.

With the luxury of an L seat all to myself, I pull Clarence's financial ledger from this year out of my bag, along with my case notebook. He either made no purchases on the day he died or he didn't have time to record them. There are no clues there about how he spent his final day. The day before is the toothpaste and socks Woolworth's purchase, and the day before that he had dinner out at Le Petit Gourmet and went to see a movie. The amount he spent implies dinner and a movie for at least two, but he doesn't have a note about who he was with.

I flip backward in the ledger to September, trying to see if Clarence did indeed get a reward from Dean O'Banion. My finger slides down the list.

+$20 work
−75¢ drinks with Liam and Keiran
+$500, Dean for services rendered

Five hundred dollars. That's a life-changing amount of money. Surely "services rendered" is a euphemism for saving Dean's life. Elzbieta did say that Dean liked to throw money around, and the timing is right, so that explanation seems most likely.

And what did Clarence do with all that money? I compare October's records to August's, before he received the money, but his spending actually decreases. That shift happens as soon as he stops dating Elzbieta. Based on these records, the five-hundred-dollar boost has no obvious impact on Clarence's life. Maybe he put it into savings?

I'm about to close the notebook in preparation for exiting the train when my eye catches on several lines of text, partially obscured by a receipt for a nice dinner with Elzbieta.

–$20 rent
–$1.74 phone
–$2.00: Cubs game with Louisa
–$500

No explanation? He spent an enormous amount of money with no annotation?

While there are times he included receipts without extra details, there are no other times that he made a handwritten addition or subtraction without some kind of explanation.

My finger pauses on the sum right as the train lurches to a stop. An addition of five hundred dollars mid-September and then a subtraction of the exact amount just two weeks later? Where did it go?

The car doors open, and I shove my notebooks back into my bag and hustle onto the platform. As I weave through pedestrians, my mind stays fixed on the five hundred dollars. I doubt Daniel knows the answer to that question, but maybe it's worth asking him since I'm here anyway.

When I arrive at his building, I follow another resident through the front door and jog up the stairs to knock on 3F. A moment later, the door opens and Daniel peeks out at me looking confused or annoyed or perhaps a combination of the two.

"Sorry to just drop in on you like this, but I have a few questions I'm hoping you can help me with." I instinctively slip my foot into the doorway. "Do you know if the police tested the glass for poison?"

Daniel blinks rapidly. "What are you talking about?"

"The glass on Clarence's bedside table. Did the police test the insides for poison?"

Daniel looks beyond me, down the hall. "Is Louisa with you?"

"Not today. Like I said, I just had two quick things to ask you. Did they test the glass?"

"Yes. Of course."

"And there was arsenic in there?"

Daniel's sigh is edged with impatience. "Yes."

"Do you know if they tested the bottle of scotch or just the glass?"

"Both. There was nothing in the bottle, just in the glass. Is that all?"

"One more thing. Do you know how Clarence spent his last day?"

His eyes latch onto mine. "I'm sure you can understand that this is all very unpleasant to revisit. It was *suicide*, Miss Sail. I hate it just as much as Louisa does, but not liking Clarence's choice isn't going to change the choice he made."

Guilt forces an acidic churn in my stomach, and I nod. "Yes, I understand this isn't easy for you, and I *am* sorry about that, but if you can just help me understand how Clarence spent his time that day, I'll be out of your hair."

Daniel sighs and shakes his head. "I have no idea. He was here when I left at eight and dead when I got home after five."

That's not as helpful as I'd like. "Do you know if he'd made any kind of large purchase recently?"

"No," he says, the gap of the door narrowing. "Please, Miss Sail. I'm begging you. Just let this go."

And he closes the door with a firm click.

CHAPTER
THIRTEEN

The reviews for *Hot Water*—tonight's feature film—have been mixed, but still the Chicago Theatre is bursting with patrons because it's Saturday and below freezing. The ticket line winds through all the stanchions, but a long wait is less bothersome when standing in a warm theater, inhaling a dizzying aroma of butter and sugar.

"For him to not make a note about where the five hundred dollars went is really out of character," I say to Mariano as we shuffle forward a few steps. "It makes me think he lost it."

"Maybe he transferred it to another account?"

"That's possible." I nod slowly. "Sometimes I have trouble discerning what's going in and out of his bank account and what's cash."

"If you're right about the five hundred originating with O'Banion, then I can guarantee you we're talking about five hundred in cash. Have you asked his sister about it?"

"No." I release a blustery sigh. "She's not going to react well. I've never seen a pedestal as high as the one she built for Clarence."

"That's one of the trickiest parts of trying to uncover the truth. Everybody tends to have their own idea of who the victim was." Mariano's fingertips graze my back as the line moves forward again. "I can't tell you how many times a mother will describe her son as loving and gentle, then the wife will say he was caustic and cruel. They experienced different facets of the same person."

I nod and drape my coat over my arm. "'I am large. I contain multitudes.'"

Mariano frowns. "Is that a quote?"

"Yes, from a poem. Only don't you dare ask me who the author is or what poem it's from. I had to pick a section to memorize for a test senior year, but that's the only part I remember. Probably because that line made me think of Lydia."

Mariano's eyebrows slide upward, silently asking *Why?*

"There was the Lydia who most people saw—responsible, well-mannered, and sweet. But also, she was sick and rather reckless." Grief rattles in my chest but thankfully doesn't spill over. "So far as Matthew was concerned, anyway."

Mariano tucks his arm tight around me, like he often does when Lydia arises in conversation. I think of Hannah's tantrum in the hallway yesterday: Are moments like this how I avoid becoming *that?* Is it like slicing steam vents in the crust of an apple pie, where letting a little pressure escape keeps the whole lot from boiling over?

A window clears and our conversation halts while Mariano purchases our tickets. After glancing at his watch, he says, "Let's find seats, and then I'll buy us popcorn. I don't want to get stuck way up front or something."

We find two seats toward the middle, and I drape my coat over the extra chair while Mariano heads back into the lobby. The houselights are still on, and people are laughing and talking loudly. There's a group of college-aged boys in the row in front of me who are trying to get the attention of the girls in the row in front of them. Their antics are being ignored, which makes me smile.

"Oh, hey."

I startle at Jeremiah's voice. He's sliding down the row in front of me, a Hershey's bar in one hand and a bottle of root beer in the other.

"Hi." My voice is a surprised squeak. "What are you doing here?"

He blinks slowly. "Well, Piper, I'm here to see a movie."

I feel my cheeks warm. "Right."

He glances at my coat, draped possessively over the seat beside me. "Mariano?"

"He's getting popcorn."

"What a gentleman."

"Mm-hmm."

We look at each other for a moment, and then I look away. Maybe interactions like this would be less awkward if the two of us had actually dated and our relationship had run its course. Then there might be some sort of common etiquette for how to handle these situations where we see each other unexpectedly. A polite hello, maybe an exchanged nicety, and then everybody moves on with their evening.

If I were the one standing and he were the one sitting, now is when I would say, "Enjoy the show," and carry on down the aisle.

But Jeremiah sinks into the empty seat in front of me. "I'll keep you company while Mariano is away. Emma tells me you're working on a case."

Perspiration gathers under my corselette. I instinctively look around, in the chance anyone is paying attention to us. "Shh."

"Oh." Jeremiah chuckles. "I didn't know it was a secret."

I fuss with the pleats of my navy dress. "It isn't, but it's also not a matter I want to discuss openly."

"Noted." Jeremiah grins and winks at me, like my case is some glorious joke.

I glance toward my left. Why is it taking Mariano forever to return?

"Let me know if I can be helpful." Jeremiah props his elbow on the seatback. "Newspapermen are excellent sources. We know all kinds of things."

He's not wrong about this, and it doesn't hurt to ask. "Fine. Do you know anything about The Foxglove Smoke Shop?"

His mouth morphs into a thoughtful line. "North Side, right? It's all a little confusing right now, with O'Banion out of the picture. I'd have to look at my notes, but it's still open as far as I know." His gaze catches on someone and his smile turns polite. "Hello."

I look up to find Mariano has returned with a large bag of popcorn, two Coca-Colas, and a polite smile of his own.

"Hi." My greeting has far more enthusiasm than normal. "Jeremiah is here to see the movie too."

Mariano arches his brows at me. "I gathered that, thank you."

"They didn't make you detective for nothing, I guess," Jeremiah says as he stands. He nods to me. "Good to see you, Piper. Enjoy the movie."

"You too," I say, my voice still coming out strained and high.

Jeremiah continues to shuffle past others as he moves down the row. When he gets to the college boys I noticed earlier, the ones trying to gain the attention of the girls in front of them, they greet him with exuberance and he takes a seat. He'll be in my peripheral vision the entire movie. Lovely.

"Sorry," I say to Mariano.

"For what?"

"That was a little awkward."

"That's not your fault." Mariano shrugs. "He wants you. I'm dating you. It'll always be a little awkward with the three of us, I think."

I gape at him.

He grins, showcasing the parentheses that form like dimples on either side of his smile. "What? I'm just stating facts, Detective Sail."

"Those are not facts. You're inferring a lot of information—"

Mariano barks a laugh and puts his arm around me. "I'm not inferring anything. I can see it plain on his face. It's a fact."

I shrink slightly in my seat. "I will happily talk about anything else."

He smiles at me as the houselights flicker, indicating it's nearly time for the movie to start. "How about your deepest, darkest fears. Is the answer still dogs and babies?"

"Still babies," I say with a nod. "And most dogs too. There's really only one dog I like."

"Sidekick is a good boy. He takes good care of you. And who knows? Maybe someday you'll decide you're okay with babies too," Mariano says. "Years from now."

I take an overly long drink of my Coca-Cola. My dress feels damp beneath my armpits. Shouldn't the lights be turning off?

"I mean, I think it'll be different when it's your own," Mariano continues. "Same as Sidekick."

I would rather put on my bathing costume and sing onstage at The Fox than talk about me having a baby.

I reach for the popcorn. "What do you think of me dressing like a cigarette girl to get inside The Fox?"

Mariano lets out a loud *ha!* that draws the eyes of several around us. "I think you really don't want to talk about your greatest fears."

"You are correct."

"And once again, I never know what's going to come out of your mouth. I can't decide if I find it cute or terrifying."

The houselights finally dim, and breathing becomes easier.

"Cute," I say. "You definitely find it cute."

"Hmm." Mariano lowers his voice to a whisper as the projection lights the screen. "I imagine you can think of a way to get the information you need without going into The Fox. You're very clever."

This is maybe true. Same as how I can go to the Lincoln Park Zoo and see lions, but it's never going to be as accurate as seeing them inside their den.

Stopping by the LeVines' house to pay a visit to Hannah seems like a good idea, until Mrs. LeVine tells me Hannah isn't currently permitted visitors due to her actions at school, but that she'd personally like a word with me since I am here.

"Oh." I swallow. "Of course."

"Tabitha just set up tea for me in the parlor. Come along." She turns and walks back into her house, spine stacked and shoulders straight.

I hesitate, then step inside and close the door. In the parlor, Mrs. LeVine moves the tea tray between two chairs. She pours me a cup before settling into her seat and taking charge of the conversation.

"Hannah has been given a week's suspension, which means she'll be out until Christmas break. It's absurd."

This isn't news to me. I'm the one who tends to the student records, including documenting suspensions. "I know. I was sorry to hear that."

"I'm not saying what Hannah did was acceptable—of course it isn't—but an entire week?" Mrs. LeVine taps her stirring spoon against her cup with such force, I'm surprised it doesn't crack. "With all the money we've given to that school? With everything our family has been through this year? Absurd."

"I don't know if this is of any comfort to you or to Hannah, but Headmistress Robinson asked me to take her out of Ms. Underhill's class. She said—"

"Wretched woman," Mrs. LeVine fumes. "And wretched teacher too, probably. I told the headmistress she should fire her, but who knows if she'll listen to me?"

I clutch my cup of tea. "I would love for Ms. Underhill to be dismissed, but at least Hannah won't have to take her class. The headmistress said I could designate a study period for Hannah and that she can work privately on—"

"I pay for her to be *taught*," Mrs. LeVine snaps. "Which is what I told Elaine when she suggested the same thing to me. I'm not paying for Hannah to sit in a room and study on her own. They need a new home economics teacher there. One who knows how to respond to smart-mouthed girls without insulting the memory of their sister." She gestures to me. "Or beating them with a ruler."

My left hand instinctively covers my right. I didn't realize Mrs. LeVine knew about that, and my cheeks burn as hot as my tea. "What she said to Hannah was far more hurtful than anything she ever did to me."

Mrs. LeVine makes a noise in her throat, but I can't tell if she's agreeing or disagreeing. I attempt a sip at the tea and stare into the crackling fire. I used to be the unwanted guest who wasn't allowed into the fancy parlor. Suddenly, not only am I invited in, I'm given the best chair beside the fire and served tea in wedding china.

"Regardless, Hannah needs to learn to control her emotions." Mrs. LeVine now sounds more tired than angry. "*Throwing* her sewing kit? Lydia never would have done anything like that."

No, but she might've eloped with the chauffeur if she'd lived long enough.

Words I will never say to Dr. and Mrs. LeVine, though. One more favor I can do for my best friend.

I pour milk into my tea to bring it to a more drinkable temperature. "Perhaps the problem is that Hannah has been *too* controlled with her emotions. I've often noticed in the last few months that Hannah seems to be angry at odd times. As if she's always angry. Have you seen the same thing?"

Mrs. LeVine hesitates. "Yes, but I think that's to be expected. She's an adolescent and her sister was taken from her . . ."

"I just wonder if she'd benefit from having someone who she can talk to about Lydia. About how she feels. Maybe she's been holding everything inside for so long—albeit imperfectly—that she just couldn't anymore."

Mrs. LeVine looks at me over the top of her tea. "She idolizes you, Piper."

"Oh, dear." I chuckle nervously. "That won't do, will it?"

Mrs. LeVine smiles, but there is tension in her lips. "A few words from you about self-control, about responding proportionally, could go a long way. You were also devastated by what happened to Lydia, but you're not ranting and raging and making a spectacle of yourself. You could explain to her how you manage your own sadness. I've tried, but I'm her mother and she's fourteen. My opinions don't count."

"I'll try," I say, "but grief looks different for different people."

And I'm not so sure Mrs. LeVine would truly like for me to counsel Hannah in this matter. I assume she doesn't want her daughter obsessively scanning newspapers for articles about those who are missing. Or lying awake imagining how she would go about looking for them—who she would talk to first, how she would get answers.

And she definitely wouldn't want Hannah throwing herself into solving the (maybe) murder of a boy she's never met, all because months ago, she couldn't save the person she loved most in the world.

FOURTEEN

"Did you hear what I said?"

I blink at Emma's amused face. Honestly, I have no clue what she said. I'm thinking about what I should wear to The Fox tonight.

"No," I say. "Sorry."

"I didn't think so." Emma fiddles with the bin on my desk for outgoing mail. "I asked, 'Do you know how Hannah is doing?'"

"I stopped by yesterday, but I only saw Mrs. LeVine." I frown at Hannah's file, still sitting on my desk from Friday. "I think the whole family is pretty upset."

"Of course they are. A teacher should really know better. Everyone says you had the magic touch and calmed her down."

"That's overstating things."

"How shocking that you're being overly modest about it." Emma's face lights, and I know this is going to be about her brother before she even says anything. "Jeremiah said he saw you at the movie house Saturday night and that you were upset when he brought up the case."

I feed a fresh piece of paper into the typewriter. "I wasn't. There were a lot of people around. That's all."

"But you're not mad at me for telling him about it? He thought you might be."

"No, it was just too public a place to discuss it. Just like he probably wouldn't want me talking loudly about some great scoop of his." I glance at the clock. "Are you keeping an eye on the time?"

Emma groans. "I don't want to go to French. We're reviewing for the final test, and it's dreadful."

"Don't go then." I shrug. "I have access to your school files, including your grades."

"Piper." Emma laughs and tucks her hair behind her ears. "Don't even joke like that."

"I wasn't joking."

Emma holds my gaze for a moment and then gives another nervous laugh. "Okay, now I *really* can't tell."

I smile sweetly. "*Au revoir*, Emma."

She disappears into the school, and I align my paper into position. Today I will be typing far more "reminding you that tuition is past due for second semester" letters than I would like. I look up to gather my thoughts, and through the glass I see Ms. Underhill entering the school. She glances into the office.

She scowls. I scowl back.

I'm on my feet and barreling through the door into the hallway before I realize I made the decision to do so.

"What you said to Hannah was completely inappropriate. How could you do that? She's fourteen!"

Ms. Underhill doesn't even flinch, just stops there in the hallway and glowers at me. A few Presley's girls loiter, and a few others glance at us and scurry away.

"Miss Sail, you may work here now, but it would serve you well to learn your place and keep your mouth shut."

"Learn my place?" I cross my arms over my chest. "When are you going to learn *your* place? Because it really shouldn't be in the classroom."

Ms. Underhill shakes her head and makes a sound that's maybe a chuckle, like this whole situation is humorous. She turns her back to me and continues down the hall. I watch in disbelief. She's simply going to walk away? She's not going to say *anything*?

"Hannah is *grieving*!" I yell at Ms. Underhill's back. "And you're just a . . . a mean old lady!"

Ms. Underhill stops in the middle of the hallway. She turns to me with a look of amusement on her face. Amusement!

"By the time you're a mean old lady, Miss Sail, you'll realize we're all grieving something. Grief doesn't make you special."

With that, she turns and continues her prim, steady walk down the hallway.

"Thanks, *Mary*!" I yell after her, just as she turns the corner. "That's really helpful!"

"Miss Sail." From my left, Headmistress Robinson says my name with a sigh.

My anger is so vibrant in my veins, I don't restrain myself from snapping, "What?"

Another sigh. "I think you'd better come see me in my office."

When I open the door, the house is fragrant with Joyce's beef and vegetable stew. For a moment, I stand in the entryway, inhale deeply, and feel the strange sense I've gone back in time. I've had a hard day at Presley's—scolded by Ms. Underhill and called into the headmistress's office—and now I return home to the comfort of Joyce Thatcher's cooking. Probably a bit of lecturing too. If Walter was here to eat an after-school snack with me while the soup simmered, I would really be reliving childhood.

Sidekick trots into the entryway as I tug off my shoes. I tell him a hurried hello and rush to the kitchen in my socked feet.

Joyce looks up when the door swings open and smiles broadly at me. "I was hoping I'd get to see you today."

I throw my arms around her, surprised by the joy that fizzes inside me. It's only been a few weeks since I last saw Joyce, but it feels much longer. "Why are you here so late?"

"Your brothers and Tim's family are coming for dinner this evening. There was a little extra cleaning to do for that, and then I had to run to the market because we were out of thyme. It's not beef stew without thyme."

"Why are Tim and Nick coming for dinner?"

Joyce releases me and turns back to her bread dough. "Just a family dinner, so far as I know. Can you stir the soup for me, honey?"

I turn to the stove and lower the wooden spoon into the pot. "How's your other job?"

"Very quiet. Cleaning office buildings in the evenings is a far cry from trying to keep this place clean when it was Tim, Nick, Walter, and you running around."

I wince. "I can't imagine we made your life very easy."

"Like trying to brush your teeth while eating blackberries." But Joyce beams as she says it. "Mrs. Sail tells me you're working at Presley's now. How do you like it?"

"Most days I like it fine. I like working there better than being a student, anyway."

Though as an employee, I found the experience of being brought into the headmistress's office even more humbling than I had as a student. Especially since I was being admonished for my childish behavior.

"What about Ms. Underhill's childish behavior?" I had asked.

"You may not like her, but Ms. Underhill isn't going anywhere, so you need to learn how to get along with her or find yourself a new job," Headmistress Robinson said coolly.

Then she'd excused herself for the morning meeting in the chapel, while I went back to my desk feeling sulky. And then feeling childish for being sulky.

"When I was a girl," Joyce says, drawing my thoughts back to the kitchen, "there were so few jobs for women. You could teach, you could be a nurse, and you could do housework, but that's all. All these options must make this a very exciting time to be a young woman."

I consider this. "You would think so, but everybody still talks as though I only need my job until I find a husband."

"Let them talk. You know the truth." She glances over her shoulder. "You can stop stirring now."

I tap the wooden spoon on the edge of the cast iron soup pot. "Have you heard from Walter recently?"

"I had a letter from him last week. Sounds like he's doing fine and doesn't mind the work he's doing, but he's ready for baseball season."

I grin, heart swelling with affection for my childhood friend. "He's *always* ready for baseball season."

"I'm heading out there for Christmas. I'll finally get to meet Audrey."

"Ooh, you'll have to report back and let me know if she's good enough for him. Any idea how that's going?"

"None. I reckon he's more open with you than he is with me. I'm his mama, after all." Joyce covers the bread dough with a towel. "Sounds like he thinks the Seals will have a good season.

I'd sure like to go out and see him play a game, but I just don't know about making a second trip out there."

"Maybe a Chicago team will sign him and he'll move here."

"Maybe. All her family is out there, though. I don't really see him coming back to Chicago, do you?"

If Walter settles on the West Coast, will Joyce move out there? Why wouldn't she? What would keep her in cold, snowy Chicago when she could be close to Walter in sunny California? Even though Joyce no longer lives with us, the idea of her moving away makes panic claw at my chest. Another piece of childhood, slipping away.

The kitchen door pushes open, and in strides Jane. "Hello, Piper, I didn't hear you come home." She radiates a smile at me, as if we're friends who haven't seen each other in a particularly long time. "Joyce, it smells divine in here!"

While I refill Sidekick's water bowl and give him a more thorough hello scratch now that I'm not as distracted, Joyce instructs Jane on where the gelatin salad is in the icebox and what time the bread should go into the oven. I soak in one more hug from Joyce before telling her good-bye.

"What would we do without Joyce?" Jane says in a bright voice after Joyce goes out the back door. "She's a gift to the whole family, hmm?"

Jane saying that feels wrong, as if she's trying to take ownership of someone who belongs to me. Which is silly, of course, because Joyce doesn't belong to any of us.

I turn away and open the icebox in search of something to eat.

"Did you have a good day at work?" Jane asks in the same enthusiastic tone.

"It was fine."

"Did Joyce mention to you that the whole family is coming for supper this evening?"

"She did."

"Excellent. Which reminds me, there was a call for you earlier—" She huffs out an exasperated sound. "Piper, don't just stand there with the door open if you don't know what you want. You're letting out all the cold air."

I select a wheel of cheese and close the door. "You said there was a call for me?"

"Yes. I wrote everything down, but I must've left the note in your father's office. One moment."

I've sliced myself several chunks of cheddar cheese by the time Jane returns with a square of paper. "Here it is."

ELLZBETTA WONDERS IF YOU ARE STILL COMING
TONIGHT. PLEASE CALL DIV 4371.

"I wish I'd known ahead of time that you have plans with a friend tonight," Jane says, "because I would've chosen a different evening to invite your brothers for dinner."

While talking to Joyce, I'd temporarily forgotten about going to The Fox. My stomach knots.

"Sorry about that," I say absently.

"Could you cancel?" Jane's voice turns bright again. "I wouldn't normally ask, but it's so difficult to find a night that both Tim and Nick can be here."

I play with the idea of canceling. I could call Elzbieta right now and tell her, *Thank you so much for your offer, but I won't be there tonight.* Then I would spend the evening in my comfortable home with people I love (and Jane) and go to bed early. Mariano would certainly prefer that.

But the mysteries surrounding Clarence Dell's death aren't going to be solved by me sitting in my dining room and staying comfortable. This is part of being a real investigator.

I suck in a bracing breath. "What time are my brothers coming?"

"Six o'clock."

"I can be here for dinner, but then I'm spending the night at my friend's house."

"Spending the night?" Jane's tone climbs with surprise. "Do you not work tomorrow?"

"I do, but it's her birthday," I lie smoothly. So smoothly that it's a little scary. "And she's been going through a rough time."

"Well, that's fine, I suppose," Jane says, like I'm ten and still need permission. "So long as you're here for supper."

"I will be." I lift the message and my plate of cheese. "I'll just call her back to confirm."

Father's office is always chillier than the rest of the house this time of year. A sweater of his hangs on the back of his chair, and I wrap it around me. Sidekick sits in the doorway and watches me with anxious eyes.

When Elzbieta answers on the third ring, I say, "Hello, it's Piper," in the warm voice I might use with Emma because Jane can probably hear me from the kitchen. Hopefully Elzbieta doesn't know any other Pipers and will overlook my familiarity.

"Hello." Elzbieta says. "Are you still coming tonight?"

I force myself to say, "Yes."

"Okay. I have some extra details for you. I was thinking

about it, and since you're supposed to be trying out the job, it'd be best if you arrived a little after me. Like a real applicant would. How does that sound?"

Terrifying. Nauseating. "Great."

"Okay, good. When you get to The Fox, there's an alley between the smoke shop and the billiards room next door. Take that around back. The door inside is guarded, but knock and tell the bouncer that you're there to see me and try out a job. That should do the trick, although I'd still like to give them a name just to make sure you don't have trouble getting in. I figure you don't want me using your real name."

Certainly not. Especially my last name, which is closely associated with the last name Cassano and won't do me any favors up north.

"Good thinking," I say.

"What name would you like to use?"

As I consider what name to give her, there are noises in the hallway that make me think Jane is rummaging about the linen closet.

"I don't know. What do you think would suit me?"

Elzbieta's laugh sounds a touch nervous. "Virginia?"

Virginia. Both Virginias I know are stuck-up girls at Presley's, but with Jane in the hallway I can't exactly start listing off names.

"Sure, that sounds fine." I pitch my voice low. "Thank you for doing this."

"It's me who should be thanking you. I mean, if Clarence really was . . . you know, then I want to do whatever I can to help."

"You're doing more than enough. See you tonight."

When I leave Father's office, Sidekick does his usual happy prance and licks my hands. Jane is indeed in the linen closet, digging around for who knows what. Strewn about her are candlesticks, vases, bundles of cloth napkins tied with string, and tablecloths that I don't even recognize.

She stands upright and smiles at me as I pass. "All set with your friend?"

"Yes."

"Everyone will be here at six," Jane calls after me, as though we didn't already discuss this. I continue to the stairs. "Please don't make me drag you out of your room tonight."

I decide this doesn't merit a reply.

In my room, I open my closet door and consider the options hanging inside. What works best for "Virginia," who's hoping for a job at The Foxglove Smoke Shop? She would, of course, wear her best dress, but it wouldn't be a fine dress. Just a good dress. I frown at my unsatisfying options. Finally in the back, I find the dress that Tim and Gretchen gave me for Christmas last year. Deep purple, with full sleeves and white velvet cuffs. Pretty, but not something I would've chosen for myself.

I slip the dress over my head, adjust the cuffs, and evaluate my reflection. "Hello, I'm Virginia. I'm here to see Elzbieta about a job."

I tilt my head to evaluate my face. I need to go heavier on makeup tonight, partly to cover up my scars, and partly because I was hardly wearing any the day I showed up at Tubs's house. I don't want him to recognize me as the girl who had her hands in his mailbox. My hair needs to be fancier too. Finger waves and maybe a sparkly clip, both of which I can do before dinner, but

I'll arouse suspicion if I leave the house in a full face of makeup. That I'll need to apply in the L station bathroom.

"My name is Virginia." I smile into the mirror and try to make the name sound normal. "My name is Virginia, but my friends call me Gin. Ginny? No, Gin. My friends call me Gin."

I nod at my reflection, confirming this detail for myself. "My name is Virginia, but my friends call me Gin, and you can trust me with all your terrible secrets."

CHAPTER
FIFTEEN

Sidekick leaps off my bed, drawing a yelp out of me. He stands by my bedroom door and looks back, expectantly. A moment later, I hear it: the low timbre of my oldest brother's voice, the high, enthusiastic greeting of my sister-in-law, and the incoherent babbles of my nephew.

I peek at my watch. Six o'clock already? My stomach dips like a boat cresting over a high wave. Spread around me are Clarence's financial journals, the photographs, his yearbooks, and my notes about the case. It looks as if I've been studying for a particularly hard test.

I put away all my case notes and tuck the box beneath my bed. After double-checking the items in my leather shopping bag— makeup, Gin's eggplant-colored dress, Nick's pocketknife—I leave my bedroom. Sidekick is curious about all the commotion, but he is also skittish about larger groups of people, so he stays close to my side, his head bumping against me every other step.

Everyone but Jane is gathered in the living room. Father sits in an armchair, while Nick, Tim, and Gretchen are all on the couch, with Howie on Gretchen's lap. The conversation halts as I enter, as though they'd been talking about me when I know they weren't. They were discussing how busy State Street is this time of year.

My sister-in-law beams at me and waves one of Howie's hands. "Hi, Aunt Piper. How are you?"

I *hate* when she does this.

"Uh, fine, Howie. Thanks for inquiring."

Howie beams at me with a smile identical to Gretchen's. I feel the corners of my own mouth lift in response.

Whatever it is that makes most females swoon over babies appears to have been left out of me when God put me together, and I will sometimes go to great lengths to avoid being around a baby. I don't like how they openly stare at you or burst into tears for no obvious reason. Even when they're done being babies, they become children, which isn't much better, with their sticky hands and awkward questions.

Even so, Howie is okay.

I take the remaining chair beside Gretchen, and she immediately exits the State Street conversation to aim a motherly smile my direction. "How are you doing, sweetie?"

Sweetie. If someone heard our interactions, they would probably think Gretchen is twenty years older than me rather than five. But Gretchen is the type of woman who seemed like a mother even before she was one. She has a thicker build, a round, smiling face, and lovely gray eyes. She talks about Tim like he invented the wheel, which is irritating but also sweet. My brother *is* wonderful, and I'm glad he has a wife who knows it.

"I'm fine, thank you. How are you?"

"Just dandy," she says. "Howie is walking everywhere now, and it's so fun."

Howie starts to make his unsteady way toward me, a long string of drool trailing clear down to the rug. I resist the urge to move my legs out of reach.

"He's getting some of his back teeth too," Gretchen says as she watches him. "That *isn't* as fun. He's been waking up a lot overnight. He was awake at twelve, two, and three thirty last night!"

"That sounds terrible."

"I just sit and rock him and he sleeps on me. It isn't so bad. Oh, you love your auntie, don't you?" Gretchen says in a squishy voice as Howie places a wet hand on my knee and makes a noise at me like *mmm, mmm, mmm.*

I feel like I should say *something.* "Hi, there."

Howie puts his other hand on my remaining knee—this one is dry, thankfully—and makes more *mmm* noises.

"You're just so sweet with him." Gretchen smiles at me like I'm doing an incredible job connecting with my nephew. "The two of you have such a tender relationship!"

Howie has dark-gray eyes just like Gretchen's, and a headful of blond curls. He gives me a gappy smile, and a thread of drool lands on my dress skirt. I pat his hand—the one that's dry—and try for a normal smile.

Jane steps into the living room and says, "Dinner is on the table," with the air of somebody who has worked very hard and is ready for everyone to come admire the fruits of their labor.

"Smells delicious, Jane," Father says as he stands.

"Sure does," Tim says, also standing.

I squash my urge to add, *Smells like Joyce made an excellent meal for us all!*

Jane stands behind her usual chair in the dining room and beams at each one of us as we file in, like we're her actual children and she's pleased to have us back under her roof for a night. The table is lavish, with crystal glasses and the fine china from their wedding, even though it's just a Monday. She really put a lot of effort into making everything look nice.

I glance at my wristwatch; not even six thirty yet. Plenty of time before I take the L up north.

Father takes his spot at the head of the table. Tim and Gretchen fill in one side of the table with Howie in a highchair between them, leaving Nick and me to occupy the other side. Once we're all seated, Father blesses the meal using what we call his "long form" of grace, where instead of simply thanking God for our food, he also throws in a sentence about how nice it is that we're all together and thank you for our health.

As soon as we've settled into eating, Jane asks Gretchen about a needlepoint project and Tim draws Father into discussing a book they've both just finished.

"I guess you're stuck talking to me," I say to Nick as I slather butter onto my slice of bread.

"As always." But Nick's smile is kind.

"How's work?" I ask as Nick says, "I saw your future father-in-law today."

He means Mariano's father, who's our father's number one client, but I'm not going to take that bait. "I'm sorry, but who are you speaking of?"

"I didn't know that Alessandro and Zola got married," Nick continues like I hadn't even responded. "And I definitely didn't know they had a baby."

I keep my focus on chewing. On breathing. Nick keeps looking at me, waiting for a reply. "You didn't?" I finally say.

"Mariano must feel strange about it."

Just keep acting normal. Chew, chew, chew. Inhale, exhale. I shrug. "He hasn't said much."

This is painfully true; the only reason I learned about Zola and Alessandro's marriage is because Jack thought I already knew. I sometimes wonder how long it would've taken Mariano to tell me if his roommate hadn't spilled. And if there are other equally monumental things he's keeping to himself.

"How would he not feel odd about it?" Nick says. "It's just as strange as if Tim and Gretchen split and she and I got married."

"No, it isn't. Tim and Gretchen are *married*. Mariano and Zola were only engaged." I tear a bite-sized piece off my bread and pop it into my mouth. "Not only that, they were still a year away from getting married when they broke up."

"You mean when she broke up with him."

An unnecessary clarification. "Thank you for that. My point is—"

"Could I have everybody's attention please?" Father says.

My point dies in my mouth as I look at my father. Thoughts of Mariano and Zola fly away. I know that expression on my father's face—the overly bright eyes, the smile tinged with anxiety—and it doesn't lead to good things.

"We're so happy to have all of you here tonight, because Jane and I have some exciting news to share."

I stop chewing.

I stop breathing.

My hand finds Nick's under the table and squeezes hard.

I can see it so clearly now. The fancy set table. The insistence that I be at supper this evening. Jane's sudden effervescence. All the evidence points to one horrifying conclusion. I might be sick. I really might be sick.

Father beams at Jane and says the exact words I'd suspected and feared: "Jane and I are expecting a baby."

For a moment, the only sounds in the room are Sidekick's panting and squashy eating noises coming from Howie in the highchair.

"How wonderful," Gretchen says in a bright voice. The brightness is forced, or at least I think it is, but she's making an effort, which is more than my brothers or I are doing. Bless her.

Jane smooths the bodice of her dress. "We expect the new arrival sometime in July. Timothy and I are absolutely thrilled."

My back teeth ache. I'm not *trying* to clench them; it's just happening. A baby. My father, whose grandson is across the table from me, is having a baby. A baby who will be younger than his grandson.

"That's . . ." Tim clears his throat. "Congratulations."

Howie, oblivious, makes babbling noises.

Jane looks at him with longing and delight. "I love that they'll be so close in age. They'll be wonderful playmates."

The burning sensation in my throat increases and now it's happening in my nasal cavity too.

"We understand you might not have expected this," Father says.

I look up and find his gaze shifting between me and Nick, the two who have not offered congratulations or even spoken. I look away. My heart pounds so hard, it sounds like it's beating right inside my head.

"I definitely didn't expect this," Nick says beside me, and the subtext is as clear as if he spoke it: *And I don't like it.*

"Babies are always good news," Jane says in a tight voice. "Expected or not."

Nick makes a chuffing sound but doesn't reply further.

I stare into my soup bowl, and it grows increasingly blurry.

"Goodness, Howie." Gretchen laughs a strange laugh. "What a mess you are. I'm going to take Howie to the washroom."

Tim is out of his chair before Gretchen has finished her sentence. "I'll help you."

Chairs scrape the floor. Gretchen murmurs to Howie. Two sets of footsteps grow quieter. All the while, I stare at my hands clasped in my lap and try to not burst into tears.

After several seconds of silence, I push back from the table. "I'm not hungry."

"Piper, don't just leave." Father's voice is soft but commanding. "Let's talk about this."

I think of Hannah in the hallway, the screaming and thrashing. I can envision myself behaving the same way. Standing up so fast that my chair knocks over. Wiping my arm across the table and sending all the beautiful plates and glasses to the ground. Screaming myself hoarse as I flip the table onto its side.

I blink away the thoughts.

"I'm not sure that's a good idea," I say in a voice barely above a whisper.

"Look, you two, I know that none of us expected to welcome another baby into this house," Father says.

And though he carries on, my thoughts stick there as if his words are a scratched record. There will be a baby living in this house. He or she will be here all the time. In *my* house.

". . . it's normal," Father is saying as I tune back in. "And your mother told me that in God's wisdom, babies take nine months to be born, and that gave me time to adjust to the idea."

"That sounds like Mother." Nick's voice has a gruff edge, like he's angry. He often sounds angry when he's actually sad.

A chair violently scrapes across the floor.

I startle at the sound and look up to find Jane scowling at all three of us, her face a blotchy red.

"The baby is *good* news." Anger makes her voice husky. "*My* good news."

She chucks her cloth napkin onto the table and marches out of the dining room. Moments later, there is stomping on the stairs and a door slams.

Father sighs. "I should go talk to her."

He sits with us for several more seconds before sighing again, wiping his mouth with his napkin, and pushing back from the table.

"I don't know why I didn't see this coming," Nick mutters to me when he's gone. "Did you see this coming?"

"No."

Tim peeks into the dining room.

"They're upstairs," I say.

He strides in, hands in his pockets. "I'm guessing we upset Jane?"

"You're correct."

"Well, Gretchen was right." Tim pushes at his glasses. "When Jane called to invite us to dinner, Gretchen said she thought this might be the reason. I told her there was no way Father would want another baby when he's this close to being rid of his youngest."

"Thank you," I say drily.

"You'll have to move out," Nick says to me. "Otherwise, Jane will have you taking care of the baby whenever you're here. You could live at my place for a while."

I give Nick a look. "You don't want me living with you."

Nick shrugs. "It wouldn't be forever. Just until Mariano is ready to pop the question."

I grimace.

Tim frowns at this. "You're still seeing Mariano?"

Now it's my turn to leave the table. "I have to go. I have plans."

"Ideal night for it, as it turns out. I would take off too, but I'm not going to let Joyce's good cooking go to waste." Nick plunges his spoon into his bowl. "Think about my offer, okay?"

I feel a rush of affection for my brother, which I swallow. I smile faintly at Tim. "Nice to see you. Tell Gretchen and Howie I said bye."

He nods, and I turn and head for the stairs, Sidekick close behind me.

On the second floor, Jane is shouting at my father about how babies are meant to be a joyful addition, and why did he have to bring up Elsie—my mother—like that? She felt humiliated. Her voice fades away as I take the second flight of stairs to my bedroom.

There's a buzz of anger in my head as I snatch my bag from my room and change my shoes. Nick is right; it's an ideal night for me to be out of the house, because Jane is still yelling at my father as I come back down the stairs, and nobody but Sidekick watches me walk out the front door.

CHAPTER

SIXTEEN

I exit the bathroom at the L station and weave my way through the people on the platform. The crowd is eclectic. Couples heading out for the evening in fine clothes, young women standing in sparkly bunches and giggling loudly, and haggard men and women in work clothes, tired after a long day.

My bag thumps against my hip with every step, heavy with the extra burden of a change of clothes and cosmetics. I've relocated Nick's knife to my dress pocket, because a girl never knows. I hope the cigarette girl uniform has a place I can hide the knife away. Ideally, the uniform will have a pocket *and* a skirt that goes down to my knees, but getting either one seems optimistic.

As I move away from Belmont Station, the crowd thins. The sidewalks are too empty for my tastes, leaving me feeling unprotected. I walk the few blocks to The Fox with my hand in my pocket, fingers curled around the knife, and scowl at anyone who decides to make eye contact with me.

The Foxglove Hotel is an unassuming, rectangular brick building of four stories nestled in a row of other unassuming, rectangular brick buildings. Above a green awning on the first floor is a neon sign reading The Foxglove Smoke Shop, and my stomach flips.

That's okay. Virginia would be nervous too.

I find the alley Elzbieta described and am relieved to see

it's well lit. Still, I don't waste any time cutting through to the back of the buildings, where I rap on the door. The man who opens the door isn't much older than me. Probably early to mid-twenties, with a long face, a broad nose, and brassy red hair.

"Name, sweetheart?" he says in a surprisingly deep voice.

Sweetheart? Ick. But Virginia wouldn't mind. She'd be expecting that sort of degrading greeting.

I make myself smile. "I'm here for Elzbieta."

"You got it. She said there was a new girl coming tonight." He doesn't even try to be subtle about dragging his eyes down the length of me. "I'm Keiran."

"Virginia." I turn my bag into a shield and wish it was even bigger. "Is Elzbieta here already?"

"Yeah, c'mon in." He steps aside, inviting me into the dim hallway. "Elz will be in the first door on the right."

"Thank you." I try for a sweet-but-shy demeanor as I smile and slip past Keiran, keeping as much distance between us as possible.

The hallway smells yeasty and sour, like a loaf of bread that's gone bad. I can hear muted male conversation and laughter, but it's hard to make out much more than that with how intensely my heart pounds. My mouth is dry, and now that I'm in here with the door closed firmly and Creepy Keiran watching me, I'm not so sure this was a good idea. Too late now.

The door Keiran directed me to is closed, and I hesitate.

"You can go on in, doll," Keiran calls. "No need to knock."

"Thank you!" I swallow hard and turn the knob, then step into the room, blessedly out of Keiran's line of vision.

The floral smell hits me before anything else, like having a dozen perfumes shoved up my nose all at once. There are probably eight or so women in various stages of donning a sequined outfit that makes me think of a fancy bathing costume. I really hope they're singers and not cigarette girls, because there's definitely no place for a pocketknife, and the only skirt is a thin row of fringe hitting mid-thigh. None of them take notice of me; they just keep tugging at their costumes or buckling high heels or shoving belongings into the row of cabinets behind them.

After a few seconds of gawking awkwardly, I say, "Um, I'm looking for Elzbieta?"

"Virginia?"

I turn to the right and find Elzbieta standing by a cabinet. Her dress is red as a stoplight, with a scoop neck and a short, flouncy skirt piped with black. The skirt is considerably higher than her knees, but hopefully it has pockets underneath those layers of tulle.

"Come on over. I'll get you a costume."

When I get close enough, she shoves a red dress my way. I clutch the fabric, wishing there was more of it, and try to breathe through my panic. This is how I find out who killed Clarence. This is how I get answers for Louisa. This is how I honor Lydia.

"You and me are the only ciggy girls working tonight," Elzbieta says as she folds a dress. "Liam is at the front door, but Tubs isn't here, which is strange. Tubs is always here." She places the dress in the open cabinet and then frowns at me. "Aren't you going to put that on?"

Oh. I'm not sure why I thought there would be some kind of private space for me to change. I unzip my dress and wriggle out of it while Elzbieta chats about the responsibilities of a cigarette girl. First, we'll fill our trays from the supply room. Then we'll head out onto the floor. There will be men at tables and men at the bar. We'll start at the tables, because they're the men gambling and spending the most money.

I shimmy into the red dress, surprised by how hard it is to tug it into place over my corselette. The bodice has a structure to it that presses into my rib cage and makes it hard to take a deep breath.

Elzbieta surveys me for a moment. "How's it feel?"

I press a hand to my compressed stomach. "Dreadful."

She grins. "Generations of women before us had to put up with this nonsense all day long. You and I just have to tolerate it for a few hours. We're spoiled."

"I don't feel spoiled," I say as I work hard to fill my lungs.

"Yours is actually a size bigger than it would be if you were a real ciggy girl. I thought you'd appreciate a longer skirt. But any bigger and you'd run the risk of"—she gestures to the scoop neck—"things falling out when you bend over."

My face burns.

Elzbieta laughs. "You are precious. I bet you'll feel better when you have your tray on."

She fits the holster around my neck and adjusts the buckle so the metal tray rests above my hip bone. "I'll do most of the talking, of course. Since you're training, nobody will expect you to know things. Lastly, the hat."

Elzbieta hands me a felt pillbox hat and a pin. I relax a tiny bit; while there's no place for my knife, a hat pin can work in a pinch if I need something sharp. Elzbieta helps me position the hat at an angle and then lets me affix the pin.

As soon as I have the hat in place, she steps back to assess her work. "Aren't you just the berries? You'll need to smile, though.

That frown isn't going to get you what you want. You catch more flies with honey, my mother always said."

And that's what this is about—catching whatever fly is responsible for Clarence's death. I put on a smile and Elzbieta nods, satisfied.

She secures her own tray with practiced ease. "Some men get handsy. Just do your best to laugh and step away."

"Am I allowed to elbow them in the throat?"

Elzbieta chuckles. "If you have all the information you need and you decide you don't want this job anymore, then sure. Get a little loose with your elbows. Ready?"

"I don't know that I'll ever feel ready, but okay."

Her smile falters into something sad and genuine. "For Clarence."

My throat tightens and I nod. "For Clarence."

I fall into step behind Elzbieta and notice immediately that she has a different walk here than at her home. She strides toward the door with her chin high and her shoulders squared. Like a singer taking the stage for a performance. The Fox is Elzbieta's stage, and tonight it will be my window into the life of Clarence Dell.

After the chatty, floral-scented changing room full of women, the floor of The Fox feels overwhelmingly masculine. The room is bigger than I expected, blanketed with a haze of smoke that stings my eyes. Men sit at wooden tables with cards or dice, puffing away. I'll probably leave here smelling like a cigar dipped in cologne.

On one end of the room is a stage, dark right now but with a piano and microphones awaiting the gaggle of sparkly women

Elzbieta and I left behind. At the other end is a bar. Bottles of illegal booze line the shelf. The barstools are nearly full, and the barkeep has his back to us, so I can only make out broad shoulders and a balding head.

"The supply room is behind the bar," Elzbieta calls over her shoulder to me. "We'll stop there first."

I try to breathe normally, but the combination of my squeezed lungs and the pungent smoke makes this difficult. A man whistles at Elzbieta as she passes. I shrivel inside but Elzbieta turns a shining smile in the man's general direction and waggles her fingers.

"Gotta get the trays filled, boys. We'll be back."

I can't do this. I cannot do this. My skin feels hot and itchy, as if the eyes of so many men upon me is causing a rash. Why did I think I could do this? Because I absolutely can't.

Yes, you can, I tell myself fiercely. *You need to talk to Liam Finnegan. Just get the information you need and get out.*

I realize I've been scowling and smooth my expression.

"Hello, Danny," Elzbieta greets the bartender as she sashays behind the counter. "Just getting our trays filled. This is Virginia. She's training."

"Good to meet you, Virginia." The bartender looks at me and the polite smile dies on his face.

I suck in a shocked breath. Danny is Daniel Becker—Clarence's roommate.

CHAPTER
SEVENTEEN

For a moment, we blink at each other. What is he doing here?

Daniel looks away. "I'm new too. Only been here a couple weeks."

His Adam's apple glides down his throat and back up. He's going to play along. He isn't going to ruin anything for me. Or is it that he's asking *me* to not ruin anything for *him*?

"How do you like it so far?" I ask.

"It's good." Daniel gives me the faintest of smiles. "I hope your training goes well, Virginia."

"My friends call me Gin, actually."

"Gin it is, then." With one more smile, he turns his back to me as he serves drinks to two men in fedoras.

Elzbieta grins at me from the tiny room behind the bar. She flicks her eyes to Daniel and then back to me. "You might be better at this gig than I expected, *Gin*," she says in a hushed voice as she loads up our trays. "I've hardly heard Danny say two words to anybody who isn't a paying customer."

She doesn't seem to know who he is, so Daniel must have chosen to keep his connection to Clarence a secret. But why?

"Cigars are fifty cents each, so keep these toward the back of the tray." Elzbieta places several where they would be hardest for a customer to grab. "Fifteen cents for a pack of cigarettes. We're out of Black Cats, so just Chesterfields and Luckys tonight."

I'm barely listening as my brain tries to work through the

mystery of why Daniel is here and why he wouldn't have told Elzbieta who he is. The temptation to tell her is ripe on my tongue, and I have to remind myself that Elzbieta is technically a suspect herself. I can't allow myself to get so comfortable with her that I start sharing details about the case.

I also can't get distracted by Daniel right now. I need to store away my questions for later so I can focus on the real goal: talking to Liam Finnegan.

"Which one is Liam?" I murmur to Elzbieta.

She glances beyond me. "Can't see him right now, but he should be by the door. He's good-looking, with brown hair and a crooked nose. He's usually wearing a flat cap. When we start working the tables, you should be able to spot him."

With our trays now loaded, Elzbieta leads us back around the bar to the dice and card tables. I follow, trying to keep my steps steady so that I don't upset any of the boxes Elzbieta stacked on my tray.

"Hello, fellas," she says as we come upon the first table. "How's everyone doing tonight?"

A few of the men keep playing without looking up. A few others smile.

"This is my friend, Gin." Elzbieta touches my shoulder. "She's new and a little bit shy, so say hello to Gin. Why don't you handsome fellas help start her night off well and buy something from her?"

Elzbieta chats easily with the men while I fumble my way through selling a pack of cigarettes to a guy with bleary eyes and a terrible hand of cards. I wish I could tell him to fold.

Elzbieta sells two cigars and then moves us to another table. "This is my new friend, Gin, and she's a little shy. Why don't you all say hello?"

By the time we arrive at the eighth table, my cheeks hurt from all my forced smiling. At the door, I catch glimpses of a man in a flat cap, but he's in a small vestibule with clouded glass, so I can't make out any of his features.

"I wasn't so sure how you were going to do at first," Elzbieta says into my ear as she nudges me toward another table. Closer to the door, thankfully. Closer to Liam. "But you're not half bad at this job."

Her eyes track the sequined ladies prancing their way onto the stage. "Oh, good. The men will be preoccupied with Deb and the girls. I can introduce you to Liam before we head over to the bar. C'mon."

I turn my back on the stage, where a woman with platinum-blonde hair and outfitted in a bright blue dress has just stepped behind the microphone to much applause and whistling.

"Do you have a plan for what to say to Liam?" Elzbieta says right into my ear. "To get him talking, I mean? Or do you want my help?"

My stomach suddenly feels like the hard pit of a peach. "I have a plan."

I'm not sure it's a *good* plan, and I had no idea Daniel would be here. That could cause problems, but there's no time to come up with something different now.

One blessing of being by the door is that the smoke is thinner. Elzbieta leads me around the vestibule toward the man I've seen obfuscated through the glass. She pulls open the door, and Liam Finnegan turns to look at us. Toffee-colored hair peeks out from beneath a flat cap. His nose is crooked enough that it draws the eye, but there's something strangely endearing about it, like he's somehow better looking like this than he would've been with a straight nose. His jaw is square and hard, but it softens when he sees Elzbieta.

"Good evening, ladies." He touches the brim of his hat and looks at me. I cut my gaze to the floor, pretending to be shy. "Who's your friend, Elz?"

"This is Gin. She's testing us out tonight, seeing what she thinks."

"You're learning from the best." Liam's voice has a nasal quality to it, as if he's recovering from a cold. "What do you think so far?"

This is all the opportunity I need.

"Everybody seems really great." I try for a giggle but instead have to clear my throat, which is scratchy from all the smoke. "I heard about this place from a boy who used to live in my building. Do either of you know Clarence?"

Liam blinks rapidly. His mouth is open, but he doesn't speak.

I look from him to Elzbieta, who appears startled. "Did I say something wrong? Does he not work here anymore? I moved out of the building a few months ago, so it's been a while since I've seen him."

Liam is still staring at me. I try to study his expression without looking as though I'm overly interested in his reaction.

"Um." Elzbieta glances at Liam and then back to me. "Sorry to have to tell you this, Gin, but Clarence died."

I've rehearsed a surprised reaction in my bathroom mirror, and I hope my practice pays off. I press my hand over my mouth. "What? When?"

"Back in October." Again, Elzbieta's gaze swings to Liam and then back to me. "I'm really sorry."

"I just can't believe that." I try to decipher Liam's expression. Shock? Suspicion? Guilt? "What happened?"

Liam averts his eyes. "Took his own life."

"*Clarence* did? We can't be talking about the same person, because I just don't believe that. The Clarence I'm talking about had a round face and green eyes and—"

"That's him." Liam cuts me off. "And he did. Kill himself, I mean."

"Good gravy, I'm so sorry to have brought that up." I fan myself, as though I might faint at any moment. "I just can't believe that *Clarence* would've done that. Are you *sure* that's what happened?"

Liam keeps his head turned away, but Elzbieta nods slowly. "You know, I've wondered recently if it's true."

Liam snaps his head to look at her. "What do you mean?"

Elzbieta gives a slight shrug. "I don't know. Just . . . like Gin said, it just doesn't seem like Clarence."

"So, what? You think somebody did him in?"

"I don't know." Elzbieta shrugs again. "Maybe?"

Liam stares at Elzbieta, his face hard with . . . something. Whatever emotion it is, there are layers of complexity there, as though he isn't just surprised—he's also hurt. Or scared.

Liam opens his mouth to say something right as the front door is yanked open and a rowdy group of men spill into the vestibule.

In an instant, Liam turns to steel. "One moment, gentlemen," he says, and Elzbieta grabs my arm and pulls me back into The Fox. Onstage, the blonde woman sings a high-energy song with a voice like velvet.

"What do you think?" Elzbieta asks, speaking right into my ear. "Did Liam do it?"

I smirk. She thinks it's that easy? "You tell me. What'd you make of his reaction?"

"Well." She glances back at the vestibule, where Liam pats down the newcomers. "He sure didn't seem to like what I said, did he?"

"No. I wish that were all the evidence I needed. What I really need is more time with him."

"I can try, but we better circulate again or I'll get in trouble. We haven't hit the bar yet."

I follow her to the bar, but my thoughts stay on Liam Finnegan. "Did he look afraid to you?" I ask as I trail after her. The music is so loud, I'm not worried about being overheard. As it is, I'm not sure how well she can hear me.

She shrugs. "He was *something*. He didn't like talking about it, that's for sure."

With that, Elzbieta puts her work face back on and turns to the first few gentlemen at the bar. "Hello, boys. Can we get you a cigar? Cigarette?"

Behind the bar, Daniel looks at me, then looks away. Could he be here for the same reason I am? Does he also suspect someone at The Fox killed Clarence? But both times I've spoken to him, he was adamant that Clarence's death came at his own hand. Was he lying? Or is he here for another reason? But then why not tell others that he knew Clarence?

"What do you recommend, doll?" the man nearest to me asks.

Something warm brushes the back of my knee, and I step away with a forced laugh that I hope sounds lighthearted.

"The Luckys are very popular tonight."

"Think they'll bring me some luck?" The man drains the last of the pale liquid in his glass and stands. "The dice weren't rolling my direction earlier."

"The night is young." I accept the dime and nickel, which he presses into my palm with an unnecessary amount of contact.

I force a smile that feels more like a grimace, then turn away and immediately ram my tray into the stomach of a man standing directly behind me. Cigars and cigarette boxes slide around on my tray, and I grapple with my balance.

"I'm so sorry, sir. I wasn't watching where I was going and—"

The rest of my sentence dissolves on my tongue as I look up into the smoky-blue eyes and scowling face of Jeremiah Crane.

CHAPTER
EIGHTEEN

"H-hi." The syllable stammers out of my mouth. "Are you"—I swallow hard—"here for work?"

"No." The word is quiet, but sharp. "Guess again."

Elzbieta shoots me a worried glance. "Gin?"

"No, thank you," Jeremiah replies tersely, barely glancing at Elzbieta. His eyes stay locked on mine. "We need to leave here. Now."

I nod, suddenly feeling overwhelmed by the smoke, the music, the raucous laughter, all of it.

I turn away from Jeremiah to Elzbieta, not entirely sure how to explain this. "I need to go. This is . . ."

How to explain who Jeremiah is? This is my friend? This is my friend's older brother? None of the labels stick quite right when it comes to Jeremiah.

"Your boss?" Elzbieta guesses.

Sure, that'll work. "Yes. Should I go out the way I came in?"

Elzbieta nods and hastily shuttles cigarette boxes and cigars onto her tray. "Leave the tray and the costume in my cabinet, okay?"

"Thank you for everything," I reply, trying to convey my sincerity while also hollering above the music. "Truly."

She touches my arm briefly. "Thank you for helping Clarence." With one last look at Jeremiah, she continues down the length of the bar with her tray.

I brave Jeremiah's scowling face. "I need to get changed and then I'll exit out back."

He shakes his head. "I'm not letting you out of my sight."

"I can't very well go home dressed like *this*, can I?"

Jeremiah glances down at my red dress, and his cheeks turn a matching shade. "Fine. I'll wait around back for you, but if you're not out in five minutes, I'm ringing your father."

Other than rolling my eyes, I don't reply to his threat, just wind my way through the tables to the changing room. The room is empty now that all the dancers are up onstage, and the aggressive floral scent doesn't seem as intense after the heavy smoke of The Fox.

I peel off the cigarette girl costume and take in a deliciously full breath. Then another. How did women survive being cinched up all those years? I hurriedly dress and take care to fold the costume nicely before putting it in Elzbieta's cluttered cabinet.

Creepy Keiran is still at the back door. He watches me approach with a lazy smile. "Done so soon, doll?"

I want to scowl at him, but I also might need to come back sometime. Best to not burn bridges quite yet.

"Something came up and I've gotta dash." I smile and waggle my fingers in an imitation of Elzbieta as I walk by. "See you next time!"

"Lookin' forward to it," he calls after me.

I drop my smile as soon as I've walked out into the fresh air. The back alley smells acrid, like old garbage and empty bottles, but it's still an improvement over the heavy smoke. A fine mist falls, and I arrange my cloche to keep the water out of my eyes. Relief rushes through me as I come around the corner and find Jeremiah standing in a circle of light from a streetlamp, waiting for me. Even if he *is* glaring, at least he's someone safe.

His gaze tracks me as I draw closer, but his mouth remains pressed into a firm line. Even here on the sidewalk, the noises of The Fox—the thrum of the music, the laughter—seep through the walls. I feel aware of the boozy, smoky odor I've brought with me.

"No coat?"

I shake my head.

He doesn't say anything, simply looks at me as if I'm going to offer some kind of explanation, but I'm not about to tell him that I left it at home because bringing my expensive coat seemed foolish.

Finally, Jeremiah says, "My car is parked this way," and turns on his heel.

I walk alongside him down the too-empty sidewalks. I forgot to wind my watch, so I have no idea what time it is. We wordlessly trek around the corner to his car, where he opens the passenger door, gives me a look like a disappointed father, and then closes me into the Buick.

I take care to straighten my shoulders and raise my chin. I refuse to act as though I owe Jeremiah Crane an explanation, an apology, or anything of the sort.

Jeremiah primes the pump several times, then pulls open the driver's side door and flops inside. But he doesn't start the car. He just sits there, staring through the misty windshield.

"I don't even know where to start," he finally says.

"I do." I turn to him, matching my cold voice to his. "Why are you here?"

Jeremiah either scoffs or laughs, I'm not sure which. "You think *that's* where we start, Piper? Not why I just found you at The Fox of all places?"

A chill seeps into my bones. I cross my arms over my chest, hoping he won't notice the slight tremble of my limbs. "I really don't see how that's any of your business."

He looks at me with wide-eyed disbelief and makes another of his scoffing or laughing sounds—a scaff. "You're behaving like *I'm* being unreasonable. I just found you inside The Fox, Piper—"

"I know where I was—you don't have to keep saying it. You're acting like you have the right to decide what's okay and what's not okay for me to do—"

"I'm acting like somebody who cares about you!" Jeremiah's eyes blaze. "Because I *do*. Should I apologize for that as well?"

I look away, out the blurry windshield and onto the empty streets. There are so few cars on the road and hardly any people. The emptiness feels unnatural, and I shiver.

"Are you cold?"

"No," I snap instinctively. The syllable is a visible vapor in the car. I take a deep breath and try again. "I'm fine. Thank you for asking."

Jeremiah nods. After a beat of silence, he says, "I'll take you home."

He starts the engine. When he pulls away from the curb, he says, "You asked why I'm here. Emma called me, because your father called her trying to figure out where you were."

"Oh." The syllable comes out so quietly, there's no way Jeremiah can hear it over the noise of the car.

I can see the scene playing out in my head—my father going to my room and finding it empty. Trying to figure out where I might've gone. Assuming I walked to Emma's. Though why didn't Jane tell him I was with a friend?

"According to Emma, he went to tell you good night and you weren't in your room. He tried Mariano first, of course, but your boyfriend didn't pick up, or was unavailable, or something along those lines." Jeremiah says all this with a sour expression, as if it's unforgivable that Mariano couldn't be reached. "So he tried Emma, and Emma called me. She asked if I had any idea where you could be because your father couldn't find you, and Emma was scared."

"I told Jane—"

Jeremiah barrels on as though I didn't speak. "Emma reminded me that you're working a case right now, and I thought back to the Chicago Theatre. When I brought up your case, you brought up The Foxglove Smoke Shop. And I thought, 'There's no way that's where she is,' but I also couldn't quite shake the idea."

I slide lower in my seat, as if I can escape the shame if I'm a bit shorter. "I told Jane what my plans were for the night."

Jeremiah scaffs again and raises his eyebrows in a way that clearly means *Really?*

"I mean, I didn't tell her my *real* plans. I told her I was spending the night with a friend, so nobody should've been worried about me at all. I don't know why Father didn't—" I think of their angry voices when I slipped by their door on my way out. "Well, it's possible they aren't speaking to one another right now. Especially about me. It wasn't a good night at our house."

Jeremiah's knuckles are white on the steering wheel. "Although even if he did speak to your stepmother—"

"Please don't call her that."

"To Mrs. Sail, she couldn't have told him where you *actually* were."

"No, but at least he wouldn't have been worried. He would've thought I was spending the night at a friend's."

"Did Mariano know where you were? Did *anybody*?"

I avert my gaze out the passenger window. I don't owe Jeremiah an explanation. I don't owe him anything.

"I'll take that as a no, which means if I hadn't remembered your question about The Foxglove Smoke Shop—"

"Then I still would've been fine. I was there with Elzbieta, and she's a friend."

Kind of. If you ignore that she's also on my suspect list.

"Who's Elzbieta?"

"The cigarette girl. The beautiful one? You thought she offered you a gin?"

Jeremiah's head shakes slowly. "I haven't a clue who you're talking about, Piper."

"It happened fifteen minutes ago. How do you not remember Elzbieta?"

"I remember the fellow at the door, because he didn't want to let me in. And then I walked in and saw you being accosted by a man at the bar—"

Now I scoff. "I had that under control."

"And at that point, I was too angry to notice anybody else. All I could think about was getting you out of there."

Even so, it seems impossible to me that Jeremiah wouldn't have noticed Elzbieta of all people. But he's gone to a lot of trouble tonight—unnecessary trouble, but trouble nonetheless—and I don't want to be dismissive of his efforts.

"I appreciate you coming all this way, but there was no need to be worried. I was safe."

"Safe?" Jeremiah's laugh is harsh. "How can you say that? You were working in a North Side casino as a cigarette girl. Nothing about that was safe, Piper."

The outrage rushes hot and fast through my body. "And Lydia got plucked right out of our neighborhood! Right off State Street. Nowhere is truly safe, Jeremiah."

He idles at the four-way stop and looks at me with such sorrow that I have to work hard to not melt into sobs.

Jeremiah pulls off his jacket. "Here, you're shaking."

"I'm fine," I say, but he's right. I *am* shaking.

Jeremiah tucks his coat around my stubborn shoulders, then resumes driving. After a few seconds, I thread my arms through the sleeves and wrap the coat tight. "Thank you," I mutter.

"Do you want to tell me about the case?"

I consider for a moment. Jeremiah stopped whatever he was doing to come find me. The least I can do is be honest with him.

"A girl at Presley's asked if I would help her figure out what happened to her brother. He supposedly took his own life, but she doesn't think he did. I'm trying to figure out who might've wanted him dead."

"And you know this girl?"

"The girl who hired me? I do now. I didn't at the time."

Jeremiah's mouth thins. "Did you know the brother?"

"No. The girl had heard about Lydia—she's friends with Hannah LeVine—and so she asked me to help her. That's all."

We're back in the bustle of downtown, heading south on Lake Shore Drive, and it feels like I can take a full breath again.

"You almost died finding Lydia," Jeremiah says as we wait our turn at a traffic light. "*Emma* almost died."

"I never meant for Emma to get involved," I say.

"I'm not saying it's your fault, Piper. I'm saying you don't have to do this." With each word, his voice grows sharper. Angrier. "With Lydia, I understood, but you don't even know this girl or her brother. You don't have to take these dumb risks to try and solve every blasted mystery that falls your way. You can say no."

"I could." I swallow and curl my fingers around the cuffs of Jeremiah's coat. "But I don't want to."

My house is the only one on Astor Street with first floor lights burning bright. As Jeremiah pulls up to the curb, Father emerges from the front door. He's silhouetted by the house lights, but his body language says relieved rather than angry. I pull off Jeremiah's coat and am still fitting my hand into the door lever when Father yanks it open for me.

"Thank God." Father pulls me out of Jeremiah's car and crushes me against him. "I was so worried."

I wait for him to say something about how I smell like I fell into a rum bucket and then lit myself on fire, but he doesn't.

"I was fine." My words are muffled in his sweater. "I had plans with a friend—"

"You have to tell me these things." Father crushes me even closer to him. "You can't just leave the house without saying anything."

Tears glass my eyes. I took such precautions to keep anyone from worrying about me, but I'd failed.

"Jane knew," I say, my voice thick. "I told her I was sleeping over at a friend's."

Father finally releases me. "I know that now, but Jane was already asleep when I checked your room and saw you weren't there. I didn't wake her until after I'd called Emma and Mariano."

He pushes a hand through his already disheveled silver hair

and looks to Jeremiah. He holds out his hand. "Thank you for bringing her home. Could Mrs. Sail and I take you out to dinner Wednesday night to express our appreciation? Piper will be there too, of course."

Supper with Father, Jane, and Jeremiah? That sounds horribly awkward.

Jeremiah glances at me. "That's kind of you, but not necessary. I was happy to help."

"I insist," Father says. "If Wednesday doesn't work, we'll find another day."

Jeremiah looks at me again, perhaps sensing this is a battle he can't win. I try to smile apologetically. "In that case, Wednesday works great."

"Splendid. How does Henrici's sound?"

"It's one of my favorites."

"I'll have Jane make a reservation for six thirty, if that suits you."

"It does." Jeremiah bows slightly. "I look forward to it."

"See you then," Father says, and then steers me up the front steps and through the door into our blessedly warm house.

Sidekick prances around my feet, his thick tail frantic.

"He's been lying by the front door, waiting for you," Father says.

The smile on his face is one I haven't seen since the summer. Relief following an extended period of worry looks different on a face than pure happiness. How fortunate that the amount of people who care about me is so small, because I can see in my father's face—just like I heard in Jeremiah's voice—I am a difficult person to care about.

The squeeze of guilt within me only tightens. "I'm really sorry I scared you."

Father slowly nods. "You really did, Piper. Being a legal adult doesn't make it okay for you to come and go as you please, as though it doesn't affect anyone else."

"I'm sorry," I say to my toes.

"Were you out drinking tonight?"

"No."

"Don't lie to me. You smell like an ashtray."

"Yeah, I know." I have to offer more of an explanation than this. "My friend wanted to go dancing, and the place was really smoky."

Father's frown deepens. "Were you at a speakeasy?"

"Not exactly."

"But they had alcohol there?"

"Yes, but we weren't drinking. We were just dancing and having fun."

"I'm aware that brand of fun isn't uncommon for young ladies your age, but you're not a common young lady, Piper Caroline. There are dangerous people in this city, people who would relish hurting you, and I just . . ."

Fears play across my father's face, twisting my guilt tighter and tighter.

"I'm very sorry."

Father studies me a moment, and then nods. "I'm sorry about a lot of things tonight. I know the announcement of the baby wasn't a welcome surprise. Maybe especially for you, since you're still living at home."

"I'm sorry I reacted poorly," I say to my shoes. "I just need some time to adjust."

"Whether you like it or not, you will always be my little girl."

Tears prick my eyes as I take in how very almost-fifty my father looks right now. The lines around his eyes. The softening around his jaw. The gray of his hair, which is probably my fault, though I think Nick deserves some blame too. While I generally don't like being thought of as a little girl, the reassurance that my father still values me is more meaningful than I would've expected.

The clock in the entryway chimes once with the arrival of eleven thirty.

Father offers a small, tired smile. "Why don't we get some sleep?"

I nod and hug him. "Good night. I love you."

He squeezes me tight, and then Sidekick follows me up the stairs to my bedroom. My body aches from the night, as if the tension of being in The Fox and then being in Jeremiah's car was rigorous exercise. I collapse into bed, but my head spins and spins: Why is Daniel working at The Fox? Why did Liam make that face when Elzbieta voiced doubt about Clarence's death? Why was Tubs nowhere to be seen? How much can I trust Elzbieta?

And what do I do next to find answers to these questions?

CHAPTER
NINETEEN

The entryway clock announces that the time is midnight, and I'm still lying here awake. When this remains true at twelve thirty, I heave myself out of bed, wrap my housecoat around me, and settle in at my desk with my case notebook. Maybe if I purge all the questions from my head, I'll finally be able to sleep.

I have a page for each suspect and come upon Elzbieta's first. I press my pencil to the page: *Can I trust her?* And I never did ask where she was the day Clarence died. I write *Alibi?* and circle it. I think of how Liam looked at Elzbieta tonight when she said she wasn't so sure Clarence had taken his own life. Whatever expression that was on his face—anger, fear, suspicion—it wasn't *trust.*

And yet Elzbieta has seemed nothing but earnest in how she speaks of Clarence. Earnest and helpful. Is that an act? A distraction technique? I tap my pencil against the page. There's nothing to do but keep talking to her and see. Time has a way of uncovering what lies beneath a shiny surface.

I flip the page and stare at Tubs's name. Why wasn't he at work tonight? Is the explanation as simple as being sick, or does it have more to do with his financial troubles? I'll have to pay another visit to his house, because so far, he has the strongest motive for harming Clarence.

The next page has *Liam Finnegan* written across the top. From what Elzbieta said, it sounded like Liam might have wanted to kill Clarence because of his own affection for Elzbieta. Tonight, however, I didn't sense that Liam's feelings were anything extraordinary. He certainly didn't look at Elzbieta like he would kill people just to get a chance with her. But I hadn't been around him for very long either, and there was definitely *something* in Liam's gaze when he'd looked at her there at the end. I think about Nick, and how when he is sad, it tends to emerge from him as anger or sometimes meanness. Maybe Liam is similar, and his anger is covering up a different emotion. But is it desire? Or guilt?

"You're trying too hard," I mutter and rub my dry eyes.

Just like with Tubs, I'll have to find another way to spend time with Liam.

I turn the page and write *Daniel Becker* at the top, and then immediately below his name, *Why is he working at The Fox? And why isn't he telling others about his connection to Clarence? Does he know more than what he told me?*

With Daniel, at least, I can go by his apartment and ask my questions. Of course, he asked that I not do that anymore, but I never promised anything, and that was before I discovered he is working at The Fox. That'll be my next step, I decide: talking to Daniel about out why he's working there and finding out anything he might've learned during his employment.

I close my notebook. Instead of feeling sleepier, I feel wide awake.

I drag the box of Clarence's things out from under my bed and go through his 1924 receipts once again. I look through ordinary purchases—groceries, the movies, Woolworth's. Those are listed in detail, but other things that I would like to know are not. Like that note of "+$500, Dean for services rendered," and then several weeks later, at the end of September, a simple "–$500."

What happened to such a large sum of money? After going through his books so many times, I've confirmed it's the only subtraction without any kind of clarification. Clarence wasn't an extravagant spender. There's the occasional nice dinner out while he's seeing Elz—Tip Top Inn, La Louisiane, Ireland's Oyster House—and he got drinks with Liam and Keiran once a week, but everything else is basic. His groceries suggest a diet of mostly sandwiches and cereal. His Woolworth's purchases are always standard items, including the day before he died. Socks and toothpaste. Aspirin and Band-Aids. Writing utensils, lined paper, and soda crackers.

No rat poison, though.

I frown at the book. Daniel said they already had the rat poison, but who purchased it? And when? I note the question and then continue to flip pages.

The clock downstairs chimes one and then one thirty, and I'm still combing through Clarence's receipts. I wish I had a way to view and assess all the information at once. At Mariano's office, I once noticed an oversized chalkboard leaning against the wall, and I feel a ping of longing.

I stand and evaluate my room. There isn't a blank wall, and even if I took down the artwork and photographs, beneath those is the rosebud wallpaper Mother picked out at my birth. I won't risk damaging that with tape or tacks.

My eyes continue to scan the room and finally land on my closet door. Instead of being long and shallow, like most closets in the house, mine is a tiny square room that you can walk into. I open the door, turn on my flashlight, close the door, and consider the blank space. This area can work. I can't write on the walls, but I can tape notes here. Take in all the evidence at once, rather than in pieces that live in a box or notebook. Joyce still does my laundry, bless her, but she leaves me to put things away where I like. If I move my laundry hamper out of the closet, there will be no reason for her to come inside.

I collect tape, a pencil, and index cards left over from an old chemistry project, then get to work writing out questions and facts on the cards. I tape them up in the closet, and when I finish, I sit on the floor and look at them.

Not much later, I realize how the chill of the night has seeped into my room. I tuck my feet into slippers and wrap my body in the white lace comforter Mother picked out for me, because she didn't yet know that her daughter wasn't a white lace kind of girl. Then I lay on the closet floor and stare at the questions, at the facts, illuminated by my flashlight and let my mind wander. Let it go where it wants to, connect what it wants to.

Louisa says Clarence always made good grades . . . but Clarence also was kicked out of Loyola for cheating. If Clarence planned to kill himself, why did he buy socks and toothpaste, especially as he was so thrifty when it came to those purchases? How long until arsenic takes effect? Did he buy the rat poison and not make a note of it? Or did he grab it on a whim from the box Daniel claimed they had? Why is Daniel working at The Fox? And if it's true that he started working there a few weeks ago, was he already employed by the time he and I first talked—so he may have met Elz by then as well? Where was Elzbieta the day Clarence died? When Clarence wrote, "I'm sorry. I just can't anymore," what did he mean? Why be so vague? What did he spend five hundred dollars on?

I stare at that last question until I become aware that my back hurts. That my left foot is asleep. That I'm cold. That my eyes are closed. I pry them open and discover I'm asleep on my closet floor, the beam of the flashlight weak. I stumble to my bed and collapse into it, causing Sidekick to grunt his annoyance and resettle.

I sleep deeply until my alarm rouses me several hours later.

I'm yawning as the phone trills. It's been a morning of nonstop telephone calls, and the harsh ring makes my head throb. Or maybe that's my abbreviated night of sleep.

"Presley's School for Girls," I say. "How can I help you?"

"I had the strangest message when I arrived at the office this morning." Mariano's voice chases away thoughts of fatigue. "It reads, 'Timothy Sail says he can't find Piper. Please call as soon as possible.'"

"Huh." I feed a fresh piece of paper into the typewriter. "That *is* strange."

"It appears you've been found."

"I have, thank you. How are you? How did that conversation with the witness go yest—"

"Nope. We are still talking about this." Mariano's voice has an *I'm serious* tone to it. If we were having this conversation in person, he would probably also cross his arms over his chest and set his jaw. "Why couldn't your father find you last night?"

"Mostly due to poor communication. I told Jane I was spending the night at a friend's, but that message didn't make it to my father because he and Jane spent the evening fighting after—" I give a sharp laugh. "Oh, I should mention that too. Father and Jane are expecting a baby. I'm going to be a big sister."

Silence. "That's . . . unexpected. I don't know why, because they're married and she's relatively young—"

"Twenty-seven." My voice sounds strained, as though I'm holding in tears, though I don't feel like I am. "A year younger than Tim."

There's more silence. "I'm sorry. I can't imagine that felt like
great news to you."

"No." I scowl at the blank page in the typewriter. "I don't know
why I brought it up, really. I don't want to talk about it."

In Mariano's silence, I can hear the other men in his over-
crowded office. He's probably sitting at his desk, wearing a tie that's
either a little too loose or a little too tight because he fusses with it
when he's uncomfortable. He's surrounded by stacks of files, always
more than he can handle, and there's likely a mug of coffee growing
cold beside him. His homburg is on the edge of his desk, there to
be grabbed if he needs to rush off. Or maybe he's still wearing it,
because he would've called Presley's as soon as he saw the note.

"We don't have to talk about it," Mariano says. "I wish I could
think of something comforting to say."

I shrug, but of course he can't see that. "What is there to be
said, really?" I fuss with the type guide on the typewriter. "Any
chance you're free for dinner? Our usual place."

"I'll try," he says. "As you know, there's only so much about
my day that's in my control."

"Lawbreakers are thoughtless like that."

Mariano huffs a laugh. "Isn't that the truth? And just so you
know, I still intend to get some straight answers about where
you really were last night."

"That's fine. I'll just bat my eyelashes at you until you forget
what we were talking about."

He laughs again, making me feel like I've won some sort of
prize. And I have, really. I've won Mariano.

I settle the earpiece back into its hook and begin typing,

though it isn't long before my mind drifts away from the letter and off to Clarence Dell.

"If you're looking for Daniel, he left for work hours ago."

I turn to find a woman standing outside the door for 3E, holding a paper shopping bag. She looks to be in her early thirties, and has a stylish black hat fitted over her dark auburn hair. I can't see her eyes very well because the hall light glints off her eyeglasses.

"Oh, rats." I look at my watch, which for once I remembered to wind. At twelve thirty, The Fox isn't even open yet, so she must be talking about a different job. "Do you know where he works?"

The woman doesn't reply immediately, just continues to look at me. I really wish I could see her eyes.

"I don't know if you know his roommate," I press on, "or *knew* his roommate, rather, but Clarence was my cousin and—"

"Oh, you poor dear," the woman says so earnestly that I feel a sharp kick of guilt for my lie. She steps closer, and the glare vanishes. Her eyes are an ordinary medium-brown color but brimming with compassion. "Clarence was such a sweet fellow. I still can't believe he's gone."

I duck my head so I don't have to look her in the eyes. "Me neither."

"We didn't talk much, but he was always so polite to me and my husband. Always offering to help if he saw me coming up with bags or boxes." The longer she speaks, the clearer I can hear her Minnesota accent. Her lips compress until they almost disappear, and she shakes her head, as though shaking away the memories. "What a tragedy. How's Daniel doing? I half expected him to move out, but I suppose he has a lease, doesn't he?"

"Yes," I say. "He does."

"He's so quiet and keeps to himself, which probably makes him well-suited for working at the college library. But I do worry for him." She frowns. "And the girlfriend. I've wondered how she must feel."

"The girlfriend," I echo. "You mean Clarence's girlfriend? Elzbieta?"

"I never knew her name, and I only saw her the one time. Beautiful girl. She had thick, dark hair and a lovely figure."

"Yes, that sounds like Elzbieta."

"I always thought they sounded like a sweet couple whenever Clarence spoke of her." The woman's smile has a touch of nostalgia to it. "His face always took on this look of pure adoration. I was surprised when he told me they'd broken up."

She appears to expect me to respond, so I nod. "Me too. I really thought she was going to be the one."

"When I saw her that day, I thought they might be getting back together. But then they fought something awful, and she was crying when she left, so I thought, 'Well, that's that.' And then the next night Clarence was gone." The woman's frown deepens. "I think of that every time my husband leaves the apartment and I'm feeling angry with him. I think, 'Catherine, you never know when it could be your last conversation. Don't say anything you'd regret in case he gets hit by a train on the way to work.' It's a bit melodramatic, I know."

Catherine's laugh is a touch self-deprecating, but my thoughts are still swirling around her saying she saw Elzbieta here. "I'm sorry, but did you say that you saw Clarence's girlfriend here the day before he died?"

Catherine leans back, like my question was a physical push. "Yes."

"And they fought?"

Catherine hesitates. "That's what it sounded like anyway. I wasn't trying to listen in, but there was some shouting, and I live right next door . . ." She shifts the shopping bag in her arms.

Elzbieta never mentioned any of this to me. Why? Maybe it wasn't her. She isn't the only girl running around Chicago with thick, dark hair and a lovely figure.

Or maybe it *was* her, and Elzbieta didn't tell me about it because she's hiding something.

"I hope I haven't upset you," Catherine says.

I push away my thoughts for later. "Sorry, I was just thinking about poor Elzbieta. She's taken Clarence's death so hard, and now I have a fuller understanding of why."

Catherine nods. "We just never know when it might be the last time we see someone."

I think of Lydia at her front gate, wearing my coat and calling a chipper "Good-bye!" to me.

I inhale deeply and put on a smile for Catherine's sake. "Thank you for your help. I'll go find Daniel at work."

"Blessings to you and your family," she says with a bob of her head.

I take several steps down the hall and then remember one of the reasons why I'd come to talk to Daniel in the first place. "Catherine?"

She pauses in her open door.

"I don't mean for this to sound offensive, but do you ever get rats in your apartment?"

Her face shows surprise, but she recovers quickly. "Not here. At our place in Minneapolis, we did sometimes, but we haven't had any here yet. Of course, we've only lived here four months." She shrugs. "Why do you ask?"

I audition several answers in my head. *Just curious. Just something I like to ask people I barely know.* "My roommate and I have them where we live. I just wondered what we should do."

"Ah. Well, I imagine we'll have them here at some point too. They're a fact of life in the city." Catherine shrugs. "Even if you get rid of them for a while, those rats have a way of popping back up."

CHAPTER
TWENTY

The university library is different from the library at Presley's or the city library. There are more tables than bookshelves, and most are occupied with students. There's an information desk, but nobody is there. I feign interest in a leaflet about the school tennis team and sneak regular glances at my watch, because I don't have much longer before I need to be back at Presley's.

I'm about to walk away when a young woman strides up to the desk.

"Sorry, sorry," she says in a rushed voice. "The machine was being cantankerous and—" She blinks at me as if seeing me for the first time. "You're not the girl who asked for a mimeograph."

"No, I'm not."

She looks around. "Well, where did she go?"

"I don't know. I've been here for about five minutes, and nobody has been at the desk."

The girl exhales sharply as she places a book and several mimeographed papers on the counter. "She better come back for these. What do you need?"

"I'm looking for Daniel Becker. Is he working?"

"Yes, but he's on his break. Which means he's next door." She exhales again. "I swear, he gets more done on his lunch break than I do all day."

"What's next door?"

"The gymnasium." Her face flickers into a scowl. "Do you not go to school here? The library is for students only."

"I'm just here to speak to Daniel. Thank you."

I turn and stride back out into the freezing afternoon. Fortunately, finding the gymnasium door takes less than a minute. It's a big room with high ceilings and wooden floors. There are a few people scattered about, but it isn't as crowded as the library. I spot Daniel relatively quickly; he's hanging off a bar, doing slow and steady pull-ups. He wears trousers and an undershirt, revealing surprisingly toned muscles. Despite having seen my brothers in undershirts plenty of times, the idea of speaking to Daniel while he's wearing only a short-sleeved shirt makes my cheeks heat.

I can't wait around, though. As it is, I'm pushing the boundaries of my lunch hour.

I straighten my shoulders and march myself over to him. "Hello, Mr. Becker."

Daniel's face had been stony with concentration, but it shifts to surprise. He drops to the ground. "Hello, Miss Sail."

"Sorry to drop by unannounced like this."

"After last night, I figured it was only a matter of time before I heard from you." Daniel reaches for a white towel nearby and wipes his face. "How did you know where I was?"

"Catherine told me. Well, she said the library, and then the girl at the desk told me I could find you over here."

When Daniel pulls the towel away from his face, he's frowning. "Who's Catherine?"

"The woman who lives in 3E."

Daniel's expression doesn't change. "With red hair?"

"That's her."

He rubs the towel along the back of his neck. "We don't speak much. Not more than 'Good morning' and 'How do you do?' anyway. I didn't realize she knew where I worked."

"Catherine seems to be the kind of neighbor who keeps an eye on what's happening. I have a neighbor like that." I smile at Daniel as though we might bond over having nosy neighbors. "Makes me crazy. My mother used to say she didn't have to worry about me when I was outdoors playing because she knew Mrs. Applegate was keeping an eye on me."

Daniel smiles, showing a glimpse of crooked teeth, before it's as if he remembers himself and keeps his lips together. "I bet you were a troublemaker. What were you doing at The Fox last night, Miss Sail?"

"I'm here to ask you the same thing."

"That's simple. Money." Daniel turns and reaches for his shirt, which is hanging on a nearby hook. "Do you know that I make as much there in one night as I do an entire week of working at the library? An entire *week*. I can't believe I didn't think of working there sooner."

For a moment, he stares off wistfully, as though he can see all those dollars he could've earned floating away.

"Nobody seemed to know about your connection to Clarence."

The wistful gaze disappears. "That's true. Do they know *your* connection, *Gin*?"

"Elzbieta does." I lean against some sort of contraption that looks like a torture device. "I'd like to keep her as the only one there who knows."

"Fine by me," Daniel says as he works the buttons of his shirt through the holes.

"I find it a little odd that you and Elzbieta never met each other while she was dating Clarence."

Daniel shrugs. "Maybe it is, but that's how it worked out. I work forty hours a week on top of a full course load. That doesn't leave me much time for socializing."

I frown. He works forty hours a week? Neither of my brothers worked while in college, and they still struggled with their course load.

"Why'd you choose to start working at The Fox?"

He looks at me. "Pardon?"

"I mean, why bartend where Clarence worked? Why not some other joint?"

Daniel considers me for a moment and then shrugs. "I guess because that was the place I knew about. Clarence liked it there. He made good money, obviously. So it was the first place I tried."

"Is that the only reason?"

"Do me a favor, Miss Sail, and ask me direct questions. If you're fishing for something, just tell me what it is."

Daniel doesn't seem irritated, maybe just a touch impatient. "Okay. I thought you might be working at Foxglove Smoke Shop because you also think someone there could've killed Clarence."

"No," Daniel says without hesitation. "I'm under no illusions about what happened to Clarence. He did himself in, and I'm working at The Fox strictly for the money. I didn't tell people about Clarence because I'm tired of everybody looking at me like I'm broken."

He concludes buttoning his shirt and looks at his watch. "Anything else you want to ask? My break is nearly up."

"Mine too, actually." I consider his offer. It isn't often that someone I'm questioning is fine with me firing away, and the change is refreshing. "What do you know about Tubs?"

Daniel blinks at me several times. "You mean my boss?"

I nod. "Elz told me he's always there, but he wasn't last night."

"Others have said he hasn't been as consistent since O'Banion was killed." Daniel shrugs. "Probably all it is. Although . . ." Daniel's gaze becomes unfocused, as though he's remembering something. "He has some personal problems going on. Not that he's said anything to me about it, but I've heard that his daughter is pretty sick. Could be related to that too."

"I've been told he and Clarence didn't get along."

Daniel shrugs. "I don't know anything about that."

I think of the five-hundred-dollar reward O'Banion gave to Clarence. Money that Tubs needed badly, based on what I saw in his mailbox. "Had Clarence made any big purchases recently?"

Daniel laughs a loud *ha*. "You asked me that before, but Clarence never made a big purchase in his life. You've never met anybody as rich yet frugal as Clarence."

Where did that money go, then?

Daniel's head tilts the way Sidekick's does when he's puzzled. "Why do you ask?"

"Just curious," I say with a vague smile. "Catherine told me that Clarence and Elz had an argument the day before he died. Do you know anything about that?"

"No." He appears to consider this and grimaces. "Did she say what they argued about?"

"She didn't know. Just said she heard lots of yelling and saw Elz leaving. Or a woman who matched Elz's description, anyway."

"Hmm. No, Clarence didn't say anything to me about it, but that doesn't mean much."

That's an interesting thing for a best friend to say, not that

I'm an expert in male friendships. "Why do you say that? Were the two of you on bad terms?"

"Not at all, but Clarence wasn't speaking much those final days. He was so quiet and brooding."

I'm careful to keep my voice light as I respond, "That's not what others say."

Daniel doesn't seem bothered. "Others didn't live with him."

"True."

And it's a good point. Besides, while Elzbieta didn't describe Clarence as "quiet and brooding" in his final days, she also didn't mention that big fight they had the day before he died.

"I have a question for you," Daniel says, leaning against a punching bag. "Who was the guy that showed up at The Fox? The one you left with? He looked angry."

"Him?" I rub at a rough edge on my thumbnail. "A friend."

Daniel raises his eyebrows.

"He is."

His eyebrows remain up. "Are you actually an investigator?"

I try to hold his eyes, but I can't seem to. "I work for one."

Daniel considers me a moment, then nods. "Okay, that makes more sense."

The lie leaves a bad taste in my mouth, but it's effective. Daniel's shoulders noticeably lower. His eyes soften. It's as if no longer having to puzzle out how I could "actually" be an investigator leaves him feeling more comfortable with me.

"Was your boss hired by the Dells or just Louisa?" Daniel asks.

How did the tables turn so that I'm now the one *answering* questions? "We're still trying to figure out if Clarence's death is something that we need to look into more. That's . . . my job, basically. To figure out if we should take the case."

Daniel's expression is tough for me to read. Is he skeptical? Doubtful? "I hope you'll tell your boss not to. And hopefully now that Louisa understands more about what happened during Clarence's final semester here, she'll be more accepting of the truth." Daniel glances at his wristwatch. "If you have anything else to ask, you'll need to do it as we walk back to the library."

It's irritating that Daniel is now the one steering the conversation. I'm supposed to be doing that.

"I do have a couple more questions." I trot alongside him, working to match his long strides. "I'm curious about the rat poison."

"What about it?"

"Did Clarence buy it or did you?"

Daniel's quiet for several steps. "I have no idea. Why?"

"You don't remember buying it?"

"No—it's just one of those things you have when you live in an apartment. Rat poison, laundry soap, bleach." Daniel makes a rolling motion with his hand to indicate an ongoing list. "Maybe *I* bought it when we first moved in. I really don't know."

"Did you have rats in the apartment?" I ask. "Catherine said they never have."

"That's thanks to us. Early on, we did, but we haven't had any for a while."

We step out into the gray, chilly afternoon.

Daniel stops walking and looks at me. "Look, Miss Sail. I understand you're just doing your job, but I hope you'll take my advice: Tell your boss there's nothing here. If he takes this case, he'll end up telling the Dells what they already know—that Clarence took his own life. Haven't they been through enough?" He swallows hard. "I know *I* have."

Not that long ago, this was me. The freshly grieving best friend. How much worse would I have felt if Lydia had taken her own life, and while I was still mourning her, someone like me came along and kept poking at what had happened? Asking questions, pulling off any scabs of peace and healing that time had allowed to form? It would've felt like my own personal hell. *That* is what I'm doing to Daniel.

I look up at him, squinting in the bright daylight. "I'm so sorry for what you lost."

Then before he can say anything else, I turn and walk away, leaving him with what little peace he has remaining.

CHAPTER
TWENTY-ONE

"Looks like quite the case, Detective Sail."

I startle to find Mariano standing over me, his mouth quirked in a smile. I'm at our favorite table at B/G, with my notes scattered across it.

My spirits lift at just the sight of him. "How are you?"

He looks worn down, and his suit is rumpled from the day's wear, but he doesn't appear as defeated as he did during our walk in the snow last week.

He bends and kisses me hello before sliding into his seat. "Better now. I thought I was on time. Didn't we say six o'clock?"

"Yes." I scrape my notes into a messy pile on my half of the table. "I didn't want to go home and be around Jane, so I came straight here. I asked Norma to bring out my dinner with yours."

"I see." Mariano removes his hat, and his dark hair falls forward, so long it brushes his eyebrows until he pushes it back. "Do you want to talk about the news your father and Jane shared or about where you were last night?"

"Goodness, we're getting right to it." I tap the papers against the table in an attempt to line up the corners. "How about, 'How was your day?' Or, 'You look very pretty.' Or, 'Tell me about your greatest fears.'"

Mariano grins and the lines framing his smile pop. "C'mon, Piper. Where were you last night?"

I tuck my stack of papers into my leather bag so I don't have to look at him. "I went to The Fox."

Mariano doesn't reply.

I finish putting my papers away, and still he hasn't said a word.

"Here you are," Norma says in a singsong voice. She lowers our plates to the table and clasps her hands together. "Can I get anything else for you two?"

I smile at her and continue to avoid eye contact with Mariano. "No, thank you."

"Holler if you need me." She walks back to the counter with efficient strides, where someone is waiting to place an order.

I finally look at Mariano. He wears the expression of someone who is trying to not show emotion. He's good at it.

"This shouldn't be a surprise." I pull my plate in front of me. "I told you I was going to do this."

"You *joked* about it." Mariano tightens his tie. "Or at least, I thought you were joking about it."

I knew he thought I was joking. I let him think that.

He drums his fingertips on the table. "Who knew that you were going to The Fox last night? Did you tell anyone?"

"Um." I poke my potato salad with my fork. "Elzbieta knew, because she's who got me in, but that was it."

Mariano's face is still the carefully neutral expression. "And why is that the end of the list? Why didn't you tell me?"

"Because . . ." *Because you might try to stop me.* "Because I didn't think to."

"With Lydia, you called me all the time to tell me your reckless plans. 'Mariano, I'm going to this lunchroom up north where they found that missing girl.' Or, 'Mariano, how do you get into a speakeasy?'" He fixes me with a searching look. "What changed? Why didn't you tell me this time?"

I poke at my salad once more. While I hadn't given my reason any conscious thought, I know immediately what the truth is. "Because what if you told me not to go?"

Mariano's dark eyes search my face. "Did you not worry about that back in June?"

"No. Back in June, you didn't matter to me the way you do now. If you disapproved, fine, but you couldn't say anything that would stop me. Now . . ." I shrug.

"You think I would've tried to stop you?"

"Wouldn't you have?"

Mariano loosens his tie as he considers. "It's possible. Or if you were really set on going, I would've come along."

And Mariano might've been recognized. Possibly as a Cassano, but more likely as a cop. Even when he isn't driving a bureau car, wearing his homburg, or dressed in one of his charcoal work suits like he is now, he has a way about him.

I lay my hands flat on the table, as if to prove I'm not hiding anything. "Elzbieta offered me a way in, and I took it. If I'm going to do this—" I pitch my voice lower. "Investigate things for people, I mean. Then sometimes I'll have to go to places like The Fox in order to talk to people. And I don't have a badge or a partner or anything like that."

Mariano looks at me for a moment and then stares at his untouched plate of food. He pulls in a deep breath. Is he about to tell me not to do this anymore? To drop the case? And if he does, what will I do?

He shakes his head, as if in disagreement with himself. "I'm struggling with what to do here, Piper. This is the sort of conversation that should have me so tied up in knots, I can't even think about eating. Especially because *you* aren't eating. But the last thing I ate today was a banana at breakfast, and I'm starving."

Mariano gives me a sheepish smile, and the tension releases with the same efficiency as opening a bottle of soda. One moment it was there, and now it's gone, replaced by fizzing bubbles of affection.

I pick up my fork, spear a cube of pineapple, and pop it into my mouth. "Better?"

His smile blooms as he picks up his sandwich. "Yes, thank you." After he takes a bite and chews, he says, "Tell me about Elzbieta. She's the ex-girlfriend of the deceased?"

"Yes. She works as a cigarette girl at The Fox. She loaned me a costume and told everyone my name was Virginia, and that I was being trained so I had an excuse to take a look around the place."

Mariano's eyebrows raise. "So you were in a cigarette girl costume?"

I feel my cheeks burning. "I was."

Mariano grins, then takes another bite and chews. "Did you learn anything useful?"

I swallow hastily and walk him through all the developments since our date at the Chicago Theatre. That I've learned Daniel has been working at The Fox for the last few weeks because the money is so good, though he hasn't told others about his friendship with Clarence. How, when I was introduced to Liam Finnegan, I said Clarence was the one who told me about The Fox and pretended I didn't know he had died. And the way Liam looked at Elzbieta when she expressed doubt over what they'd been told about Clarence's death.

"I'm aware that 'he looked at her strangely' isn't admissible in court," I say, waving my fork. "But there's something there."

Then I rush through my conversation with Daniel today, as well as what I learned from the neighbor in 3E. "She says there was a girl at the apartment the day before Clarence died, and the description sure sounded like Elzbieta. The neighbor says they fought and the girl left crying, but Clarence didn't tell Daniel about it, and Elzbieta told me the last time she saw Clarence was the twenty-seventh, at work. This fight would've happened on the twenty-ninth."

Mariano wipes his mouth with his napkin. "Might not have been her."

"I wondered that. The description matches, but it wasn't a very specific description, so it's possible this was a different girl."

"It's also possible Elzbieta lied to you."

"Yes, it is." I pick up my sandwich, which is mostly untouched. "Though she's been so helpful with the investigation, it's hard to believe she would lie about something that important. Why would she do that? Aside from the fight not looking good for her."

"That's all the motivation a person needs, usually."

We sit in silence for several seconds. While I was going through the details of Clarence's case with him, Mariano cleaned his plate. Now he alternates between tapping his fingers on the table and sipping his water.

"Piper." Mariano sits forward, elbows on the table. He tightens the knot of his tie. "Can I make a proposal to you?"

A *proposal*? My stomach dips. He's never even said he loves me. Shouldn't that come first? Is this a normal way for a man to lead into it, to ask if he can ask? Did he speak to my father already? Does he really think B/G is where we should have a moment like this?

"Uh . . ."

Mariano takes in my face and recognition dawns. "Not *that* kind of proposal." He exhales a laugh and pushes his chair onto its back two legs, then immediately brings it back down. "A *professional* proposal, I mean. An offer."

I wheeze a high, nervous laugh, take a huge bite of my sandwich, and tell my heart to slow its racing. He's not proposing. Obviously.

"What if I acted as your partner? Like a silent, unpaid partner? You can talk to me about cases, like we did just now. I can accompany you in any situations where it could be helpful to have an extra person. That sort of thing."

I blink at Mariano. He looks back at me, seeming nervous.

I swallow hastily. "You're offering to be my partner."

He nods. "Unpaid. And unofficial."

"What do you get out of it?"

"You, obviously." Mariano cuts his gaze away from mine. "And your safety."

I think of Jeremiah in the car on the drive home from The Fox. The way he'd yelled, "I'm acting like somebody who cares about you!"

I lower my sandwich back onto my plate. "I'm a little surprised that you're not trying to talk me out of the whole thing."

"The thought has definitely crossed my mind, but that doesn't seem right to me. I've known from day one what kind of girl you are, Piper. Trying to talk you out of being who you are seems unfair. Not to mention futile. And honestly . . ." He takes in a slow breath. "I don't like the danger you put yourself in, but I like the heart behind it. It's hard to watch you choose this, but also, I like that you're the kind of person who *does* choose this. Does that make any sense?"

Delight dances in my chest. Is there any better feeling in the world than someone seeing who you really are and caring for you all the same?

"It does, because I feel that way about you. Part of me thinks, 'Why can't he be an accountant or a teacher or something that would keep him safe?' But also, that would mean you being a different person than who you are, and I would never want that."

"You *do* understand." He drums his fingertips on the table. "What do you say? Will you take me on as a partner, Detective Sail?"

He holds out his hand across the table, like we truly are making a deal that we should shake on.

I reach out and slip my hand into his. "Yes. Yes, I will."

It's after seven by the time I arrive home and let myself in the front door. Sidekick had been curled up in his usual place beneath the living room window, but otherwise the house is dark and quiet. No smells of a dinner that I missed, no quiet conversations, and not even any creaking floorboards upstairs.

"Hello?"

The only response to my inquiry is Sidekick's wagging tail.

I wind through the hall, through the dining room, past the door to Father's office, and into the kitchen, which is clean and empty. There's a note taped to the icebox, written in my father's hand: *Out to dinner. Will be home late.*

"Just you and me, I guess," I say to Sidekick.

He appears pleased by this, especially when I pull his leash off the hook. It's cold outside with a biting wind whipping off the lake, so our walk is short. Once we're back home, just as I put food in his bowl, the telephone in Father's office trills.

I walk briskly to his desk, snap on the light, and answer the phone. "Hello, Sail residence."

"Piper?"

It takes me a moment to place the voice. "Elzbieta?"

"Yes," she says in a hushed tone. "Were you in trouble last night? Your boss looked angry."

I settle into Father's desk chair. "No, that's just how he is. How are you?"

"Worn out. I didn't get home until after two, and then I woke up when my brother-in-law was getting ready for work a few hours later. I'm counting down the days until I have my own place."

"I believe it." I lean back and the leather squeaks against my wool coat. "I appreciate you getting me in last night. It was very helpful."

"Something happened after you left," Elzbieta says in the same hushed voice. In the background, I can hear children, probably her nieces. "I don't know what you'll think about this, but Liam asked when you worked next. I said I wasn't sure if you were going to take the job or not, and he said something like 'Keiran will be disappointed. He was hoping we could double-date sometime.'"

A shiver runs up my spine at the memory of Keiran watching me in the hallway.

"I didn't know what I should say," Elzbieta continues. "I know it's a chance for you to talk to Liam more—and Keiran was friends with Clarence too, so that could be valuable. But at the same time, I've always said no when Liam has asked me out, so saying yes now feels strange." Her laugh is fleeting. "And I don't know that Keiran is your type."

"No. He isn't. But . . ."

"But Clarence," Elzbieta says. "I mean, that's why I would say yes. If you think Liam is involved and this will help, then I'll say yes for us. I wasn't sure what your boss would think. Or if he's decided yet to take the case."

"He's taking the case," I say absently, thinking of the way Liam looked at Elzbieta. "And we should say yes, I suppose."

"I thought you'd say that." Elzbieta sounds resigned rather than enthusiastic, like we're talking about a doctor's appointment, not a date. "I'll ring him. Does Friday night work for you?"

"One moment, let me check." I hurry to the kitchen and pull my calendar and case notebook from my leather bag. Back in Father's office, I pull the earpiece close again. "Yes, Friday is free."

"Okay. I don't want to go to some gin joint either. If we're doing this, I want a real dinner at a restaurant, with tablecloths and everything." Elzbieta's tone is grumpy, as though Liam has already suggested otherwise. Maybe he has. "Somewhere with lobster and oysters."

I try to imagine imposing those kinds of demands on Mariano and grin.

"I'm fine wherever we go, so long as we meet them there." The thought of getting into an automobile with either of those men sends a shudder through me. Mariano won't like the idea of the date . . . but he won't try to stop me.

"Yes, good idea. Liam asked for your last name, by the way. I panicked and said it was Chlebek. You don't look like you have an ounce of Polish blood in you, but it was the first name that came to mind."

"Virginia Chlebek." I echo. What a mouthful. "Gin Chlebek. Can you spell that for me?"

Elzbieta rattles off the spelling and then punctuates it with, "Sorry."

"Don't be. Anything is better than giving him my real last name."

I flip my case notebook to the page that's dedicated to Liam. "Have you ever heard Liam mention Patrick or Colin Finnegan?"

"No," Elzbieta says. "I don't think so. Why?"

"Just curious. Has he ever said anything to you about Clarence's death that seemed odd?"

"Not a thing. He was as shocked as me."

I realize that I've always imagined a police officer formally telling Elzbieta about what happened to Clarence—I guess because that's how I learned about Lydia—but they wouldn't have notified an ex-girlfriend.

"How did you hear about Clarence? About his death, I mean."

"Liam told me. Clarence hadn't shown up for work in a couple of days, which just wasn't like him. So Liam went by his place to check on him."

"Not you?"

She hesitates, and I wish I could see her expression. "Not me. Not because I didn't want to, necessarily, but . . . Everything was complicated with me and Clarence at that point. It made more sense for Liam to go."

"When was that?"

"Probably a week after Clarence had died. Close to, anyway. Liam said nobody was at the apartment, but the neighbor told him what had happened. When Liam called me, he was crying."

That gives me pause. I try to picture Liam Finnegan crying. Could he have faked that? It'd be easier on a phone call than in real life, but even so. "And you said Liam was surprised?"

"We all were. He said lots of 'I don't believe it' and 'I can't believe this happened.' That sort of thing. He'd seen Clarence that afternoon. Said he didn't seem depressed at all."

My pencil stops moving. "Sorry, but you said Liam saw Clarence 'that afternoon'? You mean the day Clarence was found dead?"

"Yeah. They'd had drinks together or something."

So Liam saw Clarence the day he died, and Elzbieta—maybe—the day before. I flip back to the page of notes about Elzbieta and see my written questions: *Can I trust her? Alibi?*

"That reminds me," I say, feigning a casual air. "I don't think I've yet asked you where you were the day Clarence died."

In the silence, I hear a squeal that sounds like a noise Howie would make, followed by the giggling of a girl.

"Watching my nieces," Elzbieta says. "Like always. And I worked that night."

"And when was the last time you saw Clarence?" My heart pounds faster. *Tell me the truth this time, Elz.*

"October twenty-seventh. At work."

I don't respond, just let her answer—her lie?—sit there on the line between us. Sidekick materializes in the doorway of Father's office and stretches in that satisfied way he does after eating. Then he sits on the threshold and keeps watch over me.

"And everything was fine between you two? You weren't arguing or anything?"

"No." Elzbieta clears her throat. "I mean, things were awkward, but that's to be expected."

"I'm sorry to press on a sore spot, but what reason did he give when he called things off?"

"Goodness." Elzbieta's laugh is high and forced. "Why are you giving me the shakedown, Piper?"

I infuse my voice with warmth. "That's not what this is."

"What is it, then?"

"Just paperwork. My boss is a real stickler for these kinds of details." I turn my voice into an apology. "I know you never would've hurt Clarence, but if I leave these kinds of details out of my report, he'll have my hide."

My pretend boss is turning into quite the asset.

"Okay. Well, Clarence was quite vague when he broke up with me. He said that we're from different worlds, he couldn't imagine it lasting long term, those sorts of things."

"Interesting," I say as I jot down her answer, despite its unhelpful nature. "In most situations, Clarence was so detailed. But then in others—like breaking up with you or the note he left behind—he doesn't offer an explanation. Or there's a note in his financial ledger where he subtracted a large sum of money, but he doesn't say where it went."

"That seems very unlike him," Elzbieta agrees, her voice low. "He was always meticulous about his money."

"I know. It's the only one like that in the book. Had he made any kind of large purchase that you know of? Or talked about an investment opportunity of some kind?"

"No." Elzbieta drags out the syllable. "Not that I can think of."

I stare at my notes. Five hundred dollars unaccounted for by a man who noted spending seventy-five cents when out for drinks with friends. And still no answers why.

"Any other questions for me, Detective?" Elzbieta's tone is light, making a joke of the conversation.

I chuckle, like I also find this humorous. "No, but thanks for your help. I think I have everything my boss will ask for."

"Okay. I'll get things arranged with Liam and Keiran and call you back with details."

"Thanks, Elz. I appreciate it."

When we hang up, I stare at my notebook, at the question *Can I trust her?*

"No," I murmur into the quiet of Father's office. "I don't think I can."

The effects of my short night of sleep press down on me like a physical weight. I trudge up the stairs to my room, Sidekick behind me, and even though it's not yet eight o'clock, I go through my nightly routine of washing my face, brushing my teeth, and changing into pajamas.

As I do so, I think about Liam having drinks with Clarence the day he died. Could he have poisoned Clarence then? But if he had, would he have cried on the phone with Elzbieta? Maybe.

I think about Daniel at the gymnasium earlier today, saying not to bother with this case. He'd hoped that Louisa would accept what Clarence had chosen once she knew about the cheating scandal, but of course that wasn't at all what had happened. Louisa had been just as stubborn about that as she had everything else.

I sigh as I flop onto my bed. Sweet Louisa, blinded by love for her brother. She just doesn't want to believe anything bad about Clarence. Though as I pull the covers over me, I must admit I agree with her about the cheating—it seems out of character for a boy who took such care with his financial records. He certainly isn't lazy. I should look into that situation more. There could be something there.

But almost as soon as I've thought this, I'm asleep.

CHAPTER
TWENTY-TWO

"My name is Elsie Piper. I'm with *The Daily Chicagoan*," I murmur to myself as I move with the crowd down the platform steps for Loyola Station. "Elsie Piper, Elsie Piper, Elsie Piper."

The clock at the station tells me I'm about to be late for my appointment with Mr. Byron, and I pick up my pace.

Falling asleep before eight o'clock last night meant that at five this morning, I was wide awake. I'd used my hours of extra time to consider Clarence's college report cards—all As—and to strategize how I could learn more about the cheating scandal.

First, I considered speaking to Daniel. But he was already tired of answering my questions, especially after yesterday, and I couldn't imagine a *fourth* interview with him going any better than the previous three. Speaking to someone at the school seemed preferable. How hard could it be to sneak into a university classroom? Though I didn't know which professors would be most beneficial, and I had no idea how to get them talking to me about Clarence.

Then my eyes had settled on the line *Adviser: Byron, Fred* listed at the top of Clarence's record, and the plan unfurled in my mind. As soon as I arrived at Presley's, I looked up the number for Loyola University, and after speaking to several people I eventually found Ms. Reid, secretary to the advisory staff, including Mr. Byron.

And now here I am, rushing along Loyola Avenue in a

tailored gray-wool dress with white embroidery, ready to introduce myself as Elsie Piper of *The Daily Chicagoan*. My hair is curled and tucked beneath a black cloche with no adornment, and instead of my usual leather shopping bag, I have a smaller black bag just big enough for a memo pad, a pencil, and a pocketknife.

"My name is Elsie Piper," I say under my breath. "I'm with *The Daily Chicagoan*."

The only other university campus I've been on is the University of Illinois, where both Tim and Nick went. I was only there a handful of times and have vague memories of bulky limestone buildings and walking paths through large, green spaces. Loyola, however, is nothing like that. Loyola's architecture is rooted in Chicago tradition, with grand brick buildings edged in stone and arched windows that look out upon Lake Michigan. I could easily feel at home here, and I wonder if Clarence did too . . . until he didn't.

I follow the signs to the administrative building, then pass through a wide, arched doorway and into a room that feels surprisingly small.

A thick woman with a long face gives me a dimpled smile. "Hello, dear. How can I help you?"

"I have an appointment with Mr. Byron. I'm Elsie Sa— Piper. I'm Elsie Piper."

She scoots back from her desk. "I'll walk you back to his office."

"Thank you."

I wrap my fingers around the loop of my small handbag, follow the woman, and say over and over in my head *Elsie Piper, Elsie Piper, Elsie Piper*. I thought choosing my mother's first and maiden name would make the assumed identity feel more natural, but of course I never knew my mother as Elsie Piper. Elsie Sail is what sounds correct to my ears.

"Did the snow let up out there?" the secretary asks as she guides me down another hallway painted the shade of natural buttercream frosting.

"Yes," I say. "The sun is out now."

"Good. I kept having to mop the entrance because everyone was slipping when they came in. Here's Mr. Byron's office." She raps on the doorframe. "Mr. Byron? Your four thirty is here."

"Thank you, Ms. Reid."

Ms. Reid smiles at me and gestures that I should enter. As I do, Mr. Byron rises to his feet behind a desk that takes up most of the office. He's a tall man, with considerable shoulders and a mustache that's as impressive as it is out of style. He looks to be in his early forties.

"Thank you so much for taking the time to meet with me, Mr. Byron." I reach across the desk to shake his hand. "I'm Elsie Piper with *The Daily Chicagoan*."

"Of course." Mr. Byron gestures toward the wooden chair. As I sit, he does too, and his chair gives a loud creak. "Ms. Reid said you're doing a story on university life?"

I withdraw my memo pad and pencil from the handbag. "Yes, sir."

His gaze narrows on my face. "Excuse me for saying so, but you don't look to be much older than a university student yourself."

I give an airy laugh and smile in a way that I hope comes across as amusement. "You flatter me. A woman my age loves to hear that." I open my pad of paper to the middle, even though it's new, and move the conversation along. "My story is about university life and the unique pressures for today's students. Is it too much? Are our secondary schools adequately preparing our kids?" I make a rolling motion with my hand. "That sort of thing. As someone who meets with and advises students, I would love to hear your thoughts on the struggles you see."

Mr. Byron's mouth has curled into a deeper frown with each question. "Well, Miss Piper, while it's not unusual for a freshman to struggle the first semester or two, most get their feet underneath them and do just fine here at Loyola. But we're also a very selective school and admit only fine students who we anticipate will perform well."

I nod along as he talks. My questions made him defensive. He wants Loyola to be spoken of favorably. I hadn't anticipated that.

"Is it always the freshmen who struggle, or do some start out strong and then falter?"

"That's not as common, but it does happen. Classes get harder, or a student gets distracted by a relationship or the other diversions of college life. Sometimes there's a hardship back home that divides their focus. If someone does struggle later in college, those are the usual culprits."

I pretend to take notes on what he says as I write *Defensive of school*. "I've been speaking with the family of Clarence Dell. Do you recognize that name?"

Mr. Byron hesitates and then nods. "Yes."

"My understanding is that Clarence was caught cheating." I raise my tone on the last word, so it comes across almost as a question.

He runs his fingers down the length of his tie, untucking it from his vest. "That's correct."

He doesn't say anything else, just looks at me.

I smile and hope that puts him at ease. "Let me reassure you, Mr. Byron, that I have no intention of making the fine institution of Loyola out to be some sort of villain in the case of Clarence Dell. I don't even intend to mention the school or Clarence by name. My article is more about secondary education and whether students are being adequately prepared. If students can understand what college life asks of them, then maybe we can help prevent situations like Mr. Dell's."

Mr. Byron leans back in his chair and seems to consider this as he runs his fingers up and down his wide, striped tie. My father used to wear one just like it, until Jane came along.

"Well." Mr. Byron drags out the word. "I'm not sure how much I can tell you. On paper, Mr. Dell was a bright young lad. His high school transcript was everything we would've asked for, and his grades here at Loyola were always strong. That was the confusing part."

"How so?" I ask without looking up from my memo pad.

"Cheating has been going on since the dawn of formal education, I assume. But typically, when we go back and look at the records, we see signs."

"What types of signs?"

"Often, the student will have struggled some. They'll have earned several bad test grades, or even received a low quarter or semester grade in a class. But then their scores magically leap to As. With Mr. Dell, I looked through all his records when the issue first came to light, and I was puzzled. He'd been a solid A student the entire time."

I frown at my written summarization of Mr. Byron's words. "So, what do you think happened?"

Mr. Byron shrugs and tucks his tie back into his vest. "Just last week, I read about the capture of a jewel thief in Europe. The article said he's possibly responsible for dozens of thefts over the years. He's stolen an unknown number of times, but he's only been caught the once. Do you see what I'm saying?"

"Comparing Clarence to a jewel thief feels like an exaggeration."

Mr. Byron smiles in response. "I disagree. Education is quite valuable, Miss Piper."

"Do you think that's the most likely explanation for what happened to Clarence? He'd been stealing his As all along, but only got caught the once?"

"I think it's possible."

"How did he get caught?"

Mr. Byron's gaze flicks down and over me, as if assessing how qualified I am for this line of work.

"Off the record, if you prefer." I make a show of marking my place with my pencil and closing the small notebook. "Like I said, I'm not going to mention any schools or students by name. I'm still in the early stages of researching this piece."

He nods. "All semester long, the professor suspected someone of cheating, but with Mr. Dell's history and stellar grades . . ." Mr. Byron shrugs. "We never would've considered him, but he had the mimeographs of multiple answer keys in his possession. That made it abundantly obvious."

"And what did Clarence say when confronted with this evidence?"

"That he didn't do it, of course." Mr. Byron's face becomes drawn. "I wish he'd been honest. I think the administration would have been more lenient if Mr. Dell had taken responsibility rather than denying it."

"Is it possible Clarence was telling the truth?"

Mr. Byron looks skeptical. "Only Mr. Dell knows the answer to that."

"True." I reopen my memo pad. "And, unfortunately, it's too late to ask him."

"What do you mean?"

I pause. The idea that they wouldn't know what had happened to Clarence hadn't occurred to me. But who would've told the staff here? He wasn't a student any longer, so there wouldn't have been a need.

I tuck my pencil into a dress fold on my lap so it won't roll to the floor. "I'm very sorry to be the one to tell you this, Mr. Byron, but Clarence Dell is dead. He died at the end of October."

Mr. Byron's eyes go wide. "No. What happened?"

I hesitate. "The police say that Clarence took his own life."

He leans back in his chair and clasps a hand over a gaping mouth.

"Sorry." I look away from the horror on his face. "I assumed the school knew."

"My God," he says on an exhale. "What a tragedy."

Seconds tick by. I have no idea what to say next. I squelch the urge to say sorry again, but I have to say *something*. "Um. Mr. Byron—"

He holds up a finger, the universal sign for *wait a moment*. I clamp my mouth shut and stare at my memo pad.

"Okay." Mr. Byron leans forward on his desk, his brown eyes bright. "Here's what you should make clear in your article."

The seriousness of his tone makes my shoulders straighten, makes me press my pencil against the page.

"You tell your readers that mistakes are going to happen.

College students are still kids. They're going to make errors in judgment. But very few mistakes are irreversible. Mr. Dell's final choice is, of course—" Mr. Byron swallows hard, and my eyes burn at the sight of his obvious emotion. "But the cheating? He could've overcome that. He could've come back here the following semester, or gone to another university; he didn't have to . . ."

Mr. Byron shakes his head and stares at nothing. "He didn't have to overreact and choose to let that decision define him, is what I'm trying to say. We have to be so careful about what we allow to define us." His gaze sharpens on me. "Do you know what I mean?"

I spent last summer on the couch, heavily bandaged but alive. I was alive while Lydia was dead, and I couldn't stop thinking, *I have to make my life count. I must've survived for something. I have to make my life count.*

"Yes." My voice is hoarse, and I attempt to clear my throat. "I know exactly what you mean."

CHAPTER
TWENTY-THREE

When I return home, I call Mariano, just like I promised him I would. "Partners check in with each other," he had told me.

"How did it go?" he asks in his brusque I'm-at-work voice.

I lean back in Father's desk chair, bringing the candlestick phone with me, and think of the raw emotion Mr. Byron had expressed. "They didn't know he had died. That was hard."

"Oh." The brusqueness is gone. "I'm sorry you had to tell him. That never gets easier."

"I imagine not." I exhale a sigh. "I learned a couple valuable things. The school is sure he cheated because he had multiple mimeographed answer keys. Though Mr. Byron *did* say that his case was unusual, because typically they can look back at grades and see when the cheating began. And I'm still not convinced he did it."

"Why not?"

"Well." I frown at Sidekick, in his usual position outside Father's office door. "Partly because of what Mr. Byron said about Clarence's grades always being high. But also because Clarence managed his financial records diligently. Maybe one thing has nothing to do with the other, but cheating is a shortcut, and Clarence doesn't seem like the kind of person who looked for shortcuts."

I recall the question written on the index card and taped to my closet door. *Is Clarence's method for keeping track of his money normal?* "Mariano, you make lots of money. How do you record your saving and spending?"

Mariano snorts. "You think I make lots of money? You are in for a lousy surprise, Piper."

"What I meant is that you make a salary, and you have for some time now. Do you have a way of tracking how much you make and how much you spend?"

"Sure, but are we done talking about the case for now? Because if so, I have work I need to finish up before I go home."

"It's related. Clarence had a system that seems overly elaborate, but I don't know much about managing finances. How do you do it?"

"To be clear, we're straying far from my expertise. I don't know if this is the right way to do things, but when you open a bank account, there's a register that comes with the checkbook. I use that, and I balance it with my statements that come every month."

"Do you think that's how most people do it?"

"Well." I can hear the slight frown Mariano makes when he's puzzling over something. "It seems logical to me, but that doesn't count for much. How did Clarence do it?"

"Clarence kept every receipt taped inside notebooks, and he made notes on the side. Who he had dinner with, if the item was a gift, that sort of thing. The Dells are a banking family, though, so I think that could be why."

"Seems probable. Also, with Clarence working at The Fox, he was probably paid in cash, right? He wouldn't have kept his money in the bank, especially if he was trying to avoid taxes. If that's true, he would've needed to develop another way to keep tabs on what he had."

"He definitely did that. You know what's really strange, though? In the middle of September, Clarence noted that he received five hundred dollars from Dean O'Banion for 'services rendered.' That's the phrase he used."

"You mentioned that before when we went to see *Hot Water*. But no note on where the money went, right?"

"Right. Two weeks later, he subtracted five hundred dollars from his record with no explanation. Why no explanation? Everything else has one. The guy didn't buy a pair of socks without writing a note about it. But all it says is minus five hundred."

"That." Mariano's voice is deep and serious. "Follow that."

"That's what I was thinking." My clear excitement makes Sidekick's ears prick and his tail wag. "It's just not like him. And he had this boss who I'm pretty sure is up to his eyeballs in debt, so I'm going to do some digging into him. Not entirely sure how yet."

"Good work," Mariano says. "Let me know if you need my help."

I flush with delight. "How has your day been?"

"There was a big shootout at a warehouse in the Levee. Real early this morning. That was . . . unpleasant. Most likely a shipment of alcohol that someone was trying to interfere with. We're still doing some identification work on the five bodies, but I'm guessing all deaths were mafia."

Any other cop might be relieved by that, but Mariano knows that one day he could show up at a scene like this, and those mafia deaths could be his brothers or cousins.

"That's a rough way to start your day. I'm sorry."

"I *am* a detective," he says in a dry voice he uses when trying to avoid emotion. "Calls like that are to be expected."

My heart feels like it's being squeezed as I consider that Mariano chose this when he could've chosen something else. *I love you.* The words swell in my mouth but stay trapped inside. Because what if he doesn't say it back?

Elsewhere in the house, a door opens. Sidekick raises his head, listens a moment, and releases a low rumble of a bark. My whole body goes still as it remembers a similar late afternoon. I'd been home alone, on the telephone, in Father's office. My brain yells, "Hide!" but I can't seem to move. I can't seem to *breathe.*

"Piper, are you still there?" Mariano's voice is far away.

I try taking in a full breath, but it's like my lungs have forgotten how to function. They keep pushing air out the moment I've managed to drag a bit in. *Hide! Hide! Hide!*

Sidekick lets out another rumbled bark.

"Piper?" Mariano's voice is still distant. The earpiece is on the ground, though I don't know how it got down there.

"Anyone home?" My father's voice.

My inhale is shaky but deep, and my brain stops shouting panicked directions at me.

"Yes." The word scrapes against my dry throat and I have to try again. "Yes, I'm in your office!"

"Piper?" Mariano's voice comes from the floor.

I take one more deep drag of air and pick up the dropped earpiece. "Sorry, my father came home."

"You had me scared for a moment." Mariano's laugh has the distinct sound of tension being released. "Did you drop the phone?"

"Yes, sorry." I try for a breezy, everything-is-fine voice. "I was startled, is all. What were we talking about?"

"I was just about to tell you that I need to go. I want to finish this paperwork and head home."

"Oh, okay. I'll talk to you tomorrow."

"Have a good night." After a moment's hesitation, Mariano adds, "Be safe."

He says the words with the same reverence as a benediction at the end of a church service. Like doing so might form a protective shield around me.

"You too," I say, wishing words really could carry that power.

I fit the earpiece back into the hook and swipe my notes into my lap before Father's steps carry him to the doorway.

"Hello, Pippy." His gaze runs over me. "You're white as a sheet. What's happened?"

"Nothing." My attempt at a lighthearted laugh sounds too high to be believable. "Just need a little more sunshine, I guess."

His gaze moves down the tailored gray dress I wore to work and Loyola. "Is that what you're wearing tonight?"

"So far," I say. "Why do you ask?"

"Well." Father frowns. "I'm not an expert on ladies' fashions, but it's not what I would've thought you'd choose for Henrici's."

"Henrici's," I echo, and then it comes back to me. Today is Wednesday, and Wednesday evening is when we have reservations at six thirty at Henrici's to thank Jeremiah for returning me home on Monday. "Oh yes. I'd forgotten. I'll go change."

Father pointedly looks at his watch. "Make it quick."

"Yes, sir." I slip past him, Sidekick at my heels, and head up the stairs right as Jane is making a regal descent.

This is the first time I've seen Jane since she stormed off Monday evening. She wears a fashionable turban over her sleek bob, a black sleeveless dress, and elbow-length gloves. I expect her to make a comment that it's nearly time to leave, but she doesn't. Just walks right by me with barely a glance of acknowledgment.

Dinner tonight should be interesting.

I reach for the first evening dress in my closet, a sleeveless, raspberry number with glass beads that sparkle when they catch the light and a V-shaped hem of fringe. Thankfully, I already took extra care to curl my hair for my meeting with Mr. Byron. I add a jeweled headband, retouch the makeup covering my scars, and pull on long black gloves. I grab a black, beaded handbag as I exit my room in what I deem to be an impressive seven minutes later.

Father and Jane stand in the entryway, speaking to each other in low voices. They end their conversation before I reach them.

Father smiles at me, though it looks forced. "Ready?"

I nod and pull my nice black coat out of the closet.

He holds open the front door for Jane and me. "Jeremiah said he'll meet us at the restaurant. His apartment is near there. Maybe you already know that."

"No, I didn't."

The drive to Henrici's is quiet. Father and Jane speak to each other, but the engine is loud enough that I'm only able to hear a few words or phrases at a time. What I do catch is of little interest to me—news about Jane's niece, plans for Father's birthday dinner in January, something about a deposition at work—so I mostly stare out the window at the people on the sidewalks, coats buttoned high and arms laden with shopping bags.

During the walk into Henrici's, Father and Jane are side by side, and I trail behind them. Looking at them now, you would never know they were arguing just two nights ago.

About the baby.

They're having a baby together. Father has talked as though this baby is an addition to our family, but to me it feels more like an entirely new family he's creating for himself. His life is moving on, and he's not the only one. So is Walter's, and because of that, likely Joyce's as well. Nick is out on his own, immersed in his last year of law school. Where do I fit in their lives now?

Father holds open the door for us both at Henrici's, and I'm enveloped by warmth and the savory smells of roasted garlic and grilled meat. Jeremiah stands several feet inside the lobby, dressed in a double-breasted suit and a bowler hat.

"Jeremiah, hello." My father steps forward to shake Jeremiah's hand. "You've met my wife, I believe."

"Yes." Jeremiah bows and smiles politely at Jane. "Nice to see you again, Mrs. Sail." He looks to me and his smile warms. "Miss Sail."

And in that moment, I remember.

This doesn't happen often anymore, thankfully, but every once in a while, Jeremiah looks at me or says something and I remember the girl I was before Lydia was taken. How I used to look forward to bickering with him after school. How the two of us were tipping ever so carefully toward dating. And I remember the *why* behind all that—because Jeremiah is as intelligent as he is handsome.

The moment is always fleeting, but I'd rather it not exist at all.

Heat rises in my cheeks. "Mr. Crane," I say to his black oxfords, which shine like they're made of onyx.

"Right this way," the maître d' says to my father.

Father looks between the two of us—face lit as though he's delighted by what he's seeing—and then he offers his elbow to Jane and follows.

Jeremiah offers his arm to me as well, and a swell of panic rises in me. His gesture is nothing more than a formality, and my response is nothing less than rude: I turn away from him and walk to the table on my own.

CHAPTER
TWENTY-FOUR

If my refusal to walk with Jeremiah into the dining room puts a damper on his mood, he doesn't let on. When we arrive at the table, he takes my coat from me and then pulls out my chair. The one moment I meet his eyes, he looks more amused than anything else. I'm already sweating, and we haven't even ordered drinks.

I force my shoulders to lower and take a deep breath. Being civil to Jeremiah isn't a betrayal to Mariano, nor is noticing that Jeremiah is attractive. It isn't as though I'm flirting with him. I'm not even being *nice*.

Father and Jeremiah sit across from each other and exchange small talk. Father reminisces about coming to Henrici's and having a bottle of beer alongside his short ribs. Jane sits across from me but shows no signs of wanting to engage in conversation. Instead, she looks at her menu, apparently reading every word.

"Yes, sir," Jeremiah replies to whatever my father said. "And I'm looking forward to not having to pick her up from school anymore. That's the downside of your father being your boss. While the other reporters are working on their stories in the afternoon, I'm chauffeuring Emma home so she doesn't have to ride the L."

Father frowns and glances at me. "Do your parents feel public transportation is too dangerous?"

"Emma is fairly delicate. I don't know that she could handle the stress of riding the L."

"Of course she could," I say. "Emma isn't delicate. What are you talking about?"

Jeremiah grins. "There you are. I was beginning to wonder if you were going to be present tonight." I scowl at him, and he winks. "And I'll have you know that Emma cried when we suggested she take the L home from Presley's."

"She's just nervous. That isn't the same as being delicate." I rearrange the skirt of my dress and accidentally bump Jeremiah's knee. I hastily pull away. "Why doesn't Emma ride home with me sometimes? She'd have to wait around an extra thirty minutes, but then she could get a little experience."

"I like that idea," Father says. "I've never liked you riding the L by yourself. Don't look at me like that, Pippy. Mariano doesn't either."

"Really?" Jeremiah says with excessive interest. "And why's that?"

I tug at the glove on my left hand, loosening each finger one at a time. "Last I checked, I don't need anybody's permission to ride the L. I have to get to work somehow, and I can't yet afford a car."

"Do you want a car?" Father's question is high with surprise. "Do you know how to drive?"

I look at my father, so loving but also so detached from my day-to-day life. "Yes."

"Who taught you that?"

"Walter. Over a year ago."

His frown deepens and he reaches for his water glass. "I'm not sure what I think about that."

I pull off my left glove and begin loosening the fingers on my right. "Let me know when you decide, but I'm pretty sure it's too late for me to not know how to drive."

The waiter appears at Father's side to discuss appetizers with him.

Jeremiah leans closer to me and points at his menu, as though we're chatting about food. "If Mariano doesn't like you riding the L by yourself"—his voice is quiet in my ear, stirring my hair—"what does he think of your activities Monday night?"

"He's very supportive of what I do."

"That's not a direct answer, Piper."

I give him an icy look. "And it's none of your business, Jeremiah."

He backs away with a bow of his head that seems more mocking than anything else. "Excuse me for caring about your safety."

"Do you kids like oysters?" Father asks in a bright voice.

We both say yes, and Father turns back to the waiter. I long ago decided on the Lake Superior whitefish for dinner, but I continue to stare at my menu because I'm afraid if I don't, I'll have to talk to Jane or Jeremiah.

"I just don't know that he can be trusted," Jeremiah mutters, just loud enough to be heard by me. "Not with who his family is."

"Mariano can't help who his family is any more than you and I can. Besides, he's a detective."

Jeremiah turns to me, elbow on the table, body angled my way. His smoke-blue eyes sear me. "Do you know how many cops I know who *aren't* taking bribes to look the other way? To make evidence disappear?" His pause, I presume, is for dramatic effect. "Zero. The city pays them peanuts and the mafia takes advantage. You think Mariano is above that?"

"Yes."

"The Cassano family has only gotten more powerful in the last year. You tell me that's not a coincidence."

I release a frustrated exhale. "I'm sure it's not, but I think it coincides more with the rise of the South Side in general than it does Mariano's promotion."

Jeremiah's expression is a challenge for me to read. If I had to label it, I would say he looks sad. "You're the smartest girl I know. I'm not going to sit here and try to convince you. Just pay attention. Be careful. Be safe."

Be safe. The same words Mariano said to me on the phone.

My thoughts flit to October. To Jack's expression when he told me about the wedding, the baby. To how Mariano turned to stone when I confronted him.

"Why didn't you tell me? Why did I have to learn about this from Jack?" I had asked him, only to receive a dismissive shrug.

"Because it was just family stuff."

Is that what he would say about this too? If he really is using his position at work to keep his family out of trouble—which he *isn't*, of course—would he shrug and say, "It's just family stuff, Piper. I didn't think you needed to know."

No, that's not what's happening. This is just Jeremiah trying to sow seeds of doubt, and I'm not going to allow that. October was an isolated incident—one that I've probably made too much of in my mind—and at the end of the day, I trust Mariano's character.

Although, if he hid something like a rushed marriage and a baby who came along a month later—neither of which were choices he made—how much more likely would he be to keep quiet if he *did* make a decision that allowed his family to prosper?

"Do you have plans for your Christmas vacation?" Isabella asks as I settle a freshly brewed pot of coffee in the teacher's lounge. She has a stack of papers in front of her and a red pen in her hand.

"It'll be a strange year." I wipe the counter where mugs have left dark rings. "My father remarried over the summer, and this will be our first Christmas with her."

"Do you like her?"

I hesitate. My feelings about Jane have grown complicated. "I don't know," I finally say. "She's not my mother."

"Mmm." Isabella nods. "She can't help that, can she?"

"She can't." I tidy the tins of tea, more to occupy my hands than because it needs doing. "What about your Christmas plans?"

"I'm going to Texas with my sister. The one you met?"

"Yes." I nod. "I remember."

Isabella smirks. "Most do with Chiara. We lost our parents two years ago, so we've begun a tradition of taking a trip over the holidays, along with her husband."

Isabella is bent over the papers, showing no signs of distress over the lost parents, but that doesn't mean there isn't any.

"I'm so sorry."

Isabella's red-lipsticked mouth presses tight for a moment. "Thank you. I have Chiara, thankfully. And William now too, my brother-in-law. Lots of people don't have any family, or they loathe the family they do have. I'm fortunate."

I think of how often I've jealously watched girls with their mothers. "Most who have lost even one parent wouldn't see it that way."

"'The happiness of your life depends on the quality of your thoughts,' after all." Isabella draws a red line through a sentence. "Marcus Aurelius."

I smile. "Yes, I figured. Why are you going to Texas?"

"We always go south for Christmas, for obvious reasons. Chiara and William are both very interested in nature and healing, so we're typically at a health resort of some kind. Not what I would choose, but they're generous enough to pay for me, so I won't complain. Chiara wanted to go to Pagosa Springs in Colorado for the healing waters, but snow makes it difficult this time of year. Last year we went to Hot Springs, and the snow—"

I whirl to face her. "Hot Springs, Arkansas?"

Isabella's dark eyes widen. "Do you know it?"

"Only a bit." I sink into a chair across from her. "What's it like? Why do people go?"

Isabella leans back as I lean forward. "All kinds of reasons. Why are you so interested?"

I could lie. That's what I normally do in these situations. I could tell her that someone mentioned Hot Springs to me, and I'm interested in going there.

Or I could tell Isabella the truth, that I'm investigating a case and one of my suspects has a wife and daughter currently in Hot Springs, Arkansas, asking for more money. What would Isabella say to that?

"Piper, what is it?" Isabella presses, all attempts to grade papers gone.

"Well." I smooth my dress over my knees. If I can't tell the truth about who I am to someone as warm and accepting as Isabella Bianchi, how will I ever be able to tell the truth to those who *aren't* receptive? "Please don't laugh."

"I won't."

"In addition to my work here at Presley's, I do a little bit of work as a . . ." I draw in a deep inhale and make myself say it. "As an investigator."

A line forms between Isabella's heavy brows. "What do you mean, 'as an investigator'?"

"A private investigator. Like if someone dies or—"

"What?" Isabella's voice raises high. "You investigate if someone *dies*?"

Her disbelieving tone causes my cheeks to flame.

"It doesn't have to be if someone dies." My fingers curl around the hem of my skirt and twist. "I mean, yes. So far, both cases I've worked on have involved people dying, but—"

"Heavens." Isabella rests a hand over her heart. "To think I go home from work and knit or listen to the radio, while you go home from work and solve crimes."

"I've only solved one, actually." I loosen my hold on my dress and smooth the fabric down. "I'm working on another, though."

"I would never have the courage to do something like that." Isabella looks at me with curiosity shining in her eyes. "Did you have to get some sort of license? Or permission from somebody?"

I smile. "As it turns out, just from myself."

From interview with Isabella Bianchi: Hot Springs, Arkansas.
A row of bathhouses (7 or 8, she doesn't remember) in
the hills of Arkansas, all built in the last 20 or 30 years to
take advantage of the natural thermal springs. Most go for
therapeutic bathing or hydrotherapy. She says there are
some other treatments available (mercury, shock treatment,

*exercise) intended to cure ailments of all kinds, but she has
never explored those.*

I pack away my notes as the train pulls into the station.
With my hat pulled low over my ears to protect them from the
cold, I set off for Tubs's house. I'm meeting Louisa at B/G at five
o'clock, but she'll forgive my being late if it's because I'm sniffing
out information about someone with a strong motive to kill her
brother.

The curtains are all drawn inside Tubs's house, but even still
I trek the unshoveled walkway to the front door and knock. No
sound comes from within the house, and after a few minutes I
turn away. The mailbox is empty, dashing my hopes of finding
more information there.

I stare up at the empty house for a few seconds before going
next door and knocking. The woman who opens the door is
short, with a thick bun of steel-colored hair and glasses set on
the bridge of a long nose.

I put on my friendliest smile. "Hi. I'm looking for your neighbor, but he doesn't seem to be home. Do you know where he is?"

She chuckles and leans against the broom she's holding. "No.
He a friend of yours?"

"No." But why else would I be here? "He asked me to come
around about a job. A cleaning job."

"Hmm. Wonder if that means his wife is coming home?" The
woman stands upright. "She and the girl have been gone about
a month. Poor, sickly thing. I'm not sure what he told you, but
I haven't seen him for a couple of days at least. House has been
shut up too."

"Is his daughter sick a lot?"

"More than a young girl ought to be, that's for sure. I doubt the doctors can do anything, though." The woman shrugs. "So far as I know, you can't cure epilepsy."

Her words seem to ring in my ears as I make my way back to the train station. I've seen firsthand the stress that happens in a family with a disease like epilepsy, and the LeVines had both money and medical expertise to find help for Lydia. But what about Tubs, who has neither of those advantages? To what lengths would he go—to what lengths *has* he gone—to find healing for his daughter?

CHAPTER
TWENTY-FIVE

Louisa concentrates her green eyes on me the moment we take a seat at my usual table at B/G. "Tell me everything. What have you found? Who have you talked to? Which person seems most likely?"

I hide from her intensity by consulting the list of details I want to discuss.

"I spoke with several people Clarence worked with. I'm still looking into his boss. Did I tell you that he and Clarence didn't get along?"

"You did, but the more I think about it, the less I think that's possible. Clarence got along well with everyone."

I don't mean to sigh, it just happens. "Louisa. As I've told you before, either Clarence took his own life or somebody took it from him. If you want me to stop the investigation, fine. I can do that. But I can't keep telling you what I've learned only to be told by you why that can't be true."

Louisa presses her mouth into a firm line. "You're saying, 'Button your lip, Louisa'?"

I bite back a laugh. "Just while I go through all this. Then you can unbutton, okay?"

She nods and pantomimes buttoning her lips.

"So, Clarence reportedly didn't get along well with his boss. It appears there was some jealousy because the owner of The Fox favored Clarence"—I glance at Louisa and find her beaming at this—"and also because Clarence had possibly caught his boss stealing from The Fox."

"Sounds suspicious." Louisa presses a hand to her mouth and winces. "Sorry, I'll take a big bite."

"It *is* suspicious, and he has the most compelling motive that I've found, but getting close to the boss has been tricky so far. I'm still working on that." I reach for my sandwich as I peek at my notebook. "Also on the list is Liam Finnegan."

Louisa's eyes widen. She raises her hand slightly, like a student tentatively offering an answer in class.

I smile at her and take on the teacher role. "Yes, Louisa?"

"I met a Liam who Clarence worked with. I don't know what his last name is."

I remember now that she mentioned this at our first dinner at Michigan Automat, but it was before I knew how important Liam was. "Tell me about what happened."

"Clarence and I were on our way to a Cubs game, and he got a flat tire. When Clarence went to change it, he discovered our spare was flat too. He said we were close to his friend's apartment, and that he might have a spare we could use."

"When was this?"

But I can visualize the entry in Clarence's financial records before she even answers. −$2.00: *Cubs game with Louisa* written just above −$500.

"Late September," Louisa says.

"Any chance you remember where Liam's apartment was?"

She nods. "It's 327 Webster Street."

I scratch the address into my notebook next to Liam's name. "*That's* impressive."

She flushes. "My birthday is March twenty-seventh, so it stuck out to me. Liam was in the middle of eating lunch when we knocked on his door, but he stopped what he was doing to help us."

"And that was the only time you met him?"

"Yes."

"Did Clarence ever say anything else to you about Liam that you can remember?"

Louisa purses her lips a moment. "When we were back in the car, I think Clarence could tell that I was a little . . . taken with Liam. He said not to bother, that Liam only had eyes for Elz."

Clarence had said that Liam only had eyes for Elz? *Very* interesting.

"Did Clarence seem upset by that?"

"Not at all. I even said to him, 'Isn't it awkward?' and he said, 'Not really.' See what I mean? He was never really *that* interested in her."

Louisa shrugs as though it really is that simple. That people always say exactly what they mean and always act in a way that reflects precisely how they feel.

"But as far as you know, Clarence and Liam were still friends when he died?"

"As far as I know." Louisa lifts her sandwich to her mouth and then pauses. "Wait, you aren't thinking *Liam* is a suspect, are you?"

She says this as though I suggested Santa Claus might've been the one to do Clarence in.

"Um, yes, actually. He's on my list."

"No." Louisa shakes her head. "You can take him off. They were friends."

"Just because somebody acts like a friend doesn't mean they are one."

Louisa shakes her head again. "What do you imagine Liam's motivation was?"

The dig at my intelligence—what do you "imagine"—causes me to clench my teeth. "Well, as you just mentioned, Liam is very fond of Elz."

"But Clarence and Elz were already broken up when Clarence died. It can't be that."

I look at Louisa's young, confident face. *You just don't know how the world works yet*, part of me wants to tell her. Sometimes people who act like your friends aren't really your friends. Sometimes people you think will always be there for you vanish from your life. Sometimes you think you know exactly what's going to happen, exactly what path your life is going to take, and you end up derailed.

I want to say all of that, and I also don't want to say any of it. I want her to remain young and innocent and confident.

I inhale slowly. "I think Liam's worth looking into, if only because he knew Clarence well. And his family has connections to organized crime."

"Really?" Louisa's naturally round eyes go rounder. "Like . . . mobsters?"

"That's right."

"But he was so *nice*."

"Many of them are very charming," I say. "Anyway, I'll keep looking into Liam. The other person on the list is Elzbieta."

Louisa nods her approval. "Did you ever find out where she was the day Clarence died?"

"She says she was taking care of her nieces."

Louisa frowns. "That's not a very solid alibi."

"Speaking of which, I've had a challenging time putting

together how Clarence spent his last day. Do you know anything about that?"

Louisa shakes her head. "I wish I did. Have you asked Daniel?"

"Yes. He told me he was at work and in classes all day, so he doesn't know. Elzbieta said Clarence had drinks with Liam that day—another reason to look into him—but that's all I've found out so far." I glance at my list. The last item is written extremely large at the top: *$500???*

"Louisa, did Clarence leave any money behind when he died?"

She had been chewing a bite of sandwich and swallows hastily. "Yes, actually. There was a locked box of cash in his nightstand drawer. I never actually saw it, but Daddy said something to Mother."

"Did he say how much was in it?"

"He was surprised by how much was in there, and said Clarence had really saved his money well. But I never heard a specific dollar amount."

That's unfortunate. I consider the money box a moment. "Do you know if Clarence had recently made any large purchases?"

"Like what?"

"Like a really extravagant purchase. Something like a car."

"He didn't have a car."

"I just meant something on that scale. There's a subtraction of five hundred dollars in his financial record, but he doesn't say what it was used for. It's bothering me."

"That's not like him." Louisa spears a slice of canned pear. "That's *really* not like him."

"Yeah, I know." I start to close my notebook when my gaze catches on the notes from my interview with Mr. Byron. "Slight change of subject, but what were Clarence's grades like in high school?"

Louisa chews and swallows. "Excellent. Always excellent." She frowns slightly. "I've always assumed so, anyway. I could look for copies of his report card at the house, if you like?"

"Please." I tuck my notebook into my bag. "I met with his adviser at Loyola to talk about the cheating incident."

Louisa makes a noise of disgust but doesn't outright protest.

"He said that typically you can see signs a student has been cheating, but that it wasn't obvious in Clarence's college records." I shrug. "His comment just made me wonder if Clarence's cheating dated back to high school. Maybe if I look at those transcripts, I can see when it began."

"You won't find anything," Louisa says, "because my brother never would've cheated. But I'll get them for you. And I owe you money, right?"

I hesitate.

Louisa reaches for her handbag. "It must be time by now. You went to Loyola. You went to Clarence's work. You met with Elzbieta. That obviously has taken more than five hours."

She holds out three dollars. "Here."

Again, I hesitate, and then I take it. "Thank you."

+$3.00 *from Louisa Dell, 20 hours of work to solve the case of Clarence Dell*

That's how Clarence would document the money. Or maybe just "for services rendered," as he wrote alongside the five hundred dollars O'Banion gave him.

"Thank you for everything you're doing," Louisa says. "I mean, I know it's your job and everything, but I appreciate it all the same."

"It's not really—" *my job*, I was going to say.

But isn't it? I spend time doing this, and I get paid for it.

How else would I define a job? When I was considering taking this case, Emma had said to me, "Maybe the only permission you really need is from yourself," and I wonder if she's right ... if everybody else can already see this is who I am, and I'm the only one who can't quite accept it.

Louisa looks at me, and I realize my half sentence still dangles between us.

I smile at her. "I'm happy to help."

"What does a girl wear on a fake double date?"

Not only is it Friday afternoon—the absolute slowest hours of the week at Presley's—but it's the last day before Christmas break. I'm passing the time by talking to Mariano on the telephone and making a list of questions that I want answered on my fake date tonight.

"Great question." Mariano's voice is a low rumble in my ear. "How about your old Presley's uniform? That's my suggestion."

I grin. "You're supposed to be my partner. Isn't that what we agreed upon?"

"Of course," Mariano says with feigned confusion. "Why do you ask?"

"This advice doesn't seem congruent with your vow to be helpful."

"Piper, which one of us is the man here? I'm telling you, a black wool skirt that goes all the way to your ankles is a good choice."

I glance at the clock. It's still three o'clock, which seems impossible. I feel like it's been three o'clock for an hour now.

Still another thirty minutes until the final bell and then another thirty minutes until I can leave.

Outside, tiny snowflakes fall, but nothing is sticking to the ground yet. I also notice the wind must be blowing pretty good, because the man striding up the Presley's walkway has a hand pressed firmly to his hat.

"As sound as your fashion advice no doubt is, I'm not sure that's what Virginia Chlebek would wear on the date."

"Well, if you choose differently, don't blame me if you can't get the men to talk. Oh, Piper, I have to go." Mariano's change of tone is abrupt. "I'll see you tonight."

"See you tonight," I say, but he's already disconnected the call.

I hang the earpiece on its hook and look at the clock: 3:01. Progress. Out front, the man who is closing in on the front door is no longer a generic man—he's Jeremiah Crane. I've barely registered this when the door swings open and Jeremiah enters, bringing a gust of cold air with him.

"Hi, how can I help you?" I say reflexively, as if he's a parent coming to collect a daughter for an appointment.

Jeremiah stands just inside the door for a moment, his jaw clenched and his eyes hard. The same way he looked at me at The Fox. "I came to speak with you."

"O-okay." I hate how the word stutters its way out of my mouth.

In three strides, Jeremiah stands at the edge of my desk. I instinctively push back in my chair.

"I had a call today from a Mr. Byron at Loyola University." Jeremiah thrusts his hand into his breast pocket and withdraws a white square of paper. From it, he reads, "'Mr. Byron wants to ask Elsie Piper what day Clarence died, because Clarence requested an appointment with him but didn't show up. Call with any additional questions she might have and best of luck on her story.'"

Jeremiah lowers the note and glowers at me. "I want you to tell me this message isn't really for you, but I'm guessing that's not going to happen."

I wince and look away.

"Piper. Sail." Jeremiah says my name through gritted teeth. "Did you tell this man that you're a reporter at *The Daily*?"

"Yes," I say to my clasped hands.

"And why did you do that?"

"I needed some information from Loyola about a student, and that was what I came up with. I'm sorry."

There's a beat of silence, and then Jeremiah asks, "What, exactly, are you sorry *for*?"

I look up, find Jeremiah's blue eyes are still blazing, and look back to my lap. "That you're angry."

"That's what I thought you'd say." He releases a sharp breath. "You're not sorry you did it, or sorry you took advantage of me, or sorry you falsely represented my family's business for your personal gain."

Heat rushes to my cheeks, and I match him with my own sharp gaze. "That's not fair. It was for a job. For my investigation."

He smiles as though I said something amusing and echoes, "Your investigation."

"Yes! I would never randomly decide to pretend I'm a reporter. I did it for the case I'm working on right now, and . . ."

Jeremiah closes his eyes, pinches the bridge of his nose, and exhales. In the single second it takes him to do that, I'm a child again, sitting in front of my father, whose patience is waning.

"You're taking this investigator thing too far, Piper," Jeremiah says quietly.

I don't know how to intelligently respond, but it doesn't prevent my mouth from trying. "Louisa hired me to help, so that's what—"

He leans on the high ledge of my desk, his expression serious. "I know ever since Lydia died, you've felt confused and lost. You miss her, and you don't know how to handle it. But, Piper, you have to stop acting like this. You're not a real investigator."

Jeremiah's words pull the air from my lungs in a gasp.

He flinches and lowers his eyes. "I'm sorry. I'm not trying to hurt you. It's only that it was bad enough seeing you at The Fox in that getup, but then I find out you claimed to work for my paper. I know you don't want to hear this, but you've gone too far."

I straighten my spine until each bone is stacked perfectly. "How far I go is not up to you. I think it's time for you to leave, Mr. Crane."

Jeremiah looks at me, jaw clenched, eyes ablaze. Then he presses his trilby firmly onto his head, and with a curt nod farewell, exits the office.

CHAPTER
TWENTY-SIX

I had a plan.

The plan was to come home from Presley's as quickly as possible to review my notes about Clarence and the questions I wrote out today. I wanted to think through the stories Virginia might tell that could steer the conversation in helpful directions. I was going to build out her backstory more, so I could answer any questions that might get thrown my way. Then I would get dressed and take the L to meet Elzbieta at Grand Street Station and walk to Ireland's Oyster House with her.

That was my plan.

That is not what I do.

Instead, I go home. I ignore Sidekick's happy prancing at my return. I immediately go upstairs to my bedroom and I fall onto my bed, shoes still on. Then I cry all the tears I've been holding in since Jeremiah turned and walked out Presley's door. I cry and cry and cry, with Sidekick alternating between pawing at me in a bid for attention and whimpering.

You're not a real investigator.

Jeremiah's right that Lydia's death wrecked me. He's right that ever since it happened, I've felt derailed. But is he right about me not being a real investigator? What does or doesn't make me "real"? I thought it was me I needed permission from, but maybe that's not enough. Maybe the outside world will never take me seriously. How much does that matter to me?

Precious minutes that I could use reviewing the case, making my plan, and transforming myself into Virginia "Gin" Chlebek slip away. But does it matter? Should I even be going tonight? Should I be taking money from Louisa and running around Chicago like this if I can never really do the job?

There's a soft knock on my door.

"What?" The word croaks out of me.

"May I come in?"

Jane. I squeeze my eyes shut. She's the last person I want to see. Well, no. *Jeremiah* is the last person I want to see right now.

Through restrained tears, I say, "Not right now, thank you."

There are no sounds of footsteps retreating.

"I brought you something," Jane says in a hesitant voice. "Should I just leave it outside?"

I frown. What would she have brought me? I wipe my slimy cheeks with my sleeve and open my door. Jane stands on the other side holding a piece of cheesecake.

Her smile had been tentative but quickly disappears. "Oh, honey. You look awful. Has something happened?"

"No." My voice is so flat, you could skip stones across it.

Jane shakes her head. "That was a stupid question. Obviously, something has happened. It's fine if you don't want to tell me, I just . . . I haven't seen you look like this since Lydia . . ."

"It's nothing like that," I say. "Just hurt feelings is all."

Jane studies me, still gripping the plate of cheesecake, which I recognize from our dinner at Henrici's. After eating my dinner, I was too full for dessert, but Father insisted on ordering me something anyway. The waiter tucked my slice of cheesecake into a box and sent it home with me.

Jane glances from the offering of cake in her hand and back

up to me. "I thought . . . Well, it's odd for you to come home and go straight upstairs like you did. Normally you take Sidekick out or you get a snack. I thought maybe you were upset, and this could help."

Much to my embarrassment, my eyes well with tears. "That was nice, thank you."

Jane's mouth curls as she hands the plate to me. "You don't have to sound so surprised."

I accept the offered cake. "I've had a bad afternoon."

"The whole week has been rough for you, I think." With the cake no longer in her grasp, Jane clasps her fingers together, twisting the enormous diamond on her left hand. "I don't know that this will matter to you, but I didn't realize the baby would be such upsetting news. I should've, probably, but I didn't. And I'm . . . sorry. For that. Not for the baby, of course, but for my lack of thought."

I can't remember Jane ever speaking to me in such a humble way.

"I'm sorry too," I say, surprised to find that I mean it. "I know how it feels to be excited about something, and for others to be upset by it."

You're not a real investigator.

"Maybe this seems silly to you, because I know how you feel about children, but all I ever wanted was to be a mother. Then I went through all of high school and all of college, and hardly ever went on a date."

Jane—with her lovely face and figure—barely dated? *Jane?*

My surprise must be evident, because she shrugs. "For a season, a lot of the boys my age were off at war, and I had a hard time meeting anyone who I was really interested in. Even when I finally met Timothy . . ." She gestures to me. "He has all three of you. He had a grandchild on the way." Jane twists her ring some more. "I thought he would say no to having a baby."

"Probably because of me. I hear I was rough."

The smile Jane gives me is perhaps the warmest I've ever received from her. "I don't think easy babies exist. Anyway, I understand you've gone through a lot of change in the last year, and that my announcement was yet another unwelcome change. I just wanted you to know that I'm sorry for that."

"Thank you," I say. "And I'm sorry I reacted so poorly."

She grins. I find myself smiling back.

Then she turns and heads down the stairs. I start to close my door, until Jane pauses and turns. "Piper? Whatever it is that has you upset, I'm sure you'll find your way through it. You're one of the strongest young women I've ever met."

I don't know how to respond to that. Other than saying, "Thank you."

I close my door with a soft click. I almost sit on my bed to enjoy the cheesecake, but instead, I carry the plate into my closet. After turning on my flashlight and closing myself inside, I stare at all the questions and facts as I eat.

"If you don't help her, who will?" Hannah LeVine said when she dragged Louisa into the office.

Maybe I'm not a real investigator. Maybe I never will be, but a so-called real investigator might not have taken Louisa's case. A real investigator—who would be a man, obviously—would never have received an invitation from Elzbieta to join her at The Fox, and as a result he wouldn't have seen the look Liam Finnegan gave her that night. And he definitely wouldn't be going out on a fake double date in a couple of hours to get more information.

Not being perceived as a threat means others will underestimate me. Like Mariano said, that is exceedingly valuable.

When we're seated in the lobster grotto of Ireland's Oyster House, Keiran hangs his arm over the back of my chair. "What'd you think of working at The Fox, Gin? You gonna take the job?"

I lean forward under the guise of reaching for my iced tea. "Maybe."

"She was the berries." Elzbieta grins at me. "Hopefully she'll get to start soon."

"Who was the guy that came to The Fox looking for you? The blond one?"

I look across the table into the cool hazel eyes of Liam Finnegan.

"Looked like a Gold Coast rich boy to me," Liam says, which I find unnervingly impressive. That's exactly what Jeremiah is. "Who is he?"

I can see the hard lines of Jeremiah's face this afternoon, his eyes bright with fury, and push the ugly memory away.

"Stepbrother?" The word comes out as more of a question than I would like. I clear my throat and take a drink of tea, as though dryness had caused the strange inflection. "He's my stepbrother. A bit overprotective. Hope he didn't cause you problems."

Liam holds his gaze steady on me; the cigarette between his fingers sends up a steady curl of smoke between us. "Nope. No problems."

The waiter arrives to take our order, and I pick out flounder broiled with mushroom sauce because it's the cheapest dinner on the menu that I can find. Elzbieta selects the Maine lobster tail a la Newberg. If she feels any embarrassment over her dinner costing one and a half times as much as anybody else's, I can't detect it. I think through the places she went with Clarence—Tip Top Inn, Henrici's, Le Petit Gourmet. The girl has expensive tastes. At least when someone else is paying.

"Elz said you knew our friend Clarence," Keiran says.

I lean back in my chair, forgetting his arm is there. His hand falls warm and possessive on my shoulder. *Don't pull away. You're fine.* I resist looking at Mariano, who took a table across the room with Jack while we were ordering our entrées.

"I did." I put on a sorrowful expression and lean into his touch. "Liam and Elz told me the news on Monday night. I was so sorry to hear."

"It was rough." Keiran looks away from me to Liam. "Clarence was a good one."

"Indeed," Elzbieta murmurs.

Liam's teeth are clenched as he stares into his lemonade. His gaze shifts upward to me. "What do you think, Gin? Do you think Elz was onto something when she said he didn't kill himself?"

My heart speeds up at the way he looks at me. The gleam in his eyes is reminiscent of the way Nick used to look at me when issuing a challenge. *You can't climb that tree* or *There's no way you're faster than me.*

"I don't know." A nervous laugh bubbles up and out. "I didn't know him that well."

Liam's head tilts slightly. "Isn't he why you applied at The Fox?"

"Yes, but I hadn't seen Clarence in months."

Liam looks at me, like he's anticipating that I'll say more. I need to stop letting him be in control of the conversation.

"But he was always very cheerful when I was around him," I continue. "I certainly wouldn't have expected him to take his own life. But also, who would've wanted him dead?"

I look at Liam. Liam looks back at me, unblinking. I turn my gaze to Keiran.

"No one I can think of," Keiran says. "Everybody loved Clarence." Liam's eyes flick to him. "Did they?"

"Sure." Keiran shrugs his beefy shoulders. "Didn't they?"

Liam reaches across Elzbieta to put out his cigarette in the ashtray. "What do you think, Elz? You're the one who said you didn't think he killed himself."

Her laugh registers a bit high, a bit loud. "Yes, but not because I have someone in mind as his murderer. Just because he was Clarence."

"I seem to remember him complaining about his boss." I sip my iced tea. "I can't remember what his name was. Something like Tubby."

"Tubs," Keiran supplies.

"That was it," I say. "What about him?"

"Tubs has a temper," Elz puts in. "If someone really did kill Clarence, he'd be at the top of my suspect list."

Liam nods his head slowly. "Possible. Tubs has a kid, though."

Elzbieta snorts. "What difference does that make?"

Keiran snaps his fingers. "What about that new broad Clarence was seeing?"

I look up at Keiran, but as his words sink in, my gaze turns to Elzbieta. There was another girl?

Elz averts her eyes and allows her hair to swing between us.

Liam's laugh is a bark. "He and Mabel only went out once. But Elz still had some feelings about that, didn't you?"

Her face flushes as she fumbles with a matchbook.

Keiran chuckles as well. "That's right. I'd forgotten."

"What's so funny?" I say, my heart pounding.

Liam looks to me, a gleam of something in his eyes. "So, Clarence and Elz used to be an item—"

"Please don't," Elzbieta says, touching Liam's arm.

"But they'd been broken up for a couple weeks when Clarence took out this other girl I introduced him to—"

"Liam," Elzbieta says.

"So Elz went to Clarence's apartment and really bawled him out." Finally, Liam turns and acknowledges her. "Clarence told me you were so angry, you said you could kill him."

Elzbieta scowls at Liam. "We all say things we don't mean when we're angry," she says in a stiff voice. "You used to say I'd never go out with you unless Clarence was out of the picture, but you don't see me pointing fingers at you."

"Don't fight, you two." Keiran removes his arm from around me. I've been so engrossed in the conversation, I forgot it was there. "Clarence wouldn't like it."

Elzbieta strikes a match, then lights a cigarette. She turns pointedly away from Liam, away from the table. Liam doesn't speak, just keeps rotating his lemonade glass over and over.

"Come on, Liam. You know Elz wouldn't have hurt Clarence," Keiran says, his voice both gruff and pleading. "Let's talk about something else."

Liam pushes back from the table. "Excuse me," he mutters as he walks away.

Keiran gives me a rueful look. "Sorry, Gin. He's not usually like this."

In that moment, Keiran doesn't seem like the creepy bouncer from The Fox. He only seems like a normal guy who's embarrassed about how this date is going.

"You've nothing to apologize for," I say.

"That's right, Keiran." Elzbieta exhales a stream of smoke. "You're not the one acting like a lunatic."

Keiran gives her an exasperated look, and I steal the moment to glance at Mariano. He sees me looking, smiles, and I look away. Acknowledging him isn't a wise thing to do, but knowing he's there makes me feel safer.

"Can you please be nicer to Liam?" Keiran says. "He's really having a hard time. He's the last one who saw Clarence alive, and the guilt is eating him up."

I blink up at Keiran with what I hope is a good damsel-in-distress face. "Poor Liam. Of course he feels awful about that. When did he see Clarence last?"

Keiran's arm drapes around me again. "They had drinks together that afternoon. Just a few hours before Clarence . . . you know. Liam feels terrible about it."

"Well, he couldn't have known, right?" I say. "Did he say anything about what Clarence was like that day?"

Keiran shrugs. "Said he seemed normal. Right, Elz? Isn't that what he said?"

Elzbieta's gaze is cool. "Something like that."

"He shouldn't blame himself, then." I look over my shoulder. "Do you think he'll come back?"

Keiran nods. "I'm sure he just went to the restroom or stepped outside for a smoke. Don't you worry, Gin."

Thirty seconds pass. A minute.

Keiran pushes back from the table. "I'll go check on him."

He walks away, and still Elzbieta doesn't look at me, just keeps smoking her cigarette.

"So." I put my elbows on the table and steeple my fingers. "You and Clarence had a big argument the day before he died?"

Her dark eyes slide my direction. "I never would've hurt Clarence. Obviously. Why would I be helping you so much if I'd hurt Clarence?" Elzbieta jerks her chin in the direction the boys went. "This is Liam trying to deflect attention from himself, make us think it could be anybody but him."

I sigh. "You should've told me the truth."

Elzbieta's gaze shifts to a point beyond me, and I turn and look. Liam and Keiran are walking back to the table. Keiran gives me a reassuring smile, and I do my best to smile warmly in return.

"Do you believe me?" Elz asks. Her voice is crisp, but her eyes are anxious.

Elzbieta has definitely lied to me, and there's no reason why I can't respond in turn.

"I do," I tell her.

"I'm sorry I didn't tell you about my argument with Clarence."

I look over at Elzbieta. Her jaw is set, and she stares straight ahead, eyes focused on a distant point across the tracks. I'm praying her train comes first because Mariano is parked nearby, waiting to take me home.

"Why didn't you?"

She swallows. "I would think my reasons are obvious."

"I would still like to hear them."

Elzbieta tightens the belt of her coat. A surprisingly nice coat, like one I would expect to see at Marshall Field's. "It's a little embarrassing, for one thing. It isn't as though Clarence and I were still dating and I caught him out with another girl. We'd been over for weeks."

"Did you know the girl?"

Elzbieta shakes her head. "She's a waitress that Liam knew. If you want to hear the really embarrassing part, I actually saw them on their date." She casts me a quick glance. "I never told Clarence this, but I knew they were going to see *Peter Pan*, and I knew what movie house Clarence frequented, so I waited around outside."

Elzbieta looks down the track, like a train might come and save her, but no trains approach. "She was a pretty girl. Probably nice too."

"What did Clarence say when you showed up at his apartment?" I ask.

"Oh, he was Clarence." Her smile is tinged with sadness. "He was calm and compassionate. 'I know this is hard, Elz, but you're going to be moving on too.' And it was like the calmer he got, the angrier I became. I've always been the type to throw really good tantrums when I'm mad. I know it's immature. Hopefully, I grow out of it someday."

A middle-aged couple staggers by us, laughing and clutching one another. They're both clearly drunk. I watch them as my mind chews on what Elzbieta just confessed to—that she's the type to throw tantrums. Is she the type to kill in a moment of passion? Maybe. Although, if Clarence was murdered, he wasn't killed in the heat of the moment. It was planned.

I wait until the drunk couple has cleared away before asking, "Is there anything else you've been keeping from me?"

Elzbieta shakes her head no.

"The fight at Clarence's apartment. How long were you there?"

"I'm not sure, exactly. Maybe twenty minutes? Long enough to really make a ninny of myself." She chuckles humorlessly.

"Did you know that Liam knew about your fight?"

"Not until tonight." A frown creases her lovely face. "I hadn't realized Clarence told him about that."

"Why do you think Liam shared that tonight?" I ask, remembering that Clarence told his sister Liam only had eyes for Elz. "He finally gets to take you on a date, something it sounds like he's been trying for a while now, and he acted like that."

In the distance, a train grinds against the tracks.

"Beats me," Elzbieta says on a sigh. "Sometimes I really don't understand boys."

"Do you think Keiran's right? That Liam feels guilty because he saw Clarence last?"

Or does Liam feel guilty because he *is* guilty? Even after he and Keiran came back, he hardly said a word.

Elzbieta shrugs again. "Sure seems like it. He didn't really act like himself tonight."

"I wonder what changed."

The train comes close enough that we can see it's Elzbieta's. She turns to me, clutching her jeweled handbag with one hand and my arm with the other. "Sorry the date went so poorly."

"That's okay," I say, though I don't think the date went poorly at all. "If I don't see you before, Merry Christmas."

She waves good-bye, and I watch her board the train. I wait until the train has pulled out of the station before I walk back down the platform and search along the curb for Mariano's Model T.

I finally find him several cars back. I jog the last few feet and pull open the passenger door.

"Thank you for waiting for me," I say as I tumble inside. His car isn't exactly warm, but it's warmer than it was up on the platform. "I waited for Elzbieta's train to arrive before coming back down."

Mariano reaches into the backseat and pulls out a blanket. "I assumed."

"Thank you," I say as I take the blanket and unfold it. "Where's Jack?"

"He has a shift tonight, so he had to leave." Mariano's gaze skims down my beaded skirt. "You didn't take my advice about clothing, I noticed."

I laugh, feeling almost giddy to no longer be pretending to be Gin Chlebek or the cloaked version of Piper Sail that I am with Elzbieta. "No, I didn't. Your advice was terrible, although I would probably be warmer now."

His arms slip around my waist and pull me across the seat, closer to him. "Warmer?"

I smile and rest my forehead against his. "Yes. This is the best part of my night."

"Mine too. I had to watch you be on a date with someone else all night."

His fingers thread into my hair, causing delightful tingles to run down my neck. He brushes his mouth over mine and the city streets melt away. It's just me and Mariano, warm and safe and close. The weight of my other worries drifts away, and then as he pulls back from the kiss, they float back into my head. Louisa, who's depending on me. Elzbieta, who kept secrets from me. Liam, who had an agenda tonight that I haven't figured out. Jeremiah and his fury this afternoon. *You're not a real investigator.*

Mariano smiles and tucks my hair back into place. "I lost you."

"Sorry." I shake my head. Foolish girl. Why didn't I just go on kissing him? "A lot on my mind right now."

"I know." He presses his mouth to mine once more. "I know you."

Then he starts the ignition and pulls away from the curb. "Was it a successful date? What'd you learn tonight?"

"Oddly, I learned more about Elzbieta than I did about Liam," I say, and then I walk him through the details of the night.

"So, Clarence had a date with another girl, and Elzbieta *followed* them?" Mariano considers this and then shrugs. "I guess I can't judge. I followed you on a date with another guy tonight."

I roll my eyes. "A fake date under my fake identity."

"Real guy, though." Mariano rubs at his chin. "What do we know about this girl? She could be important."

"She's a waitress that Liam introduced him to. And I agree." I wrap the blanket tighter around me. "I wish I'd known about her sooner. I guess Elzbieta probably thought it would make her look suspicious."

"Probably. Hiding it from you isn't any better, though."

"Or that she and Clarence had a fight where she told him she was angry enough she could kill him."

"Bet she regrets saying that now. Though"—Mariano frowns—"if I were planning to kill someone, I wouldn't say something like that. Liam claims he heard about this from Clarence?"

"Yes, and Elz confirmed that she did say that."

Mariano checks over his shoulder before changing lanes. "And Clarence told Liam this . . . when? The same day he died?"

I nod. "They had drinks together that afternoon. Supposedly, Liam is the last one who saw Clarence alive."

"You said he was poisoned. Could that have happened at drinks rather than at the apartment?"

"I think it's a possibility," I say. "Not that I know how to prove it."

"I did look up Liam Finnegan for you. If our notes can be trusted, he's related to *the* Finnegans, but he's a nephew. Clean record so far."

"Thank you," I say. "That's something I was hoping would come up tonight and never did."

Mariano laughs. "That's a hard one to work into conversation. Honestly, I'm surprised you gleaned as much as you did."

"Liam seemed to want to talk about Clarence." I try to work through this unsettled feeling rattling around in my chest. Something felt off about the night, about Liam's actions. "I'm trying to figure out what his behavior means. Elz also said he wasn't acting like himself."

Mariano shrugs. "He was probably intimidated by you."

I laugh. "Oh yes. I'm very intimidating."

"Laugh if you like, but you really can be. You have an intensity." He frowns slightly. "I'm not sure that's the best word to describe it, but I used to feel nervous every time I talked to you."

"You felt nervous around *me*?" I blink at him. Why on earth would Mariano have ever felt nervous around me?

"You do this thing with your eyes, and it feels like you're looking right through me. If I hadn't followed every single possible lead to find Lydia, I was sure that you would know, and you would skewer me." He gives me a sidelong glance. "Yes, that's it. That's the look."

I guffaw. "No, it isn't. That's just me looking at you."

"I'm used to it now, but when we first met . . ." Mariano gives a theatrical shudder.

I laugh. "You make me sound terrifying."

"I'm not saying I mind. Scare every other guy away, please. They don't know what I know." Mariano reaches over and takes my hand. "You're like a cannolo. Crunchy exterior but soft like ricotta on the inside."

His Italian heritage pops through on the word *ricotta,* making me grin. "Like *what* on the inside?"

"Ricotta," he repeats, the accent extra strong. *Ree-coat-uh.* "It's a kind of cheese."

"I've never heard of that before."

He gives an exaggerated sigh. "Next date, we will go to Ferrara Bakery and eat cannoli."

"And when will this be? Between Christmas, your work schedule, and my multiple personalities and fake dates, I'm not sure when we'll have time."

Mariano makes a sour face as he pulls down Astor Street. It's nine o'clock, but the city lights reflect on both the cloudy sky and the fresh snow, so it's easy to see his expressions.

"I don't know. Maybe around Christmas? I have the twenty-fifth off, but that isn't ideal, for obvious reasons. I don't know how your family celebrates."

"I don't know either," I say with a laugh. "My family is different this year."

"Yeah. Mine too, I guess."

Mariano will spend Christmas Day with Zola. My stomach gives an ugly twist. I imagine Elzbieta, standing outside the movie theater watching Clarence take a new girl on a date, and it doesn't seem as crazy as it once did. But that's silly because *I* am the new girl. And not only is Zola now his sister-in-law, she also has a baby. So why does jealousy rise in me every time she crosses my mind?

"What are you thinking about?" Mariano asks.

He's parked in front of my house, and I didn't even notice. I could say it right now: *I'm thinking about you and Zola. What was it about her that made you rush into an engagement, yet you've never even said you love me?*

But then what? I don't want him saying he loves me because he feels pressured. He spent his whole night sitting in a restaurant, keeping me safe while I was working. Isn't that enough for me? Actions speak louder than words, as the saying goes. I know he cares about me, and if I drag up the issue of Zola now, the night will end on a bitter note.

"Christmas," I say. Not entirely untruthful. "Just thinking about Christmas."

CHAPTER
TWENTY-SEVEN

When I ask to borrow Father's car so I can take care of some Christmas shopping, he insists on having me drive him around the neighborhood to prove that I really am capable of handling an automobile.

The Chrysler is newer and nicer than the Model T Walter trained me on, with a push start in the floor and a smoother throttle. Even though it's been at least a month since I last drove, I pull away from the curb with ease.

"I just can't believe that you learned to drive, and I didn't even know about it," Father says. "Makes me wonder what else you might be up to that I'm unaware of."

I laugh but don't otherwise respond. I need to focus on my driving, after all.

"Do you speak with Walter much these days?"

I frown. "Not as much as I'd like. He's very busy with his life out in California, and I'm busy here."

"Watch out for the stop sign ahead."

"I know about the stop sign."

Father stays silent until we're through the intersection, then releases a long, slow breath, as if we'd been in danger despite no other cars being within ten feet of us.

"Joyce is leaving to visit him the day after Christmas," he says.

"Yes, she told me. I'm a little worried that Joyce will get a taste of Christmas in California and not come back." I try for a smile but can't quite make it. "I don't see her as much as I did when she lived with us, but I would be sad if she followed Walter out there and I never saw her anymore."

"If she doesn't stay, we'll need to hire someone else to help with the baby, of course."

I keep my eyes on the road and my hands on the wheel. "Do you want me to turn on State or keep going?"

"State's fine. Keep an eye on that man up there who just got into his car. He might pull out in front of you."

I wonder what my father would think if he knew I once drove several miles north with Emma to investigate her boyfriend.

"How are you feeling about the baby?" Father asks.

I consider the question. "Fine."

"Fine?"

Yes, largely because I haven't been thinking much about the baby. Now that I am, my insides feel squirmy. "Mm-hmm."

"Well, that's good." Father seems to relax in the passenger seat. "That's great to hear. Sometimes I'm not entirely sure how I feel about the baby, to be honest."

"Really?"

"Sure. I mean, I'll be fifty next month—"

"More like two weeks."

Father grimaces. "Yes, thank you. I never planned on having a baby this late in life. Never thought I'd lose your mother so early in our marriage either."

I frown. "You'd been married at least twenty years when she died, hadn't you? Tim was at college."

"Twenty years of being married to a woman like Elsie didn't feel like near enough. She was remarkable." Father's voice is gruff with emotion. "You remind me of her every day."

My heart swells almost painfully, like it's straining my rib cage. "That's the nicest thing anyone has ever said to me."

"It's deserved."

I pull alongside our house, wipe my eyes, and find Father beaming at me. "I guess Walter really did teach you to drive."

I laugh, chasing away the last of my tears. "Did you think I was lying?"

"Not *lying*, but I thought you might be overstating. With so many people buying cars, I see more and more people on the road who think they know how to drive but don't." Father straightens the vest under his coat. "I can respect your desire to drive—you've always wanted to do things for yourself—but if you're going to do so, I insist upon you driving *well*. I'm glad that you do."

"Walter was a good teacher."

I pull on the emergency brake and feel a pang for that summer when he taught me. Summer of '23 had been full of driving lessons with Walter, Oak Street Beach with Lydia, and freshly made lemonade in the kitchen with Joyce. As I get out of the Chrysler and shiver in the chill of December, those days feel agonizingly far away.

I'm about to follow Father through our front gate when I hear a "Piper!" from down the street.

I turn to see Louisa walking down Astor Street, wrapped in her green coat and wearing a fur-trimmed hat.

Father continues on inside while I wait for her.

"I was visiting Hannah and thought I'd bring over Clarence's report cards from high school." She withdraws an envelope from her coat pocket. "And I'm curious about how last night went. Didn't you say you were getting together with Elzbieta?"

"Yes, I did." I glance up at my house. "I'd rather not discuss it here. Do you mind walking with me?"

"Of course not."

I open the envelope Louisa handed me and peek inside at the four report cards. Each one is dominated by As, with the exception of two Bs his sophomore and junior years, both in English. I frown. I was really hoping to see what Mr. Byron talked about, the dramatic rise in grades, but I don't. I'll have to take a closer look later.

"Thanks for bringing these." I tuck the report cards into my pocket and begin down the sidewalk. "Last night was interesting. I learned that Elzbieta and Clarence got in a big fight the day before he died."

"Really?" Louisa's eyes widen. "That has to mean something, don't you think?"

"It might. Especially since she was trying to hide it."

"What did they fight about?"

"Clarence went on a date with another girl and Elz was upset by it. Elzbieta says she said a lot of things she shouldn't have and feels remorseful."

"Of course she says that *now*," Louisa says in a tone that implies this is obvious. "Who was this other girl?"

"A waitress. It sounds like Clarence only went out with her once, but I haven't yet had a chance to follow up on that."

"Elzbieta is starting to sound like the kind of girl who, if she couldn't have Clarence, didn't want anybody to have him."

I nod slowly. "I think that's possible. I also think it's possible she was heartbroken and got a little carried away."

Louisa snorts.

"Okay, a *lot* carried away. The problem is that being jealous, fighting with someone, and saying things that sound bad later aren't evidence of a crime. They might point to a motive, but motive isn't actually murder."

Louisa presses her lips thin and seems to consider this. After a moment, she nods as though she finds this logic satisfactory. "What about the boss? Did you learn anything more about him?"

"Not really. I'm still looking into Tubs. And Liam. And now this waitress girl Clarence had a date with."

"Not Elzbieta?"

"Well, yeah. Her too."

Louisa comes to a stop at the corner of Astor and Burton. "Be careful around her, okay? Maybe I'm wrong, but the more I think about it, there *was* a period of time that Clarence seemed over the moon about her. And then it's like a switch had been flipped and he wasn't anymore. I think she's the kind of person you have to watch yourself with."

Louisa's unusual rhetoric of "maybe I'm wrong" makes me pay closer attention than anything else. My thoughts turn to Clarence's notebook, to all the receipts for dinners and movies and gifts for Elzbieta . . . until they stopped. That seems a little odd if Elzbieta is telling me the truth and Clarence really did just decide they weren't right for each other.

"I think you're probably right about that," I tell Louisa. "I'll be careful."

She releases a deep sigh. "This is our first Christmas without Clarence, and I really hoped to know by now what happened to him. I wish you were closer to solving this."

I try to brush away her disappointment before the comment can hurt my feelings. "I know it's hard to wait for answers, but these things take time."

Louisa squints into the distance. "Daniel says I should just let this go. He's having Christmas dinner with us, and I told him I'd apprise him on what you've learned. He said he knows it's hard to accept, but that Clarence really did . . ." She trails off and clenches her teeth for a few seconds. "Sorry, I have a hard time talking about this without getting emotional."

"I know, don't apologize." I consider hugging her, but then I don't. "And Daniel could be right. It's possible that I'll do all this digging and what I ultimately uncover is that Clarence really did take his own life."

Louisa shakes her head. "No. If I'm sure of anything, it's that. That's not Clarence."

I sigh, small and private. "Okay."

After saying farewell to Louisa, I stop in at the LeVines' to see Hannah. To my relief, she's the one who answers the door.

"Piper," she says with a smile. "Come in."

The girl standing before me is a different species from the one I held in the hallway while she screamed. Her eyes are as bright as the sky and her smile doesn't have the brittle look to it that it has had since Lydia died.

"I'm in the middle of making a sandwich. Do you want one?"

"No, thank you."

"It's just me here, which is a little strange." Hannah turns for the kitchen, and I follow. Even the way her body moves—fluid and natural—looks different than the way it has these last six months. "Sarah is at a friend's Christmas party, my parents are out shopping, and Tabitha is off this weekend."

Hannah pushes through the door into the kitchen, holding it for me. The LeVines' kitchen is the only room in the house that doesn't look poised and ready for company at all times. The black-and-white checked floor has a few scuffs, the wooden countertops typically hold evidence of a meal in progress, and the large gas range and oven often clicks and hums noisily as it heats whatever is within.

"You look a lot better than when I saw you last," I say as Hannah returns to the tuna salad she's mixing.

She laughs. "It wouldn't take much, would it? I think I scared poor Miss Bianchi half to death."

"She was very worried about you. We all were."

Hannah points her spoon at me. "Probably not Ms. Underhill. And Louisa said it's all over school that you bawled her out in the hallway for what she said to me."

"Oh." I lean against the counter. "Probably not the smartest thing I ever did, but it felt good in the moment."

"I understand that. Don't tell my mother I said this, but I don't regret what I did one bit. Even if they'd kicked me out of Presley's for good, I think it would've been worth it. I feel like myself again."

"You look like yourself. It's wonderful."

Hannah smooths tuna salad onto a piece of waiting bread. "It was like everything I'd felt since Lydia—the pain, the anger, the fear, everything—had taken over my body. I felt it all the time. I was trying to be strong for my family, because I thought that's what Lydia would've wanted, and I just couldn't do it anymore. It all came pouring out of me that day."

I think of how Hannah had clutched me, how she'd screamed

in such a way that my teeth ached from the sound. "That's what it seemed like."

"At first I didn't feel any better." Hannah pours herself a glass of orange juice and offers the pitcher to me. I shake my head. "My parents were furious, as I'm sure you know. But that night was the first time I'd slept soundly in months, and I woke up the next day feeling . . ." She trails off, her eyes unfocused. "I can't find a word for it. Cleansed, maybe? I still felt sad about Lydia, of course. I think I always will. And my voice was hoarse for days afterward from all the screaming. But I didn't feel heavy anymore. I didn't feel like a pot about to boil over."

I smile. "That's amazing."

"My parents could see the difference too. At first, I think it irritated them." Hannah chuckles. "Like I should be taking my suspension more seriously. Mother said that you told her something that helped her to understand better."

I frown. "What did I say?"

"Mother said you suggested I'd been too controlled with my emotions, holding too much in, and that maybe I needed to feel freer to talk about how I was feeling."

"Oh. Yes, I did say something like that. It's just a feeling I've observed in myself, is all."

Hannah beams at me. "It was the best thing you could've said to her. That was when she and Daddy started to understand that it wasn't that I didn't care about being suspended, it was that I was finally free of all the heaviness I'd been feeling. I'm not confined to the house anymore, and I can have friends over. Oh!" Her eyes light. "Did Louisa pay you a visit?"

"Yes, I saw her right before coming here."

"Are you close to figuring out what happened to her

brother?" Hannah punctuates her question with a large bite of her sandwich.

"Oh, I don't know." I pluck a piece of lint from my skirt. "I feel like there's lots of details that don't really add up, but I haven't found anything conclusive."

"Can I help?" Hannah asks brightly. "I'm bored silly. I'd love to have something to do."

"Well . . ." I want to say *absolutely not* because I'm not dragging Lydia's fourteen-year-old sister into this case, but her expression is so eager that I'm having difficulty actually saying the words.

And then I think of a way that she could help. "Something that's been confusing about this case is the poison that killed Clarence."

Hannah holds up a finger and rushes out of the room, shining blonde hair bouncing behind her. Seconds later, she's back with a notepad and pencil. She plops back into her seat. "Okay. Go on."

I bite back a grin. "He died from arsenic poisoning, probably mixed into a glass of scotch. But I don't understand how long the process took. Does it take hours for the poison to kill someone? Half an hour? I wondered if your father had books in his office that might talk about different poisons."

Hannah nods but doesn't look up from her writing. "Possibly. If not, he probably knows. I'll start with asking him."

"Oh." I sit up straighter. "I don't want to arouse suspicion—"

"I'll be subtle." Hannah waves away my concern. "So, you need to know how long the poison would've taken to be effective?"

"Yes." I hesitate. "But, really, I don't want to alarm your father—"

Hannah just laughs and picks up her sandwich. "Really,

Piper. Don't worry. I'll get an answer for you and report back, and Father will have no idea why I really wanted to know. I have a way."

"Okay," I say, still uneasy.

I watch her for a moment as she eats. *Sorry, Lydia*, I think. But I can't imagine Lydia minding *too* much, not when this is the happiest Hannah has seemed since June.

CHAPTER
TWENTY-EIGHT

While it's true that I want to borrow Father's car for shopping on State Street with Emma, it's not the entire truth.

I park across the street from 327 Webster, turn off the engine, and look up the length of the brick apartment building. I hope Louisa's memory can be trusted and that this really is where Liam Finnegan lives.

I look at my watch, which probably needs to be wound soon. One hour until I need to leave to pick up Emma for lunch at The Walnut Room. I watch pedestrians with shopping bags in all shapes and sizes pass by. A man comes out of 327, but he's short with a thick mustache and beard. Definitely not Liam. I check my watch and find only five minutes have ticked by.

After another five minutes, I get out of the car. Before I sit out here any longer, I at least want to verify this is where Liam Finnegan lives. Fortunately, just inside the building door is a row of metal mailboxes. On each, surnames are listed, and apartment 6 says Finnegan/O'Leary. But unfortunately, seeing Liam's last name printed on a mailbox is the closest I get to seeing him. When my watch ticks to the top of the hour, I sigh, start the engine, and drive to the Crane house to pick up Emma.

As I get out of Father's car to knock on the Cranes' door, Emma emerges, looking lovely in a forest-green coat with oversized black buttons. Lovely and—I tilt my head as I study her—tired? Sad?

"Hello," she calls down to me in her usual chipper voice.

I resist greeting her with "What's wrong?" because I've learned that not everyone likes probing questions to be lobbed at them right away.

"Hi," I say instead.

Her eyes are definitely puffy, though she's tried to hide this with layers of Maybelline. She puts on a smile as she reaches me on the sidewalk, but it doesn't transform her face the way it typically does. "It's colder than it looks out here."

"Emma—"

The Cranes' front door pops open and out steps Jeremiah. My gut clenches. He presses his hat onto his head and jogs down the steps before glancing our way. His smile starts warm, and then freezes when his gaze lands on me. "Hi."

"Hello," I say, with the polite stiffness I typically reserve for strangers. Did he tell Emma about our fight? Or about what I did?

"I called good-bye to you, but you didn't answer," Emma says to him. "Piper and I are heading to lunch at Marshall Field's."

He looks away from us. "Okay."

Emma frowns at the back of his head. "What's eating you?"

"Nothing."

Emma's frown deepens. "Are you upset I didn't invite you along? Because that's—"

Jermiah laughs and looks at his sister. "Of course not. Have fun. I'll see you on Christmas Eve."

He turns and saunters away without so much as a tip of his hat to me. He's in his car and pulling away, all within about thirty seconds.

"Golly," Emma says to his tailpipe. "I wonder why he's so cranky."

Apparently, Jeremiah has kept her in the dark about what happened between us. "Sometimes I bring that side out in people," I say.

Emma laughs as though I'm joking.

Emma drops a sugar cube into her cup of tea and stirs aggressively. "Robbie wrote to say that he's seeing somebody else."

"Oh." The sound escapes unintentionally, as though I'd been elbowed in the ribs.

"I know we weren't even together anymore, but since he was still writing to me, I thought someday, maybe . . ." Emma swallows hard. "Now it feels as though it's *really* over."

"I'm so sorry."

She taps her spoon against the rim of the cup with such force, I'm tempted to reach over and stop her. "Don't be." Her shrug is sharp. "My family sure isn't. You should've heard them. 'It's for the best, Emma. These things have a way of working themselves out.'"

Her jaw clenches as she stares into her tea, which still swirls inside the cup.

"I'm sure they have good intentions, but even if that *is* true, it doesn't mean you have no reason to be upset."

Emma looks at me through her heavily caked lashes. "Thank you."

Her eyes well, and I shove napkins in her direction. "Careful, or you'll have Maybelline everywhere *but* your eyelashes."

I can't tell if the noise she makes is a chuckle or a sob or both. She looks up at the chandeliers hanging from the high ceilings, as if admiring them, while she waits for the tears to pass.

"Should we talk about his flaws?"

Emma lowers her head and looks at me, a small smile on her face. "No, but thank you."

"Because his letter writing skills were abysmal. Not only that, I'm not sure he's smart enough to *spell* abysmal."

Emma's mouth drops open, and it's definitely a laugh this time, not a sob. "That's just cruel, Piper. Spelling is hard for some people."

I take a sip of my coffee. "Did you ever notice that he couldn't say the word *picture*?"

"What?" Emma shakes her head and spreads her napkin across her lap. "Yes, he could. You're being ridiculous."

"He always pronounced it *pitcher*. I'm not sure he knew that *picture* and *pitcher* are two different words."

"Of course he did." She rolls her eyes at me, looking nowhere near tears now. "That was just his accent."

"I'm not so sure. I think it's possible he didn't know."

She brings her teacup to her mouth, but I see the smile she's trying to hide. "We don't have to say mean things about him. But thank you."

A waitress appears and places the Field's Special in front of Emma and the chicken pot pie in front of me.

When she disappears, Emma sighs heavily. "Jeremiah always thought Robbie was too old for me. That's the worst part of it all, feeling like I should've just listened to him."

I wave my fork as if to shoo away Jeremiah's opinion. "If I waited for Tim and Nick to approve of a boy for me, I'd never date anyone."

"They don't like Mariano?"

"They would like him fine if we weren't dating." I shrug. "I will always be their little sister. I can't stop them from casting a vote, but I don't have let them be the deciding vote, if that makes sense."

"And how are things with Mariano?"

"Everything is good," I say as steam billows out the top crust. "We don't see each other as much as I'd like, between his work and my work, but when we're together, it's good."

That is, if I ignore how tense Mariano gets whenever Zola comes up. And how tense I get as well.

"How does he like having a girlfriend who is also investigating a murder?"

"He doesn't seem bothered by it." A smile plays at the corners of my mouth. "Or at least he's accepted this is who I am."

Emma has a tinkling sort of laugh, like if fairies were real. "It's just part of the price for dating you, you're saying."

"The price?" I scoff. "It's a perk."

Emma grins and presses her fork through the olive sitting on top of her opened-face sandwich. "I don't think Jeremiah would view it that way, so I guess it's good that the two of you never started anything."

I shrug and poke at my chicken pot pie.

"He told me he was really worried about you," Emma says, her tone carefully light. "He wouldn't give me many details, but he said this case you're investigating has taken you to some 'unsavory places,' as he phrased it."

I avert my eyes. "He isn't wrong, but I've been fine."

"That's what I told him. I said, 'If anyone can handle herself, it's Piper.'"

I try to not be curious, but . . . "And what did he say to that?"

"He had a whole rant about how Mariano shouldn't allow

you to do these kinds of things, and one day your luck will run out, and that luck was the only reason you and I didn't both die back in June."

I can't decide what irritates me more: the idea of Mariano "allowing" me to do things or that I don't really disagree with Jeremiah's assessment of what happened in June. Both Emma and I were incredibly lucky.

I poke at a carrot coin. "He blames me for what happened to you."

Emma waves her hand, like we're discussing something as trivial as me stepping on her toe. "That wasn't you. That was me being in the wrong place at the wrong time."

"*I* blame me," I say to my pie crust.

She presses the tines of her fork through hardboiled egg and iceberg lettuce. "No one needs to blame anybody, because I'm fine."

Guilt is thick like mucus in my throat. I swallow it down. "We could blame Robbie?"

Emma looks at me for a moment, then realizes I'm joking and grins. "Yes. Because if I hadn't started dating him, I never would've hired you. And if I hadn't hired you, then you wouldn't have been at my house that afternoon. And if you hadn't left your bag behind, I never would've brought it to your house when I did."

"It's decided, then," I say with a decisive nod. "The whole thing is Robbie's fault."

"Indeed." Emma smiles her normal, lovely smile. "Maybe by the time I graduate, you'll have enough cases that you'll need an assistant."

And Jeremiah had the nerve to call her delicate. Affection for Emma blooms in my chest. "Or a partner."

Emma beams. "Or a partner."

Christmas break provides a wonderful opportunity to haunt Liam Finnegan's street, though despite being the nephew of two gangsters, his day-to-day life is no more exciting than the average person's. Or at least, that's true for this particular Monday. Thus far, I've tailed him to the laundromat, Woolworth's, the market, and now back to his modest apartment building. But I suppose even Al Capone has menial household tasks that need doing.

I sit in the driver's seat of the car and gaze up at the brick building, wondering what Liam is doing in there, and if he plans to go anywhere else today. I really hope he isn't the sort of person who takes a nap in the afternoon—that's going to make everything even duller.

I at least thought to bring my box of Clarence's belongings. I position myself so that I'll see if anyone enters or exits Liam's building, and then I pull the envelope with Clarence's high school grade cards from the top of the box.

Just like when I looked at them initially, I see evidence of someone who has always been a diligent student. Nothing like what Mr. Byron described. I stare at the B in English his sophomore and junior years, but there's simply no other way to see this: Clarence always made good grades, just like Louisa said. That doesn't mean he didn't cheat to get those good grades, but I'm not seeing an obvious origin of his decision to cheat.

I set the grade cards aside and flip through the financial notebooks again. I stare once more at the entry *+$500 Dean, for services rendered* and then flip through several receipts of normal purchases—routine groceries, a nice dinner with Elz, his share of the rent—before the balancing entry: –*$500.*

Did he give the money back? Lose it? Spend it? Why no explanation? Clarence Dell is specific when I don't need him to be—an itemized receipt from the market—but then vague when it matters. Like the suicide note. Like how he spent the five hundred dollars. Why would he not—

Liam steps out the front door of his apartment, wearing a dark gray flat cap and a black overcoat. Instead of heading toward his car, which I know is parked across the street and to the west, he's walking the opposite way. Wherever we're going, we're going on foot or we're taking the L.

I make quick work of fitting my blonde hair up inside a brunette wig and check my reflection in my compact before pulling my cloche tight over the top.

I grab my leather shopping bag and am about to pull my door open when a car zips by. I take a deep breath, thankful to have avoided my father's car door being yanked off its hinges, and climb out. By the time I've fumbled with the key to lock the door, Liam has disappeared from sight. I take off in the direction he went and pray the gray flat cap will pop into view soon.

As I come up on the corner of Webster and Lincoln Park, I spot him waiting for a break in traffic before he crosses the street.

I slow my pace and wait until he's most of the way across Lincoln Park Way before I start to cross as well. He isn't really walking briskly, but he's walking steadily, and his legs are much longer than mine. That makes my goal of staying with him but not right on top of him much easier.

I follow him south across another two streets before he

stops, pulls on a door handle, and disappears inside. I rush ahead, slowing only when I discover that the establishment he entered is Georgie's Diner and the entire front of the restaurant is windows. After a moment's thought, I pull my compact from my handbag and hold it at face level, like I'm checking my makeup, and try to see through the windows while keeping my face hidden. The tiny mirror reflects a busy restaurant, but not much else.

Now what? There's only one door into the place. What if Liam is standing there, waiting to be seated? My wig hopefully keeps me from being instantly recognizable, and I'd opted to wear no makeup today in contrast to the two other times Liam has been around me as the heavily made-up Gin Chlebek, but no makeup and dark hair isn't a stellar disguise. If he spends any time looking at my face, he'll likely recognize me. Maybe it's better to not go inside the diner, but rather wait out here for him.

I pretend to consider the window display at the haberdashery next door as I think about what to do next. I'm still contemplating the pros and cons of following Liam inside when I catch a reflection in the window of a man walking by. He's an abnormally tall man, with his face turned toward the buildings, reading addresses. Tubs.

As I watch, he takes in the sign for Georgie's Diner and heads inside.

Well, that makes the decision easy. I'm going in there.

CHAPTER
TWENTY-NINE

I watch the door close behind Tubs.

Assuming Liam already has a table for them inside, I decide to allow one minute for Tubs to go in and get settled. Then I'll enter and find my own table, hopefully close to them.

After a minute ticks by on my watch, I take one swift, fortifying breath and approach the door. When I step inside, I do my best to look around while also keeping my face shielded by my hat. If only wide brims were the style.

The diner is narrow but nice. Booths line the windows, and I spot Liam and Tubs seated at the farthest table from the door. Liam faces the entrance, but I keep my wig of dark hair like a shield between us and assess my own seating options.

A long counter runs the length of the diner, behind which waitresses in mint-green dresses and white aprons bustle about, taking plates of food from the pass-through into the kitchen and filling drinks at the soda fountain. There's a barstool open at the very end of the counter, which will put me only ten feet away from Liam and Tubs. That feels uncomfortably close, but it's also the best option for listening in on their conversation.

I walk to the empty barstool, keeping my face averted while I rummage through my leather shopping bag, as though in search of something. With my back to the men, I slide into the empty seat.

"It's just busy all the time these days," Liam says in his slightly nasal voice. "Makes the time pass quickly, I guess. Something to be said for that."

A waitress who looks to be in her forties appears in front of me with a roll of silverware. "Hi, honey. Know what you want, or do you need a menu?"

"A menu, thank you."

She passes a paper menu to me. "I'll be back to check on you in a minute."

". . . made me curious," Tubs is saying as I resume listening. "You haven't had your car too long, have you?"

There's a stretch of silence, and I shift slightly so I can see through my strands of hair. Liam has his elbows resting on the table, the thick muscles of his arms visible even beneath his suit. "I didn't really ask you here to talk about the car, Tubs."

Tubs looks away, and so do I.

"You fellas ready to order?" says a chipper new voice. "Oh, hi, Liam. How are you?"

"Doin' fine, thanks. How about you, Mabel?"

Mabel. The back of my neck prickles, and I turn slightly, hoping to catch a glimpse of her.

"Working a lot, but I'll have some time off over the holidays. You want your usual?"

"I'll just have coffee and a piece of cherry pie today," Liam says.

"Okay, how about you, Sir?"

"I'll have the same."

"Sure thing, boys," she says. A moment later, she appears in my peripheral vision, walking to another table. She has thick hair that shines coppery brown, but that's all I can see.

"If it's not about the car, then what is it?" Tubs's voice pitches higher than before, like he's nervous.

"Have you been talking to anybody about the thing we said we weren't going to talk about?"

There's a moment of silence in which I hold my breath, then Tubs says, "Of course not."

"Made a decision, honey?" the waitress asks.

I blink at her, and it takes me a moment to register what she asked. "Oh, uh—" I glance down at the menu. "Patty melt with fries," I say, the first item my eyes land on.

The waitress scribbles on her order pad. "And to drink?"

Liam says, "I just wondered is all."

"No, of course I haven't. Why would I?" Tubs still sounds nervous.

"To drink, Miss?" the waitress asks again, louder.

"Sorry." I hand the menu back. "Coca-Cola. Thank you."

"I don't know." Liam doesn't sound nervous. His voice is low and even. If I was sitting anywhere but here, I'm not sure I'd be able to hear him. "Maybe you got spooked by somebody."

I reach into my bag for my notebook, careful to keep the brim of my hat between me and Liam's line of sight. He's leaning forward, his elbows on the table, looking intimidating.

Tubs has a matchbook in his hand that he keeps rotating. "Finnegan, I have no idea what you're on about right now."

Liam pitches his voice lower. "Has anybody come around recently to talk to you about Clarence?"

"No. But I haven't been home a lot either. I've been at work or at the hospital with Polly."

"Really? Nobody? I mean, everybody knows you hated him, so I thought—"

"I didn't *hate* Clarence." Tubs runs a hand over his tired face. "He was an arrogant kid, and I never could figure out why O'Banion thought he was the cat's meow, but I didn't *hate* him."

"You told Banks you'd have fired him if he wasn't a pet of O'Banion's."

"I've fired a lot of people. Not because I hated them, but because they were rubbish at their jobs."

"But Clarence wasn't rubbish at his job, and you know it. *That* was the problem, wasn't it?"

Silence. My Coca-Cola sits fizzing in front of me, though I didn't notice it being delivered. Behind the counter, I watch the young waitress, Mabel, plate two pieces of cherry pie. This has to be the waitress Clarence took out, right? She looks to be in her early to mid-twenties. Pretty, but in a different way than Elzbieta. A heart-shaped face with freckles across her nose. More cute than beautiful.

Behind me, Tubs says, "C'mon, Finnegan, say it plain. What's going on?"

In Liam's next stretch of silence, Mabel loads the coffee cups onto the tray with the pies and lifts it without a wobble.

"Nobody has come to talk to you about Clarence?" Liam asks.

"No." Tubs sounds exasperated, and I can't blame him. "What is this about?"

"Here you go, boys. Two coffees and two cherry pies. And here's the cream and sugar. Anything else I can get for the two of you?"

"Looks great. Thanks, Mabel."

Mabel swishes away and within seconds is speaking to customers at a different table. Liam and Tubs are silent—or talking too quietly for me to hear—and I fight off the temptation to turn around and look.

Liam finally breaks the silence. "Did you know there's a private investigator looking into Clarence's death?"

I had been jotting a shorthand version of their conversation into my notebook, and now my pencil freezes on the page. The discomfort of wearing my hat over a wig seems to increase all at once, and my scalp is hot and itchy.

"What?" Tubs says with a disbelieving laugh. "How do you know that?"

I can scarcely hear their conversation over my pounding heart.

"Because she was at The Fox the other night. Goes by the name Virginia Chlebek, but her real name is Piper Sail."

My vision turns black around the edges, and I force myself to inhale. Basic functions like breathing and thinking are failing me. Did Elzbieta tell Liam? Why would she do that?

"You mean it's a *dame* looking into Clarence's death?"

"Yeah, but not just any dame. Her father is a big-deal attorney, and she fancies herself as some kind of detective. I guess the Dell family hired her, I don't know."

"How did you learn all this?"

"The night she was at The Fox, this guy came in. I wasn't gonna let him in because he wasn't saying any of the right things, and I knew he wasn't our sort. But then he got this real desperate look on his face, slipped me some cash, and asked if I knew if a girl named Piper Sail was inside."

My back teeth press together so hard, the pain threads through my jaw. *Jeremiah Crane, you numskull.*

"He told me this whole story about how her father was looking for her and he was real worried. I asked him to describe her, and when he did, she sounded like this girl Elz had introduced me to not ten minutes before. Only she didn't say her name was Piper Sail, she said it was Virginia."

"So Elz is the one who let her in The Fox?"

"I don't think she meant to. I think this girl pulled one over on Elz, saying she was looking for a job. When Elzbieta introduced her to me, the girl—Piper—claimed she knew Clarence. Said that was why she knew about The Fox in the first place."

"Wait, I'm confused. How did Piper know Clarence?"

"She didn't, I don't think. It was just a story to . . . I don't know. See what Elz and me said."

"Does Elz know?"

"I haven't told her yet."

There's silence for a moment.

Then Tubs asks, "You think it's about the money?"

"Here you go, hon." The waitress slides my plate in front of me, and I jump. "Sorry, didn't mean to startle you."

"It's fine," I say, the words a touch wheezy. "Thank you."

She looks at me with a mixture of caution and concern, like she thinks I might be mentally unbalanced. "Can I get you anything else?"

I shake my head and try to give her a normal smile, which I'm sure guarantees I look even more deranged.

". . . suicide, so they have to be after the money," Liam is saying when I'm able to listen again. "Right?"

"But the Dells are already rich as can be. Why would they come after us?"

"That's just how rich people are. It's never enough." There's a pause and then Liam continues, "Except for Clarence, that is. He didn't have much patience for greed." His tone turns somber. "I can still picture his face when he confronted me. Sure wish I could do that conversation over again."

"I'm sorry it happened like it did," Tubs says. "I didn't like the guy, but even so."

They're silent for a bit, and I steady my breathing enough to pick up my Coca-Cola without worrying that I'm going to knock it over.

"Just watch yourself," Liam says after a bit. "I saw her again a couple nights ago. She's not a total bunny, but I wouldn't say she's smart either. Probably just smart enough to be a liability."

Tubs grunts. "Just like Clarence, huh?"

"Yeah," Liam says in a grim voice. "Just like Clarence."

CHAPTER
THIRTY

"I don't like this." Mariano wags his head slowly. "I really don't like this."

"I know."

My hands have finally stopped shaking, so that's something. As soon as Liam and Tubs cleared out of the diner, I picked at my food, left a large tip for the poor waitress who had to deal with me, and then walked the long way around to Father's car. I sped away from Liam's building as fast as the law allowed and drove straight to Mariano's office.

He leans back in his chair, his eyes unfocused as he thinks. "If they didn't actually work together to kill Clarence, they worked together on *something*."

"That's sure what it sounded like. It sounded like Liam was involved in something—something *with* Tubs—and Clarence confronted Liam about it." My brain feels like a beehive, thoughts buzzing all around, trying to make something of what I've collected. "Maybe it's related to the skimming that Tubs was doing? Maybe Liam was skimming too? Whatever it was, it was related to money, because Liam said all this after talking about Clarence not being greedy. Maybe the missing five hundred dollars is related?"

Mariano's gaze sharpens again and lands on me. "I know you don't want to hear this, but I think you should walk away from this case, Piper."

I shake my head. "I'm so close."

"I know. And if Liam didn't know who you really are, then it might be different. But he *does* know who you really are."

"Stupid Jeremiah," I mutter.

Mariano grimaces. "He thought he was helping."

"My father," I say. "He thought he was helping my father, not *me*."

Mariano's head tilts slightly as he thinks about this. "I imagine he thought it was for your own good. Probably thought he was rescuing you."

"I don't need rescuing."

Mariano places his elbows on his desk, disturbing the official-looking forms he'd been filling out when I arrived, and smiles at me. "We all need rescuing sometimes."

"Well, I didn't need it right *then*."

"You know what I need?" Mariano reaches for his homburg. "Food. Do you have time for those cannoli I promised you?"

Fifteen minutes later, we've left his paperwork and Father's car behind at the detective bureau and Mariano drives us along Taylor Street on our way to Ferrara's Bakery for my first cannolo—which Mariano informs me is Italian for just one, but he also says I will likely eat several cannoli once I have a taste.

"Do you know you have an Italian accent only when you say words like *cannoli* and *ricotta*?" I ask.

"That's not true. I just pronounce them correctly, unlike you. Like how you say *Parmesan* wrong."

I frown. "I do not."

He grins at me. "You say Parma-shan. The correct way is Parma-zan."

However you say Parmesan, Taylor Street in Little Italy smells divinely of that and baking bread and slow-simmered sauces. My stomach gives a hungry lurch.

"I think you'll love Ferrara's," Mariano says as he takes my hand and leads me toward a store with a window display full of lovely boules of bread, cookies in unfamiliar shapes, and elaborate cakes. "And I think the cannoli are going to be the best part of your day."

I squeeze his hand. "You don't think it'll be you?"

"No. I think the cannoli will edge me out."

I grin up at him, but he isn't looking at me. He's looking ahead, a smile frozen on his face. I follow his gaze to a young woman emerging from Ferrara's, pushing a pram. When she locks eyes with Mariano, I know I'm looking at Zola Capecce. Or rather, Zola Cassano.

"This is a surprise." Her dark eyes travel from Mariano's face to our joined hands to my face, all within a second. "You must be Piper. I've heard so much about you. I'm Zola."

She speaks so warmly—much warmer than I would've expected—and I tell myself to do the same. I release Mariano's hand to shake hers. "Nice to finally meet you."

She grasps my hand tightly, like we're already friends and just haven't discovered it yet. She's pretty, with skin a little darker than Mariano's and thick lashes framing her wide-set eyes.

Zola angles the pram so I can see inside. "And this is Evalina."

"Beautiful," I say, because that's what you say when someone shows you their baby. With Evalina's hat pulled down to her eyebrows and her blanket up to her chin, I really can't see much of her. She's awake, and has a tiny fist shoved in her mouth that she's sucking on. She isn't *not* beautiful, for a baby.

"It's funny we're just now meeting." Zola's gaze slides to

Mariano and she smiles at him, which makes something in my chest burn in a way that I don't like. "I was beginning to think Mariano made you up."

I laugh with more enthusiasm than I feel. "No, I'm real."

Her dimpled smile shifts back to me. "I was so sorry that you couldn't come to the wedding. I know you can't help being sick, but—"

"What are you picking up?" Mariano gestures to the Ferrara's box, tucked in a basket beneath the bundled baby.

"Amaretti, of course. For Christmas." She glances at me. "I wish you were able to come to Christmas dinner. Of course, we all understand you have your own family, but I was hoping it would work out for you to join us."

Zola hasn't even finished her sentence when Mariano begins steering me away, beneath the green awning, toward the door for Ferrara's. "We need to get going," Mariano says. "Good to see you."

"Nice meeting you!" Zola calls after me, and then pushes the pram away down Taylor Street as if the three of us all just had a lovely conversation.

My mind gallops at such a speed, I can hardly grab hold of a thought and think it through properly. She's sorry I couldn't come to the wedding. Sorry I can't be at Christmas dinner. So I've been invited to all these things . . . and Mariano is keeping me away. My hand feels clammy within Mariano's grasp, and I tug it free.

I'm dimly aware that it smells like vanilla and almond inside Ferrara's. That the display of pastry and bread options in front of me is diverse and beautiful. But it's as though all my senses are wrapped in a film, and I can't absorb anything.

"So that was Zola," I say.

"It was." Mariano sounds as stunned as I feel. "There are probably some things I should explain to you."

A dry laugh scrapes across my throat. "Probably."

"Piper, I can imagine what you're thinking, and—"

"Mariano! *Ciao!*"

He turns to the woman behind the counter, who reaches across to grab his hand. She has a crinkled smile and dark hair pulled back in a bun at the nape of her neck.

"Mrs. Ferrara, *come stai?*"

"*Bene. Molto bene. E tu?*"

"*Ci. Bene.*" He releases Mrs. Ferrara's hand and gestures to me. "This is Piper Sail. Piper, this is Serafina Ferrara. Best baker in Little Italy."

I try to smile. I think I say that it's nice to meet her. My mind is still consumed with Zola's words out on the sidewalk. *I was so sorry you couldn't come to the wedding. I wish you were able to come to Christmas dinner.*

Mariano and Mrs. Ferrara speak in Italian as she loads several cylindrical cookies into a white box. I move to the display in the window, as though I'm absorbed by the different types of baked goods. Any other time, I would be. *I know you can't help being sick*, Zola had said. Is that what she was told? Because the truth is, I didn't even know she and Alessandro had gotten married until a month after the fact.

Mariano chose to shut me out of that part of his life. Almost as if he's ashamed of me.

Mariano's touch is featherlight on my arm "You ready?"

I nod.

Mrs. Ferrara calls, "*Buonasera!*" as we exit, but I don't turn around.

Outside, Mariano opens the passenger door and I climb inside without thanking him or meeting his eyes. The shock is melting away into a pool of anger.

Mariano gets behind the steering wheel. He sits with the white bakery box on his lap, his eyes straight ahead, and his mouth shut.

"Zola said—" My throat suddenly aches in the way it does right before I cry. I breathe deeply until the sensation passes. "Zola said she was sorry that I wasn't able to be at the wedding."

Mariano nods. I wait for him to say more, but he doesn't.

"I was invited to the wedding, but you told them I was sick and couldn't come. And you didn't even tell me the wedding was happening."

For a moment, I don't think Mariano is going to respond to this either, but finally he says, "Yes. And then I did the same with Christmas dinner. Papa asked if you would be joining us this year, and I told him your family dinner was at the same time."

The ache returns to my throat. "Why?"

Mariano continues to look straight ahead, and with the brim of his hat casting a shadow, I can't make out his expression. All I can see is the hard line of his jaw. "Because I didn't want you there."

Well, there we go. I was right. He's ashamed of me.

I try to think of a way to respond that isn't as embarrassing as crying, but I might not have a choice. "And why not?"

"Because it all feels very . . ." Mariano pushes his hat off and scratches his head. "It feels like inviting you to one of my doctor's appointments or something."

"What?"

He sighs. "Like it would be too personal."

I gape at him. "The idea of me attending a family wedding or coming to Christmas dinner feels 'too personal'?"

He stops scratching and jams his hat back onto his head. "It's hard to explain."

"Please try." My throat aches so badly, I can barely talk. "Because you have seen me at my lowest of lows—but having me around your family somehow feels too personal?"

He swallows, and I watch his Adam's apple travel down his throat and back up. "That's different."

"I don't see how. Do you not trust me?"

"Of course I trust you, I just . . ." He tightens his tie, and I have to stop myself from reaching over and loosening it. "I don't want there to be *more* reasons we shouldn't be together. I know your father and Jane are hoping I'm some kind of phase for you."

"What?" The word is more air than sound. "That's not true."

"It is."

"No, it's not. And even if it was true—which it isn't—I wouldn't care."

"You might think that now, but that could change . . ."

I roll my eyes. "Why would that change? Father thinks you're wonderful."

"He doesn't, Piper. Or at least, he doesn't think I'm wonderful *for you.*"

"He's never said anything like that to me."

Mariano tightens his tie again, and this time I reach over and loosen the knot. "You're going to choke yourself. Stop that."

Mariano leans back against the headrest. "Your father is in a very tricky position, with *my* father being his primary client and all." Mariano's face is resolute, as though this isn't subjective. As though he's just reporting facts to me.

"This is all your opinion. Do you have any actual evidence?"

A smile cracks his serious face. "You sound like my boss."

"Well, do you? Because this just sounds like conjecture to me."

"Herein lie the perils of dating a lawyer's daughter." Mariano's smile fades. "I overheard a conversation between your father and Jane. Jane didn't approve of me, and your father said he didn't either, but he also couldn't afford to upset my father. He assumed you'd come to your senses, especially if Jeremiah persisted. He's a nice fellow, after all. Good family."

The ache returns to my throat. "When did you hear all this?"

His eyes briefly graze my scars. "While you were still recovering."

"That was months ago. Why didn't you tell me?"

He shrugs.

"Well, who are they to judge? I don't much approve of *their* relationship, so we're even."

Mariano shrugs again. "I can understand your father's perspective." When I make a scoffing noise, he says, "I'm serious. You're from a family of lawyers. You live in the Astor Street District. You have a private school education. Piper, I make eighteen hundred dollars a year. I will never, ever be able to take care of you the way someone like Jeremiah can."

"I don't need to be taken care of," I snap. "I don't care how much you make or who your family is. It doesn't change the fact that I love you."

As is often the case, my mouth was moving faster than my brain. The words, which I yelled, reverberate in the car.

I swallow and look away. "I didn't mean to yell."

"That's okay." Mariano's voice is warm like flannel. "I love you too."

My cheeks feel hot, and I can't seem to look him in the eyes. "You don't have to say that just because I did."

"Piper, what in our history makes you think I feel pressured to tell you that I love you? I've never been anything but honest with you. Do you believe that?"

I swallow. "I do . . . mostly. When I found out from Jack that your brother and Zola got married, it just made me wonder if there were other secrets you were keeping from me."

I'm not looking directly at him, but I still see his shoulders bow forward. For a moment, he doesn't say anything, and then finally he says a quiet, "Okay. That's fair."

"And I thought perhaps you weren't open about it because you still—" I swallow hard and force myself onward. "Have feelings for her."

"Piper." Mariano sounds hurt. "Of course not."

A laugh scrapes out of my throat. "Of course not? Mariano, you were engaged. And she's the one who broke it off, as my brother likes to remind me. Why is it so crazy to think you might have feelings for her?"

"Will you look at me, please?"

I hesitate and then lift my gaze to him. His expression is serious. Sincere.

"I don't have feelings for her at all. I promise. I'm so sorry I made you suspect otherwise."

My throat aches as I resist crying. "Okay," I say. "It's just that you were engaged to her, and it isn't that I want to be engaged"—my face heats at the thought that he might think I'm fishing for a ring—"but you'd never even said you loved me, so I started wondering if maybe you still cared for her."

"No." His fingers link through mine. "It's more that I'm hoping for a different result with you than with Zola, so I'm going about things differently. More slowly. I'm sorry I made you doubt."

We sit quietly in the car while people walk up and down Taylor Street. "I believe what you said about Father and Jane," I say quietly, "but I'm not so much worried about them splitting us up as I am about the distance you're putting between me and your family. Next time they invite me to something, can we please decide together if I should go?"

"Yes." Mariano nods. "We can decide together."

Seconds tick by, maybe minutes. My hand grows sweaty against his. "Can we please eat the cannoli now?"

I brave a glance his direction and am rewarded with his smile.

"Yes," he says. "But first."

Mariano leans forward and kisses me.

The cannoli, while delicious, do *not* edge him out, but it's a close second for the best part of my day.

When Mariano and I return to the detective bureau, I hesitate before getting out of the car.

"I liked Zola," I say. "I wouldn't have expected that, but I did."

Mariano goes still. "Okay."

"I assumed she'd be . . ." I gesture with my hand, even though I'm not sure what I'm trying to say. "I don't know. Not likable. But that's silly. Obviously, you asked her to marry you for a reason."

"Because we'd grown up together and everyone expected it," Mariano says. "Because back then, I thought that the life our families had was what I wanted."

That following in his father's footsteps was ever attractive to Mariano is news to me. I knew he'd been raised with the expectation he'd take over the family business, but I didn't know that it had ever appealed to him.

"What changed your mind?"

"I wasn't good at it. And every job I did for my father felt . . . distasteful."

I don't ask what kind of jobs.

Mariano is quiet for a minute, maybe more. "Right after Prohibition started, Papa and Uncle Lucas had us help them distribute shipments. It was me and some of my older cousins, including Matteo. Matteo was a few years older than me, and I grew up admiring him. He was great. You would've loved him."

This story won't end pretty. I reach out and take Mariano's hand.

"This happened in April of twenty, so you have to remember it was still early on. Back when the Prohibition agents actually tried to arrest gangsters rather than only taking bribes and turning away. We were sorting some new inventory when the raid started, and Matteo got shot as we were scrambling to get out of there." Mariano squeezes my hand but keeps rolling with the story. "My other cousins, they ran for the car. There was no hesitation about leaving Matteo there, no attempt to take care of him. All they cared about was getting out of there before they got nabbed too. And I— I got in the car to go with them."

He shakes his head, as though chastising the young version of himself. I run my thumb over his and wish I could think of something comforting to say that doesn't also sound trite.

"As we drove away, I turned to look, and there was a policeman sitting with Matteo. Police were the enemy. I grew up hating them, But I watched this one take Matteo's hand, cross himself, and—I don't know for certain, of course, but I think he gave my cousin last rites."

"Last rites?"

Mariano nods. "It's a Catholic sacrament for when we're close to death. If there's time, you get a priest. You give a last confession. You receive the Eucharist. There's an anointing. But if there's not time, like with Matteo, then someone else can at least say it."

"Say what?"

Mariano inhales deeply and says in a clear, authoritative voice, "'You loved him greatly in this life; now that he is freed from all its cares, give him happiness and peace forever. Welcome him now into paradise, where there will be no more sorrow, no more weeping or pain, but only peace and joy with Jesus, your son.'"

For a moment, I can't speak. "That's beautiful. I don't think we have anything like that in my church."

Mariano's smile is grim. "I memorized it when I made my decision to join the force. Watching the policeman sit with Matteo that day, as the rest of us abandoned him there, I realized that I had a choice. I could be the type of person who worked in the dark and fled under fire, or I could be the type of person who worked in the light and rushed in to help. As soon as I turned eighteen, I enrolled in the academy."

He shrugs as if this isn't some incredible feat of strength that he just described to me. As if it didn't cost him his family, his fiancée, and the only life he'd ever known.

"I can only imagine how hard it was to tell your family what you'd decided."

Mariano considers this. "I think I told you before that they were surprised, but for a while they thought my position could work to their advantage. When I made it clear that I was on the side of the law, not their side, they stopped wanting me around." He releases a long, slow sigh, like a tire gradually losing pressure. "I was naïve about the whole thing, now that I look back on it. I thought if they could see another way, they would want it too. Like they just didn't know there was this other way of viewing the world. That was dumb of me."

"I don't think it's dumb to want good things for people."

Mariano's eyes warm, but only for a fleeting moment. "I thought if Zola and I were engaged, that would make a difference. And it did for a little while, but it also didn't take long for Zola and me to realize that we weren't who we were in high school anymore. She was the brave one who ended it." The corners of his mouth lift in a humorless smile. "She said she didn't even know who I was anymore, which was so funny that I actually laughed. I had never felt more like myself."

He turns to me. "Even when it was happening, I felt a little relieved. I knew by then that we weren't good for each other."

In a way, it's not so different from how I feel about Jeremiah. Yes, for a time, he seemed perfect for me, and if my life had stayed on course, maybe he would've been. But that's not what happened.

"My family is hard for me to talk about." Mariano squeezes my hand. "But I really messed up by not telling you what was going on. And I know I need to be better, because you deserve to know." His expression turns grim. "You should know who you're involved with."

"Mariano, don't you worry about that." I rest my forehead against his. "I know who I'm involved with."

CHAPTER
THIRTY-ONE

If I drive back to Georgie's now, I can speak to Mabel.

Of course, less than two hours ago, Mariano told me he thought I should drop this case. That Liam knowing who I am changes things. I see his point, but I also can't walk away when I'm so close to gaining new information. I have to find out what Mabel knows, and if I don't go back to Georgie's now, when will I get another chance to speak with her?

Georgie's Diner is only half full now that the lunch hour has passed. I take the booth that Liam and Tubs occupied not long ago, and a minute later Mabel approaches with a smile and a menu.

"Hi, there." Mabel hands me the menu and glances at the empty seat across from me. "Will someone be joining you?"

"No." I take the menu but lay it flat on the table without looking at it. "I'm actually here to speak to you. Do you know someone named Clarence Dell?"

Mabel's sunny smile freezes. "Clarence? Yes." The smile is gone now, replaced by a look of wariness. "Why?"

I nod. "My name is Piper Sail, and I work for a private investigator. Do you have a break coming up? Because I'd like to ask you some questions, if you don't mind."

Mabel swallows hard and nods. "We're pretty quiet in here now. I'll ask Edith if she can cover my tables."

A few minutes later, Mabel returns with two coffees and a self-conscious smile. "I have about ten minutes. Is that enough?"

"Sure. Thanks for taking time to talk to me."

Mabel sinks into the booth across from me. Her pale face has become even paler, making the sweep of freckles across her nose stand out. "Are you investigating Clarence's death?"

I nod. "What can you tell me?"

"I barely knew him." Mabel pulls one of the mugs of coffee in front of her and drops in a sugar cube. "We only went out one time. When he didn't call me in the next few days, I thought maybe I'd read the situation wrong. That he didn't like me as much as I thought. I had no clue he'd died until nearly a week later when a friend of his—Liam, he's how Clarence and I met—was in here and told me what had happened."

She adds another sugar cube and a long pour of cream to her coffee.

I reach for mine, even though I don't particularly want it. "Do you mind if I take notes on our conversation?"

Mabel shakes her head.

"Thank you." I pull my notebook from my bag as I ask, "What did Liam say happened?"

"He told me Clarence had taken his own life." Mabel stirs her coffee, and the spoon bumping against the ceramic makes a light tinkling sound. "I wanted to laugh. Maybe I actually did. I don't know, I was so shocked. I guess that's normal?"

Mabel looks to me, like she's wanting me to confirm this.

"Death often feels surprising," I say. "Which is strange, I suppose, considering the statistics."

A corner of her mouth quirks. "True. None of us make it out of here alive, do we?" Her mouth flattens once more. "I was telling a girlfriend about it later, because her mother had done herself in. My friend said it was normal to be shocked, to think there was no way he'd have done something like that. She said that's how it felt when she found out too, and then it wore off and she started to remember things. Signs of what her mother was considering, I mean." Mabel presses her teeth into her lower lip. "Maybe if I'd known him longer, I would've seen things too, but I just never got over thinking it didn't fit."

"You're not alone in that." I sip my coffee, which tastes weak though the warmth is nice. "Do you mind telling me about your date?"

Mabel continues to stir her coffee. I'm beginning to doubt she'll ever actually drink it. "He took me to Le Petit Gourmet for dinner—"

"What day was this?"

"It was a Tuesday night. The twenty-eighth or twenty-ninth, I don't remember."

"What was his mood like on the date?"

"Well . . ." Mabel lays her spoon on her saucer. "It started off a little strange, honestly, because I could tell Clarence was distracted. It felt like he was *trying* to have a good time rather than actually having a good time. I wanted to say something, but that felt awkward. First date and all. Then he finally said that he'd learned something upsetting about one of his closest friends. He was trying to make a decision about what to do. He couldn't decide if he should confront him directly or speak to authorities."

My pencil moves swiftly across the page and the back of my neck prickles with the importance of this information. I know what Clarence chose—he chose to confront that friend directly, because just a few hours ago I'd heard Liam tell Tubs about it. *I can still picture his face when he confronted me*, Liam had said.

"And what did you say?" I ask.

"It's hard to remember exactly what I said. Something about how that sounded pretty serious. I mean, I can't remember a single time that I've had a conflict with a friend and wondered if I should involve *authorities*. I said maybe he should just start with talking to his friend."

I nod as I write this. "Did he say anything else about the nature of the conflict? About the friend?"

She shakes her head. "No. After that, he didn't seem bothered anymore, and we had a nice time together. We went and saw *Peter Pan*, then we talked about plans for the upcoming weekend. He said he'd be working, but maybe the next week we could go out again." Mabel curves her hands around her mug. "I guess that's why him dying by suicide just didn't seem right to me."

I skim over my notes as I think. "While you were out together, did either of you see anyone that you knew?"

"No." Mabel frowns. "Why?"

"Did he tell you he'd recently ended a relationship?"

Her frown deepens. "Yes, but we didn't talk about it much. I was also just out of a bad relationship."

My ears prick at that word *bad*. "Did Clarence say he was coming out of a bad relationship?"

"He didn't use the word *bad*."

"Do you remember what he said?"

Mabel nods, her auburn hair swishing with the motion. "He said he ended things when he discovered she wasn't who he thought she was."

Mabel's answers to my questions continue to bounce around my head as holiday festivities crowd my schedule. Christmas Eve and Christmas Day pass by in a lovely blur of church services, special foods, and a fresh covering of snow.

Nick, Tim, Gretchen, and Howie stay overnight on Christmas Eve, so Christmas morning feels like one from childhood, the house loud and warm. We sit around the tree, still dressed in our nightclothes, and pass around brightly wrapped packages. In some ways, it's the merriest Christmas we've had in recent years.

But even as I'm laughing and smiling, the moments feel touched by melancholy, as having Jane in the house causes my thoughts to regularly wander to my mother. I imagine her sitting here with us, expressing delight over having us all together. How she might've laughed when Tim demonstrated Howie's new jack-in-a-box and Howie burst into tears. Or how she would've fawned over the thick red scarf and mittens Gretchen knit to keep me warm on walks with Sidekick. How Mother would have snuck off to the kitchen to put breakfast rolls in the oven, so they'd be warm when we were done opening gifts.

Even so, having Jane do all those things instead of my mother doesn't feel as painful as it once might have.

Nick, Tim, and Tim's family depart late Christmas afternoon. Soon after, Jane goes upstairs to lie down and Father retreats to his office. I take the opportunity to shut myself into my bedroom and review the notes I took at Georgie's Diner, both during Liam and Tubs's conversation and my interview with Mabel.

Even if I decide to persist with unraveling the confusing

death of Clarence Dell—despite Mariano's warning—there's no way around the fact that approaching Liam will be different from here on out. And after Liam told Tubs not to talk to anyone, I can't imagine Tubs will fall for any kind of story I feed him in hopes of gleaning information about Clarence.

And now I have these additional insights from Mabel: Clarence was going to confront somebody—or possibly go to the police. Plus, he'd ended his relationship with Elzbieta because of something he *discovered*. This aligns with what Louisa said—that Clarence had seemed to care about her a lot, until he suddenly didn't.

I vacillate between reading over my case notes, adding note-cards to the back of my closet door, and puzzling over Clarence's financial records and the other items in the banker's box Louisa gave me. Maybe it's time to see if I've gathered enough suspicious evidence that the police would reopen Clarence's case?

Hours later, I'm staring at the card that says *$500?* when I hear Jane calling up the stairs for me. "Piper! Telephone call!"

I clatter down the stairs and find Jane at the bottom, holding a mug of something steaming and looking a bit green in the face. "Are you sick?" I ask.

She smiles wanly. "No, I'm with child."

"Oh, right." I hesitate. "Could I get you crackers or something?"

Her smile warms. "That's very thoughtful, but you'd better take your call first. It's Hannah LeVine."

"Thank you," I say as I rush off to Father's office. I grab hold of the telephone and bring it close to my mouth. "Hannah?"

"I have information for you."

Blast. I don't have my notebook with me. "Yes?"

"I've spoken to Daddy, and he has a lot to say about arsenic poisoning. Firstly, he says arsenic is very common for suicide because it's, well, so common. Do you know all the products you can find arsenic in? It's amazing in a horrifying kind of way."

I pull a piece of Father's stationery from his top desk drawer. "Clarence supposedly used rat poison," I say quietly so my voice won't carry to Jane in the living room.

"I remembered Louisa telling me that, so I asked specifically about rat poison—"

"You did?" I can't keep the alarm from my voice. "What did you tell your father this was for?"

"Never you mind," Hannah says brusquely. "I promise I was discreet, and he had no clue this was for a case you're working on."

"But why else would he think you'd be asking about—"

"Do you want my information or not, Piper?"

I bite the side of my lip as I look at the piece of paper. "Well, I *do* want it. I'm just concerned—"

"I'm telling you that doesn't need to be a concern. Arsenic comes in several more-diluted forms, but rat poison is concentrated, so it's particularly common in suicide cases."

"How long does it take to work?"

"It depends on the dosage. Lower-level poisonings will lead to something Daddy called 'gastro issues.' Lots of vomiting and diarrhea. He said with that, it could take multiple weeks to die."

I frown as I write this. "But that's not what happened."

"Yes, I know. A high dosage takes only a few hours. There would still be stomach pains, vomiting, and the like, but it would all happen much quicker. The complication with the higher dose in a murder, Daddy says, is that the victim is more likely to notice taking it."

I'm tempted to again ask Hannah how she could discuss this

so openly and yet be confident of how discreet she was, but I dismiss the idea. "But I thought it didn't have a taste."

"It isn't invisible, though. The murderer couldn't just add it to a glass of scotch, like in Clarence's case, because it would be cloudy. I suppose it's possible it wouldn't be cloudy enough for Clarence to notice, but if it killed him that quickly, it probably was. Unless he really did poison himself, that is. Then it wouldn't matter because it didn't need to be disguised. Daddy says with murder, arsenic is more likely to be mixed into something with substance. Like hot cocoa or cider, a berry pie, or maybe a stew of some kind."

My throat seems to go dry. "What about a chocolate cream pie?"

"Sure," Hannah says. "I don't see why not."

The next afternoon, my thoughts still swirl with what Hannah told me. Daniel had said there were traces of arsenic in the glass, but maybe it was too small of a dosage, so the murderer poisoned the pie too? Or maybe they added the poison to the glass after the fact to cover their tracks?

Of course, there's no way to prove that there was arsenic in the pie that Louisa gave her brother in addition to it being in the scotch glass. And if either Liam or Tubs is the murderer, how would they have poisoned the pie? They would've needed to be in Clarence's apartment, and surely he would have noticed them mixing arsenic into his slice of pie. Could they have broken in when he wasn't there?

Who else had access to it? Just Clarence and Daniel. But when Daniel left the apartment, Clarence was still there, so

Clarence would have seen him do it. Besides, Daniel has no motive as far as I can ascertain.

Elzbieta was at the apartment the evening before, though. This thought mingles with Mabel's words several days ago—how Clarence had discovered something that made it clear Elz wasn't who he thought she was. Was his discovery something Elzbieta didn't want others to know about either? When she was at the apartment during their fight, could she have mixed arsenic into the pie, knowing that Clarence would eat it eventually? That would mean that she knew the pie belonged to Clarence, that there was no chance of Daniel eating it, and that she had an opportunity to do that while at his apartment. I have a hard time imagining Elzbieta taking the risk, banking on all of that coming together for her.

A long walk is what my brain needs.

I put on my coat, clip Sidekick's leash in place, and head out onto Astor Street. The fresh snow is powdery beneath my boots, and despite the bright sun suspended in the cloudless sky, the cold makes my nose burn. I'm walking along Burton Street when I spot Daniel Becker approaching.

I wrap Sidekick's leash around my hand, anticipating his growl, and call, "Hi, Daniel."

Daniel smiles his characteristic closed-mouth smile. "I'm just on my way to your house."

I keep my friendly smile fixed in place despite how concern sparks in my chest. Why would he be coming to my house? "I wasn't aware that you knew where I lived."

"I looked you up. I need to speak with you."

Sidekick growls, and I tighten the leash. "Sorry, he's afraid of people. And I'm afraid of dogs. It's why the two of us get along so well."

Daniel gives Sidekick a wary look and keeps his distance. "I've never been a fan of dogs either, actually." He looks from Sidekick to me. "I spent some of the day with the Dells. That's why I'm here."

Sidekick growls again, and I pat his head. "He'll be fine if we walk. Do you mind?"

"Not at all." Daniel gestures that I should lead the way. "I was disappointed to hear that Louisa still doesn't believe Clarence killed himself."

"Yes, I know you were hoping that she would feel more convinced after learning about the cheating at Loyola."

"Miss Sail." Daniel stops walking and turns to face me, his expression solemn. "In light of Louisa's persistence, I have extra information about Clarence that I feel I must tell you."

Something about his tone makes my heart feel heavy. "Yes?"

Sidekick takes the opportunity to thoroughly investigate the base of the streetlamp, but he keeps an eye on Daniel as he fishes inside his coat pocket.

"You might hear this and ask why I didn't tell you before. I knew it could be helpful for you and your boss, but I didn't want word to get back to the Dells. They're a good family, and they've been through so much." Daniel meets my eyes. "I feel it's important for you to know this, but I also must insist on your discretion."

Dread lies thick in my throat. "I don't want to hurt the Dell family either."

"I believe you." Daniel takes his hat off, and the gesture elevates the moment to one of reverence. "You should know that the letter Louisa showed you is a fake."

For a moment, I'm sure I've misunderstood. "You mean *the* letter? Clarence's letter?"

"Yes, *the* letter. The one Clarence left when he died. I know it's fake, because . . ." He takes in a deep breath and releases it. "Because I'm the one who wrote it."

For weeks, that letter has bothered me. So vague, so unlike Clarence. Now an explanation is being handed to me, but I can't seem to grasp it any more than I can grasp a handful of water.

"*You* wrote it?"

He presses his hat back onto his head. "I don't feel good about that, but if you'd seen the original letter Clarence wrote, that's what you would've done too."

"Tell me more." My fingers itch to write this down, but I settle for wrapping Sidekick's leash around my hand.

"In the original letter, Clarence blamed his family for his decision. He said that his parents turned their backs on him when he was suspended from Loyola. That the way they treated him is what led to his decision." Daniel stuffs his hands into his pockets and looks at me, a pleading look. "You see why I had to do what I did?"

I inhale deeply as I think. I can well imagine the shock of it all—first finding Clarence dead, and then finding a letter like that. A letter that Daniel knew would inflict a lifetime of pain on people he cared about. Pain piled on top of the pain they were about to feel from Clarence ending his own life.

"Yes," I say softly. "I can understand that. But how did you make the handwriting so convincing? Neither Louisa nor I ever questioned that it was Clarence's handwriting."

Daniel looks away. His ears have turned red. "It wasn't hard. Our handwriting was already similar—the consequence of being trained by the same handwriting teachers. I made sure to keep it short, and I checked it against some writing samples in his room. I hoped if I was off a little bit, people might chalk it up to Clarence not being himself in those final hours.

"I'm sorry I didn't tell you earlier. It would've saved you a lot of time." He winces at this, as though that's an equally grievous part of the whole thing—my wasted time. "But I didn't know if I could trust you, and I was so worried about word getting back to the Dells."

"What happened to the original letter?"

"I burned it. Just seemed safest."

I nod slowly. I can see the sense in that, because otherwise there would always be the risk of the letter finding its way back to the Dells. Still. I would've really liked to have seen that original letter.

"I know I shouldn't have done that." Daniel kicks at the ground. "Probably makes you think *I'm* suspicious. And for what it's worth, I do hold myself responsible for his death. If I'd just been paying closer attention."

I should probably say something comforting, but my mind is preoccupied with all those questions posted on the back of my closet door. Of all the places in the city I went in the name of discovering the truth. The Fox, Ireland's Oyster House, Loyola, Georgie's Diner. Is it possible that all that time, the simplest explanation was the truth: Clarence really did take his own life? That the police were right, but the confusion happened because Daniel muddied the waters when he tried to protect the Dell family, and Louisa idolized her brother too much to accept the truth of who he was?

Sidekick strains at the leash, pulling me from my thoughts. "I appreciate you telling me. I'll speak to my boss."

Daniel gives one efficient nod. "Again, I'm sorry for my lack of candor up front. It would've saved all of us time."

"You told us now. That's what matters."

He touches the brim of his hat in a farewell. "Good luck in the New Year, Miss Sail."

"You as well, Mr. Becker."

He turns on his heel, heading back in the direction of the L station, and Sidekick and I press on, just the two of us.

This might still be murder, right? What Daniel said doesn't change the unaccounted for five hundred dollars, or the conversation I overheard between Liam and Tubs, or Clarence telling Mabel he needed to confront a close friend about something. It doesn't change the fact Clarence had discovered something unsavory enough about Elzbieta that he immediately called off their relationship, and they fought loudly the day before he died.

This could absolutely still be murder. Maybe the long suicide note that Daniel burned was fake as well, only he was just too distraught—having just discovered Clarence's dead body—to realize it? That's plausible, right?

Jeremiah's words come back to me. *I know ever since Lydia died, you've felt confused and lost.*

Or maybe, loathe as I am to admit it, Jeremiah was closer to the truth than I'd like. Maybe the problem is that, much like Louisa, I'm clinging to the idea of murder because if it really was suicide, then not only is the case closed, but there was never even a case at all.

CHAPTER
THIRTY-TWO

Daniel could be lying.

I reach up for the notecard—*If Clarence planned to kill himself, why did he buy socks and toothpaste?*—and release it from my closet door with a *pop*.

That's what Mariano asked when I spoke to him about it on the phone. "Do you think he's lying?"

But I don't think he is. I think he really did write that fake suicide note.

The questions flutter to the floor, one after another. *Where did the $500 go? Did Clarence ever say anything to Tubs about his stealing?* I'm not convinced any of them matter. Maybe there aren't even answers to all of them. Maybe Clarence himself wouldn't be able to explain why he bought socks and toothpaste the day before he took his own life.

I don't know. What I *do* know is that when you're looking into the lives of others, they're not going to make perfect sense. The facts aren't going to fit together like the pieces of a jigsaw puzzle, just like I can't make myself fit into the role of a secret investigator. Even if stripping away all my polite, Astor Street upbringing and digging into an investigation makes me feel— oddly and inexplicably—most like myself. It doesn't matter. Because facts are facts. And the fact is, I'm not a real investigator.

I scrape the worthless cards into a pile and dump them in my wastebasket. "Case closed."

As the 1924 calendar comes down off my wall and the 1925 calendar goes up, the box of Clarence's belongings continues to sit under my bed. I know I need to return everything to Louisa, but if I tell her I'm done with Clarence's case, I will also have to tell her *why*. And I'm not ready to have that conversation yet.

I know when school resumes next week, I won't be able to put it off any longer. Louisa will come find me in the office, and she'll want to know if I have any new information for her, and I'll have to tell her *something*. Which is why I keep pulling out the box and leafing through the yearbooks, the financial records, the family photos. Trying to find some way to make the answer easier. No luck so far.

I stare at the letter Clarence supposedly left behind that was actually penned by Daniel. I hold it alongside Clarence's financial records and see that he did an excellent job with his forgery, even if the words themselves were too vague to be Clarence's.

Although . . .

I tilt my head and study the *+$500 Dean, for services rendered* entry. Then I flip to where I know I'll find an even less-detailed entry: *−$500*. Clarence could sometimes be vague when doing so served someone else, like Dean O'Banion. He doesn't mention him by full name here.

I tap the *−$500*. "I wish I knew where you went."

I frown at the entry. It's written in blue pen, not black, like the other entries with the same date. Like it was added at a different time.

I scan the entries above—groceries, Woolworth's, movie with Elz, dinner with Elz.

I scan the entries below—Sears, movie with Daniel, groceries, CTA pass, dinner with Elz. The dinner with Elz, which is also the last ever dinner with Elz, is the only other entry written in blue pen.

My mind hums with the implications.

Maybe it's nothing. And maybe I don't even need to follow up on this, because I was hired to find out who killed Clarence, not where this five hundred dollars went, or why Clarence ended their relationship. But . . .

But nothing. I'm going to leave this alone. I reload the financial record in the box and secure the lid. This case is closed.

That lasts about two minutes before I hurry down the stairs to Father's office to make a telephone call.

5555 North Sheridan Road is home to the Edgewater Beach Apartments. The building soars high above Lake Michigan, resplendent and pale pink. Staring up at the luxurious exterior, my itch of suspicion turns to a sinking sensation low in my belly.

A man and woman both dressed in long fur coats approach the front door, and I follow them into the foyer, which is replete with golden mailboxes.

"Oh, good," I say as the man inserts his key into the lock of the ornate inner door. I smile and pat my large leather bag. "I thought I was going to have to dig mine out of here! Oh, this is lovely." I make a sweeping gesture at the woman's coat. "My mother has a similar one, but the color on yours is much nicer."

The woman smiles. "Why, thank you! I don't know how anyone handles the Chicago winters without a fur. You young things don't seem to mind, though."

The man holds open the door and gives me a well-mannered nod as I step through into the lobby. I remind myself to not gawk at the chandeliers or walnut paneling or white marble floors. Someone who lives here wouldn't notice how extravagantly beautiful everything is.

"The café always smells so wonderful, doesn't it?" the woman says with a nod toward a heavy wooden door, and I realize that's why the whole place smells rich and warm, like browned butter.

"Yes," I say as I join them on the elevator. I nod at the operator and say, "Third floor, please."

The elevator moves swiftly. I tell the fur coat couple good-bye after a delightfully short ride, and then step out onto the third floor. Artwork hangs in gilded frames, lit by electric sconces, and a thick rug runs the length of the hallway, like at a luxury hotel. The apartment doors must be thick as well, because I can hardly hear any of the residents. I might think everyone was out if not for the faint whispers of a radio play and the rich smell of a pot roast dinner in the oven.

My heart pounds as I walk along the lovely hallway to apartment 301.

Louisa had told me time and time again that Elzbieta was a bad egg, but I'd been blinded by her willingness to help. Or should I say her willingness to point fingers at anyone else.

I settle my face into a neutral expression and knock on the door.

Several heartbeats later, the door cracks open and Elzbieta peeks out.

I wave and force myself to grin. "Surprise!"

Elzbieta's tentative smile becomes broad, and she pulls the door all the way open. "This *is* a surprise. Come on in."

I step into the apartment. The floors are a dark, wide plank and the ceilings are at least nine feet high, maybe even ten. Most of the units in the building have lake views, but this isn't one of them. I might be able to catch a sliver of Lake Michigan, if I stand on a ladder and lean the right direction when looking out the window, but the view is largely treetops and the windows of other pricey apartments.

"Sorry to drop in on you like this," I say in a cheery voice. "I rang you at your sister's place, but she said you'd moved out. This is so lovely!"

Which is true, though the actual word I would choose to describe the apartment is *empty*. Aside from an ashtray on the floor beside the windows, the living room is completely bare.

"Thank you." Elzbieta's eyes scan the apartment, and her smile is tight. "It looks very grand, I know, but I got a good deal."

"How wonderful." I hope my feigned enthusiasm is convincing enough to cover my annoyance. How stupid does she think I am? As if there are ever "good deals" on brand-new luxury apartments. "It really is swell."

Her dress is a deep blue, hitting at just the right length. It's finer than any other I've seen her wear, even on the night Liam and Keiran took us out.

"Would you like something to drink?" She tucks a wave of hair behind her ears and gives a self-conscious chuckle. "I can really only offer water."

"I'm fine, thank you. I don't intend to stay long." I hitch my bag higher on my shoulder. "I really just came to let you know that I'm no longer investigating Clarence's death."

Elzbieta's eyes widen. "You're not? Why?"

In my head, I revisit exactly how I planned to say this. "Some new information has come forth, and we now know who likely killed him."

Elzbieta's mouth opens slightly. Her cheeks redden. "Really?"

I nod. "Yes."

She blinks at me. "Are you . . . going to tell me?"

"I'm not able to until we speak to the family."

She releases a long breath through her nose and nods once. "Sure, that makes sense. Can you"—she pauses to swallow hard—"maybe give me a hint?"

"I really can't. I understand that's frustrating." I watch Elzbieta blink away emotion and feel a twinge of doubt. Not doubt that I'm right, but doubt that I should proceed.

"Sorry, I don't know why this is hitting me so hard." Elzbieta pulls a handkerchief from her pocket and presses it to each eye. "I guess I just still can't believe it happened. Clarence was such a good man. Kind and funny and generous."

"Mmm," I say. "The kind of person whom others could take advantage of."

Elzbieta pulls the handkerchief away from her face. She blinks at me, clearly having noted the tone shift. "I suppose so."

"You know what's interesting? Rent here starts at sixty dollars a month." I clasp my hands together behind my back and look her in the eyes. "How much do you make at The Fox, Elzbieta?"

Elzbieta's mouth falls open. Her cheeks flush red. "What are you implying? You can't possibly think that . . ."

"I think Clarence was besotted with you right up until he learned something about you. Something you'd done. Something he couldn't forgive. And that's when he ended things."

"No," she says. "He just lost interest in me, that's all."

"And you got angry, didn't you? Really angry."

"What are you saying, Piper?" Elzbieta's dark eyes flit about like a cornered animal. "You can't possibly think *I* killed Clarence."

I hold out my arms, gesturing to the apartment at large. "I think I'm standing in the motive right now. Aren't I?"

"No." Elzbieta shakes her head wildly. Tiny strands of hair stick to her cheeks. "I didn't kill him. I *never* would've killed him. But I did—" She clasps her hands together and twists. "I did steal from him."

There it is. I keep my lips pressed together so I don't speak.

Despite holding a handkerchief, Elzbieta drags the back of her hand across her eyes to wipe away tears. The gesture makes her look young, like a guilty child confessing to taking a cookie.

"I need you to tell me everything, Elzbieta." I make my voice authoritative but gentle. "What happened?"

She squeezes her eyes shut, and more tears roll down her cheeks. "When O'Banion gave Clarence the money as a thank you for saving his life, he did it right in front of me. He knew Clarence, knew he wasn't the type to show off, and I think he was trying to help him look like a big man in front of me." Elzbieta's hands tremble and she clasps them together. "I'm pretty sure I'm the only one who knew about the money. I asked Clarence what he was going to do with it, and he said nothing."

"Nothing?"

Elzbieta nods. "He told me that his father's name was on his bank account, and Mr. Dell thought Clarence worked at an actual smoke shop. So Clarence deposited what he used to make at the department store in his account every two weeks, but kept all his cash in a fireproof box in his bedroom. He told me he wasn't even sure how much was in there."

I frown. "But that's not true."

Elzbieta nods. "It was a lie. I know that now."

"Why would he lie to you about that?"

Elzbieta's fingers fuss with the shiny beadwork of her dress. "I think maybe he knew."

I wait for her to finish her thought, but she doesn't. "Knew what?"

"That I was mostly interested in him for his money." Elzbieta glances at me, then looks away. Her cheeks are stained crimson from the shame of it all. "I never would've dated him otherwise. I know how that makes me sound."

"You really fooled me," I admit. "I thought you genuinely cared about him."

Elzbieta nods, her face a picture of misery. "I did genuinely care. I just didn't know it yet."

"What happened next?"

She doesn't respond right away, just looks at her hands. When her voice does emerge, it's so hushed that I have to hold my breath to make sure I can hear. "I was pretty sure he kept the key to the box on the ring with his apartment key. I suggested a restaurant that was close to his apartment, and then as we were headed to a movie, I said I needed to use the restroom."

"He didn't accompany you upstairs?"

She shakes her head. "I think he suspected what I was up to. I think he wanted to test me."

"And you failed."

She nods and wipes at her eyes, seeming indifferent to mussing her eye makeup. "He took me to dinner two days later and said we were over. He said he couldn't trust me anymore, but that he wasn't angry with me. He was so kind, and it made me feel so much worse about what I'd done." Elzbieta wipes at her eyes again. "That was when I knew I'd made the worst mistake of my life."

"Why did you do it?"

"Why does anybody steal money? Because I didn't have enough. Because I was tired of sharing a bed with my nieces. Because I thought Clarence was so rich, he wouldn't even notice."

"You didn't think he'd notice he was missing five hundred dollars?"

"Stupid, I know. But that's also what he wanted me to believe. He had loads of money in that box, and he seemed so indifferent to the money from O'Banion. I thought it'd be a while before he noticed, and maybe he'd think he'd misplaced the envelope or something. Like I said, I was stupid."

"Why didn't you give it back to him?" I ask, thinking of the blue-inked subtraction in the records. "Did you already have a down payment on this place?"

She shakes her head. "He wouldn't take it back. Said I should keep it."

Is that the truth? Clarence spent a lot of time and effort documenting his finances. He clearly cared about money.

"I know that sounds like a lie, but I swear it's true. I didn't spend any of it at first, because I felt so rotten about the whole mess. I thought maybe if Clarence saw that I wasn't spending it, that I wasn't using it, he would take me back."

"But that isn't what happened."

She looks away from me. "He said he would never be able to trust me again, that we were over, but he also said he wouldn't tell anyone. He would protect my dignity. And he did. Never told his friends, so far as I can tell. Never said a bad thing about me. Even at work, he just told people we weren't seeing each other anymore. It was more unbearable than if he'd been rude, you know?"

I can easily imagine that. The guilt already so heavy and then made all the worse by discovering what a truly honorable person she'd stolen from.

That is, if this story is true. Without Clarence here to tell his side, Elzbieta is free to shape the events however she likes. Though it does align with what I know to be true of Clarence—he *was* discreet about the reason he broke up with Elzbieta when explaining himself to his sister, Mabel, and Daniel. Daniel is the only one who has mentioned Clarence being upset by the whole ordeal, and even he didn't say anything about the stolen money.

Elzbieta wipes her eyes with the handkerchief, smearing the remains of kohl into her hairline, and then blows her nose. "Even when he took that other girl out, I was angry, but I never would've killed him. If that's what you think happened, you've got it wrong."

"I think you're probably telling me the truth this time," I say. "The new evidence that came forward makes it pretty convincing that Clarence really did take his own life."

Elzbieta gapes at me. For a moment, the only sound is a distant car honk from the street below.

"But you made it sound like . . ."

"I know what I made it sound like. I figured unless you thought you were on the hook for murder, you wouldn't come clean about what you *really* did." I cross my arms over my chest. "Like Clarence, I've learned you can't be trusted."

She continues to look at me, her expression one of indignation.

When the silence stretches on, I turn and walk to the door, my footsteps echoing in her empty life of luxury.

"How dare you judge me for lying, Piper," she says in a low, angry voice as I reach for the handle. "You're such a hypocrite."

I turn and look into her sneering face. "I may sometimes lie to get information, but pretending to be interested in a job at The Fox is far different—"

"That's not at all what I'm talking about. You work for a private investigator? *Work for*? What a lie."

I stand in the hallway, feeling as though Elzbieta slapped me across the face but trying to not show it.

Elzbieta plants her hands on her hips. "I've never seen someone who has so much brains, so much money, and so much status try to reduce herself to so little."

And with that, Elzbieta reaches out and slams her thick, sixty-dollars-a-month door in my face.

CHAPTER
THIRTY-THREE

Louisa nods slowly after I finish explaining my conversation with Elzbieta. "Yes," she says, dragging out the word. "That fits."

"You think she's telling the truth?"

"Well." Louisa casts her gaze through the window, but I have a feeling she isn't really seeing the Presley's students who are filing out of the school and onto the front lawn. "Yes, I think I do. I think that's exactly how Clarence would've handled the situation. He wanted to know the truth about her character, but he wouldn't feel the need to expose her. I think Elzbieta is being honest."

I consider this, and an alternate story spins loose in my imagination—Clarence was furious about the money and told Elzbieta that he was going to turn her in to the police. So she got angry and . . . came back later and poisoned him?

But no. This is just me trying to keep the case going.

"Your family could maybe press charges?" I suggest. "Get the five hundred dollars back."

"It sounds like Clarence handled the situation how he wanted to and was satisfied. That's enough for me." Louisa shrugs. "What else have you learned?"

I can't put this off any longer. I take a bracing breath and reach into my bag for an envelope. "Louisa, this will be hard for you to hear, but the more I look into this, the more likely it seems to me that the police had it right."

She blinks at me, her confused expression making her look more like a child than an adolescent. "I don't understand."

Because we're in the Presley's office, I don't have Clarence's box with me. All I have is an envelope with the money Louisa gave me. I hand it to her, and she looks inside at the money and then back at me. "Are you *quitting*?"

"No, I'm just not sure there's anything else for me to do here." I try for the same gentle but firm tone I used with Elzbieta, only it feels much harder with Louisa. "I always told you this might happen. That I might look into Clarence's death and find that the truth really is Clarence killed himself—"

"But he didn't." Louisa closes the envelope and hands it back to me. "My brother wouldn't do that."

I push the envelope back to her. "The evidence all points to Clarence being upset about getting caught cheating at Loyola, and the direction that his life had taken since then—"

"You mean that he was upset about being *falsely accused* of cheating? Because that's what happened." Louisa's eyes narrow. "He didn't 'get caught' because he didn't do it."

"I understand this is hard for you to hear—"

"It isn't," she snaps. "What's hard is that you're not listening to me."

The door from the hallway opens, drawing both of our attention. Emma Crane gives a tentative smile and wave. "Hello. I'm ready when you are."

"I just need a minute." I turn back to Louisa. "Emma's a friend. We can talk openly in front of her. Louisa, I really wanted to help you—"

"Then stop with all this suicide nonsense and find out what *really* happened to my brother. Stop trying to quit."

My cheeks flame. "I'm not quitting. I understand why it may look like that to you, but the conclusions of my investigation are that your brother most likely took his own—"

"No!" Louisa pounds her fist on the edge of my desk and leans so she's nearly yelling in my face. "My brother never ever would've done that. Never! Your conclusions are garbage. Not only that, but you, Piper Sail, are a complete fraud! You can't quit, because I'm firing you!"

With that, Louisa snatches the envelope from the desk and storms out into the frosty, gray afternoon.

In the silence following her departure, my ears ring with her words.

Emma presses a hand over her heart and looks at me with wide eyes. "Goodness, Piper, are you okay?"

I nod slowly. "She's just angry. She'll calm down."

"She shouldn't have spoken to you like that. It was completely uncalled for."

I shuffle the papers I'd been working on into a tidy stack. All of it can wait for tomorrow. "I'm fine. Are you ready to go? Sorry, silly question. Of course you are."

"I thought you had to stay until four o'clock?"

I glance at my wristwatch. Three fifty. "Today, it's fine. We're going out for my father's birthday tonight, so I need to get home."

But really, I don't want to be stuck in this office anymore today. I wrestle my coat off the hook by the door and head into the biting afternoon cold.

Emma and I don't converse as we walk to the train station. Offering to have Emma ride home with me on the L every day is partially an attempt to apologize to Jeremiah. When I mentioned this to Mariano, he said he thought that if I wanted to apologize,

I might have to use words like "I'm sorry" and "Please forgive me." I'm hoping he's wrong and that my ensuring Emma gets home safely so that Jeremiah doesn't have to leave work every day to do so will communicate the sentiment well enough.

The L car isn't exactly warm, but it's a nice break from the wind. I make sure Emma takes the seat by the window so I can be on the aisle, and she doesn't get jostled by anybody getting on or off.

As the train pulls away, Emma makes a huffy sound, crosses her arms over her chest, and says, "I just find myself feeling incredibly jealous of you."

I turn and gape at her. "I'm sorry, but what?"

"If I'd been yelled at like that, I would still be a puddle on the floor. You would currently be in that office trying to mop me up. But not you. Someone gets right in your face and screams, but you just keep on going. You have far too much—" Emma's hands flail, like she might be able to pull the right word from the air. "Purpose to flounder for long."

My laugh is short and sharp. "Lies. All lies."

"I'm serious."

"So am I. I just failed miserably at this case—"

"You did not."

"And me being too proud to cry about it in public is not evidence that I have purpose."

"You do, though. When Robbie broke up with me, I realized that I'd assumed I would marry him. That was my plan for who I would be as an adult—Robbie's wife. I thought I'd graduate high school and plan a wedding. What a ninny."

"Thinking you will marry your boyfriend doesn't make you a ninny, Emma. That's a reasonable thing to think."

"I don't even know what I'll do next fall." Emma moves her fingers to her mouth, as if to chew on a nail, only to get a mouthful of glove instead. "The whole situation makes me so jealous of people like you and Jeremiah. His purpose was just handed to him. He's always known that he would be a newspaperman and take over for Father someday."

I shrug. "My brothers are similar, but I've always wondered if I would feel trapped by the whole arrangement. Expected to be a lawyer because my father is a lawyer."

"I guess. Jeremiah seems to love it, but maybe he *does* feel trapped." She frowns. "I should ask him."

We ride in silence for a minute, the steady rumbling of the train and a recent history of restless nights making my eyelids heavy.

"What if I join you?" Emma asks.

Apparently, I had closed my eyes, because they snap open now. "Join me?"

"Yes. Join you. Like, when you do interviews, I can be the one who takes notes or something. I'm good at taking notes. Ooh, and typing. I can type things for you."

"Emma, you're talking like I'm a person who could actually hire you. I'm not taking any more cases. I'm done."

Emma makes the same half-laugh, half-scoffing sound that Jeremiah does. "No, you aren't."

"I am."

"You are not. You love helping people." Emma waits for me to meet her gaze before continuing. "I know things didn't work out the way you wanted with Louisa's case, but I don't believe any of this talk about you being done."

"Well, you should because I *am*. I never should've started. It's not like I was qualified to do what I was doing."

"You're not qualified to help people?" Emma elbows me. "You will take on more cases, I'm sure of it. And when you do, I want to help."

"But do you *want* to do detective work?" This is a moot point, because I'm not taking on any more cases, but it still feels worth pointing out to her. "If I wasn't in the picture, is that what you would choose to do?"

Emma looks at me as though I'm making a joke. "Detective work? No. Of course not."

"Emma, I appreciate your offer. I really do. And if I was a real investigator and I could hire somebody, I would definitely hire you. But you need to find something that makes *you* happy. That fills *you* with purpose."

She holds my gaze for a moment, and then sighs. "I hear what you're saying. I just don't have any interests that light me up."

Our train slows as it pulls into our station. I secure my bag and stand. "I was like that too, before Lydia went missing. I had no idea what I was going to do with my life. I still have no idea."

The doors open and I step out. When I glance behind me to make sure that Emma followed, my eyes catch on a familiar profile—flat cap over hair the color of toffee, a hard jawline, and a crooked nose. Liam Finnegan? Was he on the same L car as us?

People move about on the platform, and by the time I have a clear view of the window again, whoever the boy is, he's no longer there.

"Is something wrong?" Emma asks, following my eyeline and looking over her shoulder.

"No." I put on a smile. "Nothing."

Dinner at La Louisiane for my father's birthday has been a tradition for as long as I can remember. At last year's birthday dinner, Father invited Jane and introduced her to us, perhaps guessing that because it was his birthday, we would all feel more inclined to accept their relationship. Instead, I'd spent most of the night glowering into my dinner. I've never liked surprises.

Tonight, Jane sits next to Father as his wife. I'm seated beside her, and she beams first at me, then Gretchen, Tim, and finally Nick. "It's so special to have everyone together. Of course, we were all together just a couple weeks ago for Christmas, but I felt so dreadful that I could hardly enjoy it."

Father puts his arm around the back of Jane's chair. "It's great that you're feeling better."

"Much better." Jane leans heavily on the word *much* as she slides forward to take a cheese puff from the tray in the middle of the table.

Gretchen selects a cheese puff as well. "When we celebrate Timothy's birthday next year, you'll need to get someone to watch the baby, just like we did."

"That's true, isn't it?" Jane looks at me and smiles.

Nick snorts. "You aren't planning on leaving Pippy in charge, are you? Surely, you've noticed she's dreadful with children."

"Nick." Gretchen rests her gloved hand on my shoulder as if to protect me from my brother. "What a horrible thing to say about your sister. Howie *adores* his aunt. Simply *adores* her."

Father leans back as a waiter refills his water glass. "Of course we wouldn't hire Piper, because we want her at dinner with us."

"Yes, of course." Jane sounds flustered. "I didn't mean to imply otherwise."

Blessedly, the waiter interrupts to take our order. As soon as we've all put in our requests, Father says to Tim, "Not to talk shop, but did you call Lucas back?"

Even on his birthday, he can't seem to help himself.

"Piper," Jane says quietly on my left. "I really didn't mean to suggest—"

I wave away the rest of her words. "I know. Nick was making something out of nothing."

Jane's shoulders relax. "So long as *you* know I have no expectations of you becoming live-in childcare."

"You might want to be, though, Piper," Gretchen says on my right. "Good practice for you. And there's nothing like a newborn baby. They're just so sweet."

"What was Howie like as a newborn?" Jane asks, leaning closer.

I pull back as the two of them talk across me about sleeping and feeding schedules. I catch Nick's eye. He crosses his eyes at me. I cross mine back and then grin.

"I thought that was you, Jane!" A sugary voice cuts into Jane and Gretchen's conversation. A bejeweled woman stands alongside Jane's chair. "Don't you look lovely?"

"Why, Natalie! What a wonderful surprise. Have you met my family?"

Whoever this Natalie person is, she's a striking woman, with a nose like a sledding hill and a bob of wavy red hair. The shade of red reminds me of Lydia's hair, though of course hers was never cut short.

Jane introduces each of us as her stepchildren and Gretchen as her daughter-in-law, and I tune out as Natalie points out her sisters, whom she's dining with. Jane fawns appropriately, and then they exchange a whole gamut of polite-society good-byes. *I had better let you get back to your dinner. Hope you have a wonderful evening. Looking forward to the meeting next week.* On and on it goes.

"See you on Wednesday," Jane calls brightly as Natalie walks away.

Then Jane turns to me and Gretchen, and her expression is so unexpectedly dark, I lean back in my chair.

"Odious woman," she says under her breath.

I can't help it—I laugh. "What? Really?"

"Yes," Jane says emphatically.

"I would've thought the two of you were best friends, the way you were talking."

She drains the last of her water with the same vigor of a man drinking a shot of whiskey. "Absolutely not."

"Does *she* know you're not best friends?" I ask.

"I imagine the dislike is mutual." Jane takes a long, deep breath and fans herself. "I need to calm myself. I can't imagine it's good for the baby to have my heart going so fast."

Father leans into our conversation, his arm circling Jane's shoulders. "Are you okay? She has some nerve coming over here to talk to you as if nothing happened."

Gretchen leans forward. "What happened?"

"It isn't even worth talking about," Jane huffs. "Not on your father's birthday, certainly, but Natalie and I are both on a fine arts committee and let's just say . . ." Jane's mouth purses. "Let's say nothing at all. It's a special night for Timothy. We're not going to ruin it with foul talk."

"You handled yourself beautifully," Father says. "After she cheated you."

"Cheated you?" Nick says with a guffaw. "What happens on these committees?"

"They can be vicious places," Jane says in a low, serious voice. "You might assume women like that—women who have it all—wouldn't be out to get more, but they are. I had an idea for a fund-raiser, and I told Natalie. She had always seemed so nice and friendly, and she's established with the committee, so I thought it would be a good idea to speak to her first to see if she thought my idea had merit."

Jane smooths her napkin on her lap time and time again. "At first, I was glad I had done so. She hardly reacted when I told her about the idea, saying it was 'something to consider.' I felt relieved that I'd brought it to her first instead of sharing it with the group and making a fool of myself. But then at the very next meeting, the president of the committee shared *my* idea but said it was Natalie Cuthbert's."

Gretchen gasps, which makes me smile.

"What did Natalie do then?" Gretchen asks.

"Absolutely nothing. She avoided eye contact with me the entire meeting, and neither of us have ever said a word about it. We just go on like this, pretending to be friends. After all, we live here together. What else are we going to do? Confronting some-one in a situation like this can have deadly social consequences."

"How awful." Gretchen shakes her head, and her lovely dark hair swishes around her face.

"Just the price of polite society. We don't need to talk about it anymore." Jane shrugs primly. "What does everyone think about the new library that's going in on the Loop?"

As the others at the table play along with the clunky change of topic, my thoughts drift to Louisa and the way she yelled at me today. The way she's so stubbornly sure of her own opinions, that Clarence absolutely couldn't have killed himself because he seemed happy. I wish Louisa had been sitting here for the whole exchange between Jane and Natalie so I could now turn to her and say, "See? Sometimes people act one way even though they feel the opposite. Sometimes people who act like your friends aren't really your friends."

But Louisa will experience this phenomenon someday for herself and then she'll know, same as I do. She'll know that sometimes people are kind and helpful just because they want something from you, or because they're trying to cover up their own bad behavior. That sometimes people tell you things as though they're facts, but they're really not.

And that's what makes the job of uncovering the truth so challenging. How do I know if Elzbieta is more trustworthy than Liam? Or if Daniel is more trustworthy than Louisa? I don't. Because for all I know, Louisa had it right all along and her brother really was a saint who didn't take his own life, who didn't cheat. But proving he *didn't* do those things only works if I can prove that somebody else *did*.

The thought hits me with such force, I freeze.

I've told Louisa all along that if Clarence didn't take his own life, that means somebody else must have taken it from him, but that's true for the other accusation too. If Louisa is right and Clarence didn't cheat, that would mean somebody else did, and it would have to be somebody who was close enough to Clarence to frame him. Somebody who seemed like a friend, but really was trying to cover up his own bad behavior.

CHAPTER
THIRTY-FOUR

The Harvard School for Boys in Kenwood isn't as impressive as I imagined, and it fills me with an unexpected touch of school pride. The Presley's campus has a spacious green lawn—in the warmer months, anyway—wide stone steps leading up to the double doors, and Lake Michigan glinting off to the east. Despite Harvard's grandiose name, the school is a three-story brick building edged with stone that sits on an ordinary city street.

I stand outside for a moment and remind myself that I'm not Piper Sail, but rather I'm Ms. Reid, secretary to Mr. Byron. I muss my hair, tighten my coat's belt, and rush through the front door, breathing fast.

The gray-haired secretary startles as I enter. I walk forward with my hand outstretched. "Mrs. Hennings? I'm Ms. Reid from Loyola. We spoke on the telephone not very long ago."

"Yes." Mrs. Hennings blinks rapidly. "My, you got here fast! I scarcely had time to make a copy."

"As I said on the phone, Mr. Byron is awfully angry with me. I just don't know what happened to those records!"

"I understand perfectly," Mrs. Hennings says, handing an envelope across the counter to me. "I've been here for twenty years, and sometimes I swear there's something living in the cabinets and eating files. I hope your boss isn't *too* hard on you."

I clutch the envelope to my chest. "This will go a long way toward getting back in his good graces. Thank you."

With one last grateful smile, I head back out the door and hurry toward the L station. I make myself wait until I'm on the platform before I pull out the high school transcript for Daniel Becker.

Printed in black on white are Daniel's Cs and occasional Bs all through ninth, tenth, and the first half of eleventh grade. And there it is—second semester his junior year, all those Cs morph into As and Bs. Senior year is straight As.

It's possible that Daniel had some sort of transformative experience that caused him to turn his grades around. But I don't think that's what's happened.

"I think you've been lying to me, Mr. Becker," I murmur as I tuck the transcript away in my handbag. "And I intend to prove it."

"Instead of going straight home today, do you want to help me with a case?" I ask Emma as we walk to the train station.

Her eyes spark. "That sounds like a lot more fun than homework. Which case? Did you already take on a new one? I knew you wouldn't be able to resist long."

"This is still the Clarence Dell case. I think I uncovered some new information."

Emma claps her hands together. "I'm intrigued."

"About six months before Clarence died, he was suspended from Loyola University for cheating. Louisa has maintained the whole time that her brother didn't cheat, and even Clarence's adviser at Loyola said Clarence's grades didn't show the typical pattern of a student who's regularly cheating."

I summarize quickly for Emma about my lunch hour trek down south to Clarence and Daniel's alma mater, and the noticeable rise in Daniel's grades late in high school, just like Mr. Byron had described to me.

"I think it's possible that Daniel was the one cheating, and when the school caught on, he pointed the finger at Clarence."

Emma gasps. "And then *killed* him?"

I think of Daniel's grim expression when he said Clarence was dead because of him. "In a sense, maybe. He probably didn't know Clarence would get booted from school. And I doubt he expected that Clarence would ultimately grow depressed and take his own life."

Emma fusses with her uniform tie. "What a horrible thing to have to live with."

I recall Daniel seeking me out the day after Christmas, to confess to me what Clarence's original letter really said. Finding that letter, discovering the full effects of his choice, must have felt like such a kick in the gut to Daniel. "No wonder he wanted me to drop the case. The guilt must be overwhelming."

The approaching northbound train comes to a stop, and Emma and I board. I sweep my gaze through the car for Liam, like I have every day since Monday when I thought I saw him, but like always, he's not here.

"I called the library and learned that Daniel works until five o'clock." I look at my watch to confirm that it's just after four o'clock now. "That should give me at least thirty minutes to search his place and get out of there before he comes home. The apartment isn't that big."

"What are you looking for?" Emma asks. "A confession letter? 'It was actually me who cheated. Sincerely, Daniel'?"

"Boy, that'd be nice. But no. Clarence was caught with mimeographed copies of answer keys, so if I find anything, I imagine it'll be that." From my leather bag, I pull out the 1921 Harvard School for Boys yearbook. "Let me show you a picture of Daniel."

Emma blinks at me as I flip pages. "I never know what you're going to pull out of that bag. How long have you been walking around with that?"

I grin as I flip to the Bs. "Just since lunch. I stopped by my house to pick up the apartment key and thought this would be useful." I point at a picture of Daniel. "If you see this guy coming into the building, let him go through the door, and then use the lever in the lobby to ring apartment 3F. If that happens, I'll know that I need to hide or get out of there."

Emma bites on her lower lip and nods. "Doesn't seem like that would give you much time."

"It doesn't, but I haven't come up with anything else. And I'm not planning on this taking long. There are only so many places one can hide evidence in an apartment that small."

Emma studies Daniel's picture. "And what do I do if you don't come out of the apartment?"

"I'll come out."

Emma fixes me with a stern look. "Let's be smart about this. I want a plan for if you don't come out."

"Okay, okay." I consider Emma's profile. "If you're worried, ring apartment 3E. Her name is Catherine, and I think she'll let you in if you tell her you thought you rang Daniel's apartment. Also, I left a message for Mariano that has the address of where we're going and that I should be home no later than five thirty."

Emma continues to press her teeth into her lower lip. I remember the sight of her in Father's office, of blood seeping through her yellow dress, and feel a rumble of unease.

"But if you'd rather just go home, that's fine too," I say. "Maybe that'd be better, actually."

Emma ceases studying Daniel's photograph and looks at me with raised eyebrows. "There's no way I'm letting you do this alone."

"Okay." I still feel unsettled, but I smile anyway. "By the time Daniel knows someone has been there, you and I will be safe at home. Promise."

Entering another person's empty apartment, even one I have a key for, is an unsettling experience. My entire body hums with awareness, all my senses alight in search of a threat. The air smells faintly sour, as though the garbage has been left in the kitchen a day too long. On the couch is a pile of clothes that probably are waiting to be folded, and the only sound is the ticking clock above the kitchen sink, showing that Emma and I arrived here much faster than I anticipated. I glance at my watch, but it's stuck at 4:03. I twist the knob to wind it and synchronize my watch with the kitchen clock.

Daniel's bedroom door is open and holds the musky smell of sheets that are long overdue for washing. I turn on the lamp sitting on his bedside table and find that despite the odor, Daniel's room is generally clean and orderly. The bed is made, the floor is clear, and there are no piles of things on his dresser or his desk like there are on mine. I do my best to take a mental picture of the room, and then get to work searching.

I start with his desk, pulling open drawers and finding nothing more exciting than rubber bands and pencils. I move to the bookshelf, which is sparse. There's nothing hiding inside his copies of *Self-Help*, *The Art of Living*, or *Duty, Character, and Thrift*. *Self-Mastery Through Conscious Autosuggestion* does have something inside, but this turns out to be a page of handwritten notes about the text itself. I reach for a textbook from one of his financial courses. If I was going to hide mimeographed copies of tests, then I would—

Knock, knock, knock.

I yelp and then clasp both hands over my mouth, as if it's possible to suppress the sound after I've already made it. My heart gallops, and my thoughts war between hiding and not hiding. The knock means that someone other than Daniel is at the door. Maybe they'll assume no one's here and go away.

Knock, knock, knock.

Go away, I think, as though I can influence the person at the door with intense internal pleading. *Go away. Go away now.*

Maybe it's Emma? But she would say something. I hear a muffled female voice in the hallway. Catherine?

I step lightly through Daniel's room toward the door. I'm trying to move silently, but with my heart thundering in my ears, it's impossible to know if I am.

I reach the door and carefully, quietly lower myself to the ground so I can better hear what's being said.

". . . varies a lot recently," Catherine is saying. "If you like, I can let him know you stopped by."

"No, thank you. I appreciate it."

All the air seems to leave my lungs at the distinct nasal sound of Liam Finnegan's voice. What is he doing here?

"You haven't seen a girl hanging around the apartment, have you?" Liam asks in a conversational, you-can-trust-me kind of voice. "Blonde hair. About this tall."

My vision grows dim at the edges and I work hard to take a deep breath.

"Not that I can think of, no."

"Has anybody come knocking on your door asking about Clarence over the last couple of weeks?"

"No. Well . . ." Catherine's voice changes, and I squeeze my eyes shut. *Please don't remember me.* "There *was* a girl, I guess. I *think* she had blonde hair, but she didn't knock on my door. She was Clarence's cousin and came to talk to Daniel."

"Really," Liam says in a flat voice. "When was this?"

"Back in December. We didn't talk very long, and I don't think she asked me anything about Clarence. What I do remember"—Catherine chuckles—"is that she asked me about rats at the end. She wanted to know if we'd ever had rats in our apartment. That seemed odd to me."

"That *is* odd," Liam agrees, but he doesn't sound like he thinks it's odd. He sounds like he suspects why I would've asked that question, and that he doesn't like it very much. "Thanks so much, Catherine. That's really helpful to know."

Through the small crack beneath the door, I watch the shadows of Liam's feet as he shifts from side to side. The doorknob turns slowly as Liam tries to open it, but it catches. Liam curses, and several seconds later, his footsteps travel down the hallway.

Calm, Piper. You have to stay calm. I sit against the wall with my knees pulled to my chest and pant for air as though I just ran up the stairs. Each one of my scattered thoughts seem to be yelling at me: *Liam is here! Liam followed me!*

I press my eyes closed and draw in a long, slow breath. Why would Liam follow me here? Have I done something—talked to someone, uncovered information—that feels like a threat to him? After all, he'd told Tubs that I was smart enough to be a liability "just like Clarence." Is this about what I learned from Mabel—that Clarence had a friend he was either going to confront or turn over to authorities? Did Liam kill Clarence before that could happen and then made it look like suicide?

I don't have time to think through all of this. Right now, I need to prioritize looking for evidence that Daniel was the one who cheated, and I need to get out before he returns home. Liam is no longer outside Daniel's door, but is he actually *leaving*?

I move over to the window that looks down on the street and wait, thoughts turning to Emma as I do. If it really was Liam I saw on the L car on Monday, then he's seen me with Emma. Is she in danger? Should I go check on her or continue my search?

Liam comes into view, crossing the street to Thompson's Cafeteria and heading inside. He'll probably take one of the seats by the window so he can watch for me to come out. That's what I would do, anyway.

My fingers wrap around my locket, around Lydia's school picture, as I consider Emma alone down there. Part of me wants to bail on the search, find some back way out of the building, and then get Emma away from here.

But no. I came here to do a job. I came here to find proof that it was Daniel who cheated, so at the very least I can give Louisa peace of mind and clear Clarence's name about *that*. I can sort out Liam's role when I'm not in this apartment. I glance at my watch. Four thirty. I'll search for another fifteen minutes, then I'll look for a back door out of this building.

I glance down at the street one more time, where the streetlamps are already on. Liam is well-lit in the front window of Thompson's, a cup of coffee in hand. He's looking up at the building, but with the lights off in the living room, he can't see me.

"I'm coming for you next," I say, and then I return to Daniel's room.

I find nothing in Daniel's dresser except rolled socks and folded undershirts. In his bedside table, there are several diaries that appear to be time logs. I take a moment to skim through the most recent entry.

6:00 a.m.: Get dressed and brisk walk
6:30 a.m.: Shower

My eyes run along a list of equally mundane daily tasks. What about October 30? I flip back to the end of October. The day reads perfectly ordinary until:

5:00 p.m.: Return home from work. Clarence.

The single word written there makes my heart ache like when you press on a bruise. Daniel made no other entries for that day. With a twinge of guilt for having pried into a horrifying day for him, I put the diary back.

As I drag a chair over to his closet to search the top shelf, I dwell on the time logs. Daniel was as fastidious about tracking his time as Clarence was with his finances. That day at the library, Daniel's coworker told me Daniel got more done on his break than she did all day. He cares about efficiency. That's probably why he cheated in the first place, to save himself time.

I glance at my watch. Four forty-five. I better not linger much longer. I stand in the doorway of Daniel's room and survey it one more time, hunting for anywhere I might've missed. Maybe Daniel doesn't cheat anymore and that's why I can't find anything? Maybe I was wrong and he never cheated in the first place? Or maybe . . .

Maybe he doesn't keep the evidence in his own room.

If I were going to keep mimeographed copies of tests, I certainly wouldn't hide them in my own room. If they were ever found, I'd want to be able to claim ignorance.

My gaze travels across the hallway to Clarence's room.

It's empty though, of course. The closet is the only hiding place left. Once again, I get a chair from the kitchen table and carry it into Clarence's room. I hoist myself up and peer at the closet shelf.

Pushed into the back corner of the highest shelf is a small stack of papers. I'm so surprised to find anything that for a moment, I just stare at them. Then I reach back and take hold of the stack. Each one of them looks like an answer key for a test. Not only that, but a number of these tests are dated *after* Clarence died.

"Gotcha," I whisper, feeling a heady surge of delight from having guessed correctly.

I tuck the tests into my bag and glance outside. It's completely dark, which is a little odd for this hour. I return the chair and see that the clock still says it's four forty-five. But surely some time has passed . . .

I think back to when Louisa first brought me here. I'd checked the clock, and Daniel had said that wasn't the right time. That he could never get that clock to run right.

That means it's probably well after five. My whole body lights up with fear, and I rush to Clarence's room to turn off the light. I've just pulled the string and sent the room into darkness when

I hear it—a key fitting into the door lock of Daniel's apartment. I barely have time to close myself into Clarence's room when the front door swings open.

CHAPTER
THIRTY-FIVE

For a moment, I can't breathe.

I stand in Clarence's empty, dark room and listen to the sounds of Daniel moving around the apartment, whistling tunelessly. At least, I assume it's Daniel. There was no buzz up to the apartment from Emma. Maybe she couldn't see his face because it's dark outside? Or maybe . . . did Liam . . . ?

The radio snaps on, and the apartment is filled with *Rhapsody in Blue*. Now at least I feel as though I can breathe without worry that Daniel will hear. I move Nick's pocketknife out of my bag and into my dress pocket. The only shot I have of sneaking away unseen is if Daniel goes into the bathroom. I need to be ready to move as soon as that happens. I have to make sure Emma's okay.

Pots and pans rattle together. Cabinets open and close. Water runs. I catch bits of Daniel's off-tune humming with the melody of *Rhapsody* as the music rises and falls. Daniel's footsteps draw closer and I suck in a sharp breath, fearing he's about to come into Clarence's room, but then I hear the easily recognizable sound of a man relieving himself.

This is my chance.

I slowly turn the handle. The music is blessedly loud, the song at one of its many crescendos. I ease the door open, the light from the kitchen slicing into Clarence's room and burning my eyes more than I would've expected.

Daniel is still relieving himself, and with a jolt I discover he didn't close the bathroom door. He's standing at the toilet, back to me, with the door wide open.

With my heart in my throat, I ease out of Clarence's room. I'm halfway down the tiny hall when there's a loud buzzing sound from the entry. Daniel turns reflexively, and our eyes meet.

He yelps a curse. "What are you doing in here?" he yells as he struggles with the buttons on his pants.

I back away from him down the hall. "N-nothing," I stammer. "Just . . . picking up something for Louisa. Sorry to startle you."

I make a dash for the front door. I've just twisted the lock open when Daniel seizes a handful of my coat and pulls me backward.

"Wait," he says. "What are you getting for Louisa? How'd you get in here?"

"I have Clarence's key." I try to put a smile on my face that makes me being here look normal and innocent. "She thought that something was in his room—"

"But you knew nothing was in his room." His eyes are slits. "Why didn't you tell her that?"

"I thought I'd missed something," I say, hitching my bag higher on my shoulder.

Daniel's suspicious gaze shifts to the strap, which he grabs, wrenching my shoulder in the process. "What'd you take?"

"Nothing," I gasp through the pain. "Just something of Clarence's for Louisa."

Daniel reaches inside and pulls out a fistful of mimeographed papers. The blaze of horror in his eyes tells me that I was right.

"What are you doing with these?" His voice is a low, dangerous rasp.

I inch toward the door. "Louisa wanted—"

Daniel shakes the pages at me. "How did you know where to find these? Tell me what you know."

I turn and bolt toward the door, but this time Daniel grabs hold of my hair. I cry out as my scalp burns, and a moment later, my head collides with the wall. Stars dot my vision. My mouth fills with a hot, metallic taste.

"Tell me what you know," Daniel snarls into my ear. I can feel the heat of his words, but they seem far away.

"It was you who cheated," I gasp. "And you let Clarence take the blame."

"What else?"

His grip on my hair tightens, and I struggle to think about anything except the pain. *What else?* Why ask me that if he isn't afraid I know more? What else *do* I know about the cheating?

"It started in high school." My words have a slushy sound to them. "But Clarence didn't know. Nobody knew. And you didn't mean for him to get expelled. You never meant for him to kill himself."

Daniel releases his hold on my hair. "Yes," he says stiffly. "Yes, that's true. That's all there is."

I clutch my throbbing head.

"Sorry." The apology is gruff. "I didn't mean to hurt you. I've kept this secret so long that someone discovering it . . . Well, I overreacted."

His words remind me of what Mr. Byron said about Clarence, that he didn't need to overreact and let the cheating scandal define him. Only Clarence wasn't the type to overreact, was he? When Elzbieta threw her tantrum about Clarence seeing Mabel, she said he grew calmer as she grew angrier. When Clarence found out she took the five hundred dollars, he handled it quietly, and he never disparaged her to others. Even when he told Mabel about the breakup, he'd been vague about why they'd split, just like he'd been vague about the problem with his friend. *He couldn't decide if he should confront him directly or speak to the authorities.* That's what Mabel had said.

I'd assumed the friend was Liam, and the situation had something to do with money and The Fox, but what if the friend was Daniel, and "the authorities" referred to Loyola? To Mr. Byron?

I can hear Jeremiah's tight, angry voice as he read the words to me: *Clarence requested an appointment with him but didn't show up.*

What if Clarence requested the appointment because he'd discovered that it was Daniel who was cheating? What if he didn't show up because he was dead?

"Did you overreact when Clarence found out?" My question emerges slow as mud, and the light seems so much brighter than before. I fumble in my pocket for my knife in case Daniel comes at me. "Is that why you killed him, because he was going to tell Mr. Byron?"

Daniel drops the documents to the floor and takes a step closer to me. "You shouldn't talk about things you don't understand."

As he draws nearer, my hazy thoughts slide to another face that once loomed over me in the same ominous, threatening way. But that time my hands had been bound and my mouth gagged.

This time, I can defend myself. This time, I can scream.

It's as though Daniel sees the idea on my face. He lunges at me, his big hand covering my mouth just as I start to shriek. My fingers curl around the knife in my pocket, and I stab wildly at Daniel's thigh. He cries out, and I take off for the door, only I can't seem to run in a straight line. The apartment spins, and I have to lean against the wall to stay upright as I move, like

I'm on a ship in rough waters. My stomach also churns like I'm at sea.

I'm reaching for the handle when the door springs open and Liam bursts in. I'm still blinking at him, processing his arrival, when Emma materializes behind him. A fresh wave of nausea rolls through me. Her mouth turns to an O when she sees me, her blue eyes as round as marbles.

"Emma, run." I try to yell the words, but I'm not sure how well they come out. "Call Mariano."

Liam looks from me to Emma. "Knock on the neighbor's door. Tell her to call the police."

I watch as she wordlessly turns and obeys. I'm still puzzling this over when the world seems to tilt, and I'm suddenly on my hands and knees, staring at the dingy linoleum floor. Are these black-and-white tiles the last thing I'll ever see?

"Danny?" Liam says in an incredulous voice.

I look up and blink through the bleariness.

"She broke into my apartment and attacked me," Daniel cries. He has one hand clutching his thigh. "She's crazy."

Liam's gaze cuts to me, as if evaluating. Another swell of nausea rolls through my stomach. What's he going to do to me?

Liam pushes Daniel against the wall, his arm pressing against Daniel's throat and cutting off a strangled yelp. "Tell me right now." Liam's voice is a low growl. "What did you do to Clarence?"

"Nothing." Daniel tries to grab at Liam's arm, but Liam doesn't let up.

"This girl is searching for his killer, and she came to you. You tell me the truth now or you'll regret it."

Daniel's face is bright red, his fingers increasingly frantic as they pull at Liam's arm.

"You're going to kill him." My voice sounds strange in my own head, like it's echoing down a long hallway.

"If he doesn't answer soon, you're maybe right."

Daniel croaks a syllable that I can't make out.

Liam lets up slightly on the pressure. "What'd you say?"

"Yes," Daniel gasps. "It was me. Let me go."

Liam releases Daniel, and he falls to his knees, gasping for breath and clutching at his throat as though Liam still has a hold on him.

I struggle to sit and rest my throbbing head against the wall. "How did Clarence find out?"

Tears stream down Daniel's face, but I'm not sure if it's remorse or pain or maybe a combination of both. Blood seeps through his pants from where I stabbed him. "He must've grown suspicious and searched my room," Daniel rasps. "He wrote a letter to Byron, but I dug it out of the mail before the carrier collected it."

"And then you poisoned him. Not in the scotch, but in the piece of pie his sister sent home with him. Then when you came home . . ." My mouth feels like it's stuffed with cotton. So does my brain. I close my eyes and try to see the scene, but that just intensifies my nausea, so I open them again. "When you came home and he was dead, you set up the scene like a suicide."

Daniel continues to clutch at his throat as his eyes stream. I think he nods, but that could also be a trick of my mind.

I attempt to look at Liam, but the light fixture near his head causes pain to crackle behind my eyes. "I thought it was you."

Liam's smile is wry. "I'm guilty of a lot, but not that. Never that." His gaze skims over my face. "You don't look good."

"Is Emma okay?" The words slur strangely.

Liam frowns. "Maybe you should lay down."

"I'm fine." My eyes are closed, even though I don't remember closing them. The linoleum is cool against my forehead. When did I lie down? My whole body feels heavy. "Fine . . . just . . ."

Tired is the word I'm looking for, but it never leaves my lips.

"Piper." My name is high and shrill. "Piper, wake up. Piper!"

I crack open an eye and pain shoots through my head as if it had been sitting there waiting to pounce. Emma's face swims in front of mine.

"She's opening her eyes!" She jostles my shoulder. "Piper, you need to wake up. The police are here. You need to wake up."

"Any luck?" Liam's voice.

"No, she's asleep again." Emma sounds distressed.

"I'm fine," I say, although I'm not sure how discernible my words are. Or how true it is. "Stop shaking me."

"Piper, can you open your eyes? The police are here."

"Daniel . . ."

"He's tied up."

I crack open my eyes and push up onto an elbow. I'm on the kitchen floor, and I can see into the entryway, where Daniel is lying on the ground too, hands secured behind his back.

My head throbs, and I let it drop back onto the linoleum. "Liam?"

"He's okay too. Everybody's okay. Well, except you." Emma's fingers smooth hair back from my face. "You should see the goose egg on your forehead. I'm so sorry, Piper."

Footsteps pound in the hallway, and I feel the vibration through the floor. "Step aside, please," says a reedy but commanding voice. "Clear the scene. Disperse please."

"Piper, can you sit up?" Emma asks. "The police are here. They'll want to talk to you."

"Mariano?"

"I don't know. I just called the regular number."

"What's going on in here, Sir?" the reedy voice asks, in the room now.

I open my eyes and take in black, shiny policeman shoes. I struggle again to sit upright.

"This guy killed his roommate." Liam nudges Daniel with his foot. "And assaulted this girl."

"No need to sit up, Miss," the cop says. "That looks like quite a blow to the head that you took."

He's young, with a dusting of a mustache that he's probably trying to grow to make himself look older, but it only makes him appear younger.

Liam frowns at me. "Piper, stop trying to sit up. Somebody should really take a look at her, Officer."

The cop crouches beside me. "Can you tell me what happened, young lady?"

Young lady. Like I'm decades younger than him instead of maybe five years at the most.

Liam shifts his weight from foot to foot, his arms crossed over his chest like he's guarding the door at The Fox. "He killed his roommate, Clarence Dell." Liam points a thick finger at Daniel. "He made it look like a suicide, and it was good enough that it fooled you guys. Not her, though." He nods at me. "She's been all over this city trying to get answers."

I finally manage to get up on one elbow. My head pounds so hard, it's a struggle to keep my eyes open.

"Wait, I'm confused." The officer holds up his hands like he's directing traffic. He turns a skeptical eye to me. "Who are you?"

"My name is Piper Sail." I try to ignore the dizziness and press on. "And I am a private investigator."

With that, I bend and vomit onto the young officer's shiny black shoes.

THIRTY-SIX

After we've given separate statements to the police and they take Daniel away for questioning, Liam and Emma help to shield me from the gathering crowd of curious residents and keep me upright all the way outside. The neon lights of the stores hurt my head, and I'm thankful I can look down and trust the two of them to guide me safely across the street.

"We need to get you to a hospital," Emma says. "That bump looks nasty."

"What time is it? Where's Mariano?" My words are still mushing together.

"Six," Emma says. "I left another message at his office. The receptionist said he hasn't been back all afternoon, but as soon as he walks in the door, she'll tell him."

"Who's Mariano?" Liam asks. "Let's get her to this bench over here."

"Piper's boyfriend. He's a detective. He was supposed to meet us here."

"We should wait for him," I say. "I'm fine."

Liam snorts a laugh and eases me onto a wooden bench. "Have a seat. My car is a couple blocks away. If you two wait here, I'll go get it."

Emma's hands twist together as she watches me. "I need to call her father. Probably my brother too. Will you sit with her just a minute while I ring them?"

"Don't call my father," I say, but she's already striding toward the telephone booth on the corner. "She's so stubborn."

Liam smirks and plops onto the bench beside me. I crook my elbow into a makeshift cushion on the back of the bench and rest my aching head against the wool of my coat. I could easily fall asleep if I wasn't so curious about Liam's side of the story.

I crack my eyes open. "When did you know Clarence didn't kill himself?"

Liam frowns down at me, his gaze on the swell of my head rather than my eyes. "It never seemed right. As you know, I saw him that afternoon, and he was angry with me. I thought, 'How did he go from *that* to supposedly offing himself an hour later?' It just didn't add up."

I try to look at him, but there's an abnormally bright street-lamp just behind him. "Why was he angry with you?"

Liam is silent.

I shield my eyes so I can look at him without the sharp pain. "I'm not going to tell anyone. You're the reason I'm alive."

Liam smirks and rubs at the scruff of his jaw. "Clarence was smart. Real smart. Back in September, he realized Tubs was stealing from The Fox, and he asked what I thought he should do. And I . . ." Liam swallows hard and looks at his hands. "I told him that Tubs had a little girl with epilepsy and that's why he was doing it. I knew if I told Clarence about the daughter, he'd drop it. Pretend he didn't see. But Tubs was skimming well before she got sick."

"And you knew that because you were in on it too."

Liam looks at me briefly. "Clarence didn't figure that out right away, but eventually he put it together. When we got together for drinks that afternoon . . ." He swallows hard. "Like I said, he was real mad at me. And I just couldn't see him confronting me like that and then doing himself in. It didn't fit. But also"—Liam shrugs—"the police said suicide. What are you gonna do?"

"Hire me."

"I'll know that for next time," Liam says. I can hear his smile. "I've been following you for a bit. When I realized what you were doing, I wanted to know who you were looking into. And when you went to Clarence's apartment, I thought, 'It has to be the roommate.'"

"Funny. When you knocked on the door, I thought it meant it had to be you."

"I sat across the street and waited for you to come out. It didn't take long for me to notice your cute friend. She kept pacing and looking up at the window, so I walked across the street and asked her what was going on. I made it sound like you and me were friends."

I groan. "We'll have to work on that."

"Jeremiah was still at the office, so he'll be here in just a few minutes," Emma announces as she returns. "Piper, I swear that bump looks worse every time I see you."

I don't bother with opening my eyes. "I'm okay."

"Why would Daniel have come to work at The Fox?"

I crack open an eye to find Liam staring pensively up at the apartment building.

"I asked him about that. He said money. He made more there in a night than an entire week at the library. But I'm not so sure that's the whole story. I think he envied what Clarence had there. I think maybe he was trying to find some of that success for himself."

"Piper!"

Mariano sprints down the sidewalk, tie so tight it's amazing he can breathe, much less run.

"What happened?" he asks breathlessly as he joins us. "Look at your head!"

I smile and try to keep my eyes open. "You should see the other guy."

"That's true," Liam chimes in. "He was bleeding pretty good when they took him away."

Mariano glances at Liam before fixing his eyes on me again. "I'm so sorry I wasn't here sooner. I came as soon as I got your message."

"Jeremiah is on his way," Emma says. "We need to get her to a hospital."

"I'm okay," I say, though I can tell it comes out more like *mmkay.*

Mariano's hair—always a little too long—falls forward into his eyes as he frowns down at me. His hat is nowhere in sight, and if I could reach up and loosen his tie, I would.

"You should loosen your tie," I say. "How can you breathe with it like that?"

I close my eyes again.

"Is her head the worst of it?" Mariano's touch is featherlight, first on my arm, then on my cheek, like he's making sure I'm not swelling anywhere else. "What happened?"

I drift in and out of sleep as Liam and Emma fill in Mariano on the details of the last couple hours. Then my hand is being squeezed and Mariano says, "Jeremiah's here with the car. We're going to move you, okay?"

I open my eyes and wince at the intense glow of the street-lamp. There's a roll of nausea in my belly. "I just want to sleep."

"No, we're going to the hospital." Mariano's arm threads around me. "C'mon. I'll help you stand."

"Piper." Jeremiah says my name on an exhale.

I catch only a glimpse of him—wide-eyed and slack-jawed—before I have to shut my eyes again. "Thanks for coming. I know you're mad at me."

"Oh, Piper. None of that matters now." Jeremiah's arm comes around the other side of me, and he and Mariano pull me to my feet. "Let's get you to the hospital."

I lie in the backseat of Jeremiah's car, my head on Mariano's lap, and doze restlessly as Emma fills Jeremiah in on what happened.

"We need to call my father," I murmur to Mariano during a lucid moment.

"Emma already did. He's meeting us at the hospital." His hand keeps running up and down my arm. "I'm afraid, Detective Sail, your days of being a *secret* investigator are over. You'll have to be a plain ol' regular investigator now."

Around Louisa and me, the Michigan Automat buzzes with its usual cacophony of clinking plates and lunchtime chatter, but she hasn't spoken for at least a minute. Maybe more. She sits there, eyes unfocused, hands cupping her mug of tea.

"So, you were right all along," I say in a gentle voice. "Your brother didn't cheat, and he didn't take his own life."

She looks at me, eyes sharpening. She nods and drags in a breath. "You don't have to tell me *that*, Piper. I never doubted either of those things."

I hide my amused smile by taking a bite of roast chicken.

Louisa slowly inhales. "Although I suppose I was wrong about a number of other things. Like Daniel." She frowns. "I really thought he loved Clarence."

"He maybe did at one point," I say. "But ultimately, he loved himself more."

Louisa sets down her tea and splays her fingers on the table. "Let me make sure I understand this. Daniel had been cheating at school for years."

I nod. "That's how he managed to work as many hours as he did while taking a full class load. And with his job at the library, he had easy access to the mimeograph machine."

"He's always been very ambitious." Louisa drums her fingers on the table. "Of course, Clarence was too."

"Lots of people are ambitious without it going this far."

"How did he make it look like it was Clarence?"

"I called Mr. Byron yesterday. Clarence's adviser? He was horrified to learn they'd expelled the wrong student. He told me that a professor noticed an answer key wasn't where it was supposed to be, and he confronted his class about it. Daniel told him that he'd found the answer key in Clarence's room. Daniel must have decided it was a matter of time before he was found out, and that he needed to control the narrative."

I think of every time I talked to Daniel about Clarence, how remorseful he'd seemed. Even when he confessed to the police at his apartment, he'd seemed genuinely sad about what had happened. There was something unnerving about that, about listening to the story of a young man who had never set out to murder his friend but had done it anyway. One choice led to another choice, escalating along the way until he found himself covering up a murder.

"That's how he went unnoticed in the cheating scandal," I say. "By putting himself in a position to tell the story, he was overlooked. And it's the same way he handled Clarence's death. He was the one who 'found the body,' and so he got to tell the story."

"And the poison was actually in the pie?"

I nod. "That's what Daniel told the police. Clarence had uncovered that it was Daniel who'd framed him, and he wrote a letter to Mr. Byron explaining the whole thing. Unfortunately, when Clarence was leaving that day, Daniel caught sight of who the letter was addressed to. He waited until Clarence left, and then he went downstairs and dug the letter out of the outgoing mailbox."

"Wouldn't somebody have seen him?"

"This is the drop box at the building, not one out on the street. Even if someone did see Daniel doing that, I'm sure he just made up something about forgetting to put a check in the bill he was paying. Something like that."

Louisa bites her lip. "So he put poison in the pie and . . . what? Just hoped Clarence would decide to eat it that day?"

"Daniel didn't say, but I'm guessing that he was trying to kill Clarence before he had another chance to tell people about what Daniel had done, while also making sure he had an alibi and suspicion wouldn't fall on him. I think Daniel assumed that Clarence would probably eat the pie that day—it was his favorite, after all—and that even if his plan was delayed slightly, that would probably be okay because Clarence would be waiting for a reply from Mr. Byron. What Daniel didn't know is that Clarence changed his course of action. Instead of waiting, he went to the school to try and speak to Mr. Byron. He was out sick that day, so Clarence set up an appointment for the next day. Only it was too late, of course."

Louisa's jaw clenches for a moment. "My parents couldn't believe it when the officers knocked on our door and told us what had happened." She looks down at her steaming tea. "They'd like to have you over for dinner, by the way. Mother and Daddy. To thank you."

"That's very kind of them."

Her gaze drifts to the side of my head. "That looks really painful."

"It's getting better," I say.

The swelling is significantly less, even after just a few days, but the bump is still noticeable, and the grayish, purplish bruising is hard to cover with makeup. My father had been furious when he showed up at the hospital and learned how I'd been injured.

"You were investigating a case? That's the most ridiculous thing I have ever heard," Father had said, before rounding on Mariano. "This is your fault. She would never have thought to do something like this if it wasn't for you."

"Timothy," Jane said, admonishment in her tone. "When has your daughter ever not been able to think for herself? This isn't Mariano's fault." She had looked at me then, her eyes both assessing and surprisingly compassionate. "This is just who Piper is."

Even if I'd been my healthy self in that moment, I'm not sure I would've known what to say. I had reached out my hand for Jane's and she'd smiled tearfully as she'd taken mine and squeezed.

After that, Father was reduced to grumbling privately. Even now, days after the fact, he seems determined to avoid referencing my investigation.

Louisa draws my attention back to the present by sliding an envelope across the table to me. "Here. For you."

I open the flap wide enough to see the green of dollars.

"I'm sorry I took the money back from you," Louisa says. "I felt rotten about that afterward."

I shake my head, and then wince. Moving it still hurts. "You shouldn't."

"You'd earned it, though. Even if I was angry with you at the time, you'd still worked really hard to figure out what happened to my brother."

"I wish discovering the truth had the power to change it," I say, my eyes prickling. "I wish I could undo what happened."

Louisa's smile is tinged with sadness. "You did what you could. That's all any of us can do."

I slip the money into my leather bag. *+$5 for solving the death of Clarence Dell* is how he would document this. Maybe that's how I'll do it too. My first money earned as Piper Sail, Private Investigator.

After having lunch with Louisa, she heads home to be with her parents, who have requested to have her taken out of school for a few days as they grieve anew the loss of Clarence. I, unfortunately, have to go back to work.

Outside the automat, I find Mariano idling in the detective bureau car, which isn't that surprising considering nobody seems keen on me being alone right now. Usually I'd protest, but since it's misting outside, and I don't often have excuses to see him in the middle of the day, I don't really mind too much.

I spend the short drive relaying to him my conversation with Louisa, and by the time he pulls up outside of Presley's, the mist has turned to rain. "I'll park and walk you up to the door," he says. "I have an umbrella."

"I don't mind. It'll be plenty warm inside the school."

Mariano sighs heavily. "I wasn't there to stop that guy from slamming your head against the wall. Will you at least let me protect your head from the rain?"

I roll my eyes.

Not that it's a horrible chore, having to share an umbrella with Mariano. With one hand, he holds it over us, while the other arm stays wrapped around my waist so that our hips bump together as we walk. I'm glad he insisted, because everything from my knees down gets soaked on the walk to the door and the rain is so cold, I'm surprised it's not turning to ice upon hitting the ground.

When we reach the front door, it's clear that Mariano held the umbrella more over me than himself. His left side is drenched.

"Mariano," I admonish.

He glances at his shoulder and shrugs. We're only steps away from where we first met. From when he showed up and split my life into two halves—before Lydia went missing and after.

I cup my hand around his cheek, push up on my toes, and kiss him good-bye. "Thank you."

Mariano raises his eyebrows. "For . . . ?"

"Sticking around." I mirror his expression and raise my brows as well. "I'm not the easiest person to care about."

He grins. "You don't have to thank me for that. I don't think I have much of a choice at this point."

He kisses me one more time, swift and warm, and then

pulls the school door open for me. Once I'm inside, he turns and strides back to his car. I watch him go, even though the umbrella obscures him.

"Miss Sail?"

I jump and my hand lands over my racing heart as I notice a student standing alongside my desk. "I didn't see you there."

"Sorry to scare you." The girl twists her hands together. "I was hoping you could help me with something."

"Yes, of course." I come around the edge of my desk, where a pile of notes have gathered in my absence. I push them to the side and reach for a pencil and my notepad. "What can I help you with?"

"Well . . ." The girl swallows and looks away. "I was talking to Emma Crane, and I'm wondering . . . are you available to work on a new case? Because I have a problem."

I look at the student for a moment. Then I push aside my Presley's notepad and pull a different notebook from my leather bag.

"Sure." I smooth a fresh page. "Why don't you tell me what's going on? If I can help you, I will."

ABOUT THE HISTORY
IN THIS BOOK

Something I love about the historical fiction genre—both as a reader and a writer—is the chance to learn more about a specific time or situation in history. If you're like me, now that you've finished the book, you're curious about what is true and what I made up.

Many places referenced in the book are real, like Astor Street, Harvard School for Boys, Marshall Field's (and its famous restaurant, The Walnut Room), B/G Sandwich Shop, and most other restaurants mentioned. While Presley's School for Girls isn't a real place, I graduated from an all-girls high school that had been in operation since the early 1900s, so much of the inner workings and life portrayed at Presley's are rooted in my own experiences.

The Edgewater Beach Apartments exist to this day in all their pink glory. When they were built, their express purpose was to provide residents with resort-style living and the amenities of a luxury hotel, which made them the perfect choice for the lavish lifestyle Elzbieta coveted. However, Edgewater Beach Apartments inconveniently didn't open until 1928, so I had to adjust history there a little.

The Foxglove Smoke Shop—or "The Fox"—isn't a real place, though it's modeled after another casino Dean O'Banion was involved with called Hawthorne Smoke Shop, which was known as "The Ship." Originally, I set out to have Clarence,

Elzbieta, Liam, and the others all working at The Ship, but this became complicated for a couple reasons. The location moved a number of times during its two years of operation, and even though O'Banion *did* make money from the casino, it was largely owned and operated by Joe Torrio and Al Capone. All that history made The Ship fascinating to learn about, but frustrating to work into the story because it's a bit too complex for the purposes of the book.

Since Dean O'Banion made an estimated one million dollars a year (in the 1920s!) and had a variety of revenue streams, it seemed plausible that he might have other casinos on the North Side, a territory he controlled. Because he was known as the florist gangster, I named his casino after a flower.

Despite my best efforts to research and fact-check, it's likely there are still inaccuracies lurking in these pages. If you find one, please let me know via my website, StephanieMorrill.com.

ACKNOWLEDGMENTS

Since *The Lost Girl of Astor Street* released in 2017, many readers have asked me, "When will there be a sequel?" If you're one of those who asked, thank you. I doubt I'd have had the audacity to write this book if readers hadn't continued to ask for it.

What a gift it is to partner with Blink. Thank you, Megan Dobson, for believing in Piper's stories and making space for them at Blink! Thank you, Katherine Easter, for seeing the potential in *The Secret Investigator of Astor Street* and helping shape the story into a much better version than the one I initially sent you. Jacque Alberta, thank you for your pickiness, your queries, and your encouragement. I am so fortunate to have such talented editors!

Jennifer Showalter Greenwalt and Dawn Cooper, thank you for working so hard to make the cover absolutely perfect. It was a joy to be included in the process. Denise Froehlich, the insides are beautiful, and I'm grateful for all the work you did to make them so! Abby Van Wormer and Sara Merritt, thank you for your dedicated work to get the Piper Sail Mysteries in the hands of readers. I'm thankful for you!

Amanda Orozco, the balance you strike of sharing industry insights while simultaneously encouraging me to write what I care about makes you a rock star of an agent. Thank you for your guidance and patience over the years.

I wouldn't be able to write books without the support of my husband, Ben, or my kids, McKenna, Connor, and Eli. The four of you are the absolute berries, as Piper would say, and your enthusiasm keeps me going on hard days. McKenna, thank you for completely freaking out when I told you I was going to write this book and for giving me confidence boosts whenever I need them.

Mom and Dad, thank you for big things, like encouraging my love of writing and reading from the beginning, as well as small things, like not being offended when I don't answer the phone because I'm writing. I love you and appreciate how supportive you've been every step of the way!

Thank you, Roseanna White, for being there for me when I'm looking for a shoulder to cry on, or when I have questions about where to put a comma, or if I have an issue that falls somewhere in between. Thank you, Jill Williamson and Shannon Dittemore, for "getting it," whether writing life feels particularly stressful or wonderful. And many thanks to Julie Collett, Lindsey Fisher, Anna Mathew, and Kristin Jacobsen. Each of you is a loving, encouraging, supportive presence in my life, and I'm fortunate to have you.

DISCUSSION QUESTIONS

1. This book begins somewhat shortly after Lydia LeVine's disappearance and Piper's investigation that led to solving her best friend's murder. How do you think those events affect Piper throughout the book, including how she handles Louisa and the mystery around Clarence?

2. How did the setting of 1924 Chicago help shape the story? Did any historical details or moments really stand out to you?

3. In addition to Piper and Louisa, many characters in the story are dealing with loss—including Hannah, Liam, and Piper's father. How does grief affect each of these characters? Do you think they handle it realistically? Are there ways you would have handled it differently?

4. Piper has different types of relationships with people like Emma, Mariano, Hannah, Elzbieta, and even Jane. How do each of these connections show us who she is? How do you think those relationships impacted her decisions? And which relationship was your favorite to read about?

5. Piper must make some big choices that aren't easy, including how she chooses to see herself. Which of her dilemmas stuck out to you most? Would you have handled it the same way or done something different? What did you think of her final decisions?

6. Throughout the book, Piper also has to deal with a lot of sudden changes in her life, including trying to figure out her life while everything begins to shift in her family at the same time. How do the comments her family makes affect Piper and how she views her future? Does her family and how she grew up/the way they see her life motivate her, or do they hold her back in different moments?

7. Piper doesn't exactly fit the typical mold for what women were expected to be like in the 1920s. What moments show her pushing back against those expectations? Are there any places where you feel she could have pushed back even more?

8. As Piper investigates, she often finds herself inadvertently caught between Mariano and Jeremiah due to the situations she encounters. Compare and contrast their two characters and how they view Piper, including the risks she takes. How do those views reflect the bigger themes and tensions in the book? And which person do you think is a better "fit" for Piper in the long run? Why do you feel that way?

   And if you read *The Lost Girl of Astor Street*—the first book in this series—do you feel things between Piper and Jeremiah would be different now if Piper had never started investigating in the first place? Why or why not?

9. What was your reaction to the way Clarence's death was pieced together? Were the clues easy to follow, or did some twists catch you off guard? How did you think the book would end?

10. What parts of the story had you on edge? How did the author make scenes, like those at The Fox, feel mysterious or suspenseful?

11. BONUS QUESTION: If you had to step into Piper's shoes and solve a mystery in your own town, who's the first person you'd team up with? Why do you think they'd make a good crime-solving partner?

THE LOST GIRL OF ASTOR STREET

"Why, I can't believe my eyes. Is that possibly Miss Sail walking alone?"

I turn and find Jeremiah Crane standing along the walkway of Presley's the next afternoon. His trilby tips at an angle, his mouth is set in a smirk, and his hands are in the pockets of his trousers. The combination of which makes up a rather rakish picture.

I hesitate, and then step out of the flow of girls to join Jeremiah. "And how are you today, Mr. Crane?"

"Very well, thank you." Jeremiah makes a show of glancing about. "Where is your Miss LeVine this afternoon? I hardly recognized you without her."

Of course. Lydia's red hair and lovely face have always attracted male attention. I tip my face up to the warm sunlight in hopes that Jeremiah won't read into any disappointment that might be evident. "At home, I believe."

Probably suffering from punishment so severe, she couldn't have even imagined it.

"Have they come for you, Miss Sail?" Jeremiah asks teasingly.

I look to Jeremiah and find him grinning, his gaze attached to something behind me. But when I try to follow his eye line, I see nothing but vehicles and parents. My confusion must be clear because Jeremiah nods toward the street. "See those two men who just got out of the touring sedan by the streetlamp?"

"Yes." One looks near Father's age, and is thick, with a belly that implies he doesn't let Prohibition tamper the amount of beer he drinks. The other is trim with olive skin and, from this distance at least, seems quite young. Maybe only three or four years older than me.

"That car they just got out of is a detective bureau vehicle." Jeremiah leans against the railing and crosses his arms over his chest. There's a spark of mischief in his slate-blue eyes. "Have pastries gone missing from the teacher's lounge again, Miss Sail?"

My cheeks heat. "I can neither confirm nor deny that."

Jeremiah releases a loud laugh. "What other response would I expect from a lawyer's daughter?"

"Surely you Cranes have plenty to discuss at the dinner table." I clap a hand to my hat as a gust of wind sweeps across campus. "It seems you wouldn't have to sink to mere secondary school gossip."

"Is it mere gossip that you slid down the stairwell banister in only your bathing costume?"

My face burns even hotter. "That . . . that's being taken out of context."

"Or that you stole a frog from the science teacher's classroom?"

"*Liberated* is the word I would choose, but that's never been proven."

"Or that you have the highest marks in the school?"

Why's he razzing me so hard? It's not like I went out of my way to talk to him. *He* called out to *me*.

"I believe it's time for me to be going, Mr. Crane." I take a step backward. "Good day."

"Wait, Miss Sail. Do you . . ." Jeremiah clutches his hat in his hands, rotating it in an absent manner. "Do you go to the movies often?"

My breath catches in my chest. Is he . . . ?

"Emma and I saw *The Thief of Baghdad* last night." Jeremiah mashes his hat back onto his head. "I thought maybe you might like to see it. That maybe, if you were free this Friday evening, we could go together."

There's no longer mischief lighting Jeremiah's eyes. My brain is incapable of forming an intellectual response. A date? He's asking *me* on a date?

"Excuse me? Are you Miss Piper Sail?"

I turn toward the unfamiliar baritone and find myself face to face with the two detectives Jeremiah pointed out to me minutes ago. "Yes, I am."

The older man is several steps up on the stairway, as if he were leading the way to the school doors. But the younger one stands on the same step as me. Both tip their hats, and the younger one speaks. "I'm Detective Cassano, and this is Detective O'Malley. Could we have a minute of your time to ask a few questions?"

What could they possibly . . . ? "Of course. About what?"

As if their heads are connected, both detectives look to Jeremiah.

"I don't mind if he hears." I straighten my shoulders, remind myself of the truth. "I haven't done anything wrong."

"Of course not, Miss," says Detective Cassano. "We're here in service of the LeVine family."

My surroundings dim with two exceptions—the grave expression on the detective's face, and the way my heart seems intent to fly right out of my chest. "The LeVine family?"

"Dr. Charles LeVine?"

"Yes, I know. I'm best friends with their daughter."

"That's why we're here. We hoped you could provide insight to her whereabouts."

Oh, Lydia. What have you done?

"H-her whereabouts?" I swallow to steady my voice. "How do you mean?"

My stomach turns to ice as both detectives sweep their hats off their heads.

"I apologize to have to tell you, Miss Sail. We thought you would know by now." Detective Cassano's words are measured, as if being selected carefully. "Lydia LeVine has been reported missing."

The Lost Girl of Astor Street

Lydia has vanished. And Piper Sail is determined to find her.

Lydia LeVine is the type of girl who had never broken a rule, other than falling for a boy below her on the social ladder—and in the eyes of her best friend, Piper, is everything "proper" she can't seem to be. So when Lydia disappears from their wealthy neighborhood without even saying good-bye, Piper knows something terrible has happened.

Convinced the police are looking in all the wrong places, Piper begins her own investigation in hopes of solving the mystery behind Lydia's disappearance. With the reluctant help of a handsome young detective, she searches for answers in the dark underbelly of 1924 Chicago, determined to find Lydia at any cost—even if it means uncovering the secrets around her and risking her own life for the sake of the truth.

From the glitzy homes of the elite to the mob-run streets, Stephanie Morrill's Jazz Age mystery shows just how far a girl will go to save her friend.

Within These Lines

Separated by war, injustice, and hatred ... they must find their way in a world divided.

Evalina Cassano's life in an Italian-American family in 1941 is ordinary ... until she falls in love with Taichi Hamasaki, the son of Japanese immigrants. Despite the fact interracial marriage is illegal in California, Evalina and Taichi vow they will find a way to be together. But anti-Japanese feelings erupt across the country after Pearl Harbor, and Taichi and his family are forced to move to an internment camp.

The degrading treatment is so difficult, Taichi doubts he will leave the camp alive. His only connection to the outside world is letters from Evalina. Feeling that the only way to help Taichi is to speak out on behalf of all Japanese Americans, Evalina becomes increasingly vocal at school and at home.

With tensions high and their freedom on the line, Evalina and Taichi must hold true to their values and believe in their love to make a way back to each other against unbelievable odds.

Available wherever books are sold!

BLINK·

ABOUT THE AUTHOR

STEPHANIE MORRILL writes books about girls who are on an adventure to discover their unique place in the world. She is the author of several contemporary young adult series, as well as two historical young adult novels, *The Lost Girl of Astor Street* and *Within These Lines*. *Within These Lines* was a Junior Library Guild Gold Standard selection, as well as a YALSA 2020 Best Fiction for Young Adults pick. Since 2010, Stephanie has been encouraging the next generation of writers at her website, GoTeenWriters.com, which has been on the Writer's Digest Best Websites for Writers list since 2017. She lives in the Kansas City area, where she loves plotting big and small adventures to enjoy with her husband and three children. You can connect with Stephanie and learn more about her books at StephanieMorrill.com.

Did you ♥ this book?

Please consider leaving a review on any of your preferred retail sites or tag us on social media sharing your thoughts! Follow us on social media:

♪ : @blinkyabooks

⊙ : @blinkyabooks

f : @blinkyabooks

For FREE educator guides for this book and other Blink titles, visit BlinkYABooks.com.

BLINK